For Neetha

Linwood Barclay is married with two children and lives near Toronto. He is a former columnist for the *Toronto Star* and is the author of two previous number one bestsellers: *No Time for Goodbye*, the Richard & Judy Summer Read Winner of 2008, and *Too Close to Home*.

Check out his website at
www.linwoodbarclay.com

FEAR THE WORST

It was the worst day of Tim Blake's life. His seventeen-year-old daughter, Sydney, was staying with him while she worked a summer job at the Just Inn Time hotel — father-daughter time to help with the after-effects of his divorce. Syd didn't arrive home at her usual time. Then, worryingly, she didn't answer her phone. And when the people at the Just Inn Time told him they'd no Sydney Blake working at the hotel, he was plunged into the abyss every parent dreads most. Where had she been every day, if not working at the Just Inn Time . . . ? To find his daughter Tim must discover who she really was, and what could have made her step out of her own life without leaving a trace.

Books by Linwood Barclay
Published by The House of Ulverscroft:

NO TIME FOR GOODBYE
TOO CLOSE TO HOME

LINWOOD BARCLAY

FEAR
THE WORST

Complete and Unabridged

CHARNWOOD
Leicester

First published in Great Britain in 2010 by
Orion Books
an imprint of The Orion Publishing Group Ltd.
London

First Charnwood Edition
published 2011
by arrangement with
The Orion Publishing Group Ltd.
An Hachette UK Company
London

British Library CIP Data

Barclay, Linwood.
    Fear the worst.
    1. Fathers and daughters- -Fiction. 2. Missing
persons- -Fiction. 3. Suspense fiction.
    4. Large type books.
    I. Title
    813.6–dc22

ISBN 978–1–44480–499–7

Published by
F. A. Thorpe (Publishing)
Anstey, Leicestershire

Set by Words & Graphics Ltd.
Anstey, Leicestershire
Printed and bound in Great Britain by
T. J. International Ltd., Padstow, Cornwall

This book is printed on acid-free paper

Acknowledgements

As always, I want to thank my terrific agent, Helen Heller, and everyone at The Paul Marsh Agency. At Orion UK, and Hachette in Australia and New Zealand, more people than I can count have supported this book and contributed to the success of those that have preceded it. My editor Bill Massey's insights went a long way to making this book what it is.

My friends Carl Brouwer and Mike Onishi, two retired car salesmen who've both persuaded me over the years that I really did get a good deal, were generous with their time in explaining how their business works. Dale Hopkins filled me in on credit card fraud, and told me a slew of private detective stories I hope to rip off from him one day.

Finally, none of this would mean anything without Neetha, Spencer, and Paige, who deserves a special thanks. Eating the eggs I'd made her one morning, she said, 'Suppose you came to pick me up at my job, and found out I'd never worked there?'

Prologue

The morning of the day I lost her, my daughter asked me to scramble her some eggs.

'Want bacon with it?' I shouted up to the second floor where she was still getting ready for work.

'No,' Sydney called down from the bathroom.

'Toast?' I asked.

'No,' she said. I heard a clapping noise. The hair straightener. That noise usually signaled she was nearing the end of her morning routine.

'Cheese in the eggs?'

'No,' she said. Then, 'A little?'

I went back into the kitchen, opened the fridge and took out eggs, a block of cheddar and orange juice. I put a filter into the coffee maker, spooned in some coffee, poured in four cups of water and hit the button.

Syd's mother Susanne, my ex, who'd recently moved in with her boyfriend Bob on the other side of the river in Stratford, would probably say I was spoiling her, that our daughter was old enough at seventeen to be able to make her own breakfast. But it was such a treat to have her stay with me for the summer I didn't mind pampering her. Last year I'd found her a job at the Honda dealership where I work, just this side of that same river here in Milford. While there were moments when we wanted to kill each other, overall it had been a pretty good

1

experience sharing digs. This year, however, Sydney had opted not to work at the dealership. Living with me was enough. Having me keep an eye on her while she worked was something else again.

'Have you noticed,' she'd asked me last year, 'that every guy around here I talk to, even for a minute, you tell me something bad about him?'

'It's good to be forewarned,' I'd said.

'What about Dwayne, in Service?' she'd said. 'His rag was too oily?'

'Sign of bad character,' I'd said.

'And Andy?'

'You're joking,' I'd said. 'Way too old. Mid-twenties.'

So this year she'd found a different job, but still here in Milford, so she could live with me from June through Labor Day. She'd got herself hired at the Just Inn Time, a hotel that catered to business travelers only looking to stay a night or two. Milford's a nice place, but it's not exactly a tourist destination. The hotel had been a Days Inn or a Holiday Inn or a Comfort Inn in a previous life, but whichever conglomerate had owned it, they'd bailed, and an independent had come in.

I wasn't surprised when Sydney told me they'd put her on the front desk. 'You're bright, charming, courteous — '

'I'm also one of the few there who speaks English,' she'd countered, putting her proud father in his place.

It was like pulling teeth, getting her to talk about the new job. 'It's just work,' she'd say.

Three days into it I heard her arguing on the phone with her friend Patty Swain saying she was going to look for something else, even if she was making good money, what with there being no income tax.

'This is off the books?' I said when she got off the phone. 'You're getting paid under the table?'

Sydney said, 'You always listen to my phone calls?'

So I backed off. Let her solve her own problems.

I waited until I heard her coming down the stairs before I poured the two scrambled eggs, a few shavings of grated cheddar mixed in, into the buttered frying pan. It had occurred to me to do something I hadn't done for Sydney since she was a little girl. I took half of the eggshell I'd just cracked and, using a soft pencil from the cutlery drawer, drew a face on it. A toothy grin, a half circle for a nose, and two menacing-looking eyes. I drew a line from the mouth to the backside of the shell, where I printed, 'Smile, damn it.'

She shuffled into the kitchen like a condemned prisoner and plopped into her chair, looking down into her own lap, hair hanging down over her eyes, arms lifeless at her sides. She had a pair of oversized sunglasses I didn't recognize perched on her head.

The eggs firmed up in seconds. I slipped them onto a plate and set them before her.

'Your Highness,' I said, talking over the sounds of the *Today* show coming from the small television that hung beneath the cabinet.

Sydney rose her head slowly, looking first at

the plate, but then her eyes caught the little Humpty-Dumpty character staring at her.

'Oh my God,' she said, bringing up a hand and turning the salt shaker so she could read what was on the egg's backside. 'Smile *yourself*,' she said, but there was something bordering on playful in her voice.

'New shades?' I asked.

Absently, like she'd forgotten she'd just put them there, she touched one of the arms, made a minor adjustment.

'Yeah,' she said.

I noticed the word 'Versace' printed in very tiny letters on the glasses. 'Very nice,' I said.

Syd nodded tiredly.

'Out late?' I asked.

'Not *that* late,' she said.

'Midnight's late,' I said.

She knew there was no point denying when she got in. I never got to sleep until I heard her come into our house on Hill Street and lock the door behind her. I guessed she'd been out with Patty Swain, who was also seventeen, but gave off a vibe that she was a little more experienced than Syd with the kinds of things that kept fathers up at night. I'd have been naïve to think Patty Swain didn't already know about drinking, sex and drugs.

But Syd wasn't exactly an angel. I'd caught her with pot once, and there was that time, a couple years back, when she was fifteen, when she came home from the Abercrombie and Fitch store in Stamford with a new T-shirt, and couldn't explain to her mother why she had no

4

receipt. Big fireworks over that one.

Maybe that's why the sunglasses were niggling at me.

'What did those set you back?' I asked.

'Not that much,' she said.

'How's Patty?' I asked, not so much to find out how she was as to confirm Syd had been with her. They'd been friends only a year or so, but they'd spent so much time together since then it was as if their friendship went back to kindergarten. I liked Patty — she had a directness that was refreshing — but there were times I wished Syd hung out with her a little less.

'She's cool,' Syd said.

On the TV, Matt Lauer was warning about possibly radioactive granite counter-tops. Every day, something new to worry about.

Syd dug into her eggs. 'Mmm,' she said. She glanced up at the TV. 'Bob,' she said.

I looked. One of the ad spots from the local affiliate. A tall, balding man with broad smile and perfect teeth standing in front of a sea of cars, arms outstretched, like Moses parting the Red Sea.

'Run, don't walk, into Bob's Motors! Don't have a trade? That's OK! Don't have a downpayment! That's OK! Don't have a driver's license? OK, that's a problem! But if you're looking for a car, and you're looking for a good deal, get on down to one of our three loca — '

I hit the mute button.

'He is a bit of a douche,' Syd said of the man her mother, my ex, lived with. 'But those commercials turn him into Superdouche. What

5

are we having tonight?' Breakfast was never complete without a discussion of what we might be eating at the end of the day. 'How about D.A.D?'

Family code for 'dial a dinner.'

Before I could answer, she said, 'Pizza?'

'I think I'll make something,' I said. Syd made no attempt to hide her disappointment.

Since last summer, when Syd and I were both working at the same place and she was riding in with me, Susanne and I had agreed to get her a car for nipping around Milford and Stratford. I took in a seven-year-old Civic with low miles on a trade and snatched it up for a couple thou before it hit our used car lot. It had a bit of rust around the fender wells, but was otherwise roadworthy.

'No spoiler?' Syd cracked when it was presented to her.

'Shut up,' I said and handed her the keys.

Only once since she'd gotten this new job had I dropped her off at work. The Civic was in for a rusted-out tailpipe. So I drove her up Route 1, what I still thought of as the Boston Post Road, the Just Inn Time looming in the distance, a bleak, gray, featureless block on the horizon, looking like an apartment complex in some Soviet satellite country.

I was prepared to drive her to the door, but she had me drop her off at the sidewalk, near a bus stop. 'I'll be here the end of the day,' she said.

Bob's commercial over, I put the sound back on. Al Roker was outside mingling with the

Rockefeller Center crowd, most of them waving signs offering birthday greetings to relatives back home.

I looked at my daughter, eating her breakfast. Part of being a father, at least for me, is being perpetually proud. I took in what a beautiful young woman Syd was turning into. Blond hair down to her shoulders, a long graceful neck, porcelain skin, strong facial features. Her mother's roots go back to Norway, which accounts for her Nordic air.

As if sensing my eyes on her, she said, 'You think I could be a model?'

'A model?' I glanced over.

'Don't sound so shocked,' she said.

'I'm not,' I said defensively. 'I just never heard you talk about it before.'

'I never really thought about it. It's Bob's idea.'

I felt my face go hot. Bob encouraging Syd to model? He was in his early forties, like me. Now he had my wife and — more often than I liked — my daughter living under his roof, in his fancy five-bedroom house with pool and three-car garage, and he's pushing her to model? What the fuck kind of modeling? Pinup stuff? Webcam porn to order? Was he offering to take the shots himself?

'*Bob* said this?' I asked.

'He says I'd be a natural. That I should be in one of his commercials.'

Hard to pick which would be more demeaning. *Penthouse*, or hawking Bob's used cars.

'What? You think he's wrong?'

'He's out of line,' I said.

'He's not a perv or anything,' she said. 'A douche, yes, but a perv, no. Mom and Evan even kind of agreed with him.'

'Evan?'

Now I was really getting steamed. Evan was Bob's nineteen-year-old son. He had been living most of the time with his mother, one of Bob's two ex-wives, but now she was off to Europe for three months, so Evan had moved in with his dad, which meant he was now sleeping down the hall from Syd, who, by the way, liked her new bedroom very much and had pointed out several times that it was twice the size of the one she had in my house.

We'd had a bigger house, once.

The idea of some horny teenage boy living under the same roof with Syd had pissed me off from the get-go. I was surprised Susanne was going along with it, but once you moved out of your own house and into someone else's, you lost a bit of leverage. What could she do? Make her boyfriend kick his own son out?

'Yeah, Evan,' Sydney said. 'He was just commenting, is all.'

'He shouldn't even be living there.'

'Jesus, Dad, do we have to get into this again?'

'A boy, a nineteen-year-old boy, unless he's your actual brother, shouldn't be living with you.'

I thought I saw her cheeks flush. 'It's not a big deal.'

'Your mother's cool with this? Bob and his boy telling you to be the next Cindy Crawford?'

'Cindy who?'

'Crawford,' I said. 'She was — never mind. Your mom's OK with this?'

'She's not having a shit fit like you,' Syd said, shooting me a look. 'And besides, Evan's helping her since the thing.'

The thing. Susanne's parasailing accident in Long Island Sound. Came down too fast, did something to her hip, twisted her knee out of shape. Bob, behind the wheel of his boat, dragged her a hundred yards before he knew something was wrong, the dumb fuck. Susanne didn't have to worry about parasailing accidents when she was with me. I didn't have a boat.

'You never said what you paid for the shades,' I said.

Sydney sighed. 'It wasn't that much.' She was looking at several unopened envelopes by the phone. 'You should really open your bills, Dad. They've been there like three days.'

'Don't you worry about the bills. I can pay the bills.'

'Mom says it's not that you don't have the money to pay them, you just aren't very organized, so then you're late — '

'The sunglasses. Where'd you get them?'

'Jesus, what's the deal about a pair of sunglasses?'

'I'm just curious, is all,' I said. 'Get them at the mall?'

'Yeah, I got them at the mall. Fifty per cent off.'

'Did you save your receipt? In case they break or something?'

9

Her eyes bore into me. 'Why don't you just ask me to show you the receipt?'

'Why would I do that?'

'Because you think I stole them.'

'I never said that.'

'It was two years ago, Dad. I don't believe you.' She pushed her eggs away, unfinished.

'You come down here in Versace sunglasses, you think I'm not going to ask questions?'

She got up and stomped back upstairs.

'Shit,' I said under my breath. Nicely played.

I had to finish getting ready to go to work myself, and heard her run down the stairs while I was in my bedroom. I caught her coming out of the kitchen with a bottled water as I came down to say goodbye to her as she headed out to the Civic.

'Being with you for the summer is going to suck if you're going to be like this all the time,' she said. 'And it's not my fault I'm living with Evan. It's not like he's raping me every five minutes.'

I winced. 'I know, it's just — '

'I gotta go,' she said, walking away and getting into her car. She had her eyes fixed on the road as she drove away, and didn't see me wave.

In the kitchen was the receipt for the sunglasses, right next to the eggshell character she'd flattened with her fist.

★   ★   ★

I got into my CR-V and headed to Riverside Honda. We were just this side of the bridge that crosses over into Stratford, where the Housatonic empties into the sound. It was a slow morning, not enough people dropping in for my turn to come up in the rotation, but shortly after noon a retired couple in their late sixties dropped by to look at a base model four-door Accord.

They were hemming and hawing over price — we were seven hundred dollars apart. I excused myself, said I was going to take their latest offer to the sales manager, but instead went into Service and scarfed a chocolate donut from a box at the coffee stand, then went back and told them I could only save them another hundred, but we were going to have a custom pinstriper on site over the next couple of days, and if they took the deal, I could get the Accord custom-pinstriped for free. The guy's eyes lit up, and they went for it. Later, I got a ten-buck pinstriping kit from parts and attached it to the order.

In the afternoon, a man interested in replacing his decade-old Odyssey van with a new one wanted to know how much his trade was worth. You never answered that question without asking a few of your own.

'Are you the original owner?' I asked. He was. 'Have you maintained the car?' He said he'd done most of the recommended services. 'Has the vehicle ever been in an accident?'

'Oh yeah,' he volunteered. 'Three years ago I rear-ended a guy, they had to replace everything up front.'

I explained that an accident translated into a

much lower trade-in value. His counter-argument was that all the parts in the front of the car were newer, so if anything, the car should be worth more. He wasn't happy with the number I gave him, and left.

Twice I called my ex-wife in Stratford where she worked at one of the car lots Bob owned, and twice I left messages, both asking how thrilled she was with Bob's plan to immortalize our daughter on a bathroom calendar at the local Goodyear tire store.

After the second call, my head cleared some, and I realized this wasn't just about Sydney. It was about Susanne, about Bob, about how much better her life was with him, about how much I'd screwed things up.

I'd been selling cars since I was twenty, and I was good at it, but Susanne thought I was capable of more. You shouldn't be working for somebody else, she said. You should be your own man. You should have your own dealership. We could change our lives. Send Syd to the best schools. Make a better future for ourselves.

My dad had passed away when I was nineteen, and left my mother pretty well fixed. A few years later, when she died of a heart attack, I used the inheritance to show Susanne I could be the man she wanted me to be. I started up my own dealership.

And fucked the whole thing up.

I was never a big picture guy. Sales, working one-to-one, that was my thing. But when I had to run the whole show, I kept sneaking back onto the floor to deal with customers. I wasn't cut out to manage, so I let others make decisions for me. Bad ones, as it turned out. Let them steal from me, too.

Eventually, I lost it all.

And not just the business, not just our big house that overlooked the sound. I lost my family.

Susanne blamed me for taking my eye off the ball. I blamed her for pushing me into something I wasn't cut out for.

Syd, somehow, blamed herself. She figured that, if we loved her enough, we'd stay together no matter what. The fact that we didn't had nothing to do with how much we loved Syd, but she wasn't buying it.

In Bob, Susanne found what was missing in me. Bob was always reaching for the next rung. Bob figured if he could sell cars, he could start up a dealership, and if he could start up one dealership, why not two, or three?

I never bought Susanne a Corvette when I was going out with her, like Bob did. At least there was some satisfaction when it blew a piston, and she ended up getting rid of it because she hated driving a stick.

On this particular day, I went home, somewhat reluctantly, at six. When you're on commission, you don't want to walk out of an open showroom. You know, the moment you leave, someone'll come in, checkbook in hand, asking for you. But you couldn't live there. You had to go home some time.

I'd been planning to make spaghetti, but figured, what the hell, I'd order pizza, just like

Syd wanted. It'd be a kind of peace offering, a way to make up for the sunglasses thing.

By seven, she had not shown up, or called to let me know she'd be late.

Maybe someone had gone home sick, and she'd had to stay on the front desk for an extra shift. Ordinarily, if she wasn't going to make it home in time for dinner, she'd call. But I could see her skipping that courtesy today, after what had happened at breakfast.

Still, by eight, when I hadn't heard from her, I started to worry.

I was standing in the kitchen, watching CNN, getting updated on some earthquake in Asia but not really paying attention, wondering where the hell she was.

Sometimes she got together with Patty or one of her other friends after work, went over to the Post Mall to eat in the food court.

I called her cell. It rang several times before going to message. 'Give me a call, sweetheart,' I said. 'I figured, we'd have pizza after all. Let me know what you want on it.'

I gave it another ten minutes before deciding to find a number for the hotel. I was about to make the call when the phone rang. I grabbed the receiver before I'd checked the ID. 'Hey,' I said. 'You in for pizza or what?'

'Just hold the anchovies.' It wasn't Syd. It was Susanne.

'Oh,' I said. 'Hey.'

'You've got your shorts in a knot.'

I took a breath. 'What I don't get is why you don't. Bob and Evan giving Syd the eyeball?

14

Thinking she should model?'

'You've got it all wrong, Tim,' Susanne said. 'They were just being nice.'

'Did you know when you moved in there with Sydney that Bob was taking his son in? That OK with you?'

'They're like brother and sister,' she said.

'Give me a break. I remember being nineteen and — ' The line beeped. 'Look, I gotta go. Later, OK?'

Susanne managed a 'Yeah' before hanging up. I went to the other line, said, 'Hello?'

'Mr Blake?' said a woman who was not my daughter.

'Yes?'

'Timothy Blake?'

'Yes?'

'I'm with Fairfield Windows and Doors and we're going to be in your area later this — '

I hung up. I found a number for the Just Inn Time, dialed it. I let it ring twenty times before hanging up.

I grabbed my jacket and keys, and drove across town to the hotel, pulled right up under the apron by the front door and went inside for the first time since Syd had started here a couple of weeks ago. Before heading in I scanned the lot for her Civic. I'd seen it the odd time I'd driven by since she'd started, but it wasn't there tonight. Maybe she'd parked out back.

The glass doors parted before me as I strode into the lobby. As I approached the desk I hoped I would see Syd, but there was a man there instead. A young guy, late twenties maybe,

15

dirty-blond hair, his face cratered by the ravages of acne a decade earlier. 'May I help you?' he asked. His nametag read 'Owen'.

'Yeah,' I said. 'I was just looking for Syd?'

'I'm sorry. What's his last name?'

'It's a she. Sydney. She's my daughter.'

'Do you know what room she's staying in?'

'No, no,' I said, shaking my head. 'She works here. Right here on the desk, actually. I was expecting her home for dinner, just thought I'd swing by and see if she was going to be working a double or something.'

'I see,' said Owen.

'Her name's Sydney Blake,' I said. 'You must know her.'

Owen shook his head. 'I don't think so.'

'Are you new here?' I asked.

'No. Well, yeah.' He grinned. 'Six months. I guess that's new.'

'Sydney Blake,' I repeated. 'She's been working here two weeks. Seventeen, blond hair.'

Owen shook his head.

'Maybe they've got her working someplace else this week,' I suggested. 'Do you have an employee roster or a schedule or something that would tell you where I could find her? Or maybe I could just leave a message?'

'Could you wait just a moment?' Owen asked. 'I'll get the duty manager.'

Owen slipped through a door behind the front desk, returning a moment later with a lean, good-looking dark-haired man in his early forties. His nametag read 'Carter', and when he spoke I pegged him as from the South, although

16

what state I couldn't guess.

'Can I help you?' he asked.

'I'm looking for my daughter,' I said. 'She works here.'

'What's her name?'

'Sydney Blake,' I said. 'Syd.'

'Sydney Blake?' he said. 'Don't recognize that name, at all.'

I shook my head. 'She's only been here a couple of weeks. She's just working here for the summer.'

Carter was shaking his head, too. 'I'm sorry.'

I felt my heart beating more quickly. 'Check your employee list,' I urged him.

'I don't need to be checking any list,' he said. 'I know who works here and who doesn't, and there's nobody here by that handle.'

'Hang on,' I said. I dug out my wallet, fished around in a crevice behind my credit cards, and found a three-year-old high school photo of Sydney. I handed it across the desk.

'It's not real recent,' I said. 'But that's her.'

They took turns studying the picture. Owen's eyebrows popped up briefly, impressed, I guessed, by Sydney's good looks. Carter handed it back to me.

'I'm real sorry, Mister — '

'Blake. Tim Blake.'

'She might be working at the Howard Johnson's up the road a bit.' He tipped his head to the right.

'No,' I said. 'This is where she said she works.' My mind was racing. 'Is there a day manager?'

'That'd be Veronica.'

'Call her. Call Veronica.'

With great reluctance, Carter placed the call, apologized to the woman on the other end of the line who answered, and handed me the receiver.

I explained my situation to Veronica.

'Maybe she told you the wrong hotel,' Veronica said, echoing Carter.

'No,' I said firmly.

Veronica asked for my number and promised to call me if she heard anything. And then she hung up.

On the way home, I went through two red lights and nearly hit a guy in a Toyota Yaris. I had my cell in my hand, phoning Syd's cell and then home, then her cell again.

When I got back to the house, it was empty.

Syd did not come home that night.

Or the next night.

Or the night after that.

1

'We've also been looking at the Mazda,' the woman said. 'And we took a — Dell, what was it called? The other one we took out for a test drive?'

Her husband said, 'A Subaru.'

'That's right,' the woman said. 'A Subaru.'

The woman, whose name was Lorna, and her husband, whose name was Dell, were sitting across the desk from me in the showroom of Riverside Honda. This was the third time they'd been in to see me since I'd come back to work. There comes a point, even when you're dealing with the worst crisis of your life, when you find yourself not knowing what else to do but fall back into your routine.

Lorna had on the desk, in addition to the folder on the Accord, which was what Lorna and Dell had been talking to me about, folders on the Toyota Camry, the Mazda 6, the Subaru Legacy, the Chevrolet Malibu, the Ford Taurus, the Dodge Avenger, and half a dozen others at the bottom of the stack that I couldn't see.

'I notice that the Taurus has 263 horsepower with its standard engine, but the Accord only has 177 horsepower,' Lorna said.

'I think you'll find,' I said, working hard to stay focused, 'that the Taurus engine with that horsepower rating is a V6, while the Accord is a four-cylinder. You'll find it still gives you plenty

19

of pickup, but uses way less gas.'

'Oh,' Lorna said, nodding. 'What are the cylinders, exactly? I know you told me before, but I don't think I remember.'

Dell shook his head slowly from side to side. That was pretty much all Dell did during these visits. He sat there and let Lorna ask all the questions, do all the talking, unless he was asked something specific, and even then he usually just grunted. He appeared to be losing the will to live. I guessed he'd been sitting across the desk of at least a dozen sales associates between Bridgeport and New Haven over the last few weeks. I could see it in his face, that he didn't give a shit what kind of car they got, just so long as they got something.

But Lorna believed they must be responsible shoppers, and that meant checking out every car in the class they were looking at, comparing specs, studying warranties. All of which was a good thing, to a point, but now Lorna had so much information that she didn't know what to do with it. Lorna thought all this research would help them make an informed decision, but instead it had made it impossible for her to make one at all.

They were in their mid-forties. He was a shoe salesman in the Connecticut Post Mall, and she was a fourth-grade teacher. This was standard teacher behavior. Research your topic, consider all the options, go home and make a chart, car names across the top, features down the side, make check marks in the little boxes.

Lorna asked about the Accord's rear leg room

compared to the Malibu, which might have been an issue if they had kids, or if she'd given any indication they had any friends. Then she was on to the Accord's trunk space versus the Mazda 6. I really wasn't listening. Finally, I held up a hand.

'What car do you *like*?' I asked Lorna.

'Like?' she said.

My computer monitor was positioned between us, and the whole time Lorna was talking I was moving the mouse around, tapping the keyboard. Lorna assumed I was on the Honda website, calling up data so I could answer her questions.

I wasn't. I was on findsydneyblake.com. I was looking to see whether there'd been any recent hits on the site, whether anyone had emailed me. One of Sydney's friends, a computer whiz — actually, any of Syd's friends was a computer whiz compared to me — by the name of Jeff Bluestein had helped me put together the website, which had all the basic information.

There was a full description of Syd. Age: 17. Date of birth: April 15, 1992. Weight: approximately 115 pounds. Eye color: Blue. Hair: Blond. Height: 5 feet 3 inches.

Date of disappearance: June 29, 2009.

Last seen: Leaving for work from our address on Hill Street. Might have been spotted in the vicinity of the Just Inn Time hotel, in Milford, Connecticut.

There was also a description of Syd's silver Civic, complete with license plate number.

Visitors to the website, which Jeff had linked

21

to other sites about runaways and missing teens, were encouraged to call police, or get in touch with me, Tim Blake, directly. I'd gone through as many photos as I could find of Syd, hit up her friends for pictures they had as well, including ones they'd posted on their various Internet sites like Facebook, and plastered them all over findsydneyblake.com. I had hundreds of pictures of Syd going back through all her seventeen years, but I'd only posted ones from the last six months or so.

Wherever Syd might be, it wasn't with extended family. Susanne's and my parents were dead, neither of us had siblings, and what few relatives we had out there — an aunt here, an uncle there — we'd put on alert.

'Of course,' said Lorna, 'we're well aware of the excellent repair records that the Hondas have, and good resale value.'

I'd had two emails the day before, but not about Sydney. They were from other parents. One was from a father in Providence, telling me that his son Kenneth had been missing for a year now, and there wasn't a moment when he didn't think about him, wonder where he was, whether he was dead or alive, whether it was something he'd done, as a father, that had driven Kenneth away, or whether his son had met up with the wrong kind of people, that maybe they had —

It wasn't helpful.

The second was from a woman outside Albany who'd stumbled on the site and told me she was praying for my daughter and for me, that I should put my faith in God if I wanted Sydney to come home safely, that it would be through God that I'd find the strength to get through this.

I deleted both emails without replying.

'But the Toyotas have good resale value as well,' Lorna said. 'I was looking in Consumer Reports, where they have these little charts with all the red dots on them? Have you noticed those? Well, there are lots of red dots if the cars have good repair records, but if the cars don't have good repair records there are lots of black dots, so you can tell at a glance whether it's a good car or not by how many red or black dots are on the chart? Have you seen those?'

I checked to see whether there were any messages now. The thing was, I had already checked for messages three times since Lorna and Dell had sat down across from me. When I was at my desk, I checked about every three minutes. At least twice a day I phoned Milford police detective Kip Jennings — I'd never met a Kip before, and hadn't expected that when I finally did it would be a woman — to see what progress she was making. She'd been assigned Sydney's case, although I was starting to think 'assigned' was defined as 'the detective who has the case in the back of his or her desk drawer'.

In the time that Lorna had been going on about Consumer Reports recommendations, a message had dropped into my inbox. I clicked on it and learned that there was a problem with my CitiBank account and if I didn't immediately confirm all my personal financial details it would be suspended, which was kind of curious considering that I did not have a CitiBank account and never had.

'Jesus Christ,' I said aloud. The site had only been up for three weeks — Jeff got it up and running within days of Syd's disappearance — and already the spammers had found it.

'Excuse me?' Lorna said.

I glanced at her. 'I'm sorry,' I said. 'Just something on my screen there. You were saying, about the red dots.'

'Were you even listening to me?' she asked.

'Absolutely,' I said.

'Have you been looking at some dirty website all this time?' Dell's eyebrows went up. If there was porn on my screen, he wanted a peek.

'They don't allow that when we're with customers,' I said.

'I just don't want us to make a mistake,' Lorna said. 'We usually keep our cars for seven to ten years and that's a long time to have a car if it turns out to be a lemon.'

'Honda doesn't make lemons,' I assured her.

I needed to sell a car. I hadn't made a sale since Syd went missing. The first week I didn't come into work. It wasn't like I was home, sick with worry. I was out eighteen hours a day, driving the streets, hitting every mall and plaza and drop-in shelter in Milford and Stratford. Before long, I'd broadened the search to include Bridgeport and New Haven. I showed Syd's picture to anyone who'd look at it. I called every friend I could ever recall her mentioning.

I went back to the Just Inn Time, trying to figure out where the hell Syd was actually going every day when I'd believed she was heading into the hotel.

I'd had very little sleep in the twenty-four days since I'd last seen her.

'You know what I think we're going to do?' Lorna said, scooping the pamphlets off the desk and shoving them into her oversized purse. 'I think we should take one more look at the Nissan.'

'Why don't you do that?' I said. 'They make a very good car.'

I got to my feet as Lorna and Dell stood. Just then, my phone rang. I glanced at it, recognized the number on the call display, let it go to message, although this particular caller might not choose to leave yet another one.

'Oh,' said Lorna, putting something she'd been holding in her hand onto my desk. It was a set of car keys. 'When we were sitting in that Civic over there,' she pointed across the showroom, 'I noticed someone had left these in the cup holder.'

She did this every time she came. She'd get in a car, discover the keys, scoop them up and deliver them to me. I'd given up explaining to her it was a fire safety thing, that we left the keys in the showroom cars so that if there were a fire, we could get them out in a hurry, time permitting.

'How thoughtful,' I said. 'I'll put these away someplace safe.'

'You wouldn't want anyone driving a car right out of the showroom, now would you?' she laughed.

Dell looked as though he'd be happy if the

huge Odyssey minivan in the center of the floor ran him over.

'Well, we might be back,' Lorna said.

'I've no doubt,' I said. I wasn't in a hurry to deal with her again, so I said, 'Just to be sure, you might want to check out the Mitsubishi dealer. And have you seen the new Saturns?'

'No,' Lorna said, suddenly alarmed that she might have over-looked something. 'That first one? What was it?'

'Mitsubishi.'

Dell was giving me dagger eyes. I didn't care. Let Lorna torment some other salespeople for a while. Under normal conditions, I'd have tolerated her indecision. But I hadn't been myself since Syd went missing.

A few seconds after they'd left the showroom my desk phone trilled. No reason to get excited. It was an inside line.

I picked up. 'Tim here.'

'Got a second?'

'Sure,' I said, and replaced the receiver.

I walked over to the other side of the showroom, winding my way through a display that included a Civic, the Odyssey, a Pilot, and a boxy green Element with the suicide rear doors.

I'd been summoned to the office of Laura Cantrell, sales manager. Mid-forties with the body of a twenty-five-year-old, twice married, single for four years, brown hair, white teeth, very red lips. She drove a silver S2000, the limited production two-seater Honda sports car that we sold, maybe, a dozen of a year.

'Hey, Tim, sit down,' she said, not getting up

26

from behind her desk. Since she had an actual office, and not a cubicle, like the lowly sales staff, I was able to close her door as she'd asked.

I sat down without saying anything. I wasn't much into small talk these days.

'So how's it going?' Laura asked.

I nodded. 'OK.'

She nodded her head in the direction of the parking lot, where Lorna and Dell were at this moment getting into their eight-year-old Buick. 'Still can't make up their minds?'

'No,' I said. 'You know the story about the donkey standing between two bales of hay that starves because he can't decide which one to eat first?'

Laura wasn't interested in fables. 'We have a good product. Why can't you close this one?'

'They'll be back,' I said resignedly.

Laura leaned back in her swivel chair, folded her arms below her breasts. 'So, Tim, any news?'

I knew she was asking about Syd. 'No,' I said.

She shook her head sympathetically. 'God, it must be rough.'

'It's hard,' I said.

'Did I ever tell you I was a runaway myself once?' she asked.

'Yes,' I said.

'I was sixteen, and my parents were ragging on me about everything. School, my boyfriends, staying out late, you name it, they had a list. So I thought, screw it, I'm outta here, and I took off with this boy named Martin, hitched around the country, saw America, you know?'

'Your parents must have been worried sick.'

Laura Cantrell offered up a 'who cares' shrug.

'The point is,' she said, 'I was fine. I just needed to find out who I was. Get out from under their thumb. Be my own self. Fly solo, you know? At the end of the day, that's what matters. Independence.'

I didn't say anything.

'Look,' she said, leaning forward now, resting her elbows on the desk. I got a whiff of perfume. Expensive, I bet. 'Everyone around here is pulling for you. We really are. We can't imagine what it's like, going through what you're going through. Unimaginable. We all want Cindy to come home today.'

'Sydney,' I said.

'But the thing is, you have to go on, right? You can't worry about what you don't know. Chances are, your daughter's fine. Safe and sound. If you're lucky, she's taken along a boyfriend like I did. I know that might not be what you want to hear, but the fact is, if she's got a young man with her, already she's a hell of a lot safer. And don't even worry about the sex thing. Girls today, they're much savvier about that stuff. They know the score, they know everything about birth control. A hell of a lot more than we did in our day. Well, I was pretty knowledgeable, but most of them, they didn't have a clue.'

If I'd thought any of this was worth a comment, I might have said something.

'Anyway,' Laura said, 'what I'm working up to, Tim, is you're going to come in this month at the bottom of the board. I mean, unless there's some sort of miracle in the last week of the month. It's already the . . . ' She glanced at the wall calendar that showed a Honda Pilot driving over a mount of dirt. 'It's July twenty-third. That's too late to pull one out of the hat. You haven't sold a car yet this month. You know how it works around here. At the end of the day, it's all about selling cars. Two months at the bottom of the board and you're out.'

'I know how it works,' I said. She'd only said 'at the end of the day' twice in this conversation. Most chats, regardless of duration, she managed to get it in three times.

'And believe me, we're taking into account your situation. I think, honestly, it would take three months at the bottom of the board before you'd be cut loose. I want to be fair here.'

'Sure,' I said.

'The thing is, Tim, you're taking up a desk. And if you can't sell cars from it, I have to put someone in there who can. If you were sitting where I am you'd be saying the same thing.'

'I've been here five years,' I said. Ever since the bankruptcy, I thought, but didn't say aloud. 'I've been one of the top — if not *the* top — salesman for all of them.'

'And don't think we don't know that,' she said. 'So listen, I'm glad we had this chat, you take care, good luck with your daughter, and why don't you give that couple a call, tell them we can throw in a set of mudguards or something? Pinstriping, hell, you know how this works. At the end of the day, if they think they're getting something for nothing, they're happy.'

Bingo.

2

I didn't turn off onto Bridgeport Avenue on the way back from work. I usually got off Route 1 there, went half a mile up to Clark, hung a left and drove over the narrow bridge that spans the commuter tracks, hung a left onto Hill, where I'd lived the last five years after Susanne and I sold our mini-mansion, paid off what debts we could with the proceeds, and got much smaller places of our own.

But I kept going up the road until I had reached the Just Inn Time on the right, turned into the lot and parked. I sat in the car a moment, not sure whether to get out, knowing that I would. Why should today be any different than every other day since Syd vanished?

I got out of my CR-V. I got to drive this little crossover vehicle for free, but if and when Laura canned me I'd be on my own for wheels. Even though it was after six, it was still pretty hot out. You could see waves of humidity coming off the pavement just before Route 1 went under 95 a little further to the east.

I stood in the lot and scanned as far as I could see in all directions. The HoJo's was up the street, and beyond that the ramp coming down from the interstate. An old movie theater complex a stone's throw to the west. Hadn't we taken Sydney there to see *Toy Story 2* when she was seven or eight? For a birthday party? I recalled trying to corral a pack of kids into one row, the whole kittens-in-a-basket thing. The hotel was just down from where the road forked, Route 1 to the north, Cherry Street angling off to the southwest. Across Cherry, the Kings Highway Cemetery.

There were a couple dozen other businesses that, if I couldn't actually see from standing in the lot here, I could see the signs for them. A video store, a clock repair shop, a fish and chip takeout place, a florist, a Christian bookstore, a butcher's, a hair salon, a children's clothing store, an adult book and DVD shop.

They were all within walking distance of the hotel. If Syd had left the car parked here every day, she could have been to any of these businesses in just a few minutes.

I'd been into almost all of them at some point since she'd gone missing, showing her picture, asking if anyone had seen her. But stores had different staff working in them depending on the day and time, so it made sense to make the rounds more than once.

Of course, Syd didn't have to be working secretly at any of those outfits. Someone else with a car could have been meeting her every day in this lot, taking her God knows where from nine to five.

But if she had been working at one of these businesses within eyeshot of the hotel, why didn't she want her mother or me to know? Why would we care if she worked at a clock repair place, or a butcher's, or a —

An adult book and video shop.

My first time along that business strip, it was the one store I hadn't been in. No way, I told myself. No matter what Syd was doing, no matter what she might be keeping from us, there was no way she'd been working there.

Not a chance.

I was actually shaking my head back and forth, muttering the words 'no way' under my breath as I leaned up against my car, when I heard someone say, 'Mr Blake?'

I glanced to my left. There was a woman standing there. Blue jacket and matching skirt, sensible shoes, a Just Inn Time badge pinned to her lapel. She had some years on me, but not many. Mid-forties I guessed, with black hair and dark brown eyes. Her corporate uniform wasn't sufficiently dowdy to hide what was still an impressive figure.

'Veronica,' I said. Veronica Harp, the manager I'd spoken to on the phone the night Sydney disappeared, and seen a number of times since. 'How are you?'

'I'm fine, Mr Blake.' She paused, knowing that politeness called for her to ask the same, but she knew what my answer would be. 'And you?'

I shrugged. 'You must get sick of seeing me around here.'

She smiled awkwardly, not wanting to agree. 'I understand.'

'I'm going to have to go back to all those places,' I said, thinking out loud. Veronica didn't say anything. 'I keep thinking she must have been going to a place she could see from here.'

'I suppose,' she said. She stood there another moment, and I could tell from her body language she was struggling with whether to say something else, or go back into the hotel and leave me be. Then, 'Would you like a coffee?'

'That's OK.'

'Really. Why don't you come in? It's cooler.'

I walked with her across the lot toward the hotel. There wasn't much in the way of land-scaping. The grass was brown, an anthill spilled out, volcano-like, between two concrete walkway slabs, and the bulb shrubs needed trimming. I glanced up, saw the security cameras mounted at regular intervals, and made a disapproving snort under my breath. The glass front doors parted automatically as we approached.

She led me to the dining area just off from the lobby. Not a restaurant, exactly, but a self-serve station where the hotel put things out for breakfast. Single-serving cereal containers, fruit, muffins and donuts, coffee and juice. That was the deal here. Stay for the night, help yourself to breakfast in the morning. If you could stuff enough muffins into your pocket you were good for lunch.

A petite woman in black slacks and a white blouse was wiping down the counter, restocking a basket with cream containers. I couldn't pinpoint her ethnicity, but she looked Thai or Vietnamese. From southeast Asia, I guessed. Late twenties, early thirties.

I smiled and said hello as I reached for a takeout coffee cup. She shifted politely out of my way.

'Morning, Cantana,' Veronica said to her.

Cantana nodded.

'I think the cereals will need restocking before breakfast,' Veronica said. Cantana replenished the baskets from under the counter, where there were hundreds of individual cereal servings in peel-top containers.

I filled my takeout cup, handed an empty one to Veronica. She sat down at a table and held out her hand to the vacant chair across from her.

'Just tell me if I asked you this already,' she said, 'but you did ask at the Howard Johnson's?'

'Not just at the desk,' I said. 'I showed her picture to the cleaning staff, too.'

Veronica shook her head. 'Aren't the police doing anything?'

'As far as they're concerned, she's just another runaway. There's no actual evidence of any . . . you know. There's nothing to suggest anything has actually happened to her.'

Veronica frowned. 'Yeah, but, if they don't know where she is, how can they — '

'I know,' I said.

Veronica sipped her coffee, then asked, 'You don't have other family to help you look? I never see you here with anyone.'

'My wife — my ex-wife — has been working the phones. She hurt herself a while back, she can't walk without crutches — '

'What happened?'

'An accident, she was doing that thing where you're hooked up to a kite behind a boat?'

'Oh, I would never do that.'

'Yeah, well, that's cause you're smart. But she's doing what she can, even so. Making calls, looking on the net. She's torn up about this just

34

like I am.' And that was the truth.

'How long have you been divorced?'

'Five years,' I said. 'Since Syd was twelve.'

'Is your ex-wife remarried?'

'She has a boyfriend.' I paused. 'You know those commercials for Bob's Motors? That guy yelling at the camera?'

'Oh my, that's him? That's her boyfriend?'

I nodded.

'I always hit the mute when that comes on,' she said. That made me smile. First time in a while. 'You don't like him,' she said.

'I'd like to mute him in person,' I said.

Veronica hesitated, then asked, 'So you haven't remarried or anything.'

'No.'

'I can't see someone like you being single forever.'

I'd been seeing a woman occasionally before Syd disappeared. But even if my life hadn't been turned upside down in the last few weeks, that relationship's days had been numbered. Spectacular in the sack can trump needy and loony for a week or two, but after that, the head starts to take over and decides enough is enough.

'You think it's possible,' I said, 'my daughter was meeting someone here? Not working here formally, but, I don't know, doing something off the books? Because I think she was getting paid in cash.'

I'd taken one of my many pics of Syd from my pocket, put it on the table, just to look at her.

'I'm going to be honest with you here,' Veronica said.

'Yes?'

'Sometimes,' and she lowered her voice slightly, 'we don't do everything on the up and up here.'

I leaned in slightly. 'What do you mean?'

'What I mean is, a lot of times, that's what we do. We pay the help under the table. Not everything, of course. But here and there, saves us a bit with the taxman, you know?'

'Sure.'

'But what I'm saying is, even if your daughter'd been here, getting paid in cash, and that could end up biting us in the ass, pardon my French, I'd tell you, because no parent should go through that, not knowing what's happened to his child.'

I nodded, looked down at Syd's face.

'She's very beautiful.'

'Thank you.'

'She has beautiful hair. She looks a little bit . . . Norwegian?'

'From her mother's side,' I said. My mind wandered. 'Too bad your cameras don't work. If Syd had ever met someone in your lot . . . '

Veronica hung her head, embarrassed. 'I know. What can I say. We have the cameras mounted so people will think there's surveillance, but they're not hooked up to anything. Maybe, if we were part of a larger chain . . . '

I nodded, picked up Syd's picture and slipped it back into my jacket.

'May I show *you* a picture?' Veronica asked.

I said of course.

She went into her purse and pulled out a

computer printout snapshot of a boy, no more than six months old, wearing a Thomas the Tank Engine shirt.

'What's his name?'

'Lars.'

'That's different. What made you choose that?'

'I didn't,' she said. 'My daughter did. It's her husband's father's name.' She gave me a second to let it sink in. 'This is my grandson.'

I was momentarily speechless. 'I'm sorry, I thought — '

'Aren't you adorable,' Veronica Harp said. 'I had Gwen when I was only seventeen. I don't look so bad for a grandmother, do I?'

I had pulled myself together. 'No, you don't,' I said.

Pregnant at seventeen.

'Thank you for the coffee,' I said.

Veronica Harp put the baby picture away. 'I just know you'll find her, that everything will be OK.'

★ ★ ★

We are renting a place on Cape Cod, right on the beach. Sydney's five years old. She's been to the beach in Milford, but it can't compare to this one that seems to go forever. Sydney is mesmerized upon first seeing it. But she soon gets over her wonderment and is running down to the water's edge, getting her feet wet, scurrying back to Susanne and me, giggling and shrieking.

After a while, we think she's had enough sun,

and we suggest going back to the small beach house — not much more than a shack, really — for sandwiches. We are trudging along, the sand shifting beneath our feet, trying to keep up with Syd, pointing at her tiny footprints in the sand.

Some kids are coming through the tall grass. One of them has a dog on a lead. Sydney crosses in front of the animal just as its snout emerges from between the grass. It's not one of your traditionally mean-looking dogs. It's some kind of oversized poodle with short-cropped black fur, and when it sees Sydney it suddenly bares its teeth and snarls.

Sydney shrieks, drops her plastic pail and shovel, and starts running. The dog bolts forward to go after her, but the kid, thank God, has a tight grip on the leash. Sydney runs for the beach house, reaches up for the handle to the screen door, and disappears, the door slamming behind her.

Susanne and I run the rest of the way, not making the kind of speed we want because the sand won't allow us a good purchase. I'm in the door first, calling out, 'Sydney! Sydney!'

She doesn't call back.

We frantically search the house, finally finding her in a makeshift closet — instead of a door, there is a curtain to hide what's stored inside. She is crouched down, her face pressed into her knees so she can't see what's happening around her.

I scoop her into my arms and tell her everything is OK. Susanne squeezes into the closet and puts her arms around both of us, telling Sydney that the dog is gone, that she's safe.

Later, Susanne asks her why she ran into the beach house, instead of back to us.

'I thought he might get you guys too,' she says.

★   ★   ★

I sat in the car, parked out front of the adult entertainment store, XXX Delights, which had a florist shop on one side and the clock repair place on the other. The windows were opaque to protect passersby from having to see any of the merchandise. But the words painted on the glass in foot-high letters left no doubt as to what was being offered. 'XXX' and 'ADULT' and 'EROTICA' and 'MOVIES' and 'TOYS'.

Nothing from Fisher-Price, I was guessing.

I watched men heading in and out. Clutching items in brown wrappers as they scurried back to their cars. Was there really a need for any of this these days? Couldn't this all be had online? Did these guys have to skulk about with their collars turned up, baseball hats pulled down, cheap sunglasses hiding their eyes? For crying out loud, go home and make out with your laptops.

I was about to go in when a heavyset, balding man strode past the florist and turned into XXX Delights.

'Shit,' I said.

It was Bert, who worked in the service department at Riverside Honda. Married, so far as I knew, with kids now in their twenties. I wasn't going in while he was there. I didn't want to have to explain what I was doing there, and I didn't want him to have to explain what he was doing there.

Five minutes later he emerged with his purchase, got into an old Accord, and drove off.

I was actually grateful for the delay. I'd been steeling myself to enter the place, not because of the kind of business it was, but because I couldn't imagine Sydney having a connection to it.

'This is a waste of time,' I said under my breath as I got out of the car, crossed the lot, and went inside.

The place was brilliantly lit with hundreds of overhead fluorescent tubes, making it easy to see the covers of the hundreds of DVDs displayed on racks throughout the store. A quick glance indicated that no niche market, no remotely obscure predilection, had been ignored. In addition to movies and magazines, the store carried a wide assortment of paraphernalia, from fur-lined handcuffs to life-size — if not entirely lifelike — female dolls. They were slightly more realistic than the blow-up variety, but still not take-home-to-meet-the-folks quality. Only a few steps from the entrance, surveying the empire from a raised platform like a pharmacist at the back of a drug store, was the proprietor, an overweight woman with stringy hair reading a tattered paperback copy of *Atlas Shrugged*.

I stopped in front of her, looked up, cleared my throat, and said, 'Excuse me.'

She lay the book down, open, and said, 'Yeah.'

'I wonder if you could help me,' I said.

'Sure,' she said. When I didn't speak up right away, she said, 'Go ahead, tell me what you're looking for, I've heard everything, and I don't give a shit.'

I handed her a picture of Sydney. 'You ever seen this girl?'

She took the pic, glanced at it, handed it back. 'If you know her name I can put it into the computer and see what movies she's been in.'

'Not in a movie. Have you ever seen her here, in this store, or even in the area? Going back about three weeks?'

'We don't have a lot of girl customers,' she said flatly.

'I know, I'm probably wasting my time — '

'And mine,' she said, her hand on the book.

'But if you wouldn't mind taking another look.'

She sighed, lifted her hand off the book and took the picture a second time. 'So who is she?'

'Sydney Blake,' I said. 'She's my daughter.'

'And you think she might have been hanging around *here*?'

'No,' I said. 'But if I only look in the places where I think she might have been, I might not ever find her.'

She studied the picture for two seconds and handed it back. 'Sorry.'

'You're sure?'

She looked exasperated. 'You need help with anything else?'

'No,' I said. 'Thanks anyway.' I let her get back to Ayn Rand.

As I stepped out, a thin, white-haired woman was locking up the flower shop. A young man, mid-twenties, was obediently standing by her, like a dog waiting to be told what to do. The woman looked my way briefly but turned her head before we could make eye contact. You didn't want to be making eye contact with men coming out of XXX Delights.

'So we'll see you in the morning,' the woman said to the man.

'Yup,' he said.

I'd talked to this woman before, shown her Syd's picture, maybe a week ago. She'd actually taken the time to study the photo, and seemed genuinely sorry when she wasn't able to help me.

'Hello,' I said.

She didn't turn my way, although I was sure she heard me. 'Hello,' I said again. 'We spoke last week?' I didn't have to struggle hard for a name. The sign in the window said 'Shaw Flowers'. I said, 'Mrs Shaw?'

I took a couple of steps toward her and she turned warily. But when she saw in my hand the photo the woman in the porn shop had returned to me, she seemed to relax.

'Oh, I remember you,' Mrs Shaw said.

I nodded my head toward the store I'd just come from. 'Still asking around.'

'Oh my,' she said. 'You didn't find your daughter there, did you?'

'No,' I said.

'Well, that's good,' Mrs Shaw said.

Like finding Syd there would be worse than never finding her at all.

'Hi,' I said to the young man standing next to her.

At first, I'd put him in his mid-twenties, but now I wasn't sure. There was a boyishness about him, his skin soft and milky white, his short black hair cut perfectly, as though he'd just jumped out of a barber's chair. He had the kind of looks that would make people think, even when he was in his forties, that he'd just finished school. He was slim, and stood a full head taller than Mrs Shaw, and his eyes always seemed to be moving.

'Ian, say hello,' she said, like she was talking to a six-year-old.

'Hello,' he said.

I nodded. 'You work here?' I asked him. 'Because I don't remember you when I was here the last time.'

He nodded.

'Ian's out on deliveries all day,' Mrs Shaw said, pointing to a blue Toyota Sienna minivan parked near my CR-V. 'Shaw Flowers' was stenciled on the rear door windows. 'Remember my telling you?' she said to Ian. 'About the man who came by looking for his daughter?'

He shook his head. 'I don't remember. You didn't tell me.'

'Of course I did. Oh, you never listen.' She smiled at me, rolled her eyes and said, 'He's always off somewhere else even when he's there. Or he's got those little wires in his ears.'

Ian looked down and away.

'You should show Ian her picture,' Mrs Shaw said. 'He lives right here. He's taken the

43

apartment behind the store.'

A man went into the porn shop and Mrs Shaw scowled. 'We were here long before them,' she said to me quietly. 'But I'll be damned if I'm going to move my shop. We tried a petition before to get rid of them and it looks like we're going to have to do it again.'

I handed the picture to Ian. 'Her name's Sydney.'

He took the shot, barely glanced at, handed it back and shook his head. 'I don't know her,' he said.

'But have you ever seen her around?' I asked.

'No,' he said. Abruptly, he gave Mrs Shaw a light hug and an air kiss and said, 'I'll see you tomorrow.'

Then he walked around the corner of the building and disappeared.

★ ★ ★

There was someone waiting for me when I pulled into the driveway.

Susanne and Bob were sitting in his black Hummer. Both front doors opened when I pulled up. As I was putting my car in park and unbuckling my seatbelt, Susanne was coming up around the back. Last time I'd seen her she'd been on crutches, and now she was using a cane, grasped firmly in her right hand. She wasn't moving a whole lot faster, but she did manage to plant herself by my door as I got out.

I wondered whether I should get ready to defend myself. The first time I saw Susanne after

Syd had vanished, she and Bob had driven over from Stratford and she'd strode up to me on her crutches and balanced herself long enough to slap me across the face, shouting: 'It's all your fault! You were supposed to be looking after her!'

And I took it, because it was an opinion I shared.

Not much had changed since then, at least from my point of view. I still felt responsible. Still felt it was my fault Syd had slipped away from me, on my watch. There had to have been signals I'd missed. Surely, if I'd been paying better attention, things never would have gotten to this point.

Even though I still felt that way, I wasn't in the mood today for an attack. So as I got out of the car, I braced myself.

But she wasn't raising a hand to me. She had both arms extended, cane dangling, and there were tears running down her cheeks. She fell into me, slipped her arms around me as Bob watched.

'What is it, Suze?' I asked. 'What's going on?'

'Something's happened,' she said.

3

'What?' I asked her. 'What's happened?'

Bob Janigan stepped forward, caught my eye and said, 'It's nothing really. I told her not to — '

I held up a hand. I wasn't interested in what Bob had to say, at least not yet. 'What's happened?' I asked Susanne again. 'You've heard from Syd? Has she gotten in touch? Is she OK?'

Susanne pulled away from me and shook her head. This was it, I told myself. Susanne's heard something. She's heard something bad.

'No,' she said. 'I haven't heard anything.'

'What is it, then?'

'We're being watched,' she said. I glanced at Bob, who shook his head back and forth in small increments.

'Who's watching you? Where? When did this happen?'

'A few times,' she said. 'They're in a van. Watching the house.'

I look at Bob again. 'Your house, or Susanne's house?'

'Mine,' he said, clearing his throat. Susanne's house was sitting empty, and I knew she was on the verge of putting it on the market, waiting to see how things worked out with Bob. The three of us checked the house regularly, on the chance Syd might be hiding out there, but there was no evidence she'd as much as popped in.

Bob said, 'Suze thinks some guy's been

46

keeping an eye on the place.'

Even in the midst of all that we were dealing with, it rankled that Bob used the same diminutive for Susanne I always had. Would it kill him to call her Sue, or Susie? But I tried to stay focused.

'What guy?' I asked. 'Who is it?'

'I don't know,' Susanne said. 'I couldn't get a look at him. It was night, and the windows were tinted. Why would someone be watching us?'

'Have you seen him?' I asked Bob.

He let out a long sigh. He's a tall guy, better looking in person than in his commercials, where he goes for an 'everyman' kind of look in khakis and short sleeves and slicked-back hair, what there was of it. But in person, he's all designer. Little polo players stitched to his shirts, perfectly creased slacks, expensive loafers without socks. If it were a little cooler he'd have a sweater tied around his neck, yuppie-style.

'I've seen a van,' he admitted. 'But it was halfway down the block. It's been there two, maybe three times over the last couple of weeks. I think there's usually been someone in it, but it's kind of hard to tell.'

'What kind of van?' I asked.

'Chrysler, probably,' he said. 'An older one.'

I wondered if it could be cops. You normally expected to see them in a Crown Vic or an Impala, but cops working undercover could easily be in a van.

'You think it was watching the house?' I asked him. A van parked halfway down the block didn't have to mean anything.

47

'You have to understand,' Bob said, 'we've all been under a lot of stress lately. This thing with Sydney, it's taking its toll.'

This thing with Sydney. He made it sound like we were having a stretch of bad weather. *Hope this thing with Sydney passes soon so we can put the top down on the car.*

'I'm sure it's been very hard on you,' I said to him.

He gave me a look. 'Don't start, Tim. I'm trying to help here. And all I'm saying is, everybody's radar's on high alert. Every time a girl goes by, we're looking to see if it's Sydney. We hear a car pull into the driveway, we rush to see if it's her being brought home by the police. So Suze — both of us — we're looking at the world different, you know what I'm saying? So we see a car parked on the street we just wonder what's going on.'

'He was smoking,' Susanne said, her voice sounding very tired. 'It was like a little orange dot behind the steering wheel, every time he took a drag on the cigarette.'

'Did you call the police?' I asked.

'And say what?' said Bob, even though he wasn't the one I was asking. ' 'Officer, there's a van parked perfectly legally down the street. Could you check it out?' '

'I wonder if it has to do with Sydney,' Susanne said, taking a tissue out of the sleeve of her pullover top and dabbing at her eyes.

'First of all,' I said, 'you don't know that it has anything to do with Sydney or you or anyone at all. Bob might actually be right about this. We're all under a terrible strain. You don't look like you've slept for weeks — '

'Thanks a lot,' she said.

I tried to backtrack. 'Neither of us has been getting the sleep we need. You get so tired you lose perspective, you start misinterpreting things people say to you, misconstruing their meaning.'

'That's right,' Bob said to Susanne.

'I just want you to take me seriously about this,' Susanne said to me.

'I am,' I said.

'I didn't belittle your concerns, years ago,' she said.

'What?'

'You remember,' she said. 'When you thought someone was going around, asking questions about you?'

I hadn't thought about that in a very long time. It had to have been ten, twelve years ago. The feeling that someone was looking into my background. A couple of people I knew said they'd had a call from someone, said I'd given them as a reference. What did they know about me? Was I reliable? As though I'd been applying for an apartment or a new job or a passport, except I wasn't applying for any of those things.

And then it stopped, and I never heard another thing.

'I remember,' I said. 'And I'm not belittling your concerns. If you think someone's watching the house, I believe you.'

'That's not all,' she said. 'Things have been disappearing. Bob bought me a Longines watch, and I don't know what happened to it. I'm sure — '

49

Bob said, 'Honey, you just misplaced it, I'm sure.'

'And what about the money?' she asked him. 'That cash? It was nearly a hundred dollars.' She looked at me. 'In my purse.'

'Has there been a break-in?' I asked.

'I don't know,' she said. 'But something's going on.'

The back door on the Hummer's driver's side opened. I hadn't realized anyone else was in the car. Evan slithered out of the back seat like a piece of boneless chicken — if I'd ever known which wife Bob made this kid with I'd since forgotten.

'Could you like turn on the car so I could put the A/C on?' he asked. He had a handful of scratch-and-win lottery tickets — what Sydney and I call 'scratch-and-lose' tickets — with panels already rubbed off. He had a penny pinched between the thumb and index finger of his other hand. 'It's roasting in there.'

'In a sec, Evan,' his father said. I'd only met Evan three or four times — just once since Syd had disappeared — and I don't think he'd said more than ten words to me on all those occasions put together. Nineteen, out of high school — I didn't know whether he'd left with a diploma or not — and not planning to go anywhere in the fall, so far as I knew. Since Bob had brought him back to his house, he'd been doing little more than hanging around there and a few odd jobs on one of Bob's lots. He was tall like his father, with dark locks of hair hanging sheepdog-like over his eyes.

'Are we getting some food on the way back?' he asked. He hadn't even looked at me.

'Hold on, for Christ's sake,' Bob said, rolling his eyes, and for a moment there, you had to wonder whether he was thinking the wrong kid went missing.

'I need to go inside for a minute,' Susanne said. She started hobbling toward the front door, putting a lot of weight on the cane.

'You OK?' I asked.

'I just . . . I need to go in and sit down for a moment,' she said. 'My hip's really throbbing today.'

I tried to catch Bob's eye, give him my 'Nice boat driving' look, but he looked away.

'The house is locked,' I said, handing her my set of keys. She might still have had a key to the house on her key ring, but I wasn't sure. I hadn't had the locks changed since our split. It wasn't as if I expected her to sneak back and make off with the furniture. Anything decent we still had after the divorce went to her place, anyway. It looked as though, ultimately, it would end up at Bob's place.

'You said we were going to stop and get something to eat,' Evan said, waving the scratched lottery tickets in the air to blow off the leftover debris.

'Just get in the car,' Bob said. 'Open the doors if you need some air.'

Once Susanne was in the house, I said to Bob, 'How is she?'

He looked down at the ground. 'She's fine, she's good. Getting better every day.'

51

'What were you doing anyway?' I asked. 'Watching teenage girls sunbathing on the beach while Suze got dragged behind the boat?'

He glared.

'Any of them look like future models? I know how you're always on the lookout for prospects.'

He shook his head in exasperation. 'For fuck's sake, Tim, let it go. I told you, weeks ago, that was a totally innocent comment. OK, maybe it was inappropriate, I get that now. But for Christ's sake, can we move on?' He stopped the head shake, lowered his voice. 'Don't you think there are bigger things to worry about right now?'

'Of course,' I said, keeping my voice even.

'Susanne, she's on the phone night and day. Calling shelters across the state. Police departments. Faxing pictures.' He shook his head disapprovingly. 'She can't do this all alone, Tim. She needs help.'

'Excuse me?'

'You have to pick up some of the slack. Syd's your daughter, too, you know.'

'Are you fucking kidding me?'

'I know you're not a detail guy, Tim, that you kind of let things slip a bit, that that's how you lost the business and all, but you gotta pick up the ball and run with it this time, you know what I'm saying?'

I wanted to slam his head into the Hummer.

'Suze can't do it all,' Bob said. 'The other day, she wanted me to drop her off at the Stamford Town Center so she could wander around, look at all the kids who were there in case she spotted

Syd. You know how huge that place is, and with that pit-like thing in the middle with the tiered seating? And her on a cane, likely to fall over half the time if she's not careful?'

I turned away for a moment, forcing the anger down, like trying to swallow a Brussels sprout as a kid.

'This van on your street,' I said.

'Yeah?'

'You think it's watching the house?'

'I don't know. It seems pretty crazy to me.'

'Any reason why anyone would want to be watching you?'

'You mean us?'

'I mean you. If there really was someone watching your house, maybe they were watching you, maybe it's got nothing to do with Suze, or Syd.'

'What's that supposed to mean?'

'Did you sell somebody another Katrina?' I asked him. 'They might be coming around looking for payback.'

'Oh for crying out loud, Tim, you really never let anything go. I sell one car, a car I bought in good faith three years ago from a wholesaler who swore it was clean, and OK, it turned out to have been underwater for a while in New Orleans, and it made the news. I'm not happy it happened, but sometimes in this business you get jerked around. Maybe, if you'd hung in running a business instead of just working at one, you'd have a better understanding of that.'

My neck felt like it was on fire.

'I run an honest business, Tim,' he added.

53

I didn't bother to mention the Honda S2000 sports car he'd tried to wholesale to me once, arguing it would sell faster off an authorized Honda lot than any of his. Said he wanted to do me a favor, that the car was pristine, low miles, still loads of warranty left. Almost got me, too. I checked the car out, top to bottom, and it wasn't until I looked at the washers under the bolts that held the fenders to the frame that I noticed they weren't original Honda parts. So then I took down the VIN number, made some calls, traced the car back to a dealership in Oregon that had reported it stolen ten months before. The car had been finally recovered, at least what was left of it. It had been stripped of wheels and seats and airbags and enough other parts to make half a car. The insurance company paid off on the vehicle, acquired its remains and auctioned them off. The buyer replaced the missing parts, sold the Honda to Bob, who then tried to fob it off on me as an original.

Bob hadn't gotten to where he was today without cutting the occasional corner.

'Find another sucker,' I'd told him at the time.

Today, he said, 'I'm clean, Tim. I've got nothing to hide. You want to come in and see my books, check the history of the cars on my lot, be my guest.'

Neck still prickling, I said, 'A jealous husband, then.'

Bob was briefly speechless. Then, 'How dare you even suggest I'd be seeing another woman.'

The thing was, I had no reason to suspect Bob of stepping out. The words were out of my mouth before I'd given much thought to them.

'Sorry,' I said.

'I love Susanne,' he said, and after a couple seconds added, 'And I love Syd, too. I'm sick to death about this. She's a great kid. I want to do anything I can to help.'

I didn't want to hear him say he loved my daughter, no matter how he meant it. I said, 'What's all this about her missing watch, and stolen cash?'

Bob shook his head sadly. 'Like I said, I think it's the stress. Susanne gets distracted. She could have lost the watch anywhere. And the cash . . . I don't know. She could have spent it on something and it slipped her mind.'

I supposed it was possible.

'About Syd,' Bob said.

'Go ahead.'

'There's a guy I know.'

'A guy?'

'I mean, the police, what are they really doing, right? She's just another runaway to them. They're not going to do anything unless, like, a body turns up, right?'

The comment cut like a knife. My eyes narrowed. For a second, the houses on Hill seemed to blur.

'OK,' he said. 'Bad choice of words. But if the cops aren't going to put any effort into this, then maybe we have to bring in someone who will.'

'I'm working on this every day,' I told him. 'I've got the website, I'm making calls, I'm driving around, going to the hotel, I'm — '

'All right, I know, I know. But this guy, he's a

good guy. The thing is, he owes me a favor, so I thought I could let him pay me back by asking around, check this and that, beat around the bushes a bit.'

My first inclination was to tell Bob to forget it. That would have been pride talking. At some level, I wanted to be the one who found Syd. But more than anything, I just wanted her back. If someone else got to take the credit, I could sure live with that.

'So, this guy,' I said. 'What is he? Private detective? Ex-cop?'

'He's in security,' Bob said. 'Name's Arnold Chilton.'

I thought about it for a moment. I didn't like Bob, and I didn't like accepting help from him, but if he knew someone professional with the skills to find Sydney, I wasn't going to say no.

It took all I had in me to do it, but I reached my hand out to him. He took it, but I could tell the gesture caught him off guard, like he was expecting me to be palming a joy buzzer. 'Thank you,' I said. 'I appreciate it.' I dug a little deeper. 'And thank you for looking after Susanne through all of this. She really needs your support, on several fronts.'

'Yeah, sure,' he said, still taken aback.

We walked back to our house. Evan was leaning up against the back of the Hummer, in a world of his own, singing a song quietly to himself, playing air guitar. He thought he was the next Kurt Cobain. Since she wasn't out front, I guessed Susanne was still in the house.

'We going?' Evan asked Bob, taking a break

from his music. 'I need to get home. I got stuff to do on the computer.'

'I guess,' he said. To me, he said, 'You want to tell Susanne we're ready to take off?'

I nodded and went into the house. I thought she might be resting in the living room, but she wasn't there.

'Susanne?' I called.

I heard sniffing coming from Sydney's bedroom. The door was partially closed, so I gently pushed it open and saw my ex-wife standing in front of our daughter's dresser, the cane leaned up against the wall. She had her back to me. Her head was bowed, her shoulders trembling.

I closed the distance between us, put one arm around her and pulled her close to me. She was dabbing her eyes with one hand, touching various items on Syd's dresser with the other. Syd didn't have quite as much stuff here as I imagined she did in her room at Bob's place in Stratford, but there was still plenty of clutter. Q-Tips in a Happy Face coffee mug, various creams and moisturizers and cans of hairspray, bank statements with balances of less than a hundred dollars, various photos of herself with friends like Patty Swain and Jeff Bluestein, an iPod Shuffle music player, no bigger than a pack of matches, and the stringy earphone buds that went with it.

'She never went anywhere without this,' Susanne said, touching the player lightly with her index finger, as though it were a rare artifact.

'She didn't usually take it to work,' I said. 'But

any other time, yeah.'

'So if she was going to go away somewhere, if she'd planned to go away, she would have taken it,' Susanne whispered.

'I don't know,' I said quietly. But that made sense to me. Syd hadn't packed anything. The bag she used to bring her things from Bob's place was here. All of her clothes were either in her closet, or, as was often the case with her, scattered across her bed and the floor.

The iPod was recharged by plugging it into Syd's laptop, which sat a few feet away on her desk. We'd already been through it, with the police, checking out Syd's emails, her Facebook page, the history of sites she'd visited in the days leading up to her disappearance. We hadn't come up with anything useful.

Susanne turned into me. 'Is she alive, Tim? Is our girl still alive?'

I took the player and placed it into the recharging unit that was already linked to the laptop. 'I want it all ready to go for when she gets back,' I said.

4

The next morning I took Syd's tiny music shuffler with me on the way to work, plugging it into the car's auxiliary jack. When I was little, and my father was away on business, like when he made his annual trek to Detroit to see the new models before anyone else got to see them, I would wrap myself in one of his coats when I went to bed.

Today, I would surround myself with my daughter's music.

The gadget was set to play tunes in a totally random order, so first I heard Amy Winehouse, then the Beatles ('The Long and Winding Road', one of my favorites; who knew Syd liked this?), followed by a piece by one of those two Davids who faced off at the end of a recent season of *American Idol*. I hadn't quite gotten to the end of it when I pulled into the parking lot of the donut shop.

I arrived at the dealership with two boxes, a dozen donuts in each. I went into the service bay where the mechanics were already at work on several different Honda models. It had been a while since I'd left donuts for the guys — and two gals, who worked in parts — out here, and the gesture was overdue. You didn't work in isolation at a car dealership. Or if you did, you were an idiot. Just because you worked in sales didn't mean you could ignore people in other parts of the building. Like on a Friday night at the close of business, and you couldn't pry the plates off a trade-in to transfer them to a new car a customer was picking up, and you needed someone from service to help you out with a bigger socket wrench. If you hadn't made any friends in there, you might as well sit on your tiny wrench and rotate.

Most days, when my mind wasn't preoccupied with bigger things, I loved coming in here and hanging out. The whirs and clinks of the tools used by the service technicians, as they preferred to be called, echoed together in a kind of mechanical symphony. The cars, suspended in mid-air on pneumatic hoists, looked somehow vulnerable, their grimy undersides exposed. Ever since I was a kid, when I would come down to the dealership where my father worked, I'd loved looking at cars from a perspective few people saw. It was like being let in on a secret.

'Donuts!' someone shouted when I set down the boxes.

The first one over was Bert, who was all smiles. 'You are the best,' he said. If he had any inkling that I'd witnessed his visit to the porn shop, he didn't let on.

He wiped his hands on the rag that had been peeking out his front pocket, then reached into the box for a cherry-filled. Then, reconsidering, he held it out to me.

'Cherry's your favorite, right?'

'No,' I said. 'It's all yours.'

'You're sure?' he asked, the filling oozing out the side of the donut and over his fingers.

'Positive,' I said. I took a double chocolate to make the point.

'How you doin'?' he asked.

I smiled. 'OK,' I said. I figured he was referring to Syd. It was a topic few around the building wanted to address directly with me. I was the guy with the missing kid. It was like having a disease. People tended to steer clear; they didn't know what to say.

When Syd had worked here last summer, she'd spent a lot of time with Bert and everyone else out here, and they'd all come to love her. She was the dealership gofer, doing anything and everything she was asked. Cleaning and polishing vehicles, changing license plates, doing coffee runs, restocking parts in the right bins, jockeying cars in the lot. She'd barely had her driver's license, and wasn't insured to take any of the cars in stock out on the road, but she moved them around the property like nobody's business. She could practically back up an Odyssey van blindfolded, mastered the stick in an S2000. That was the thing about Syd. You only had to show her once how to do something.

Some other mechanics wandered over, grabbed a donut, mumbled some thanks, gave me a friendly punch in the arm, returned to work. Barb from the parts department, fiftyish, married four times, rumored to have given a tumble to half the guys out here, came out of her office and said, 'There better be a chocolate one left in there.'

I held one out to her.

'No fucking coffee?' she said.

'Bite me,' I said.

'Where?' she asked, her eyes doing a little dance.

I went into the showroom and dropped into the chair behind my desk. My message light was flashing. I dialed immediately into my voicemail, but all I had was a call from someone wondering how much his 2001 Accord ('V6, spoiler, mags, metallic paint, really mint, you know, except I have a dog, and there are some urine stains on the upholstery') might be worth.

Another message: 'Hey, Tim, I called yesterday, didn't leave a message, thought I'd try you today. Look, I know you're going through a lot right now, what with Sydney running away and everything, but I'd really like to be there for you, you know? Is it something I did? Did I do something wrong? Because, I thought we had something pretty good going. If I said something that made you angry I wish you'd just tell me what it was and we could talk it out and whatever I did I won't do it again. We were having some real fun, don't you think? I'd really like to see you again. I could make you some dinner, maybe pick something up, bring it over. And listen, they had a sale the other day? At Victoria's Secret? Picked up a couple things, you know? So give me a call if you get a chance. Or I can try you at home tonight. So, gotta go.'

Kate.

I fired up my computer and went to the website about Sydney. No emails, and judging by the counter that recorded visits to the site, no one had dropped by recently. My guess was the last person who'd been to the site was me, shortly after I'd gotten up that morning.

Maybe it was time to put another call into Kip Jennings.

'Hey, Tim,' said a voice from the other side of my semi-cubicle wall.

It was Andy Hertz, our sales baby. He was only twenty-three, and had been with us a year. That was the thing about selling cars. You didn't necessarily need a lot of education. If you could sell, you could sell. And the thing you had to remember was that you weren't selling cars, you were selling yourself. Andy, good looking in his smartly tailored clothes and brushcut, and undeniably charming, had no problem in that area, particularly with older women, who looked at him like he was their own son.

Like a lot of guys new to the business, Andy started out hot. Came close to the top of the board a number of times. But again, like a lot of newbies, he seemed to hit a wall several months in. The mojo was gone. At least I had an excuse for not selling any cars this July, even if Laura Cantrell seemed unimpressed that it was a pretty good one. Andy'd hit a dry spell, and it was just one of those things.

His normal cheerfulness was not in evidence when I wheeled my chair around to see him.

'Andy,' I said.

'Laura wants to see me in five,' he said.

'Any last words you'd like me to pass along to your family?'

'Tim, really, I think she's going to carve me out a new one,' he said.

'We all hit these kinds of stretches,' I said.

'I haven't sold a car in two weeks. I had that one guy, I was sure he was going to get the Civic, I call him up, he got a Chevy Cobalt. I mean, come on, give me a fucking break. A Cobalt?'

'Happens,' I said.

'I think she's going to fire me. I've tried working my contacts, even family. I've already sold my mom a car, but my dad still refuses to buy Japanese. Says that's why the country's going into the toilet, we're not buying from Detroit. I tell him if Detroit hadn't been so slow to get its head out of its ass and stop making big SUVs, it would have been fine, and then he gets all pissed and tells me if I like the Japs so much maybe I should go live over there and live on sushi. I don't know if I can pay my rent this month. I'd rather kill myself than move back in with my parents. Things keep going like this, I'll be making sperm bank donations to get lunch money.'

'Been there, done that,' I said, recalling desperate times in college. 'You run the risk of repetitive strain injury.' Despite everything, Andy grinned. 'Get out the used car ads,' I told him.

'Huh?'

'From the newspapers, online, anything in this area. See who's selling their cars privately.'

Andy looked at me. It was taking a minute for him to figure this out.

'You call them up, you say hey, I saw your ad for your Pontiac Vibe or whatever it is, you don't want to buy it, but you wondered whether they'd made up their mind about a replacement vehicle, that we have great financing and lease rates on at the moment, and if they'd like to come in, you'd love to get them into a new Honda, bring their current car in for a trade.'

'That's a fucking awesome idea.' He smiled giddily. 'So I tell Cantrell I'm working a whole bunch of new leads.'

'Just be ready when she rips a page out of the phone book and hands it to you.'

'Why would she do that?'

'She'll say, 'Leads, you need fucking leads? Here's a whole page of them.' She has one phone book in there, all she uses it for is to rip out pages.'

'Hey, you're first up, right?' Andy was looking over my shoulder. I turned around, saw a stocky, wide-shouldered, middle-aged guy who looked to have cut himself shaving a couple of times that morning, like he didn't do it that often but today he wanted to make a good impression and it backfired. He had on a crisp, clean work-shirt, but his worn jeans and scuffed work boots betrayed him. It was like he was thinking, if the top half of me makes a good impression, no one'll notice the rest of me.

He was admiring a pickup truck in the showroom.

'Hi,' I said, out of my chair. As I headed over to him I caught Laura out of the corner of my eye, summoning Andy, the poor bastard.

'Hey,' said the guy. He had a deep, gruff voice.

'The Ridgeline,' I said, nodding at the blue truck. 'Gets a 'recommended' rating in Consumer Reports.'

'Nice truck,' he said, slowly walking around it.

65

'What are you driving now?' I asked.

'F-150,' he said. The Ford. Also a good truck, recommended by Consumer, but not something I felt needed pointing out. I glanced out the showroom window, looking for it, but instead what caught my eye was a plain, unmarked Chevy, and Kip Jennings getting out.

'Would it be possible to take one of these for a test drive?' he asked.

'Sure thing,' I said. 'I just need a driver's license from you, we make a photocopy.'

He fished out his wallet, gave me his license, which I scanned. His name was Richard Fletcher, and I extended a hand. 'Mr Fletcher, good to meet you, I'm Tim Blake.' I handed him one of my business cards, which included not only my work number, but my home and cell numbers.

'Hey,' he said, slipping it into his pocket.

I walked the license over to the girl at reception so she could make a copy, all the while glancing out into the lot at Jennings. She was short — she probably topped out at five feet — with strong facial features. A woman my mother might have referred to as handsome instead of pretty, but the latter word was also apt. I would have handed Mr Fletcher off to Andy, but he was in Laura's office getting chewed out. If I had to let a customer cool his heels while I found out what had happened to my daughter, tough. But Jennings was on her cell, so I took another moment to get this guy set up for a test drive.

I instructed one of the younger guys in the

office to track down a Ridgeline, hang some dealer plates off it, and bring it up to the door ASAP.

'We'll have one ready for you in just a couple of minutes,' I said to Fletcher. 'Normally I'd tag along for the test drive — '

Fletcher looked dismayed. 'Last place I went let me take it out alone. Not so much, you know, pressure?'

'Yeah, well, I was about to say, if you're OK going alone, I just have to talk to this person — '

'That's perfect,' he said.

'One of the fellows will be bringing up one of our demo trucks in a second. We can talk after?'

Even though Jennings was still on her phone, I bolted out of the showroom and walked briskly across the lot toward her. She saw me coming, held up an index finger to indicate that she'd be just another second. I stood patiently, like a kid waiting to see the teacher, while she finished her call.

It didn't exactly sound like police business. Jennings said, 'Well what do you expect? If you don't study, you're not going to do well. If you don't do your homework, you're going to get a zero. It's not rocket science, Cassie. You don't do the work, you don't get the marks . . . Yeah, OK . . . I don't know yet. Maybe hot dogs or something. I got to go, sweetheart.'

She flipped the phone shut and slipped it into the purse slung over her shoulder.

'Sorry,' I said. 'I didn't mean to listen in.'

'That's OK,' Kip Jennings said. 'My daughter. She doesn't think it's fair that you get a zero when you don't hand in an assignment.'

'How old is she?'

'Twelve,' she said.

Out of the corner of my eye, I saw Richard Fletcher get into the gleaming new pickup and drive it off the lot. But I was focused on Jennings, what she might have to say.

She must have seen the look on my face, a mixture of hope, expectation and dread, so she got to it right away. She took half a step back so that when she looked up at me she didn't have to crane her neck so much.

'You have time to take a ride with me?' she asked.

'Where?' I asked.

Please don't say the morgue.

'Up to Derby,' she said.

'What's in Derby?'

'Your daughter's car,' Jennings said.

5

'Where did you find it?' I asked, sitting up front in Kip Jennings's gray four-door Chevy. It had none of the trappings of a regular police car. No obvious markings, no rooftop light, no barrier between the front and back seats. Just lots of discarded junk food wrappers and empty coffee cups.

'I didn't find it,' Jennings said. 'It was found in a Wal-Mart lot. It had been sitting there a few days. The management finally called the cops to have it towed.'

'Was there anyone . . . ' I hesitated. 'Was there anyone in the car?' I was thinking about the trunk.

Jennings glanced over at me. 'No,' she said, then looked at the tiny satellite navigation screen that had been stuck to the top of the dash. 'I always have this on even when I know where I'm going. I just like watching it.'

'How long's the car been there?'

'Not sure. It was parked with a few others, no one really noticed it for a while.'

I closed my eyes a moment, opened them, watched the trees go by as we headed north up the winding two-lane Derby Milford Road, about a twenty-minute drive.

'Where's the car now?' I pictured a brilliantly lit forensics lab the size of an airplane hangar, the car being gone over for clues by technicians in Hazmat suits.

'In a local compound, where they take cars they've towed for parking illegally, that kind of thing. When they brought the car in they ran the plate, which I'd had flagged in the system. That's when they called me. Look, I haven't even seen the car yet. You know the car, you can tell me if you notice anything out of the ordinary about it.'

'Sure,' I said.

Everything about this was out of the ordinary. My daughter was missing. At times over the last couple of weeks I'd tried to find comfort in the thought that while Syd might have run off, that didn't have to mean harm had come to her.

The first couple of days she was gone, I told myself it was about the fight we'd had. My questioning her about the Versace sunglasses, asking about the receipt. That had pissed Syd off big time, and I could imagine her wanting to punish me for thinking she might have stolen them.

But as the days went on, it seemed unlikely that argument had sparked her disappearance. Then I tried to tell myself something else that had made her angry enough to run away. Something I'd done, or maybe Susanne.

Maybe she was punishing both of us, I wondered. For splitting up. For ruining what had been, for a long time, a pretty decent little family. For making her shunt back and forth between houses for five years, for having to move now, at seventeen, into Bob's house. Sure, it was a bigger place, he had more money, could give her things I couldn't, but maybe all this change was unsettling, messing her up.

Now, though, there were more logistical questions. I wasn't just asking myself why she was gone. I was asking myself how. If she didn't have wheels, how had she gotten to wherever she'd gone? Why leave the car behind?

I couldn't think of any reasons that made me feel optimistic.

Jennings hung a left at the end of Derby Milford Road, went another couple of miles, straight past the Wal-Mart where I presumed Syd's silver Civic had been found, then pulled off onto a gravel lot where a couple of tow trucks were parked outside a low cinder block building that adjoined a fenced-in compound full of cars.

Jennings found a badge in her purse and flashed it ut someone in the office window. The metal gate that led into the compound buzzed, Jennings went through and beckoned me to follow her.

The Civic was tucked in between a GMC Yukon and a Toyota Celica from the 1980s. Syd's car looked the same as the last time I'd seen it, yet it was somehow different. It wasn't just Syd's car now. There was something ominous about it, as though it was sentient, that it knew things it didn't want to tell us.

'Don't touch it,' Jennings said. 'Don't touch anything. In fact, put your hands in your pockets.'

I did as I was told. Jennings set her purse down on the hood of the Celica and took out a pair of surgical-type gloves. She pulled them on, giving them a good snap at the wrist.

I walked slowly around the car, peering into

the windows. Sydney was proud of this little car, and kept it tidy. Unlike Jennings's vehicle, there were no discarded Big Mac boxes or Dunkin' Donut cups.

'Do you have the keys?' I asked.

'No,' Jennings said, and sniffed. 'But the car was found unlocked.'

She was walking around it in a crouched position, looking at it in a trained, professional way. She seemed to be studying the handle on the driver's door.

'What?' I asked from the other side of the car.

She held up one gloved hand, index finger pointed up, as if to say, 'Give me a sec.'

I came around the back of the car, stood there and watched as she gingerly opened the door with one finger, slipping it under the handle and lifting very carefully.

'What are you doing?' I asked.

Again, she said nothing. Once she had the door wide open, she looked down, next to the driver's seat, and reached down. There were a couple of small levers there, one for the gas cap and one for the trunk. Next thing I knew, the trunk lid, right in front of me, clicked and popped open an inch.

Even though Jennings had said earlier that no one had been found in the car, the unlocked trunk provoked an overwhelming sense of dread.

'Don't open it,' Jennings said. 'Don't touch anything.'

I didn't have to be told.

She came around to the back of the car and slipped a gloved index finger under the far right lip of the lid, where someone would be unlikely to have touched it, and slowly lifted. There was nothing inside except for the first-aid roadside emergency kit I'd put in there myself when I got Syd the car. It didn't appear to have been touched.

'Anything missing?' Detective Jennings asked.

'Not since the last time I looked in here,' I said.

She left the trunk open and returned to the open front door. She leaned in over the driver's seat, still careful not to touch anything. Her short frame was twisted awkwardly, unable to touch any part of the car for balance as she looked about.

Then, suddenly, she jumped back. It was as though something in the car had sprung up and shoved her.

My heart thumped. 'What?' I asked.

She spun her body around and let out an enormous sneeze over the Celica. 'Sorry,' she said. 'I felt this tickle coming, and I didn't want to contaminate the car with my own DNA.'

Once I'd had a moment to recover, I said, 'DNA?'

Jennings said, 'I'm going to want the crime scene investigators to go over this car.'

'Why?' I asked. 'Is that just routine? Is that something you always do?'

Jennings studied me for a moment, weighing something. Then, 'Come here.'

Delicately, she moved the door back three-quarters closed, drew me closer, and pointed to the outside handle. 'You see those smudges?'

I did. Smears of something dark. Reddish brown.

She pulled the door wide again and pointed to the steering wheel. 'Don't touch it,' she said again. But she pointed to the wheel. 'You see that?'

More smears of what appeared to be on the door handle.

'I see it,' I said. 'It's blood, isn't it?'

'That'd be my guess, yes,' Kip Jennings said.

6

'We're going to need to get a sample of your daughter's DNA,' Jennings said during the drive back. 'A hair from her brush would do the trick. And then we can compare that to the blood sample.'

'Yeah,' I said, but I was barely listening.

'Can you think of any reason why your daughter would be in Derby? Did she have friends there? A boyfriend, maybe?'

I shook my head.

'I'm having the car brought in, we'll go over it thoroughly, and as soon as I know anything, I'll pass that information on to you and your wife. Sorry, your ex-wife. And I'll have someone come by your house later today, for something we can use to get a DNA sample.'

I nodded slowly. 'You're suddenly taking this seriously.'

'I've never not taken this seriously, Mr Blake,' Kip Jennings said.

'I'm sorry,' I said.

'You OK?' she asked.

'I have to make a call,' I said.

'I have another question for you,' she said. 'A favor for my counterparts over in Bridgeport. If you don't mind.' I shook my head absently, neither refusing to answer nor agreeing. 'I'm sure there's no connection here, but there was an incident around the time that your daughter disappeared.'

'Someone else is missing?'

'Not exactly. You ever heard someone name of Randall Tripe?'

'What was that again?'

'Tripe. Really. And he usually went by Randy instead of Randall.'

'Went by? Not any more?'

'No. Do you recognize the name?'

'No. Should I?'

'Probably not,' she said.

'What happened to him?'

'Something that could have been expected sooner or later,' she said. 'He was a lowlife entrepreneur. A bit of prostitution, theft, moved stolen property, sold guns, even ran something of an employment agency. And he still found time to work in the odd stretch in prison. He was found in a dumpster down by the docks in Bridgeport the day after you reported Sydney missing. He'd been shot in the chest. Judging from the wound, he might have survived if someone had got him some help, but instead he got dumped in the trash and was left for dead.' She rooted through her purse on the console between us, trying to look inside it and watch the road at the same time. 'I've got a mug shot here someplace.'

'I don't understand what it has to do with Sydney.'

'Nothing, I suspect.' She was starting to drift across the center line, looked up, corrected, went back to the purse. 'Here it is.' She handed me a folded sheet of white paper. I opened it up. A police arrest sheet, dated more than a year ago. Randall Tripe was white, unshaven, fat, forty-two

76

at the time, balding, and looked like no one I knew or would ever want to know.

I gave it back. 'I don't recognize him.'

'OK,' she said, tucking the sheet back into her purse.

'This can't be good news,' I said.

'Hmm?'

'Blood on the car.'

'We'll see,' she said. 'We'll have to wait and see.'

We drove on for another minute. I felt I was drifting into some kind of dream state, that none of this was happening.

'Your daughter,' I said.

'Excuse me?'

'When you were on the phone. Her name is Cassie?'

Kip Jennings nodded. 'Short for Cassandra.'

I nodded. 'Cassie have any brothers or sisters?'

'No, it's just us,' Jennings said.

I nodded, catching some hidden meaning there. A single mother.

'What's happened to her, Detective?' I asked. 'What's happened to my little girl?'

'We're back,' she said, turning into the dealership.

*   *   *

Andy Hertz was sitting at his desk, a sheet torn from a phone book in front of him. As I sat down, he said, 'I got the D's.'

'Not now, Andy,' I said. I had to get out of here. I just had to get out.

77

'That guy?' Andy said.

'What?'

'The one who took out the Ridgeline for a spin? He left it out there at the far end of the lot, dropped off the keys with me when he couldn't find you. He only came back about five minutes ago. Longest test drive ever, you ask me. Where the hell did you disappear to? You've been gone over an hour. Anyway, he left, went across the street and got into a yellow Pinto. I didn't even know any of those were still on the road. Wasn't there something, years ago, about those things blowing up or something?'

It was before his time.

I got up, scooped the truck keys off Andy's desk, and went outside.

Once I had the dealer plates off and the truck where it belonged in the back lot, I'd take off. Drive around Derby, find more places where teens might hang out, show Syd's picture around.

As I approached the vehicle I noticed something unpleasant wafting my way. The closer I got to the truck the worse it got.

I opened the driver's door and as I lifted myself up to get inside, I happened to glance back into the pickup bed. It was filthy. There was some kind of brown debris — at first glance it looked like topsoil — smeared all over the place and up the side walls.

I hopped down, came around to the back of the truck and dropped the tailgate, which, on the inside, was an even greater mess. Some of it got on my hand.

'Shit,' I said. The word was more than just an

78

expression of anger. It was descriptive.

The son of a bitch had used the truck to deliver a load of manure.

* * *

I came back into the showroom, determined to get the hell out of there — I couldn't get the image of blood on Syd's car out of my head and needed to get away from these people — but Patty Swain was sitting in one of the chairs across from my desk. She had one leg up over the arm, her other leg sticking out the other way, in a pose that was pretty provocative even though she was in a pair of jeans.

She'd dropped by nearly every day — if not here, then at my house — since Sydney had gone missing.

Patty was the girl who comes home at dawn. The one who has no fear of walking through a bad part of town after having too much to drink. The one who wears skirts that are a bit too high and tops that are a bit too low. The one who has a couple of condoms in her purse. The one who curses like a sailor.

She worried me, but her independent streak was hard not to admire.

Syd met Patty last year at summer school. Sydney had failed math and had to spend four weeks making up her credit, squeezing in her dealership job around the classes. The thing was, Sydney had no trouble doing calculations in her head when it mattered. If you'd promised her five dollars an hour to clean up the garage and she'd spend six hours and forty-five minutes at it, she'd be able to tell you to the penny how much you owed her without the aid of a calculator. But no matter how good you may be with figures, if you don't do the homework and don't study for the tests, well, you end up at summer school.

A couple of days into her summer classes, Patty appeared. They ended up sitting together, and found they had more in common than their contempt for a system that would have them sitting in a classroom when everyone else was outside catching some rays.

Music, movies — they both had a closet love for Disney flicks from their childhood — boys, junk food. Everything seemed to click, with the possible exceptions of their backgrounds.

Sure, Syd was now from what she liked to call 'a broken home', but if ours was broken, Patty's had been hit with a cruise missile. She didn't have what you'd call a strong support system, from what I'd heard. Her mother, according to Syd, was pretty much an alcoholic. She had a hard enough time getting through the day herself, let alone monitoring Patty's behavior. Her father, if I remembered right, worked in a liquor store, for now, but didn't tend to keep jobs for long. Despite his sketchy financial situation, he still found different women happy to take him into their homes for varying periods of time. Sydney said Patty had told her he'd walked out on them when Patty was little. But he'd occasionally drift back into their lives for a few days or weeks, until her mother got tired of having him in her bed and kicked him out.

'I'm sort of glad,' Syd had said to me, 'that when you and Mom split up, that was it. This getting back together and then breaking up, over and over, that would drive me crazy. You'd get your hopes up, and then everything would go to shit again.'

Evidently, it hadn't always been that way with Patty's parents. They'd started out living the American dream. Good jobs, a house with a rec room, a station wagon in the driveway, a week in Florida every year, a day at Disney World. But then Patty's dad lost his job at Sikorsky after it was found he'd been stealing tools, and life was a never-ending downward spiral after that. He left Patty and her mother to fend for themselves when Patty was just a toddler. The mother started drinking. Patty learned early to look after herself.

Susanne and I — separately and together — offered Syd plenty of words of caution. This girl's had a lot of tough breaks, we get that, but don't let her lead you down the wrong path. Don't let her get you into trouble.

Syd assured us we had nothing to worry about. And she insisted that despite Patty's somewhat wayward behavior, she was a good kid, and a good friend. 'She's like this soulmate I've always been waiting for,' Syd told me once. 'We say things at the same time. We finish off each other's sentences. All I have to do is look at her and she cracks up. I'll be thinking about her, and right then, swear to God, my cell will ring and it's her.'

81

When Syd was staying at my house, Patty seemed to be there more than half the time. And when Syd was at her mother's, Patty was often hanging out there. (I didn't know whether this was true now that Susanne and Syd had moved in with Bob.) Patty, for all her hard knocks and cynicisms, devolved into a little girl when it came to making a batch of chocolate chip cookies. It seemed Syd had a moderating effect on Patty, rather than Patty having a negative influence on Syd.

'I like it here,' I heard her tell Syd when they were at my house. 'No one's screaming at each other or falling over pissed.'

My heart went out to her.

Despite her apparent recklessness, Patty had an instinct for survival. No rose-colored glasses for her. She saw the world for what it was. A cruel place where you couldn't count on anyone but yourself. That was one reason I liked her, and at some level, admired her. She'd been dealt a bad hand, and was trying to play it as best she could.

I hadn't seen her stroll in this time, but she usually turned heads when she came to visit, breasts bobbing and hips swaying as she wound her way through the roomful of Hondas. Patty knew what she had and didn't mind using it to effect. Today, in addition to the low-cut jeans with rips at the knees and thighs, she was wearing a dark blue tee that didn't come down far enough to hide her pierced navel, but did come down low enough to offer a tease of a lacy black bra. Her hair was dirty blond with a few narrow pink streaks going through it, and she seemed to be without makeup except for some very bright red lipstick.

As I sat down in my chair she said, 'Hey Mr B. You look like shit. You OK?'

I nodded. 'Hi, Patty.'

'What's going on? You look kind of pasty.'

'Just . . . nothing.'

'That sucks.'

'Yeah, it does.'

She wrinkled her nose. 'What's that smell?'

'Manure,' I said.

Then, another greeting: 'Hey Mr Blake.' I looked around, didn't immediately see anyone.

'Jeff tagged along,' Patty said. 'He's over there.'

She pointed to an Accord. Patty's friend Jeff Bluestein was sitting behind the wheel, touching the buttons on the dash, fiddling with knobs. Whenever he came by, he found a car to sit in and stayed there.

'Hey, Jeff,' I said, offering half a wave.

He smiled and waved back. Through the windshield he said, 'Website still working OK?'

'Yeah,' I said.

'Lots of hits?'

'A few.'

Jeff went back to looking at the dash. In the meantime, Patty had been taking in the showroom, looking at the posters for various models. 'You think I could get a job here?' she asked.

'Doing?'

'Selling cars,' she said, the 'duh' left unsaid. 'I

83

don't know how to fix them or anything, so about the only thing I could do is sell them.'

I didn't think it was her intention to suggest that if you were without any skills, this was about the only job left for you.

I said, 'So you're into cars now.'

Patty shrugged. 'I guess not. And I guess I'd have to get a bit of a makeover. The whole crack-whore thing I've got going on might put off Mr and Mrs Upstanding when they come in for a minivan to take their tiny Republicans to the mall.'

'It might,' I said. Patty usually had a job, but it was rarely the same one she'd had a couple of months ago. She'd worked a lot of retail, usually in trendy clothing outlets frequented by similarly dressed clientele. Only six months ago she'd been working at a sports footwear store in Stratford. Now she had something in an accessories shop where she sold cheap jewelry, hair bands and scarves.

'Can I tell you something, honestly?' She was moving her jaw around, like she was chewing gum, but there was no gum.

'I'd expect nothing less, Patty.'

'This whole thing about putting DVD players in vans, is that like, evidence of the fucking collapse of civilization or what? Are they thinking, like, little kids aren't getting enough of a chance to watch TV, that they've got to put them in their cars, too?'

You see what I mean? She had her moments.

'I get what you're saying,' I said. 'When Syd was little, and we were driving around together,

84

she'd always be asking what everything was. She liked to ask what all the different kinds of cars were. By the time she was six, she could tell a Honda from a Toyota from a Ford. That wouldn't have happened if she was watching *The Little Mermaid* instead of looking out the window.'

I felt a lump in my throat and tried to swallow it away.

'My point exactly,' Patty said. A few more seconds went by where she didn't say anything. Maybe she was thinking about the fact that she never spent a lot of time riding around in a car with her father.

Jeff got his awkward, lumbering frame out of the Accord and got behind the wheel of a Civic. You could almost hear him making 'vroom' noises under his breath as he gripped the wheel.

Patty said, 'Syd and I actually watched *The Little Mermaid* together a few months ago and we cried like we were in fucking second grade.' It was difficult to picture the girl sitting before me now being entranced by anything remotely Disney.

'You know that cartoon about the monsters?' I said. 'How they all work for a big company and their job is to scare little kids?'

'*Monsters, Inc?*'

'That's the one,' I said. 'I took Sydney to that when she was, what? Ten? The ending, I started tearing up myself. You know the part I'm talking about?'

Patty Swain nodded. 'Oh yeah. My mom took me to that. She snuck in a can of Coke that actually had rye in it. She's taught me everything I know.' She grinned, hoping she could shock me.

I leaned forward. 'Patty, did Sydney have any friends up in Derby?'

She looked taken aback. 'I don't think so. Derby? Fuck, no. Nobody in Derby. Why?'

I weighed whether to tell her about Syd's car, decided against it.

'So I'm still putting the word out,' she said. 'Facebook, shit like that.' The leg she'd propped over the chair arm was swinging back and forth, plus she was doing some flicking thing with the fingers of her left hand.

'I appreciate that. You're probably reaching more people that way than I am.' I watched the leg swing. 'You OK, Patty? You seem a bit on edge.'

She stopped all the seemingly involuntary body movements. 'I'm cool.'

'You're not, you know, high or something, are you?'

She laughed. 'Shit, Mr B, you're something.'

Laura Cantrell was doing a slow walkabout through the showroom, graceful as a gazelle despite the five-inch heels. She swept by my desk, not saying a word to either of us, wandered between the cars. It felt as though the thermostat had been turned down.

Laura slipped back into her office. Patty had been aware of her the whole time.

She said, 'Seriously, that chick needs to get banged.'

'I know I've asked you this a thousand times,

Patty, but where could she have gone?' I asked. 'If she wasn't working at that hotel, where was she?'

'I don't know. It's totally fucked up.'

'I've been all up and down Route 1, going into every shop and business. No one knows anything about her.'

That made me think, just for a second, about Ian, from Shaw Flowers, how he could have looked at Syd's picture a little longer before saying he hadn't seen her.

'You were her best friend,' I said. 'And yet she didn't tell you what she was really doing.'

She nodded. 'I swear, I thought she was working at that place. She never told me any different. The thing is, she's not like me. She wouldn't be looking for trouble. I was born for it.'

I flashed her a weary smile. 'Thanks for dropping by. If you think of anything . . . '

She nodded, blinked furiously several times, like maybe she was warding off tears. 'Sure,' she said, getting out of the chair. 'The thing is, I was wondering . . . '

'What is it, Patty?'

'You know this new job I got at the mall?'

'At the jewelry place?'

She nodded, like this was no big deal. 'Yeah. So you have to work for a month before you get your first paycheck, and my mom, well, you know, she's kind of tapped out herself at the moment, and it's not like my dad's sending me a check every month.'

'You can't be asking me for money, Patty,' I said.

'Sure,' she said, her face flushing. 'I get that.'

I looked at her a moment, then took a twenty out of my wallet and handed it to her. She took the bill and stuffed it down the front pocket of her jeans. They were on so tight she had trouble getting her fingers in there.

'Thanks,' she said. 'You want me to grab something tonight?'

Trying to fill the gap left by Sydney, Patty had dropped by half a dozen times in the last few weeks with surprise deliveries of McDonald's or Burger King or Subway, then hinted she was broke and made no objections when I paid her back.

'I don't think so, not tonight,' I said.

I could see the disappointment in her eyes. 'That's OK,' she said. 'Catch you later.'

As she walked past Andy Hertz's desk, hips swaying, she said, 'Hey there, Andy Panda,' and kept on walking.

Andy, who was working his way through the page from the phone book, making cold calls, mumbled a 'hey'.

Patty had been in here enough to know Andy, but that seemed a little familiar.

Jeff got out of the Civic and ran to catch up to Patty, dropping a set of keys on my desk as he went by. 'Someone left these in the car,' he said.

7

I used to wonder how people did it.

You'd watch the news, and there'd be some couple who'd lost a child in a fire. The mother of that girl who went missing in Bermuda and was never found. A father whose son was killed in a bar fight. Once, there was a story about a girl whose class went on a skiing trip, and there was an avalanche and she was buried under several feet of snow and the rescue workers couldn't find her. And there were her parents, weeping, holding out hope their daughter was still alive, and you knew there was simply no way.

How the hell do they do it? I'd say to the TV.

I figured, something like that happens to a loved one, everything just stops. How can it not?

But I was realizing that everyone does go on. You get up. You have breakfast. You go to work. You do your job. You come home, have some dinner, go to bed.

Just like everybody else.

But it's always there. You go on, but you don't go on. Because there's this weight, and you can feel it all the time, like you've got a cinder block sitting on each shoulder, pushing you down, wearing you out, making you wonder whether you'll be able to get up the next day.

And son of a bitch, you do get up. That day, and the day after, and the day after that. With those blocks on your shoulders.

Always there.

*   *   *

On my way out, I picked up, from reception, the photocopy of the driver's license of Richard Fletcher, my manure delivery guy. I made a mental note of his address, on Coulter Drive. I folded the sheet and slid it down into my pocket.

Once in the car, I turned Syd's iPod on again and listened to some Natasha Bedingfield (I'd heard Syd listening to her one night in her room and asked who it was), an Elton John number from my own youth, and, astonishingly, pianist Erroll Garner's 'Misty'. I'd mentioned him to Syd one weekend a few months back, and she'd gone and downloaded one of his songs.

'You're something else, sweetheart,' I said, as though she were in the seat next to me.

I didn't head home. Instead, I drove over to the original Bob's Motors used car dealership and pulled up by the office — a disguised forty-foot trailer with the wheels hidden behind decorative vinyl skirting.

As I went up the steps, the door opened and Evan came rushing out, his face red, his jaw set angrily. He looked ready to explode.

'Hey,' I said, but he brushed past without seeing me, charged off between the used cars, then stopped abruptly next to a red Jetta with a 'One Owner!' banner in the windshield, and kicked the rear fender with everything he had.

'Fuck!' he shouted. 'Fuck her! Fuck that bitch!'

And then he stormed off, heading down the sidewalk, away from the lot.

I went inside, where Susanne was posted at a desk just to the right of the door, the crutches she'd been managing without leaned up against the wall, the cane hanging from a coat hook. She was shaking her head, then looked up when she saw me.

'Geez, perfect timing,' she said. She was obviously rattled. 'Did he run into you?'

'He just beat up a Volkswagen,' I said. 'What's going on?'

'All I did was ask him about the petty cash,' she said.

'What petty cash?'

'In the desk here. I swear, there was two hundred dollars there yesterday, and today there's forty. I asked him whether he'd had to go into it for something and he flies off the handle, says I'm calling him a thief. I never did any such thing. All I did was ask him whether he — '

She stopped herself, looked at me. 'What's happened?'

'They found Sydney's car,' I said.

Her face didn't move. She waited.

'In Derby. Left in a Wal-Mart lot. It may have been there since she vanished. There are traces of blood on the door handle and steering wheel.'

Her face still didn't move. She took it in, waited a moment, and said, 'She's not dead. I refuse to believe she's dead.'

'She's not,' I said, because that's what I had to believe, too. 'They'll have to do DNA tests to know whether it's Syd's blood.'

'It doesn't matter,' Susanne said. 'She's not dead.' She raised her chin, as though defying unseen forces.

The door flung open and Bob walked in. Before he'd set eyes on either of us he barked, 'What the hell did you say to Evan?' Then, seeing me, he said, 'Oh.'

To Susanne, I said, 'I'll go. I'll keep in touch.' To Bob, I said, 'Take care of her. And if I ever hear Evan call Susanne a bitch again I'll put his head through a windshield.'

★ ★ ★

I'm not sure how I got home. I had no memory of driving there. Hot blood was clouding my vision.

There was a police vehicle parked out front when I got there. A van instead of a cruiser. A nattily dressed black man identified himself as from the city's forensic investigations unit. He'd been sent by Detective Kip Jennings to retrieve a DNA sample of Sydney's. I let him in, showed him Syd's room and the bathroom she used to get ready for work in the morning. He zeroed in on the hairbrush.

While he was doing that, I went down to the kitchen. The light was flashing on the phone. I hit the button to hear the message.

'Hey.'

Kate Wood.

'I just wondered how you were doing. I don't know whether you got my message at work. My offer still stands. I could bring something over. I

92

know you probably don't feel like cooking. You could even come over here if you want. Anyway, get back to me? OK?' And then she rhymed off her cell number, which I knew better than my own, she'd reminded me of it so many times.

I deleted the message.

I went upstairs to the spare bedroom where I keep my computer and pay the bills and went online to see if there'd been any action on the website.

Nothing.

I sat there for a while, stared at the screen.

The guy from the forensics department popped his head in, said he'd find his own way out.

'Sure,' I said. 'Thanks.'

Finally, I went back down to the kitchen. I opened the fridge and stared into it for a good twenty seconds, thinking if I looked long enough something edible would magically appear. I hadn't bought groceries in a couple of weeks, and — on the nights when Patty didn't show up with fast food — was surviving mostly on a cache of microwaveable dinners that had been collecting in the freezer over the last year or two.

I closed the door and put my palms on the kitchen counter, leaning into it. I took several deep breaths, letting each one out slowly.

If this was supposed to relax me it wasn't working, because suddenly with the back of my arm I swept everything off the counter in front of me — toaster, salt and pepper shakers, a day-by-day *New Yorker* cartoon calendar I hadn't turned the page on in three weeks, an electric can opener — crashing to the floor.

I was filled with all this pent-up rage and frustration. Where was Syd? What had happened to her? Why did she leave?

Why the hell couldn't I find her?

I wanted to explode. I had so much anger and no place to direct it.

I'd only been home a few minutes but I needed to go out again. Every moment I spent here, alone, reminded me that Syd was not here. I couldn't sit around. I had to burn off some steam. Drive around. Keep looking.

The phone rang. I snatched the receiver off the cradle before the first ring was finished.

'What?' I shouted.

'Whoa.'

'I'm sorry,' bringing my voice down, not knowing who it was. 'Hello.'

'I called earlier. Did you get my message?'

Then I knew. 'I just got home, Kate.'

It had started about six months ago. I'd met her in a rather unconventional way. She was backing her Ford Focus out of a spot at Walgreens and hit my bumper on the other side of the aisle. I was behind the wheel, engine off, listening to the end of a newscast before I went into the store, and jumped out when I felt the jolt.

I had a number of lines set to go. *Are you blind? Where the hell were you looking? Did you get your driver's license off the net?*

But when she got out of the car, the first thing out of my mouth was, 'Are you OK?'

I think that had a lot to do with the fact that

she was such a striking woman. Maybe not beautiful, not in some supermodel sense (and here, I would defer to Bob anyway, of course), but arresting, with short brown hair, brown eyes, a slightly Monroe-esque figure. But instead of a squeaky Betty Boop kind of voice, her words came out soft, and low, throaty.

'Oh my God,' she said. 'That was totally my fault. Are you hurt?'

'I'm fine, I'm fine,' I insisted. 'Let's see if your car's OK.'

It was fine, and there was only a minor scratch on my bumper. Even though it was not something worth repairing, I offered no objection when Kate wanted to give me her name and phone number.

'You know, later, you might have whiplash or something,' she said. Like she was hoping.

The next day, I called her.

'Oh my God, don't tell me you have a concussion or something.'

'I wondered if you wanted to get a drink.'

She told me, over a beer, that when I called she figured I'd be faking a spinal injury and suing her for a million dollars' worth of hospital bills because that's the kind of thing people do, that's the kind of world we're living in.

That should have been a clue.

But I didn't pick up on it, because things between us seemed to be clicking pretty good. They ended up clicking pretty fast.

We moved on from drinks to dinner, and from dinner to my house. Five minutes after we'd come through the front door we were in bed. I hadn't had sex in several months, and it's possible I made that apparent more quickly than I would have liked. But it was a long evening, and I was able to redeem myself.

Kate seemed, at first, almost perfect.

She was warm. Attentive. Sexually uninhibited. She was addicted to DVD sets of television series. I worked so many evenings I'd never much gotten into TV, so she introduced me to shows I'd only heard of, including one about these people whose commercial jet crashes on an island, and somehow this is their destiny, they've all been brought to this island for a reason, it's all part of some big plan — I could hardly make any sense of it. But Kate was obsessed with it, how everyone's lives were being manipulated by unseen forces. 'That's so what happens,' she said. 'Other people are always pulling the strings behind the scenes.'

That should have been another clue.

The thing was, she was fun to be with. And I hadn't been with anyone fun in quite some time. But it was when she started opening up about herself that things started to go off the rails.

She'd been divorced three years. Her husband was a commercial pilot. He fooled around. She got totally screwed over in the divorce. Her lawyer, she believed, was a friend of her husband's, although she couldn't actually prove it. Some kind of deal got cooked up behind closed doors, she said, otherwise she would have ended up with the son of a bitch's house. But guess what? He was still living there, and she was stuck in some shithole apartment in Devon half a block from a bar and Friday nights you were likely to find some guy taking a leak on your front tire.

OK.

And if that wasn't enough, she was being treated totally unfairly at work. She was clearly the next in line to be head buyer at Jazzies, the clothing store where she worked in New Haven, but they went and gave it to this woman named *Edith*, if you can believe that any woman with a name like *Edith* would have a clue about what's fashionable.

'Edith Head?' I said. 'The Oscar-winning costume designer?'

'Are you making that up?'

Anyway, she knew they had it in for her at work, that they didn't like her, and the most likely theory as far as she was concerned was that it was because she was so much more attractive than the others. They felt threatened. Well, they could all go fuck themselves, that's what they could do.

At first, I welcomed her calls at work. I was quite OK with her telling me, in some detail, what she wanted to do to me the next time we were together. But sometimes, when you're trying to clinch a deal for a $35,000 loaded Accord, you have to end things, no matter how much you might be enjoying them.

Kate's feelings got hurt easily.

The more she called my work and home phones, and my cell, the less I called back. 'Give me a chance to be the one to make the call,' I suggested gently.

'But I told you that in my message,' she said. 'I told you to call me back.'

It certainly wasn't all phone sex. It was often more stories about how her ex was hiding money from her, or how they still weren't recognizing her talents at work, or how she thought her landlord had been in her apartment when she was out, going through her underwear drawer. Nothing was out of place, but she just had a feeling.

One night, when I had intended to break it off, I somehow allowed her to talk me into letting her meet Sydney.

'I'm dying to see what she's like,' Kate said.

I'd been in no rush to introduce them. I didn't see any need for Sydney to meet every woman I dated, and in the last year or two there certainly hadn't been many. I figured, if it got to the point where things were getting serious, that might be the time for introductions.

But Kate persisted, so I arranged for the three of us to meet at lunch one Sunday. Syd, a seafood fan, picked a spot down along the waterfront that, for all I knew, got its so-called 'fresh' catch of the day from an ocean half a planet away.

Kate thought it went fabulously. 'We so hit it off,' she told me.

I knew Syd would have a different take.

'She was very nice,' she said later when we were alone.

'You're holding out on me,' I said.

'No, really.'

'Spill it,' I said.

98

'Well, you know she's crazy,' Sydney said.

'Go on.'

'She was the only one who said a word all through lunch. And it was all about how this person doesn't like her and that person she had a problem with, and how she didn't get along at this job because the people were all against her and gave her an unfair job review, and then she got this other job and even though it's going OK she knows people are talking about her behind her back, and how she's pretty sure that she got overcharged by the guy where she gets her dry cleaning done and — '

'OK,' I said. 'I get it.'

'But I understand,' Syd said.

'What do you mean, you understand?'

'She's hot. I mean, it's a sex thing, right?'

'Jesus, Sydney.'

'I mean, Dad, come on, what else would it be? If I had a rack like that I'd be the most popular girl at my school.' I tried to think of something to say, but before I could, Syd added, 'But she's very nice.'

'But she's a bit crazy,' I said.

'Yeah,' Sydney said. 'But a lot of crazy people are very nice.'

'Did she ask you a single question about yourself?'

Sydney had to think about that one. 'You know when you went to the can? She asked me my opinion of her earrings.'

The thing was, Syd had nailed it. Kate was self-obsessed. She thought everyone was against her. She saw conspiracies where none existed.

She jumped to conclusions. She was pushing too hard when I wanted to slow things down.

The day after the lunch, Kate, who had initially felt it went well, called me at work and said, 'Sydney hates me.'

'That's insane,' I said. 'She thought you were very nice.'

'What did she say? Exactly?'

'She liked you,' I said, leaving out the references to *crazy* and *rack*.

'You're lying. I know you're lying.'

'Kate, I have to go.'

We still saw each other, occasionally. Out of guilt, fearing I was using her, I made excuses not to sleep with her.

Most of the time.

After Syd disappeared, I stopped returning any of her calls. I had enough on my plate. Occasionally, I'd pick up without checking the caller ID.

'Let me be there for you,' she'd say.

I was reluctant to accept her offers of comfort.

'So you didn't mind my being around when you need to get off,' Kate said at one point, 'but you don't want me there when the going gets tough?'

And now she was on the phone as I stood here in my kitchen, the floor littered with debris after my explosion, still unable to think of anything but my daughter's car, bloodstains on the door and steering wheel.

'Hey, you there?' Kate asked.

'Yeah,' I said. 'I'm here.'

'You sound terrible.'

'Long day.'

'Are you alone?'

'Yeah.'

The truth was, I felt very, very alone.

'I know you've got a lot on your mind,' she said.

'Yeah,' I said.

Neither of us spoke for a moment.

'Have you eaten?' she asked.

I had to think. Hadn't I just been staring into the fridge? That must have meant I'd not had dinner.

'No.'

'I'll bring something over. Chinese. And I've got some new DVDs.'

I thought a moment, and said. 'OK.' I was hungry. I was exhausted. And I felt very alone.

I said, 'Can you give me an hour? No. An hour and a half?'

'Sure. I'll be there.'

I hung up without saying goodbye, stared out the kitchen window. There was still an hour or more of good light left.

I locked the house, got in the car, checked Susanne's empty house again, then drove up to Derby. Cruised through plazas, drove slowly through the parking lots of fast-food joints, always looking, scanning, searching for anyone who might be Sydney.

No luck.

I knew, in my heart, what a futile gesture this was, that somehow, by chance, I was going to spot my daughter walking down the street. How likely was it she'd be taking an evening stroll, or sitting by the window of a McDonald's as I happened to drive by.

But I had to do something.

I was heading back south when a street sign caught my eye.

Coulter Drive.

I hit the brakes and hung a right before I'd even had a chance to think about the decision. I pulled the car over to the shoulder and reached down into my pocket for the sheet of paper I'd taken from the dealership.

I unfolded it, studied the photocopy of Richard Fletcher's driver's license. He lived at 72 Coulter. I glanced at the closest house, which was 22. The next one down was 24. I took my foot off the brake and moved slowly down the street.

Fletcher's house was set back from the street, shrouded in trees. It was a simple two-storey house, four windows, a door dead center. The front lawn was spotty and full of weeds. Used tires, several rusted bicycles, an old lawnmower and other bits of assorted junk were crowded up against a separate one-car garage. In the drive were the yellow Pinto Fletcher had used to make his escape earlier today, as well as a Ford pickup that had seen better days. The hood was propped open, and I could just make out someone leaning over the front to examine the engine.

Richard Fletcher, I guessed. The son of a bitch.

I came to a stop at the end of the gravel driveway. Any other time, I might have had the sense to drive on. So the guy pulled a fast one.

Took a truck out for a spin, used it to pick up some manure. Next time you'll know better, you won't let a guy test drive a truck without tagging along. Fletcher got lucky with me today. Not next time. Live and learn.

I was too on edge to be that rational.

I got out of the car and started striding up the driveway. A dog I'd not seen before started loping up the lane toward me. But this was no guard dog. He was a mutt of undetermined heritage, limping, gray in the snout. His frame had the same sag in it as the Fletcher house roof. His weary tail wagged liked a sideways metronome at the slowest beat.

I walked on past the dog. As I came up around the truck, I saw that it was, indeed, Richard Fletcher staring into the engine well. He had his elbow on the rad, and his head was resting on his hand. He held no tools, wasn't actually repairing anything. He was looking at the engine the way a washed-up fortune teller might gaze into the bottom of a teacup. Trying to come up with answers, not having much luck.

'Hey,' I said, an edge in my voice.

He looked over at me. His eyes narrowed. He was trying to place me.

'Next time you take a truck for a test drive, you mind cleaning out all the shit before you bring it back?'

Now he knew.

Fletcher straightened up, ran his hand back over his head and looked at me, not saying anything.

'You're a real fucking piece of work, you know

103

that?' I said. 'Who the fuck do you think you are? I got a bulletin for you. We're not a fucking truck rental agency.'

He moved his mouth around, like he was trying to think of what to say to me, but couldn't find the words.

The front door of the house popped open, squeaking on its hinges. Fletcher turned his head around. A young girl poked her head out and said, 'I've got dinner ready, Dad.'

She was maybe ten, twelve years old. I couldn't see that much of her. Just enough to see that she was on some kind of metal braces.

Fletcher said, 'Be right in, sweetheart.'

He turned back to look at me. 'You'll have to excuse me,' he said. 'I've got to go have dinner with my daughter.'

He walked back to the house, climbed the steps to the front door. I stood there, watched him go inside, and suddenly felt very small.

★   ★   ★

I spotted Kate Wood's silver Ford Focus in the drive as I came down my street. She was standing by the back of it, a large brown takeout bag in one hand, and what appeared to be a bagged bottle of wine in the other.

I parked, came over to her, and something primal took over. I needed her. I needed her to comfort me. I slipped my arms around her and pulled her close, resting my head on her shoulder. Her hands still full, she squeezed me with her outstretched arms.

104

'Oh baby,' she said. 'It's OK, it's OK.'

I didn't say anything. I just held her.

'Has something happened?' she asked. I still had no words. 'Come on, let's go inside. Come on.'

I found my house key on the ring as she led me to my own door. Once inside she said, 'I'll get some plates, we'll get some food into you, we'll talk. I swear, you look like you've lost ten pounds.'

I'd noticed my pants had seemed looser the last few days but hadn't really given it much thought.

'You want to open the wine?' Kate asked.

'Let me check something first,' I said.

'When you get back I'll tell you what's happened with Edith,' she said. 'She totally fucked up an entire order.'

'In a minute,' I said.

'Good God!' she said as she entered the kitchen. 'What happened here?'

My earlier outburst. 'Don't worry about it,' I said.

I went up the stairs, two at a time. I didn't even bother to sit in front of the computer, just leaned over, moved the mouse around, hit the button to see whether there had been any responses to the websites, other than for discounted Viagra.

There were two messages. One said there was a problem with my eBay account. I did not have an eBay account. I deleted it.

Then I opened the second email.

It began:

'Dear Mr Blake: I'm pretty sure I've seen your daughter.'

8

I was trembling even before I sat down.

The email, from a Hotmail address that was preceded by the letters 'ymills' and a series of numbers, read:

'Dear Mr Blake: I'm pretty sure I've seen your daughter. I work at a drop-in shelter for teens in Seattle — '

Seattle? What the hell would Syd be doing in Seattle? No, wait. What mattered was: *Syd was alive.*

Having just seen traces of blood on my daughter's car, this email already had me fighting back tears.

I started reading again. 'I work at a drop-in shelter for teens in Seattle and because I'm in that line of work I'm often scanning websites about kids who are missing and I came to your site and when I saw the pictures there of your daughter Sydney I recognized her because she's very pretty. At least I am pretty sure that it was her but of course I could be wrong. I don't think she said her name was Sydney, I think she might have said Susan or Suzie or something like that.'

She was using her mother's name. I wondered, for a moment, whether there was something wrong with the computer because the cursor was jiggling all over the place. I glanced down and saw that my hand on the mouse was shaking.

'Feel free to get in touch at this email address,'

the note continued. 'It must be very stressful not to know where your daughter is and I hope that maybe I can help.'

The note signed off with: 'Yours in Christ, Yolanda Mills.'

From downstairs, Kate shouted, 'Come get this while it's hot! This chow mein looks pretty decent.'

I hit the reply button and wrote: 'Dear Ms Mills: Thank you so much for getting in touch with me. Please tell me how to reach you other than email. What is the name of your drop-in shelter? What is the address in Seattle? Do you have a number where I can reach you?'

I was typing so quickly I was making numerous typos, then backspacing and fixing them.

'Tim? Everything OK up there?'

I typed, 'Sydney went missing nearly a month ago and her mother and I are frantic to find her, to know that she is OK. When did you see her? How long ago? Has Syd been in there several times or just once? Here's how you can get in touch with me.' I then typed my home phone number, my cell number, my number at the dealership. 'Please get in touch the moment you receive this email. And call collect, please.'

I double-checked that I hadn't entered in any of the phone numbers wrong, typed my name at the end, and hit Send.

'What's going on?' Kate said. She was at the door, leaning into the frame.

I turned, and I know I must have had tears on my cheeks, because Kate suddenly looked horrified, as though I'd just gotten bad news.

'Oh my God, Tim, what's happened?'

'Someone's seen her,' I said, feeling overcome. 'Someone's seen Syd.'

Kate closed the distance between us, pulled my head to her breasts and held me while I tried to pull it together.

'Where?' Kate asked. 'Where is she?'

I pulled away and pointed to my screen. 'This woman in Seattle. She works at a drop-in shelter. Some place, I guess, where runaways can go.'

'Seattle?' Kate asked. 'What would Syd be doing in Seattle?'

'I don't know and right now I don't care,' I said. 'Just so long as I know where she is I can go get her and bring her home.'

'Have you got a number? Call this woman. It's what, three hours earlier out there? She might even still be at work.'

'She didn't send me a phone number,' I said. 'I just wrote her back, asked her for one.'

'How about the shelter? Did she say what it was called?'

'No,' I said. 'I don't know why the hell she couldn't have been a bit more specific.'

'What's her name?'

I glanced back at the screen. 'Yolanda Mills.'

'Shove a bum,' Kate said, motioning for me to get out of the computer chair. I stood while she sat down. 'We go to the online white pages, find her, call her.'

Kate tapped away on the keyboard, went to a site with some empty fields where she entered the woman's first and last name and the city where she lived. 'OK, let's see what we've got . . . We got nothing yet. Three Y Mills but none of them Yolanda.'

'So maybe she's married and the phone number is listed under her husband's name. Her last name might still be Mills.'

'Let me see how many Mills there are.' Kate whistled under her breath. 'OK, there's like more than two hundred of them.'

I put a hand on the edge of the computer table to steady myself. Blood was pulsing in my ears.

'We could wait for this woman to get back to you, or we could just start calling all of them.'

'Maybe we can narrow it down another way,' I said. 'Do a search on teenage drop-in shelters in Seattle.'

Kate's fingers danced across the keyboard. 'Holy shit,' she said. 'There's all kinds of them. Not as many shelters as there are Mills in the Seattle directory, but there's quite a few. Hang on, I think I can narrow it down. Some are men's shelters so we can skip those . . . let me see. OK, look here.' She pointed to the screen. There were half a dozen listings for Seattle area shelters aimed at youths.

I grabbed a pen and a scratchpad and scribbled down web addresses. 'I'll grab Syd's laptop and work on these downstairs. I'll use my cell, and you can use the land line for some of the women's shelters. She might be attached to one of those for all we know.'

'I'm on it,' Kate said. She snatched the receiver off the cradle and punched in a number as I ran downstairs, grabbing my daughter's laptop on the way. The house was equipped for wireless, so I could use Syd's computer anywhere. I found my cell in the pocket of my jacket that was hanging over a kitchen chair, and dialed the first of the five numbers that came up on the screen once I had the laptop up and running.

'Refuge Place,' a woman answered.

'Hi,' I said. 'I'm trying to get hold of Yolanda Mills. I think she might work at your shelter.'

'Sorry,' she said. 'No one here by that name.'

'OK, thanks,' I said, ended the call, waited a beat, and then dialed the second number. Upstairs, I could hear murmurs of Kate on the phone.

'Hope,' a man said.

'Is this the shelter?' I asked.

'Yeah, Hope Shelter.'

'I'm calling for Yolanda Mills.'

'What's that name again?' he asked.

I repeated it. 'I think she may be an employee there.'

'I know everyone here,' he said. 'We got no one by that name.'

I thanked him and hit 'end'.

'How's it going?' Kate shouted from upstairs.

'Nothing yet,' I said. 'You?'

'Ditto.'

There were two plates of shrimp fried rice, chow mein, sweet and sour chicken and egg rolls on the counter, but I wasn't hungry. I had next to nothing in my stomach and already felt like I was going to lose what was there.

I tried the next two numbers, struck out with

both. I was just entering the last of the five I'd jotted down when Kate shrieked: 'Tim!'

I flipped my phone shut and bolted up the stairs two steps at a time. 'You got somebody?' I said breathlessly as I came into the computer room.

'You have mail,' she said, hopping out of the chair and letting me sit down.

It was Yolanda Mills. Her reply read:

'Dear Mr Blake: Thank you for getting back to me. That was foolish of me not to give you more information. I work at a Christian youth center called Second Chance in the west part of the downtown area. There's a number there but I'm in and out all the time (one of the things I do is arrange for the meals there, so I'm out a lot getting groceries and things) but I always have my cell with me so you can usually get me on that. Here it is.' The number followed.

I had the receiver in my hand and was dialing, looking back and forth between the screen and the phone.

'What if she's a nut?' Kate asked as I hit the last digit. 'What if it's someone just running a scam or something? A lot of people, they're always thinking up ways to get innocent people to fall for things.'

I knew that, in a nutshell, was Kate's world view, but realized it was something I had to consider. As the phone began to ring at the other end, thousands of miles away, Kate said, 'If she starts asking about money, about whether there's a reward, that'll be your tip off that she's — '

I held up my hand for her to stop talking,

expecting the cell to be answered at any second.

And then it was.

'Hello?'

A woman. It was only one word, but she sounded on the young side.

'Is this Yolanda Mills?'

'Is this Mr Blake?' she asked.

'Oh God,' I said, breathing a huge sigh of relief. 'We were trying to track you down using the online phone directories and Google and everything and then you got back to me. Thank you so much. You don't know what this means to me.'

'I just don't know how much help I can be.' I wasn't picking up any noticeable accent. And trying to pick up someone's age from their voice is tricky, unless the person is very young or very old. Yolanda Mills sounded right in the middle.

'When did you see Syd?' I asked.

'Who?'

'Sydney,' I said. 'I call her Syd.'

'It was two or three days ago, I think.'

'How was she? Was she OK? Did she look hurt? Was she sick?'

'She looked fine. I mean, assuming it was her. She came in a couple of times to get something to eat.'

Jesus Christ, my daughter eating in a shelter for runaways. What had brought her to this? Why was she on the other side of the country?

'Did you speak to her at all?'

'Nothing much. Just, you know, 'How ya doin', darlin'?' That was about it.'

'Did she say anything?'

112

'She just kind of smiled.'

'Was she with anyone? Was she traveling alone?'

'As far as I could tell, she was by herself. I have to say, she looked sad.'

It was as if someone had reached into my chest and given my heart a twist.

'And you said you last saw her a couple of days ago?'

'OK, let me think a minute,' Yolanda Mills said. 'I think the first time I saw her was about four days ago, then she came in two days after that when we were serving lunch. And that was the day before yesterday.'

Which meant that Syd had been in Seattle for a while. Maybe she was popping into Yolanda's drop-in every couple of days. So if I got out there, hung around the shelter long enough, she might show up.

'Do teens, runaways, do they come to your place to eat even if they aren't staying there?'

'Oh sure. We only have so much space. And this isn't meant to be someplace where you come to live permanently. It's a stopgap measure, you know? So kids, sometimes they find a place to bunk in with a friend, or they sleep in a car, and sometimes, I hate to say it, sometimes they just find a place in the park or something for the night.'

Syd, sleeping on a bench. I tried to push the image out of my head.

'How did you find out about Syd?' I asked.

'Didn't I tell you, in the email? Because of where I work, because I know so many of these

113

kids are runaways and homeless, and because I know they've got parents who are looking for them, I Google websites where parents post pictures of their kids who've run away or are just missing. This is just the second time I've seen someone who's actually been in our shelter.'

'Were you right the other time?'

'As a matter of fact, I was,' she said proudly. 'There was a young man, his name was Trent, and he was from just outside of El Paso, and his parents were going out of their minds trying to find him. And he was actually staying at the shelter, and this time, I was sure it was him, and I thought about telling him that I knew his parents were looking for him, that he should call them, but I thought that might scare him off, so I called his folks instead and they were on the next flight up here.'

A flight. I would have to book a flight the moment I was done talking to Yolanda.

'If she comes in again, don't tell her you've spoken with me,' I said. 'I don't know why she's run off, I don't know whether I did something, I just can't figure it out. I've been wracking my brain, trying to think why she'd do something like this and — '

'That's what a lot of the parents say, but sometimes I think they know the answer and they're just not acknowledging it, you know what I'm saying?' Yolanda said.

'I suppose.' As grateful as I was to Yolanda Mills for giving me a lead on where to find Syd, I didn't want to get into a discussion with her about why all this might have happened.

114

'Here's the thing,' she said. 'I can't say for a hundred per cent that that's your little girl. I could be wrong.'

'But you might be right,' I said.

'Would it help if I sent a picture?'

I felt as though I might fall out of my chair. 'A picture? You have a *picture* of Sydney? In Seattle?'

'Well, it's not a very good one. I've had this phone for ages that will take pictures but I've never been able to figure out how to do it, you know? I'm not really a gadget person. So I was fiddling with it at the shelter, taking random shots just to see if I could figure out which buttons to push, and your daughter happened to walk by when I was taking one of them. Her and a few others, but there's one shot where it's just her.'

I knew that if I saw that picture, I would know.

'Can you email it to me?' I asked.

'I know that can be done, but like I was saying, it's been all I can do to figure out how to make it take a picture. I haven't any idea how to upload it or download it or whatever it is you do, to a computer? But my husband understands all that and he'll be home in the morning. He works an overnight shift. But when he gets home I could have him do it.'

Even though things suddenly seemed to be happening quickly, it would be an eternity waiting until morning to see that picture.

Kate, who'd been standing a few feet away, unable to hear the other end of the conversation, gently tapped my shoulder, rubbed her thumb and two fingers together, the money sign.

'Listen,' I said to Yolanda Mills, 'is there any way I can repay you for this? Are you looking for a reward or anything?'

'A reward?' she said, and nearly sounded offended. 'That wouldn't be very Christian, would it?'

9

When I finished my call with Yolanda Mills, I felt I'd had twenty coffees injected directly into my bloodstream. My body was shaking, and I couldn't decide what to do first.

'I have to call Susanne,' I said. 'No, not yet. This woman, she's going to send me the picture in the morning. I need to call the detective. Kip Jennings. She could get someone from the Seattle police to put out one of those APB things or whatever on Syd. They could get the entire police force — '

'Tim,' Kate said. 'Just hold on a second. You have — '

'I have to book a flight,' I said. 'Maybe there's a flight out tonight.' I whirled back around in the chair and started tapping at keys.

'You just need to take a minute,' Kate said. 'You don't even know for sure it's Syd. You won't know that until you see the picture, and even then, you may not know. Those cell phone shots, they're not always the best. And you just wait. Whoever that Yolanda woman is, you can be sure she's going to be wanting some kind of reward at some point. If it's one thing I've learned it's that everyone's always got an agenda, you know what I'm saying? They smile at you but they're just lying through their teeth, trying to figure out how they can screw you over. What you should do is — '

117

I turned and snapped, 'For fuck's sake, Kate, enough.'

She put a hand to her cheek as though I'd slapped her.

'Everyone's always out to get you, aren't they?' I said. 'Your ex-husband, the people you work with, your landlord? Is there anyone out there who isn't making your life a living hell?'

She looked at me and said, 'Evidently not.'

'Oh, so now I'm doing it, too.'

She studied me a moment, then seemed to come to a realization. 'You've used this whole thing with your daughter as an excuse to break off with me.'

I was too stunned to say anything right away. Then, I almost laughed. 'What?'

'You never return my calls. I know you look and see if it's me calling and don't pick up.'

'Kate,' I said.

'Is that what I was for you? A good fuck and now it's over?'

'Kate, I don't have time for this discussion right now. I have to book a flight.'

'You see? You're doing it right now. It's what my therapist calls an avoidance strategy.'

'Your therapist?'

'Just tell me, Tim. Is your daughter actually missing? Or is she just off at summer camp somewhere? Were you even *talking* to some woman from Seattle just then?'

I leaned back in my chair, let my arms hang down at my sides. Exhaustion, defeat, take your pick.

'I have a lot to do, Kate,' I said, keeping my

voice as even as possible. And then I said something that was probably very stupid. 'What do I owe you for the Chinese food?'

'Fuck you,' she said and went down the stairs.

I got out of the chair as if to follow, then decided there really wasn't any point. I heard some containers of Chinese food being thrown around the kitchen, then the slamming of a door.

I'd clean up later.

I dropped back into the chair, grabbed the receiver and called the police. Not the emergency number, but the line for the office Kip Jennings worked out of. A fellow detective said she was off duty. I explained that it was urgent and asked whether they could relay a message and have her call me.

He said he'd see what he could do.

I hung up and turned back to the computer to look up flights. I nearly booked a 1:59 p.m. US Airways flight out of LaGuardia, then just before confirming my arrangements noticed that I had to switch planes in Philadelphia.

'Fuck that,' I said.

Then I found a Jet Blue flight that departed the same time, and was $300 more, that went non-stop to Seattle. It was a six-hour flight, which would put me into Seattle around five p.m. local time. Assuming it took me an hour to get into the city, I could be looking for Yolanda Mills, and my daughter, by early evening.

I didn't know when to book a return ticket for, so I didn't book one at all. I confirmed my choice, provided all my credit card info, then waited for the ticket to be emailed to me and printed it out.

The phone rang. I had the receiver in my hand before the first ring had ended.

'Mr Blake? Detective Jennings here.' She sounded nasal.

'Hi, thanks, listen, I have a lead on Sydney.'

'Really,' she said, with less enthusiasm than I might have expected. 'She's been in contact with you?'

'No.'

'What's this lead?'

'A woman who works at a drop-in for teenage runaways read about Syd on the net. She got in touch. She's *seen* Syd. I've already booked a flight out at two tomorrow.'

'Mr Blake, I'm not sure that's wise.'

In the background, I could hear a shouting, 'Mom! I'm ready!'

'It's all I've got right now. I can't sit around here in Milford.'

'The thing is, it could be someone trying to scam you.'

'She didn't ask for anything,' I said. 'She said it wouldn't be Christian.'

Kip Jennings made a snorting noise.

'This woman may not be asking now, not yet. But once you've flown all the way out there — Cassie! I'm on the phone! I'll be up in a minute!' A sigh. 'Once you get out there, that's when she'll suddenly come up with a reason why you need to pay her. Or she'll be asking about a reward. You'll think, you've come so far, you'll

120

give her whatever she wants. I've seen this kind of thing before.'

'I don't think it's like that. It doesn't feel like that.' I didn't want to believe this was a shakedown. 'A few hours ago, when we went up to see my daughter's car, I started thinking, maybe things aren't looking so good. Syd's car abandoned . . . the blood. But this, this is good news. This is solid.'

'How?' Jennings said. 'You've got the word of a woman you don't know who . . . how did she even connect up with you?'

'She checks websites about missing kids, sees if they match up with any of the kids in her shelter.'

'It sounds fishy,' Jennings said.

I refused to let her defeat me. 'What would you do,' I asked, 'if it were Cassie?'

A long pause at the other end of the line. 'Mr Blake, did you call just to tell me you're heading out there, or is there something specific you want me to do?'

'Call the Seattle police. Have them put out an APB or whatever it is on her.'

'I'll call them, but I have to be honest. A runaway teen isn't going to be a high-priority for them. I'll tell them about finding the car, that this may be more than a simple runaway, but I wouldn't get my hopes up that they're going to jump all over this.'

'That blood,' I said. 'That was on Syd's car. Did you find out whose it is?'

'That'll take a while, Mr Blake. Maybe, by the time you get back from Seattle, we'll know something. And if your daughter ends up coming home with you, maybe it won't matter.'

★ ★ ★

I went down to the kitchen, cleaned a container's worth of chow mein off the floor. The boxes Kate hadn't dumped contained some breaded shrimps, beef with broccoli, and some plain rice.

I ate it cold.

Then I went back upstairs and packed a small, over-the-shoulder case. Something I could carry straight on to the plane. I didn't want to be waiting around for checked luggage.

I had a little room left over in my bag, so I went into Syd's room and looked at the stuffed animals she had on display in various places. In her chair, on her bookshelves, tucked in around her pillows. Tiny dogs and bunnies. A small, once-furry, moose given to Syd, when she was two, by my late mother. It had endured so many years of snuggling it was nearly threadbare. Some things little girls never outgrow, even when they're leaving the house in fishnets with studs in their nose, purple streaks in their hair.

Her stuffed friends weren't arranged this way the day she disappeared. She'd gone to work leaving her bed unmade. The animals had been tossed all over the place. But when a week had gone by, I made the bed and put the animals in position to welcome Sydney home.

They were probably as tired of waiting as I was.

I thought one of them should accompany me to Seattle.

I picked the moose. His name, according to the tag, was Milt. He wouldn't have been my first choice. His puffy antlers made him more difficult to pack. But I knew he was Syd's favorite.

I got under the covers, expecting not to sleep. But I guess the tension I'd been living with for the last few weeks had ebbed slightly with Yolanda's news.

I just hoped her husband would sort out sending the picture in the morning, as promised.

I was up before six, checked the computer before doing anything else. No news. I showered and shaved, went back to check the computer again.

Still nothing. Then I remembered it was only a little after three in the morning in Seattle.

That didn't stop me from checking every five minutes.

Shortly after nine, there was mail.

A short note from Yolanda: 'Hope this is her. Let me know.' There was a picture attached.

I was afraid to open it. Up to now, I had convinced myself that the girl she'd seen was Sydney. It had to be Sydney. I had my ticket, my bags were packed. I was going to Seattle to bring back my girl.

But what if the picture turned out not to be her? What if this clearly was some other girl?

The time had come to find out one way or another. I double-clicked on the attachment snapshot and it opened up before my eyes.

123

I let out a whoop I was sure everyone on the street must have heard even with the windows closed.

It was my girl.

It was Syd.

10

Not that the picture was perfect. It was no more than a fleeting shot of Syd. The background was nothing more than a builder's beige wall and a small glass door, maybe two feet square, with the words 'FIRE EXTINGUISHER' stenciled on it in red, the first 'I' nearly worn off. The letters are more in focus than Syd, who is moving through the frame, right to left, just about to move out of the picture. She's in profile, leaning forward into her stride, her head tilted down so her blond hair is hanging forward. There's not much of her face to see but the tip of her nose, and I'd know that nose anywhere.

But it wasn't just Syd's nose that convinced me it was her. It was the light, summery scarf she wrapped fashionably about her neck. Coral in color, crinkly in texture, thin and wispy, with a fringe at the end. Her mother had bought it for her a few months ago on a shopping excursion into Manhattan.

I had a reputation in my house as someone who wouldn't notice if his wife or daughter walked into the room in a neon wedding gown. Different eye shadows and nail colors eluded me. But I remembered the first time I saw Sydney wearing that scarf, the smart way she'd tied it, the blazing coral contrasting with her blond hair.

When Syd got in the car one recent morning wearing it, I'd said, 'That's sharp.'

And Syd had replied, 'Whoa. Get your cataracts fixed?'

The scarf, matched with the hair, the tilt of the girl's head, the nose, left no doubt in my mind.

I doublechecked that I had everything I needed for my trip. Before grabbing my bag and heading out the door, I emailed Yolanda a brief message: 'It's her. I'll be in Seattle this evening. See you then. Thanks so much.'

There was one stop to make along the way. I wheeled into Riverside Honda just after ten. There were sales staff on the floor, but that early in the morning, unless it was a Saturday, was not a busy time. I saw Andy Hertz was at his desk, but instead of popping by mine, I went straight to Laura Cantrell's office. I rapped not so lightly on the open door.

'Hey,' I said.

She looked up from some sales report she was reading, removed the glasses she wore for that kind of detail work, and set them on her desk. 'Tim,' she said.

'I'm taking some time off,' I said. I wasn't asking for permission.

The perfect eyebrows went up a quarter of an inch. 'Oh?'

'I have a lead on Syd,' I said. 'I'm going to Seattle.'

Laura pushed back her chair and stood up, took a couple of steps toward me. 'You've found her?'

'I know she's been out there. She's been seen a couple of times at a drop-in place.'

'That must be a huge relief,' she said. 'To know that she's not . . .'

126

'Yes,' I said. I'd learned that as bad as it was to have a daughter who was missing, it was better than having a daughter who was missing that you knew to be dead. 'I'm catching a flight in three hours. I could be a couple of days, but I could be longer. I simply don't know.'

Laura nodded. 'Take as much time as you need.'

Was this the same Laura who threatened to give my desk to someone else if I didn't get my sales numbers up?

'Thanks,' I said.

'I'm sorry,' she said.

'Excuse me?'

'About the other day. I gave you a hard time.' She'd taken another step closer to me. I could smell her perfume.

'Yeah, well, I guess you do what you have to do,' I said.

'You know they're leaning on me, too,' she said. 'You know how it goes. At the end of the day, it's all about numbers. I'll bet, when you had your dealership, you had to ride people hard.'

That was part of the problem. I didn't. I was always the nice guy, the one who understood, the one who said, hey, you need some time, take some time. Used to drive Susanne crazy.

'Sure,' I said.

'Maybe,' Laura said, 'when you get back, and bring Cindy home with you, we should have a drink or something.'

I couldn't be bothered to correct her this time. 'Sounds great, Laura,' I said. 'I've got to be going.'

I headed for my desk. Andy was scouring the

used car classifieds in the *New Haven Register*, circling numbers.

'Morning,' I said. Andy glanced up, grunted a greeting. He looked stressed.

My phone was flashing. I had a message from a couple who'd bought a van from me four years ago. Their kids were older now and they were thinking of getting into an Accord or a Pilot. I scribbled down their phone number, tore off the sheet, and handed it to Andy.

'Probably an easy sale. Good people. Tell them I had business that took me out of town, that I asked you, personally, to look after them.'

'Jesus, Tim, thanks.'

'No problem.'

'I owe you.'

'No kidding.'

He asked where I was going and I told him. Said I'd be gone at least a couple of days.

'I hope she's OK,' he said.

★ ★ ★

Sydney, eleven years old:

A boy named Jeffrey Wilshire walks her home from school. It's the second time he has done this. His attentions do not go unnoticed by Susanne or me.

I am driving her to an evening dance class. This was just before she gave up ballet. This whole prancing about in tights thing no longer appealed to her. It hadn't for some time, but her mother kept pressing her to take it. 'If you drop it, you'll be sorry.'

128

Finally, Syd did, and she was not.

So I am driving her to her lesson and say casually, 'So this Jeffrey fellow, he seems to be taking an interest in you.'

'Please,' Syd says.

'What's that mean?'

'He's always waiting for me to come out at the end of the day so he can walk with me. I keep hoping Mrs Whattley will give us a detention so maybe he'll get tired and go home.'

'Oh,' I say.

We drive a bit further, and Syd says, 'He likes to blow up frogs.'

'What? Who likes to blow up frogs?'

'Jeffrey. He and this other boy — you know Michael Dingley?'

'No.'

'Anyway, Mom does, because Mom and his mother used to be volunteer drivers when we did that trip to the fire station last year.'

'OK. Tell me about Jeffrey.'

'So they catch frogs, and then they stick firecrackers into their mouths and then they light the firecrackers and blow the frogs up.'

'That's sick,' I say. Detonating animals was not, at least in my case, a rite of passage on the way to adulthood.

'They think it's really funny,' Syd says.

'It's not funny.'

'I mean, I know we eat animals and everything,' she says. 'Didn't Mom used to be a vegetarian?'

'For a while.'

'Why'd she stop?'

I shrug. 'Cheeseburgers. She felt life wasn't

129

worth living without cheeseburgers. But it's one thing to kill an animal for food, and another to take pleasure in its suffering.'

She thinks about that a minute. 'Why would someone do that?'

'What?'

'Kill something for fun?'

'Some people are wired wrong.'

'What's that mean?'

'I mean, some people think it's fun to make others suffer.'

Syd looks out her window. 'I'm always thinking about what the other person is feeling.' A pause. 'Or animal.'

'That's what makes you a good person.'

'Doesn't Jeffrey know that the frog feels pain?'

'If he does, he doesn't care.'

'Does that make Jeffrey evil?'

'Evil?' The question throws me. 'Yeah, maybe.'

'He said, one time, he put a live hamster in a microwave and turned it on.'

'Don't let him walk you home from school anymore,' I say. 'How about, for the next couple of days, your mother or I will pick you up?'

* * *

I listened to some more of Syd's tunes on the way to LaGuardia. I had to turn it off halfway through Joe Cocker's 'You Are So Beautiful to Me'. I didn't want to tear up on the 95. I didn't want to end up in a story under the headline 'Weeping Father Makes Fatal Lane Change'.

130

At the airport, I bought a couple of magazines — the new *Car and Driver* and *The New Yorker*. I had my doubts I'd be able to concentrate on either of them, but the first one would have lots of pictures of shiny cars and the latter would have cartoons. Sitting in the stale, soulless departure lounge at LaGuardia, I got out my cell and put in a call to Susanne at work.

She'd been working with Bob nearly two years now. I gathered, listening to Syd, it was not always the best of working relationships. And now that everyone was living together as one big happy family, troubles from the lot sometimes erupted at home. For example, Bob was often critical of the way Suze kept the books. Reporting all your income, he felt, was highly overrated.

Sitting shoulder to shoulder in the crowded departure lounge didn't afford me much privacy, so I relinquished my seat and walked over by one of the windows where I could watch jets landing and taxiing in.

'Bob's Motors,' Susanne answered. There was no joy in her voice. There hadn't been for several weeks now.

'It's me,' I said.

'Hey,' Susanne said, her voice sharpening, cautious. A call from me, these days, could mean very good news, or very bad news.

'I'm at the airport,' I said. 'I'm going to Seattle.'

A short intake of breath. 'Tell me.'

'I have a lead, not a bad lead, that Sydney might be out there.'

I filled her in. She listened. She interrupted with a couple of questions. Had I told Kip

Jennings? Could I believe this woman on the phone?

Yes. And I hoped so.

'I'll pay for your flight,' she said.

'Don't worry about that.'

'I should be going with you.'

'You need to take it easy.'

'I'm not a fucking invalid, you know.'

'Actually, at the moment, you are.'

'I'm doing pretty good with the cane. I may not be ready for the marathon yet, but — '

'It's OK. Just let me do this.'

'I know. I'd just slow you down. I just hope . . . I hope I haven't fucked something up permanent. The hip's killing me, and the knee still hurts like a son of a bitch.'

'It just takes time.'

'Thanks for not rubbing it in.'

'Rubbing what in?'

'About Bob, about my doing a stupid thing like parasailing, thinking I'm eighteen or something. It shows a lot of restraint, not making wisecracks to me about it.'

'Doesn't mean I'm not thinking them,' I said. She laughed softly. When she didn't say anything for a moment, I said, 'Suze.'

'Yeah, I'm here.'

'What's going on? With Evan?'

'I really can't get into it, Tim. I mean, he's Bob's son. What am I going to say?'

'I can tell something's going on. When he came out of the office, he was furious.'

'He's . . . he's a good kid, mostly.'

'Mostly.'

'He's just . . . he hardly ever comes out of his room. He's on the computer all the time.'

'Kids do that, talking to their friends.'

'No,' she said quietly. 'It's something else.'

'Porn,' I said. 'He's whacking off to porn.'

'No,' Susanne said, stretching the word out, wondering. 'I don't think it's that either. I think it's something . . . worse.'

'Have you talked to Bob about this?'

'I've told him . . . that there are things I've noticed.'

'What? What have you noticed?'

'I think Evan's stealing.'

'The petty cash,' I said. 'And you mentioned your watch went missing, and money from your purse.'

'All of that. Bob says I'm just stressed out, that it's making me absent-minded, forgetful.'

'You think he's right?'

'I think he's full of shit. And the watch came back. I know exactly where it was, in my drawer, and it was gone. And this morning, it was back.'

'What do you make of that?'

'I think Evan might have pawned it. And I think Bob bought it back.'

'He's covering for him.'

'Bob's very defensive about Evan.'

'Move out, Suze,' I said. 'Get out of there. Go back to your own house.'

She shot back, 'Oh yeah, that's the answer. Don't try to work things out, just wash my hands of them. Is that what you'd like?'

'You have enough to worry about. You don't need to be living under the same roof with some kid who's stealing from you.'

'I can't talk about this. I can't. Just find Sydney.'

'OK,' I said.

'You know,' she said, 'I really blew it with you.'

I didn't say anything. I was watching one of the terminal clocks. My flight was due to board shortly.

'I never should have pushed you,' she said. 'Our life was good.'

'I know.'

'I got caught up in the whole . . . I thought, if we had more, that'd be good for all of us, right? I mean, sure, I like nice things, I admit that. I was thinking about myself, but I also believed that what I wanted would be good for all of us, good for Sydney. You'd make it big, we could get her nice things, a bigger room, a top-notch college, a better future, you know?'

'Sure.'

'So I pushed you. But it wasn't what you wanted. It wasn't what you were good at. I should have been smart enough to see that from the beginning.'

'Suze, you don't have to — '

'And then it all went to shit. I pushed you because I wanted more for us, for Sydney, and ended up with so much less. Sometimes, I think she hates us. Hates me. For letting things fall apart. I keep thinking that maybe, if we'd stayed together, this never would have happened. Syd wouldn't have left.'

'There's no way to know that.'

'Somehow, things would have been different.'

'I think they're calling my flight,' I said.

'You'll call.'

'I promise.'

★　★　★

The thing about driving is, you feel like you're doing something to get yourself there. You're in charge. You're in control. It helps funnel the tension. You're reading the map, finding a different radio station, looking for an opening so you can pass a pickup driven by an old guy in a hat.

But in a plane, you just sit there and slowly go out of your mind.

Of course, driving to Seattle was not an option. A six-hour flight was preferable to a three-day drive. But the fact that I could do nothing more than look out the window, leaf through my magazines, or watch in-flight entertainment that, even with headphones, could barely be heard over the drone of the engines made the trip interminable.

But it did finally end. While I may have been screaming in my head while I waited for everyone in the seats ahead of me to get their luggage together and exit the plane, I managed to keep my cool. Once I was off the plane I powered up my cell phone and checked to see whether I had any messages.

I didn't.

I found my way to the taxi stand, got in the back of one and said to the driver, 'Second Chance'. I offered him the address but he waved me off.

'I've been driving a cab in Seattle for twenty-two years,' he said. 'I know my way around.'

I settled into the seat, gazed out at the unfamiliar territory, feeling like a stranger in a strange land.

I'm coming, Syd. I'm coming.

11

The taxi was heading into downtown in the middle of the afternoon commute home. The regular traffic would have been bad enough, but we got bogged down where three lanes were being narrowed to one for an accident. Just before six, we were pulling up in front of the Second Chance shelter, a light rain coming down. I'd lost all sense of direction coming in, couldn't guess north from south, east from west, especially with no sun in a western sky visible.

I paid the cabby and grabbed my bag. I was in an older part of town. Used record shops, discount clothing stores, pawn shops. This must have been the only block in Seattle where there wasn't a Starbucks. Second Chance looked more like a diner than a refuge. There were tables pushed up to the windows, young people in scruffy clothes seated at them, drinking coffee out of cardboard cups. They had an aimless look about them, as though they'd already been sitting there a long time, that if I came back a couple of hours from now they'd still be there.

Already I was looking. Scanning the sidewalk in both directions, searching the faces. Satisfied that Syd wasn't hanging around the street, just waiting for me to show up, I entered Second Chance.

Once inside, I started doing the same thing. I scanned. A couple of dozen teens — some actually looked older than that, late twenties maybe, even one who could have been in his early thirties — milling about, but none of them was Syd. They seemed to sense that they were being studied, and several of them subtly turned their backs to me.

I was expecting something like a hotel front desk, I suppose, but what I found off in the corner of the room was a door resting on two sawhorses, and sitting behind it, peering through wire-rimmed glasses at a computer, was a man in his late thirties, prematurely balding but with enough hair at the back to make a short ponytail, dressed in a plaid shirt and jeans.

'Excuse me,' I said.

He held up one finger, resumed typing something, then hit, with some fanfare, one button. 'Send,' he said. He turned in his chair and said, 'Yeah?'

'My name is Tim Blake,' I said. 'I just flew in from Connecticut.'

'Good for you,' he said.

I wasn't in the mood for attitude, but pressed on. 'Is Yolanda around?'

'Beats me,' he said. 'Who's Yolanda?'

'She works here,' I said.

'News to me.' He shrugged, as if to say, *So what if I don't know who works here*? 'Is there something I can do for you?'

'I'm trying to find my daughter,' I said. 'Sydney Blake. She's been in here a couple of times in the last week, I think. We've been going out of our minds, her mother and I, wondering what's happened to her. Hang on, I've got a picture.'

138

I reached into my jacket pocket for reprints of the photos of Sydney that were on the website. I handed a sampling of them to the man who glanced at them quickly and then put them on his desk.

'Never seen her,' he said.

'What's your name?' I asked.

'Len,' he said.

'Len, would you mind just taking another look?'

He gave the shots another cursory glance and said, 'We get a lot of kids through here you know. It's possible she's been around, but I don't recognize her.'

'You here all the time?' I asked.

'Nope. So maybe she was here when I was off. How did you hear that she's been in here?'

I didn't want to tell him that Yolanda had tipped me off. She might have violated privacy rules by getting in touch. I was betting one of the reasons runaways felt comfortable coming here was because it was understood the management wasn't in the habit of ratting them out to their parents.

So instead of answering directly, I said, 'There was a tip to the website I set up when my daughter went missing. That she might have been here. So then I was in touch with Yolanda Mills.'

'OK,' Len said.

'Has Yolanda gone home for the day?'

'Like I said, I don't know her.'

'Is this her day off? Does she work a different shift?'

'What's the name again?'

'Yolanda Mills.'

Len had a blank look on his face. 'And she works here? At this shelter?'

'That's what she told me,' I said.

'You spoke to her?'

'Yes. By email, and over the phone,' I said. I was getting a strange tingling at the back of my neck.

'Can you give me a second?' Len got up from behind the desk and went through a door that led down a dark green hallway dotted with notices that had been taped directly to the wall. I saw him go into a room halfway down the hall. He was in there no more than twenty seconds, then came back.

'We got nobody working here by that name,' he said.

'That's not possible,' I said, feeling my anxiety level go up a notch. 'I spoke to her. Who were you talking to back there?'

'Lefty.' My look must have told him I thought he was jerking me around. 'Morgan. She's the boss. We just call her Lefty. You want to talk to her?'

'Yes.'

'Great. She loves interruptions.'

He led me down the hall, stuck his head in the doorway and said, 'Guy wants to talk to you, Lefty.'

She was nearly hidden behind a desk stacked with paper-stuffed folders. Forties, probably, although the thin gray streaks in her brown hair and the wire-rimmed John Lennon glasses suggested to me that she might be older. A blue long-sleeved sweater hung off her thin frame,

140

and when she stood up I could see that she'd cinched her belt tight to keep her jeans, a couple of sizes too large, from falling off her.

'Yeah?' she said.

'I'm Tim Blake,' I said, extending my right hand. Instead of returning the gesture with her own right hand, she stuck out her left. She had no right arm. The right sweater sleeve, hanging empty, was tucked into a pocket. I was glad I hadn't called her 'Lefty'.

'Morgan Donovan,' she said. 'This is my empire.' She waved her hand majestically at the chaos that was her desk. 'You're looking for somebody?'

'Two people, actually,' I said. 'My daughter, Sydney Blake. And a woman who works here. Yolanda Mills.'

'Nope.'

'Excuse me?'

'No one by that name works here.'

'She told me she worked at Second Chance. Is there another drop-in place with this name?'

'Maybe in some parallel universe,' Morgan said. 'But we're the only one in Seattle.'

'I don't understand,' I said.

'Maybe you got the name wrong. She works for some other shelter. God knows the city is full of them.'

'No, I'm sure I have it right,' I said. I put the pictures of Syd on the top of one of the folders. 'This is my daughter, Sydney Blake. Yolanda Mills said she'd seen her here. Twice.'

Morgan gave the pictures a more thorough examination than Len had. 'I'm good with faces,' she said. 'But this girl, she's not familiar. She's a looker. If I'd seen her, I'd have remembered her. So would Len.' She rolled her eyes. 'Especially Len.'

'But you're back here in the office,' I said. 'She could have come in and you wouldn't have seen her.'

She nodded. 'Yup,' she said. 'But if there was a Yolanda Mills working for me, that I'd know. I sign the checks.'

'Maybe she's a volunteer. Do you have volunteers here?'

'Some. But none by that name.'

I took out a slip of paper on which I'd written the shelter's address, my flight info, and several phone numbers, including Yolanda's. 'I've got her number right here.'

Morgan asked me to read it out to her. 'That's not the shelter number,' she said.

'It's her cell,' I said. 'I called this number last night and talked to her. She said she helped with the food orders here, that she was out all the time picking up groceries.'

Morgan Donovan just looked at me.

'Hang on,' I said, got out my cell, flipped it open, and punched in the number. 'I'll get her on the phone and you can talk to her yourself.'

'Why the hell not,' she said tiredly. 'It's not like I have anything else to do.'

I let it ring a dozen times, thinking that eventually it would go to message, but it didn't. I ended the call, then immediately tried the number again. I let it go another dozen rings, then snapped the phone shut.

Morgan said, 'You don't look so good.'

12

I was having a déjà vu moment. First Syd's not working where she says she is. Now the mysterious Yolanda.

'You want to sit down?' Morgan said.

'Something's wrong,' I said. My legs were rubbery, my stomach was doing a slow somersault. 'Where the hell is she?' I said, more to myself than the woman sitting behind the desk.

Morgan sat down, leaned back in her chair, and sighed tiredly. 'You might as well fill me in.'

So I did. Syd going missing. The hotel. The car. Then, a hit on the website I'd set up from a woman claiming to have seen her in Seattle.

'And she said she worked for us,' Morgan said. 'That's some story. Sounds like a scam. Maybe some kid, jerking you around.'

'No,' I said. 'It didn't sound like a kid, and she didn't ask me for anything. Didn't want a reward.' Wheels were turning. 'If you knew someone here was sending tips to parents, telling them their kids were here, would that be against the rules?'

'Big time,' she said. 'We'd like nothing more than for these kids to get back together with their mothers and fathers, but some of those moms and dads don't deserve to have them back. You got no idea the kind of crap a lot of these kids have had to put up with. Not that they're all angels. Seventy per cent of them, I'd probably

143

kick them out myself if they were mine. But they're not all trouble. Some of these girls, when their stepdads weren't using them for punching bags, they were trying to get into their pants. We got kids out there whose parents are drunks and drug dealers. We had a girl here last year, her mom was pimping her out. She was getting a little too old in the tooth to do it herself and figured her daughter could take over the family business.'

'Jesus,' I said.

'Yeah, well, he seems to be MIA at the moment. We had a kid here last week, his skin was a mess, like it had all peeled off and was growing back on again, especially his face. Anything that wasn't protected. His dad was pissed he hadn't taken a shower when he'd told him to. So he hauls the kid out to the driveway, takes a power washer to him. You ever feel the pressure off one of those things? You can strip paint with them.'

I said nothing.

'So we're not exactly going to put a call into mommies and daddies like that and say hey, guess what, we found your little angel, why don't you come on down and take them home.'

'I get it.'

'These kids trust us. They have to be able to trust us or we can't help them.'

I was thinking. 'So then, if you did have someone on staff who was doing this, who was trying to reunite kids with their parents, and you found out, they'd be fired.'

'Very likely.'

'So maybe whoever called me works here but didn't use her real name.'

Morgan Donovan considered that a moment. 'Why would someone have to give you a name at all? She could have gotten in touch with you anonymously.'

'I have an email address for her,' I said.

Morgan asked for it and wrote it down on the back of an envelope. 'There's no one here with that address that I know of. A Hotmail address ain't exactly that hard to get.'

'I know,' I said.

'So like I said, maybe someone's yanking your chain,' she said. When I couldn't think of anything to say to that, she said, 'Wanna coffee or something? I'd offer you something stronger but it's a church foundation that tops up our budget and they take a dim view of my keeping scotch in my bottom drawer. Not that there isn't a bottle in there right now. We've got a pot of coffee that's been going continuously since 1992. Want some of that?' My face must have given away my reluctance. 'A Diet Coke then?'

I said sure.

'Hey, Len!' Footsteps scurrying down the hall, then Len poked his head in. 'Can you grab us a couple cans of DC?'

Len continued further on down the hall, where I could hear an old-fashioned fridge open and then latch shut, and then he was back with one can and a paper cup. 'We're running a bit low,' he said, putting both items on her desk and leaving.

Morgan got up and started clearing some papers

145

off a wooden chair so that I could sit down.

'Let me get that,' I offered, but she held up her arm to deflect me, then used it to scoop up the files.

'I'm pretty good at this,' she said. 'Although you know what pisses me off? Those taps in public washrooms, where you only get water so long as you're pressing down? So as soon as you let go of the tap to get your hand under it, there's no fucking water. I've just got the one fist, but if I could find the guy who invented that goddamn tap I could knock his teeth out.'

I smiled awkwardly.

'You can ask,' she said.

'Sorry?'

'How I lost it.'

'It's none of my business,' I said.

'You ever hang your arm down the outside of the door when you're in a car?'

Slowly, I nodded.

She smiled. 'My husband's driving, I'm chilling out in the passenger seat, my arm dangling out the window, the asshole runs a red and we get broadsided. I lost my arm in the front grill of a Ford Explorer. Maybe, if the two of us hadn't been three sheets to the wind it wouldn't have happened. Getting your wife's arm cut off tends to put a strain on a marriage, so rather than look at me every day and be reminded of what he'd done, he hit the road. At least I had the one arm left to wave goodbye, the son of a bitch.'

She popped the Diet Coke can, filled the paper cup to the rim and handed it to me. She

146

sipped what was left in the can and returned to her spot behind the desk.

I sat in the chair she'd cleared for me.

'I don't think you answered my question,' she said. There had been a question? I was still processing the lost arm story. Morgan refreshed my memory. 'Why couldn't this person have just sent an anonymous tip? Why give you a fake name?'

'I guess she wanted me to know she was legit,' I said. 'And she was. I'm sure of it. She even sent me a picture of my daughter.'

'A picture?'

'Sydney was caught in the frame of a shot she took with her cell phone.' I sipped Diet Coke from the paper cup. I hadn't realized, until that moment, how parched I was. 'It was her. In the picture. I'm positive.'

Morgan shook her head slowly back and forth. 'Maybe she wanted you to know your daughter's out here, she wants you to believe her, so she gave you a name. But maybe there was some reason why she couldn't reveal her true identity to you.' Morgan laughed. 'Makes her sound like Wonder Woman or something.'

'It wasn't you, was it?' I asked. The idea popped into my head.

Morgan Donovan was too worn down by her job to register any surprise by my question. She said tiredly, 'It's all I can do to get these kids to have some breakfast, let alone reunite them all with their families.'

'I'm taking a lot of shots in the dark these days,' I said.

147

'Where are you staying?' Morgan asked me.

'I don't know. I didn't book anything before I left. I thought, maybe, if I found Syd right away, we'd catch a red eye back home tonight.'

She smiled pitifully at me. 'An optimist. It's been so long since I ran into one of those I almost forgot they existed. Give me your cell number. I'll put some of your snaps up on the bulletin board, tell everybody to see me if they know anything. Then I'll call you. That a deal?'

'Sure,' I said. 'I'd really appreciate that.' A couple more swallows and I had finished my cup of Diet Coke. 'Would you mind if I asked the other people who work here if they've seen Syd, or heard of Yolanda Mills?'

'Actually, yes, I would,' Morgan said. 'I'll do what I can for you, but I don't want you stirring things up around here.'

I didn't like her answer much. I got up from the chair, nodded, and said thanks. She went back to the mounds of paper on her desk. When she noticed I hadn't left yet, she said, 'Was there something else?'

'You were going to put my daughter's picture on the bulletin board,' I said.

'So I was.' She brushed past me on her way out of the room, went down the hall and into the main reception area where kids were still milling around. There seemed to be more here than before I'd gone into Morgan Donovan's office. She crossed the room and stuck Syd's face to a bulletin board and wrote under it 'If you've seen this girl, see Lefty.'

The board was a collage version of a

148

graduating class photo. Hundreds of photos. Boys and girls. White, black, Hispanic, Asian. Some as young as ten or twelve, others who looked to be in their thirties. The moment Morgan stepped back from the board Sydney's face blended into all the others. Not one lost daughter, but the latest addition to a lost generation.

I stared hopelessly at the wall.

'I know,' Morgan said. 'It's a bitch, isn't it?'

*   *   *

I asked Len for a sheet of paper from his printer before I left. I leaned over the door that was his desk, positioned a photo of Syd in the middle, and wrote above it: 'HAVE YOU SEEN SYDNEY BLAKE?' Below the shot I printed my own name and cell phone number, adding: 'PLEASE CALL.'

I left and found a drug store with a photocopying machine, positioned the picture in the center of the sheet and placed the two items on the glass. I set the counter to one hundred and pressed Print. Once I had the copies I went up and down the street. I figured if Syd had been in this area at least a couple of times, she might have frequented other businesses. Maybe she'd even have gone into some of them looking for work. She'd always been a pretty resourceful kid, and I could see her looking for odd jobs so that she could afford to feed herself.

Most of the shopkeepers politely took the flyers, glanced at them, put them aside. Some just said, 'Sorry.' Others glanced at the sheet and crumpled it up.

There wasn't time to get angry with any of them. I just moved on to the next shop.

I did that until about nine. There was a diner across from Second Chance, and I managed to get a seat by the window. I put my cell phone on the table and ordered a hot open-faced turkey sandwich and coffee and sat there, rarely taking my eye off the front of the drop-in center. There was a street lamp on the sidewalk there, and it cast enough light that if Syd appeared, I was confident I could spot her, even through the off-and-on drizzle.

I ate my dinner mechanically. Put the food in my mouth, chewed, swallowed. Drank my coffee.

I tried the Yolanda Mills number again. No answer, no way to leave a message.

I'd no sooner put the phone down than it rang. I grabbed it so quickly I knocked my fork to the floor. I didn't stop to see who was calling before I flipped the phone open and put it to my ear.

'Yes?' I said.

'It's me,' Susanne said.

'Hey,' I said. 'What are you doing up? What time is it? It must be after midnight where you are.'

'I've been sitting here by the phone all night, waiting for you to call.'

'I'm sorry,' I said. 'The lead . . . hasn't panned out.'

'You sound . . . beat,' she said.

'I'm going to find a place to stay. There's a

150

Holiday Inn or something up the street. I'll get an early start tomorrow. See if I can find the woman who called me, hit all the other shelters I can find, see if Syd went to one of those.'

'You haven't connected with the woman who called you?'

'No one's heard of her.'

'That doesn't make any sense.'

'I know.'

I could sense Susanne's frustration thousands of miles away. 'I shouldn't have got my hopes up.'

'Yeah,' I said. 'I know.'

I propped my elbow on the table and rested my head in the hand that wasn't holding the phone, still watching the Second Chance shelter across the street.

A girl stood in the doorway of the shelter. Blond.

'It's just, you get some hint that maybe this is it, you grab on and hold on with everything you've got,' she said. 'If you hear anything, you'll call?'

'I will,' I said. Switching gears, I said, 'Susanne, how close are Evan and Sydney? I mean, before she disappeared.'

'I don't know,' she said. 'Not that close, as far as I could tell. I mean, they'd be civil with each other at the dinner table, but it's not like they hung out together, or anything.'

'What do you think he's into?'

'What do you mean? Into?'

'You think he's stealing from you, he's always on the computer with the door closed. You don't

151

think it's porn. What's your best guess?'

'I don't know. I mean, it may be nothing. He's really into music. You know they've got all these programs where you can create music on the computer. Maybe he's doing that, with the headphones on so we don't hear it.'

But she didn't sound convinced.

I kept watching the girl across the street.

'Do you think Evan might have dragged Syd into whatever he's up to?' I asked.

'I never saw anything to suggest — '

'Susanne? Hello?'

'Sorry. I just closed the study door. I don't want to wake Bob. Anyway, no, I don't think Syd was mixed up in anything Evan's up to. But there's something I have to tell you.'

The girl kept moving in and out of the shadows. She'd move in close to the shelter entrance where I could barely see her, then poke her head out to watch the cars go by, the streetlights catching her blond hair.

Come on, come on, step out, step out all the way.

'I saw that van again tonight,' Susanne said.

'What van?' I said. The girl took a step forward, the light hitting her face for less than a second. She glanced down the street, then retreated into the shadows.

'The one on our street? The one Bob doesn't think is a big deal?'

I knew what van she meant the first time, but I was having a hard time keeping track of the conversation while I watched the girl.

'When did you see it?' I managed to ask.

152

'Tonight. A couple of hours ago. After it got dark, I happened to look outside and saw a van parked a few houses down, and when I went out and walked down to the end of the driveway the van started up and backed up to the corner and took off.'

A boy — a young man — was approaching the shelter from the right. He came up to the door, and the girl threw her arms around him, kissed him. He had his back to me, and all I could really see of the girl was the top of her head and her arms.

'Susanne . . .'

'It's freaking me out. Bob says I'm getting paranoid about everything because of Syd. Why the fuck wouldn't I be?'

The girl stepped out from the entrance, into the streetlight, but the way she had her arms wrapped around the boy, her head tucked down onto his chest, I couldn't see her face. But my gut said it wasn't her. There was something not quite Syd about her. This girl's legs, they seemed a little shorter.

They started walking up the street. In another moment, they'd be gone.

'So I'm thinking, is someone watching our house? Or one of the other houses on the street? If it's our house, are they watching me, or are they watching Bob? Or has this got something to do with Evan?'

Then the girl leaned her head back, tossed her hair back over her shoulder.

I'd seen Syd do that a thousand times.

'Susanne, I have to go for a second. Hang on.'

153

'What? Why — '

I bolted from the diner, leaving my bag behind, my phone on the table. I threw open the door and ran into the street, forcing drivers coming from both directions to hit the brakes. Horns blew, someone shouted, 'Asshole!'

They were thirty yards ahead, forty, twenty. Arm in arm. She had an arm around his waist, her thumb in a belt loop.

'Syd!' I shouted. 'Syd!'

Before the girl had a chance to turn around I was on them, grabbing her by her free arm, using it to swing myself around in front of her.

'Syd!' I said.

It wasn't Syd.

The girl jerked her arm back as her boyfriend shoved me away forcefully with both hands. I stumbled back, tripped over my own feet, landed on my ass on the sidewalk, my head narrowly missing a brick wall behind me.

'Fuck's your problem?' he said, grabbing the girl and taking her across the street.

13

The next morning I debated renting a car, but Seattle isn't exactly laid out like New York. I wanted to hit as many teen shelters as possible, and didn't want to waste time attempting to navigate the city's winding streets, so I talked to a cabby out front of the hotel and cut a deal to have him take me from shelter to shelter, and wait while I was at each one, for $200.

'That'll take you to noon,' he said.

'We'll see where we are then,' I said. 'Let me go find a cash machine.'

The hotel — not a Holiday Inn, not even close — at least had a computer in the lobby I could use, and I went online to get a list of local shelters. The desk clerk said the printer was busted, so I had to write down names, addresses and phone numbers on a pad I'd found next to the phone in my room.

I handed the sheet, and the cash, to the cabby and said, 'Let's hit the closest first and work our way out to the others.'

'You don't have to worry about me running you all over the place. You've already paid me, the meter's off, and with gas costing what it is we're doing the shortest route possible.'

'Great.'

He delivered me to all the shelters on my list by half past eleven. It was the same story everywhere. I showed them Syd's picture, left them some flyers with my cell phone number on them. I stopped kids at random, pushed the photo under their noses.

No one recognized Syd.

Nor had anyone heard of Yolanda Mills. Every place I stopped I asked for her, too.

After the last shelter, I dropped into the back seat of the taxi. 'You know of any other places that aren't on this list?' I asked.

'I didn't even know there were this many,' the cabby said, turning in his seat to look at me. The Jesus bobble head stuck to his dash, which had been bouncing madly during our drive around Seattle, had had a chance to calm down. My driver was heavyset, hadn't shaved in a couple of days, and spent most of the time as we wandered the city talking on his cell phone to his wife about what they could do to find somebody to marry his sister. She was, from what I could tell, unlikely to be named Miss Washington in the near future, and this was a major stumbling block.

'All right,' I said, dejected. 'Is there a main police headquarters?'

'Sure.'

'Drop me off there and that'll be it,' I said.

'Tough about your daughter,' he said.

I hadn't discussed Syd with him, but given that we were hitting all the shelters for runaways, and I had a stack of flyers in my hand, you didn't have to be Jim Rockford to figure out the nature of my mission.

'Thanks,' I said.

'Sometimes,' he said, poking Jesus with a finger and making him shake, 'you just have to

156

let them do what they want to do, and wait until they realize they need your help, and they come home on their own.'

'What if they're in trouble?' I countered. 'And they're waiting for you to find them?'

The driver thought about that for a moment. 'Well, I guess that's different,' he said.

★ ★ ★

The Seattle police headquarters was on Twelfth Avenue. I went into the lobby and up to the counter and told the woman there I needed to speak to someone about a missing teenage girl.

An officer named Richard Buttram came out to see me and led me to an interview room. I told him about Sydney, when she'd gone missing, how I'd been led to Seattle. That I'd lost touch with Yolanda Mills since I'd gotten here, and that I'd had no luck finding my daughter.

I gave him one of my flyers, told him about the website.

He listened patiently, nodded, stopped me to ask the occasional question.

'So you don't really know,' he said, 'whether your daughter's here in Seattle, or whether she ever was here in Seattle.'

Slowly, not wanting to admit, I said, 'I suppose that's true.' Then, trying to sound more confident, I continued, 'But this woman told me she was here. That she had seen her. She even sent me a picture that I'm as sure as can be was of my daughter.'

'What was the number she gave you?'

I opened my cell phone, found it, read it off to Buttram, who scribbled it down on a notepad. 'Let me try it,' he said, dialing the number from his desk phone. He let it ring a good thirty seconds, then hung up.

'Give me three minutes,' Buttram said and left the room.

I sat there for nearly fifteen, staring at the empty tabletop, the unadorned walls. I looked at the clock, watched the second hand make sweep after sweep.

When Buttram returned he looked dour. 'I went to see one of our detectives who knows a lot about cell phones and various exchanges and all that kind of thing.'

'OK,' I said.

'It's his guess that this is a throwaway phone. He did a quick check of the number, made a call, told me it's one of those ones you can buy at a 7-Eleven or whatever, use for a short period of time, then ditch it.'

I felt like I was slowly slipping under water.

'None of this makes any sense,' I said.

Buttram said, 'I'll hang on to this flyer, put the word out, but I don't want to raise your expectations that we're going to find your daughter.'

'Sure,' I said.

'This woman who called you, she wasn't sniffing about for a reward?'

'No,' I said.

Buttram shook his head as he stood up and walked me to the lobby. 'Then I don't know what to make of it.'

'I don't know what to do,' I said. 'I'm starting

158

to think Sydney's not here in Seattle, that she never was, but I'm afraid to fly home. I keep thinking, if I walk around that neighborhood, where the shelter is, just one more time, I'll spot her.'

'You've put the word out,' he said. 'Morgan, at Second Chance, I know her, and she's the real deal. If she says she's going to keep her eye out for your girl, that's exactly what she'll do.'

He shook my hand and wished me good luck. I stood on the sidewalk out front of the police headquarters for five minutes before walking back to my hotel and checking out.

I booked myself on a Jet Blue flight that didn't leave Seattle until shortly before ten, and would arrive, considering the time change, at LaGuardia at six in the morning. That gave me time to go back into the Second Chance neighborhood and keep looking for Syd.

I managed to grab the same table in the same diner where I'd eaten the night before and stared across the street at the door to the shelter for the better part of four hours. I ordered food, then a coffee about every half hour.

I never saw her, or anyone else who looked remotely like her.

From there I cabbed it to the airport and sat around in the departure lounge like some sort of shock trauma victim, staring straight ahead, hardly moving at all, while waiting for my flight to be called. My cell rang twice. The first call was from Susanne, hoping for good news, but knowing there'd be none since I had not gotten in touch.

159

And then the phone rang again.

'Yeah,' I said.

'I'm really sorry.'

'Hey, Kate,' I said.

'I kind of flipped out the other night.'

I didn't say anything.

'You went, right? To Seattle? I noticed you weren't back yet.'

So she'd been driving by my house.

'Kate, I really can't talk now.'

'I know I said some things, and I just wanted to apologize.'

Maybe, if I hadn't been so tired and discouraged, I might have found a way to be more diplomatic.

I might not have said, 'Kate, this isn't working out. We're done. It's over.' And I certainly wouldn't have finished with, 'Life's too short.'

But that was what I said.

Kate waited a few seconds before coming back with, 'You're a total asshole, you know that? You're a goddamn fucking asshole. I knew it the first time I met you. And you know something else? There's something not right with you, you know that? Something just not — '

I ended the call, turned the phone off, and slipped it into my pocket.

★ ★ ★

I'm not normally able to nod off on a plane, but this overnight flight was an exception. Exhaustion overwhelmed me and I spent almost the entire trip asleep. I was more than bone weary. I

160

was depressed, crushed, burdened by despair. I'd traveled clear across the country thinking I was going to bring my daughter home with me.

And I was coming home alone.

We landed on time, but the pilot had to wait for a gate to clear, so it was nearly seven before I got off the plane, and what with several traffic jams, a couple of pit stops, and everything else, it was shortly before noon before I pulled into my driveway on Hill Street back in Milford.

A defeated soldier coming home from war, I trudged up to the door, bag slung over my shoulder. I put my key into the lock, and swung open the door.

The house had been trashed.

14

'So run through it again for me,' Kip Jennings said.

'I got home, I opened the door, it's like somebody tossed a grenade in here,' I said.

'When was this?'

I glanced at the clock hanging on the kitchen wall, one of the few things still in its place. 'About an hour and a half ago.'

'Have you touched anything since then?'

'I put that clock back on the mantle,' I said. 'It was my father's.' The gesture was akin to straightening your cap after you've been run over by an eighteen-wheeler.

There were a couple of uniform cops wandering around the house, taking pictures, muttering amongst themselves. They'd found a basement window that had been kicked in.

'You'd been gone how long?'

'About forty-eight hours. I left here early two days ago. After nine. So two days and four hours, give or take.'

'Seattle,' Jennings said.

'That's right,' I said.

'And your daughter?'

'I didn't find her,' I said.

Jennings's eyes softened for a moment. 'So you got home, you opened the door,' she said. 'Did you see anyone? Was anyone running away from the house when you pulled into the driveway?'

'No,' I said.

I told her what I'd found. In the living room, cushions tossed from the furniture, then cut open, the foam scattered about in chunks. Every shelf cleared, every cabinet emptied. Books thrown about, CDs all over the place. Audio equipment pulled from the shelves, some components still hanging from them by their wires, hanging precariously like a truck on a cliff in an Indiana Jones movie.

In the kitchen, every cupboard emptied. And then, the boxes that were in the cupboard, emptied. Corn flakes all over the floor. Things pulled out of the fridge, the door hanging open.

It was the same story everywhere. All the drawers in my bedroom dresser pulled out and turned over. So many clothes on the floor you couldn't see the carpet. Socks, underwear, shirts. Items ripped off hangers in the closet, thrown here and there.

Syd's room was no different, although she didn't have quite as much stuff to trash as I did, since most of her clothes were still at her mother's house. The dresser had been emptied. Unlike my bed, which didn't appear to have been touched, Syd's mattress had been cut open. The contents of the closet were on the bedroom floor.

In my computer room, all the desk drawers had been opened, the shelves cleared off.

The basement damage was minimal. The washer and dryer had been opened, and a box of Tide detergent had been emptied onto the floor. The toolbox on my workbench had been dumped out.

Our boxes of stuff — those things you accumulate through life that you don't know what to do with but haven't the nerve to pitch, like your children's kindergarten drawings, photos, books you'll never read again, old files and business papers from your parents' house — had been opened and rummaged through, but only a couple had been dumped out.

Standing amidst the wreckage in the living room, I asked Jennings, 'What kind of little bastards would do this?'

'You think it was kids?' Jennings asked.

'You don't?'

We went slowly through the house, our shoes crunching on corn flakes as we went through the kitchen. She walked and talked. 'Have you noticed whether anything was stolen?'

'How could you tell?' I said, surveying the wreckage. 'I really haven't had a chance to go through the place and check.'

'Your computer missing?'

'No, it's still up there.'

'Your daughter's laptop?'

I recalled seeing it, nodded.

'Laptop's pretty easy to walk off with,' Jennings said.

'Yes.'

'How about silverware?'

I had noticed it earlier dumped from a buffet drawer onto the living room carpet. 'It's here. Would kids even steal silverware?'

'How about iPods, little things like that that are easy to pocket?'

'I don't know. I don't have one. Syd does, but

it's in my car. But they didn't take the small TV here.' I pointed to the set hanging from the kitchen cabinet. Someone would have needed a screwdriver to free it from its bracket.

'They didn't break it, either,' Kip Jennings said. 'You keep any cash in the house?'

'Not a lot,' I said. 'Some, in this drawer over here. Just a few bills, fives and tens, for things like pizza, charities, stuff like that.'

'Have a look,' she said.

I opened it. The cash was normally tucked between the edge of the cutlery tray and the side of the drawer.

'It's gone,' I said.

'Other than the cash, anything jump out at you as being missing?'

'Not really. What are you getting at?'

'You think maybe it was kids, and maybe it was. But you see any spray paint on the walls? Any TVs kicked in? Doesn't look like anyone's defecated on your rug.'

'A silver lining to everything,' I said.

'It's the kind of thing kids will do.'

'So you don't think it was kids,' I said.

'I'll tell you this much. I don't think anybody came in here to steal stuff at random. They were looking for something. They were looking for it pretty hard, too.'

'Looking for what?' I asked.

'You tell me,' Jennings said.

'You think I know and I'm not telling you?'

'No. At least, not necessarily. But you know better than I what you might have hidden in this house.'

'I don't have anything hidden,' I said.

'Maybe it wasn't you who hid it,' she said.

'What are you saying?'

'I'm saying your daughter's missing and we don't know why. She said she was working at that hotel but no one there's even heard of her. That tells me your daughter wasn't exactly being honest with you about everything. So maybe she was hiding something in this house — or at least somebody thought she might have been — that she didn't share with you.'

'I don't believe that.'

Kip put her hands on her hips and studied me. 'This is a pretty thorough search. In all the years I've been with the police, I've seen very few places torn apart like this. I've never even seen cops tear apart a place like this. This took a while. Looks like they weren't too worried about you walking in the door unexpectedly. Looks like they knew they had time.'

Our eyes met.

'Who knew you were going to Seattle?' she asked.

Who had I told? Who knew? Kate. My boss, Laura Cantrell. My colleague in the showroom, Andy Hertz. Susanne, of course, and no doubt Bob and Evan. And anyone else any of these people might have told.

I was missing the obvious, of course.

Yolanda Mills, whoever she was, knew I was off to Seattle. She'd practically invited me there.

'Maybe I was set up,' I said.

'Come again?' Jennings asked.

'I was set up. The woman who called me, who

166

said she'd seen my daughter. She knew I wasn't going to be home.'

'Refresh my memory.'

I told her about Yolanda Mills, how I couldn't find her in Seattle, how the cops out there believed she'd called me from a disposable cell phone.

'Seattle's about as far away as someone could send you and still be in the country,' Jennings said. 'Once you were on your way to the airport, they knew they had at least a couple of days to go through your house.'

'But she had a picture of her,' I said. 'She sent it to me. It was a picture of Syd. I'm as sure of that as I can be.'

'Can I see it?'

'Computer,' I said.

I led us into the study, stepping over tossed books and dumped shoeboxes spilling out receipts. While the computer tower and monitor had been shoved about, they were reasonably intact. I fired it up, opened the email program, and found the message and attached photo from Yolanda Mills. I opened it for Detective Jennings to see.

'It's not the greatest picture in the world,' she said. 'The way her hair is falling, you can't see much of her face.'

'You see this?' I said, pointing to the coral, fringed scarf that Syd had tied about her neck. 'I know that scarf. Syd has one just like it. You put that scarf with that hair, and that bit of nose you can see there, and that's her. I'd bet my life on it.'

Jennings leaned in close to the screen and studied the scarf. 'I'll be back in a minute,' she said.

I sat there at the computer, checked to see whether anyone else had been in touch in the last two days. There had been hardly any hits on the website for Syd, and my emails were all junk.

Jennings appeared in the doorway, something bright and colorful wadded up in her hand. She held up a scarf.

'The color caught my eye when I was looking in your daughter's room earlier,' she said. 'It was dumped out onto the floor with everything else.'

I stood, reached for the scarf and held it as though it might dissolve in my fingers.

'Is that the scarf?' she asked.

I nodded very slowly. 'That's the scarf.'

'So if you're daughter was supposedly wearing this scarf in Seattle a few days ago, what's it doing here in your house?'

That was a really good question.

I didn't have much time to ponder it. A minute later, one of the uniformed cops poked his head into the study and said to Jennings. 'I think we found what they were looking for.'

15

'What?' I said.

The cop said nothing. He led Jennings to my bedroom and I followed. One of the pillows had been stripped of its case, and was slit open. A clear plastic freezer bag that was filled with a white powdery substance lay on the bedspread.

'I noticed a funny bump under the pillow case,' he said.

Detective Jennings pinched the corner of the bag between thumb and forefinger, lifted it up for an inspection.

'Lordy, lordy, what do we have here?' she said.

'Is that what I think it is?' I asked.

'I don't know,' Detective Jennings said, eyeing me, the cop in uniform studying me as well. 'What do you think it is?'

'I think it might be cocaine.'

'If that turns out to be right, what do you think it's doing in your pillow?' she asked.

'I have no idea,' I said.

'Want to hazard a guess?'

Slowly, I shook my head. 'No.' I thought a moment. 'Yes.'

'Go ahead,' she said.

'Someone put it there,' I said.

The cop made a small snorting noise.

'I'd have to agree with you there,' Jennings said.

'I slept on that bed two nights ago. There was

nothing in that pillow then. Someone put it there while I was away.'

'So what are you saying?' Jennings said. 'That there were two different break-ins while you were away? That someone came in here and hid this what-may-prove-to-be cocaine in your pillow, and then someone else broke in trying to find it?'

'I don't know,' I said. 'To be honest, as strange as this is, I'm a little more concerned about how my daughter's scarf can be here if she had her picture taken wearing it in Seattle.'

'One thing at a time,' Jennings said. She set the clear bag on the bed. 'Let's say, for the sake of argument, that someone other than yourself snuck in while you were away and hid this in your pillow. Wouldn't that be pretty stupid? First time you get into bed, you put your head on the pillow, you notice it's there.'

'I agree, that'd be pretty dumb,' I said. 'About as dumb as my inviting you into my home to find it. And if this house really was broken into twice, once to hide those drugs, and then a second time by somebody else trying to find them, then how the hell did they overlook them? It took your officer here ten minutes to stumble on them. I mean, look around. This house has been turned fucking upside down. And that pillow's just sitting there full of drugs. Does that make any sense at all?'

Jennings said nothing. She was standing there, one hand held thoughtfully over her mouth and chin. She was trying to work it out.

'Unless whoever put those drugs there did it after the house was torn apart,' she said. 'A place

170

that's already been searched is a great place to hide something.'

'Even if that's what happened,' I said, 'my pillow is still a stupid place to hide anything. I'd find it.'

She turned her head and looked at me. 'Unless you're the one who put it there.'

'For Christ's sake,' I said.

'Do you have a lawyer, Mr Blake?' Detective Jennings asked.

'I don't need a lawyer,' I said.

'I think maybe you do.'

'What I need is for you to believe me. What I need is for you to help me figure out what's going on. What I need is for you to help me find my daughter.'

That stopped her for a moment. 'Your daughter,' she said. 'She certainly wouldn't have to break through a basement window to get in.'

'What are you getting at?'

'She could get in here any time she wants. She has a key.'

'What? You think Sydney was here? You think my daughter's been back? That she'd come back, and not let us know she's OK? That she'd hide cocaine in my pillow?'

Kip Jennings closed the distance between us. And even though she was considerably shorter, she managed to get right in my face. 'Now let's talk about that scarf.'

'I can't explain it.'

'Take a shot at it,' she said. 'That scarf, the one she's wearing in a picture supposedly taken in Seattle, is here, in this house.'

171

I shook my head. 'Maybe Syd was out there, and came back.'

'Just how well do you know your daughter, Mr Blake?'

'Very well. We're very close. I love her.' I paused. 'How well do you know yours?'

She ignored that. 'Do you know all of Sydney's friends? When she goes out late at night, do you always know where she is? Do you know who she talks to on the Internet? Do you know if she's ever tried drugs? Do you know whether she's sexually active? Do you know the answer to any of those questions with any certainty?'

'No parent would,' I said.

'No parent would,' she repeated, nodding. 'So when I ask you how well you know your daughter, I'm not asking you how close you are to her or how much you love her. I'm asking whether it's possible she could be involved in things, involved with people, you might not approve of.'

'I don't know,' I said.

'Do you think Sydney could have been involved in drugs?'

'I can't believe that.'

'Your daughter's missing. Her car was abandoned. And there was blood on it. You need to start waking up to the fact that something's going on.'

'You think I'm not — '

'You need to wake up to the fact that it's possible, just possible, that Sydney may have been mixed up in some nasty things. She may have been hanging out with some nasty people. She told you she was working at that hotel. If she was lying to you about that, what else was she lying about?'

I walked out of the room.

'Get out,' I said to a cop standing at the bottom of the stairs as I headed for the kitchen.

'What?'

'Get out,' I said. 'Get the fuck out of my house.'

'You're not going anywhere, Talbott,' Kip Jennings told the cop from behind me. 'Mr Blake, you can't order these officers out of here. Your house is a crime scene.'

'I have to start cleaning up, put this place in order,' I snapped at her.

'No, not yet,' she said. 'You won't be doing anything around here until I say so. And you're going to have to make arrangements to sleep someplace else tonight.'

'You're not kicking me out of my own house,' I said, turning and pointing a finger at her.

'That's exactly what I'm doing. This house is a crime scene, and that includes your bedroom. Especially now.'

I shook my head in frustration. 'I thought you were trying to help me.'

'I'm trying to figure out what happened, Mr Blake. I hope that ends up helping you. Because my gut's been telling me, up to now, that you've been playing straight with me, that you've been telling me what you know, that you haven't been holding out on me. But things are a bit cloudy now. That's why I think it would be in your

173

interest to talk to a lawyer.'

'You're not seriously thinking of charging me with drug possession or something?'

She looked me right in the eye. 'I'm giving you good advice here, and I think you should take it.'

I held her gaze.

She continued, 'Has it crossed your mind, if you really were conned into going to Seattle so someone could go through your house, that it was your daughter who sent you out there?'

'That's crazy,' I said. 'The woman I spoke to on the phone was not my daughter.'

Jennings shrugged. 'She wouldn't have to be working alone.'

Of all the things Jennings had suggested or intimated, this struck me as the most ridiculous.

But instead of reacting angrily, I held up my hands in a defensive, let's-cool-this-down gesture, because there was something else on my mind I needed to discuss with her.

'Regardless of what you may think of me, or what you may think is going on here, there's something else you need to be aware of,' I said.

'OK,' she said.

'It's about my ex-wife. Someone's watching her house.'

Jennings's brow furrowed. 'Go on.'

'Susanne's noticed someone parked down the street a few times. She says you can see a little light, like he's smoking.' I paused, a thought just occurring to me. 'It's not the police, is it?'

'Not that I'm aware of. She got a plate number?'

'No,' I said.

'Tell her, next time, get it,' Jennings said. 'And I'll see whether we can have someone take a run by there every once in a while.'

I muttered a thank you, turned, and my eye caught the open kitchen drawer that had, until recently, held some cash.

And a name came to mind. Evan. We needed to have a word.

★ ★ ★

On the way to Bob's Motors, I got held where they were merging two lines down to one for roadwork. Feeling briefly charitable, I let a Toyota Sienna that was trying to get into my lane go ahead. Through tinted glass I saw the driver's hand wave thank you.

As the Sienna straightened itself out in front of me, I noticed it was the delivery truck for Shaw Flowers, the florist shop next to XXX Delights. I was guessing that was Ian, the young man who'd been with Mrs Shaw the other day when she was closing up the place, behind the wheel.

He'd given Syd's picture such a cursory glance when Mrs Shaw had suggested I show it to him, that I thought he deserved another chance to look at it.

Ian put his right turn signal on. I did the same.

I followed him into an old residential area with trees so mature they formed a canopy over the street. As he came to a stop in front of a two-storey Colonial I drove on past and turned into a driveway half a dozen houses up.

Ian got out, white wires running down from his ears and into his shirt pocket. I was guessing he had one of those mini iPods like Syd's. He went around the passenger side of the van, slid open the door to get a large bouquet of flowers, and walked it up to the house.

I backed out of the drive and pulled up across the street. I waited by the van while Ian rang the bell. A woman answered, took the flowers, and then Ian was walking briskly back down the sidewalk.

He looked startled when he saw me standing by his vehicle.

'Ian?' I said.

He still had the wires running to his ears and yanked them out. 'What?'

'It's Ian, right?'

'Yeah. Can I help you?'

'We met the other day, at the shop, when Mrs Shaw was closing up. I showed you a picture of my daughter.'

'Oh, yeah,' he said, moving past me to the driver's door.

'I wonder if you'd mind taking another look,' I said, taking a photo from my jacket and following him.

'I already told you,' he said. 'I don't know her.'

'It'll only take a second,' I said. He had the door open, but I put my hand on it and eased it shut. He didn't fight me.

'Sure, I guess,' he said.

I gave him the photo. This time, he studied it a good five seconds before handing it back. His eyes seemed to dance around the whole time, like he was never really focusing on Syd's face.

'Nope,' he said.

I nodded, took my hand off the van door. 'Well, I appreciate you taking another look.'

'No problem.'

'Mrs Shaw said you live behind the shop?'

'Yeah,' he said.

'There's an apartment back there?'

'Kinda. Nothing big. Big enough for me.'

'That's handy, living right where you work,' I said. 'You all by yourself?'

'Yeah.'

'You worked long for Mrs Shaw?'

'Couple of years. She's my aunt. That's why she lets me stay there, since my mom died. Some reason why you're asking me all these questions?'

'No,' I said. 'No reason.'

'Because I've got other deliveries.'

'Sure,' I said. 'Don't let me hold you up.'

Ian got in, closed the door, buckled his seatbelt, and hit the gas hard as he sped off down the street.

Sometimes, I'll get a customer who, once he's made an offer on a car, starts to panic. He's not worried the offer will be rejected; he's scared to death it'll be accepted. He'll have the car of his dreams, but now he has to find a way to pay for it. Between the time he signs the offer and learns whether the sales manager will accept it, he fidgets, he licks his lips, he looks for water because his mouth is dry. He's gotten in over his head and doesn't know how to get out.

Ian had that look.

★ ★ ★

'Evan?' Susanne said. 'What did you want with Evan?'

I'd just walked into the sales office at Bob's Motors. Bob was out on the lot somewhere, no doubt trying to persuade someone looking for an econobox that what they really needed was an SUV that could go over boulders. I hadn't seen Evan out there.

'I just want to ask him a couple of questions about Syd,' I said.

'Believe me,' said Susanne, sitting behind her desk, 'I've asked him.'

'Maybe he needs to be asked again.'

'You look rattled. Has something happened since you got back from Seattle?'

She had a right to know what had happened, but I didn't want to get into it with her now.

'I'm fine,' I said. 'Is he around?'

'He's out back, in the garage, shining up a car, prepping it for delivery.'

I left the office without saying anything. I made it around to the back of the building, where Bob's Motors had a secondary building, about the size of a double-car garage. Bob was strictly a sales operation. Once you bought a car from him, it was up to you to find a place to have it serviced. But he did need a place to do minor repairs, and get cars cleaned up before their new owners came to pick them up.

Evan had been put to work on a three-year-old Dodge Charger.

He had all four doors open and didn't hear me

178

approach because he was leaning in, going at the rear carpets with a Shop-Vac.

'Evan!' I said.

When he didn't respond, I flipped the switch on the top of the vacuum canister.

'Huh?' he said, whirling around. He didn't look happy when he saw it was me. 'Turn that back on,' he said.

'I want to talk to you,' I said.

'My dad says this car has to be ready in an hour.'

'You want to waste time arguing, or just help me out so I can get out of your hair fast as possible?'

'What do you want?' He brushed some hair away from his eyes, but it fell back immediately.

'My place got broken into,' I said.

'That's too bad,' he said.

'They tore the place apart,' I said.

He brushed the hair away again. 'Whaddya want from me?'

'I want to know anything you can tell me about Sydney and what might have happened to her.'

'I don't know anything about that.'

'You liked her living in your house, I'll bet.'

'No big deal. So we lived under the same roof a few weeks. She had her life and I had mine.'

'Did you spend time together?'

'Huh?'

'Did you hang out?'

'We had meals together. Sometimes I had to tell her to move her ass so I could use the bathroom.' That seemed unlikely. Bob's house had several.

179

'You didn't think it was kind of cool? Her moving into your dad's place?'

'You make it sound like something it wasn't,' he said.

'Did you introduce her to your friends?'

'You don't know anything about my friends. You don't know anything about me.' He glared.

'You do drugs, Evan? Do any of your friends sell drugs?'

'You're crazy. I have to get this car cleaned up.'

I asked, 'Why are you stealing?'

'What?'

'You heard me.'

'Fuck you.'

'The petty cash, Susanne's watch that went — '

'She found that watch.'

'So I hear. You don't want to deny the petty cash, too?'

That caught him off guard. 'Does my dad know you're talking to me?'

'Should we go get him? Then I can ask you, with him present, whether you broke into my house.'

'Why the fuck would I do that?'

'I don't know. You tell me.'

'I don't know where this is coming from, but you're totally nuts.'

'What are you doing on the computer all the time?'

He grinned. 'She's telling you all this shit, isn't she?'

'She?' I said.

'She's not my mother, OK? Just because she's

my dad's girlfriend doesn't give her the right to spy on me, and then go blabbing to you about what she's found out.'

'Evan, can I tell you something? Right now, I'm cutting you a whole lot of slack, because the other day I heard you refer to my ex-wife as a bitch, and right now, all I really want to do is rip your head off. But I've decided to be nice, because all that matters to me is finding Sydney. And there's something about you, I don't know what it is, but it's like a bad smell, and I can't help but think that whatever's happened to Syd may have something to do with you.'

He shook his head and tried to laugh it off. 'You're a piece of work.'

He hit the switch on the vacuum and turned away from me. I was about to grab him by the shoulder when I heard someone shout: 'Tim!'

I turned. Bob Janigan was standing in the open garage doorway. He shouted my name a second time.

I strode over to him, said, 'You need to find out what's up with your boy,' and walked back to my car.

★   ★   ★

Back on the road, my cell rang.

'What happened?' Susanne asked.

'Our — my house was broken into while I was in Seattle. The place was trashed, searched from top to bottom. Some cash got stolen. Maybe some other stuff, too. I don't know. And when the police looked around, they found what I'm

181

guessing was cocaine.'

'What?'

'I think Evan knows more than he's saying.'

Susanne said, 'Bob says if you ever go near Evan again he'll kill you.'

'It's my other line, Suze. I have to go.'

★ ★ ★

It was a criminal lawyer named Edwin Chatsworth. He was part of the firm I used whenever I needed legal matters dealt with. Like a failed business, but also property matters, title transfers, that kind of thing. Once, a dissatisfied customer had threatened to sue me personally, as opposed to the dealership that employed me, over a used car that turned out to be a genuine lemon.

I'd put a call in to the firm between leaving home and going to see Evan. They said it sounded like a job for Edwin, and promised he would get back to me.

I spelled it out for him the best I could.

'Just guessing,' he said, 'but I'd be very surprised if they go ahead with any charges over the coke, assuming it is coke, and not a Baggie full of baking soda.'

'Because?'

'Like you said. You invited the cops into your home. The place had been broken into. People other than you had an opportunity to put the drugs in your bed. A judge would toss it out before they'd finished their opening arguments.'

'You sure?'

182

'No. But that's what my gut tells me. And this Detective Jennings, you don't talk to her any more.'

'But she's also looking for my daughter. I can't not talk to her about that.'

Chatsworth mulled that one over. 'Don't trust her. She starts veering the conversation to what was in the house, you say nothing without me being there. There's no way they can prove those drugs were yours.'

'They weren't. They're not my drugs.'

'Hey, did I ask you that?'

★   ★   ★

The bag I'd packed for the trip to Seattle was back in my car. I'd walked into the house with it but, after discovering the state my place was in, never unpacked. And now that Kip Jennings wasn't going to let me sleep in my own house that night, I'd hung on to the bag.

I went into the mall and had a slice of pepperoni pizza in the food court. I watched all the young people walking by. Tried to catch the faces of all the teenage girls.

You never stopped looking.

Then I got back in the car and drove over to the Just Inn Time. Carter and Owen, the two men who'd been on the front desk the night I'd come in trying to find Syd, were on once again.

I walked up to the counter and said, 'I'd like a room.'

16

And that's just what it was.

A room. A generic, nondescript, plain room. A patternless blue spread covered the double bed in the center. Dull white shades covered the lamps flanking the bed. The bedroom walls were beige, much like the bathroom and the towels and the halls and everything else in this budget-minded hotel.

But that said, it was also clean and well kept. The bathroom came equipped with soap and shampoo and a hair dryer. The closet had one of those mini-safes you can program with a four-digit code, suitable for holding a passport, a video camera and a few thousand in unmarked bills.

The hotel hadn't yet moved to fancy, flat-screen wall-mounted TVs. And while the bulky set sitting atop the dresser seemed to be from a couple of decades ago, you could still order up movies — including ones with titles like *She'll Be Cummin' Round the Mountain When She Cums* — if you were so inclined.

I flipped through the channels, left Dr Phil on in the background to exploit some miserable family stupid enough to air their dirty laundry for the entertainment pleasure of millions, and looked out the second floor window. I don't know what I was expecting, exactly. Maybe I thought staring at the Howard Johnson restaurant and hotel up the street, the cars and trucks whizzing past on I-95, would somehow provide a clue as to where Syd had gone after I'd dropped her off out front of the Just Inn Time.

It didn't.

Watching those hundreds of cars and trucks and SUVs racing by, I couldn't help thinking that if you were in one of those vehicles, in a few short hours you could be anywhere in New England. Boston or Providence, up to Maine. Maybe Vermont or New Hampshire.

You could head west and north, be up in Albany in under three hours. Or closer to home, but harder to find, in Manhattan.

And that would just be the same day you got in one of those cars. By now, weeks later, a person could be almost anywhere.

If that person was alive.

I'd been trying very hard, since the moment she'd gone missing, not to let my mind go there. As long as there was no definitive evidence that harm had come to her, I had to believe she was fine. Lost — at least to Susanne and me — but OK.

The image of that blood on Syd's Civic was a hard thing to get out of my head.

And there was an audio loop running through my head. It had been playing for weeks, always below the surface, like a hum, like background noise.

The loop was made up of questions that I kept asking over and over again.

Where are you?

Are you OK?

What happened?

Why did you run?

What scared you?

Why won't you get in touch?

Did you leave because I asked about the sunglasses, and then something happened that kept you from coming back?

Why can't you just let me know you're OK?

So around nine o'clock, a time of day when, as I've gotten older, I'm often ready to nod off, I wasn't the slightest bit tired.

I went through the motions anyway. I unzipped the bag I'd taken to Seattle, and there was Milt the stuffed moose looking up at me.

'Oh shit,' I said, feeling slightly overwhelmed. I took him out and set him on one of the pillows.

I took my cell phone from my jacket and put it by the bed. I brushed my teeth, stripped down to my boxers, threw back the covers and got into the bed. I channel-surfed for another ten minutes, then hit the light.

Stared at the ceiling for half an hour or so.

Light from Route 1 — passing cars and trucks, the neon glow of the commercial strip — was flooding into the room. I thought maybe pulling together the drapes more tightly would block out the light and help me get to sleep.

I got out of the bed, padded across the industrial carpet, and grabbed one of the drapery wands. But before giving them a pull, I gazed out over this part of Milford again. Traffic was thinning, except on the interstate, where it always seemed to be busy. Cars always appeared to be moving so slowly when viewed from some height.

186

The view of the nearby businesses from up here was actually pretty good. I could see many of the places I'd visited in the last few weeks. The Howard Johnson's to the right, the other small operations to the left.

I could clearly see the blood red neon letters of XXX Delights, and half a dozen cars parked out front. I watched men, always alone, go into the store empty-handed, emerge a few minutes later with their evening's entertainment packaged in plain brown paper.

A man coming around the corner of the building, where the flower shop was, caught my eye.

He walked across the lot, pointed a remote, and then the red lights of a van pulsed once. He opened the driver's door and got in. I wasn't certain, but it looked like the Toyota van belonging to Shaw Flowers.

Seemed kind of late for a delivery. Maybe Ian had use of the van any time he wanted. Maybe he had a hot date.

The van backed out of its spot, then nosed up to the edge of Route I, waiting for a break in traffic.

The knock at the door nearly made me jump.

I turned away from the window, walked across the darkened room, and squinted through the peephole. Veronica Harp, the day manager.

'Hey!' I shouted through the closed door. 'Give me a sec!'

I flicked on the bedside table lamp, found the pants I'd draped over a chair, pulled them on hurriedly, threw on my shirt, and was still buttoning it when I opened the door.

'How are you?' I said.

She had traded in her corporate uniform for something more casual. Crisp, tailored jeans, heels, and a royal blue blouse. With her black hair and soulful eyes, you didn't look at her and immediately think 'grandmother'.

'Oh no,' she said, looking at my bare feet and the buttons I had left to do up. 'I caught you at a bad time.'

'No,' I said, 'it's OK. I couldn't sleep anyway.'

'I just popped in and Carter told me you were actually staying in the hotel,' she said. 'I was so surprised.'

'I needed a room,' I said.

'Did something happen to your house? A fire?'

'Something like that,' I said. 'I'm hoping I'll be able to go back tomorrow. Get the place cleaned up.'

'That's a terrible shame,' Veronica said, still framed in the doorway.

It seemed rude to make her stand there so I opened the door wider for her to come inside. She took half a dozen steps in, and I let the door close behind her on its own. She glanced over at the unmade bed.

'Well, I'm delighted you chose this hotel. There are certainly nicer ones around,' she conceded.

'I guess, these days, I know this one best,' I said, and offered her a wry smile.

'I suppose you do,' she said, and smiled back.

I sidestepped back toward the window, took a quick look outside. It was more difficult to see, what with the room lights reflecting in the glass.

'Looking for something?' Veronica asked.

The van was gone.

'No, just, no, nothing,' I said.

'You know what?' Veronica said. 'I'm intruding. A person should be able to check into a hotel without being pestered by the management.'

'No, that's OK,' I said, stepping away from the window and doing up the last of my buttons. I felt a bit self-conscious about my bare feet, but thought it would be silly to pull my socks on at this point.

'So how's that grandson of yours?' I asked.

Veronica brightened. 'Oh, he's wonderful. He's always watching everything going on around him. I think he's going to grow up to be an engineer or architect. He has these oversized building blocks in his crib and he's playing with them all the time.'

'That's great,' I said. Then, 'Why did Carter tell you I was here?'

Veronica smiled. 'He knows you and I've spoken a few times, and he knows how hard you've been working to find your daughter.'

'Maybe he's tired of seeing me hanging around the parking lot,' I said.

'Well,' she said, and her voice trailed off. 'No one could blame you. Anyone else in your position would be doing everything he could. So this fire? How bad was it?'

'It wasn't a fire,' I said. 'There was a break-in.'

Her hand went to her mouth. 'Oh my. Did they take a lot?'

I shook my head slowly. 'No. A bit of cash.'

'That's an awful thing. You feel so violated.'

'Yeah,' I said. 'Can I ask you a weird question?'

'Go ahead.'

'Would the hotel have a pair of binoculars?'

'Binoculars? What are you doing? Spying on someone?'

'No, never mind, forget it.'

'Why would you want binoculars?'

'Just passing the time, watching the cars go by. Looking at the trucks on the interstate.'

Veronica Harp's eyebrows popped up briefly in puzzlement, but she didn't pursue it. 'Is there anything else I could get you? We don't have room service here, but if you wanted a pizza or something I could arrange to have it delivered and we could add it to your room bill.'

'No, I'm good.'

She walked further into the room, ran her hand across the top of the rumpled bedclothes, then asked, 'Is your room OK?'

'Of course. It's fine.'

She turned and faced me head on, very little space between us.

'I feel that you're such a sad man,' she said.

'I'm kind of going through a rough patch,' I said.

'I can see it in your eyes. Even before your daughter disappeared, were you sad?'

I wanted to change the subject. 'Are you . . . what does your husband do?'

'He passed away two years ago,' she said, and pointed to her chest. 'Heart.'

190

'He must have been young for a heart attack.'

'He was twenty years older,' she said. 'I miss him very much.' She reached out a hand and touched my chest.

'I'm sure you do,' I said.

'If you didn't know I had a grandchild, would you have guessed it?'

'No,' I said, honestly. 'Not in a million years.'

She leaned in, tilted her head up. Before she could kiss me, I turned my head slightly and rested it on her shoulder, held her lightly for several seconds before gently moving her away and creating some distance between us.

'Veronica . . .'

'It's OK,' she said. 'You think it would be wrong, with your daughter . . .'

'I . . .'

'I know about sadness. I do. My life has been one sadness after another. But if you wait for all of them to be over before you allow yourself any pleasure, you'll never have any.'

Part of me would have been happy to forget my problems. To put them aside, however briefly, for some human contact, sex without strings. But nothing about this felt right.

When I didn't say anything, she understood we were done. She went to the bedside table and wrote a number on a pad bearing the hotel logo. She tore off the sheet and handed it to me.

'If you want to talk to me, or need anything, you call me. Any time.'

'Thank you,' I said, and held the door for her as she slipped back into the hall.

I leaned my back against the door for a

second, let out a breath, then killed the lights and went back to the window.

There was something about Ian I couldn't get out of my head. Something was off about the guy. Something was not quite right.

I wanted to know more about him. And for now, that meant watching the flower shop from my perch up in this hotel room.

But Ian had just left in the van. He could be gone for hours. What was I going to do? Just sit here all night and stare out the window?

I grabbed the remote, tuned the TV into CNN for background noise. I heard Anderson Cooper's voice, but didn't listen to anything he had to say.

There was one cushy chair in the room — the one I'd used to hang my clothes on — and I dragged it over by the window so I could sit comfortably while I conducted my amateur surveillance. I leaned my head up against the glass, frosted it with my breath. I turned the TV so the screen didn't reflect in the window.

This was dumb. What the hell was I doing, staring out the window, waiting for some flower delivery guy to return to his apartment? Maybe I was doing it because I couldn't think of anything.

I got up, grabbed a pillow, sending Milt on a tumble, and put it between my head and the glass. As awkward as I must have looked, I was actually pretty comfortable.

So comfortable that I drifted off to sleep.

I woke myself up with my own snoring, the TV still blaring. I lifted my head away from the window and the pillow fell to the floor.

I was groggy and disoriented. For several seconds I didn't know where I was. But quickly things started to make sense. The clock radio by the bed read 12:04.

I'm at the Just Inn Time. I'm staying here because my house has been trashed.

It was all coming back to me.

And I was watching the florist shop.

I blinked a couple of times and looked out the window. There were fewer cars on the road now. Only a couple of pickups were at the porn shop, which was still open.

The Toyota van was back. How long it had been there, I had no idea. But clearly Ian was back home and tucked in his —

Hang on.

Someone was coming around the back of the van and up the passenger side. The van must have just returned, and Ian had just gotten out the driver's door.

He opened the passenger door, but no one stepped out. He leaned in, like he was undoing the seatbelt for someone. But he stayed in that position for several seconds, like he was trying to get hold of something.

Then Ian eased slowly back out of the van, very carefully. He was carrying something large and cumbersome. It looked as though he had something slung over his shoulder, like a sack.

He backed up far enough to clear the door, slammed it shut. A streetlight was casting a soft glow in his direction. There was just enough light to see that Ian was carrying someone over his shoulder. Someone smaller than himself.

Someone with long, possibly blond, hair.

A girl.

And she wasn't moving a muscle.

17

I started running for the door in my bare feet, stopped, grabbed my shoes, figuring I could slip them on and lace them up in the elevator.

'Phone,' I said, jerking myself to a stop a second time in as many seconds. I bolted over to the bedside table, reached for the phone, and ended up knocking it down between the bed and the table.

There wasn't time to look for it.

I threw open the door and ran down the hall and hit the down button between the two elevators. I glanced up, saw they were both down in the lobby. Quickly, I slipped my shoes over sockless feet, hopping on one foot, then another, then, almost as quickly, did up the laces.

Neither of the elevators had budged from the lobby.

I realized I'd hit the button — the kind that doesn't actually depress but senses your finger there — so quickly it hadn't registered.

'Fuck it,' I said and ran to the end of the hall for the stairs. I took them two steps at a time, leaping down them like I was in some sort of new parkour Olympic event. I came through the fire door on the first floor so hard it flew back and hit the wall. I sprinted down the hall and shouted to Carter as I passed him at the front desk: 'Call the police!'

The motion-sensitive doors leading out of the

hotel weren't fast enough for me and I almost crashed through them, hitting the brakes just in time, then slipped through the opening the moment it was wide enough.

I realized then I didn't have my keys, but even if I had I don't know that I would have taken the time to get into my car and start it up. I was running flat out now and I didn't want anything slowing me down.

I crossed Route I on an angle, only having to slow to let a taxi get by. There wasn't much traffic at this hour. The small plaza with XXX Delights, Shaw Flowers and a couple of other businesses was about a hundred yards ahead. I could feel my heart pounding in my chest and even as I ran I tried to remember the last time I'd run like this and prayed I didn't have a heart attack before I reached Ian's apartment.

It's Syd, I told myself. *It's her. He's got her. He's had her all along.*

But what the hell was he doing with her in the van? Moving her from one location to another? Actually, maybe that made some sense. He could hardly keep someone hidden in an apartment right behind the shop. Mrs Shaw would hear something, notice something, wouldn't she?

I'd reached the van and ran right past it.

It was dark around the back of the shop, but there was a single door with a light over it and a small curtained window to the side. There were lights on in the apartment.

I didn't bother to knock.

I tried the door but it was locked. I put my shoulder into it, tried to force it open, but it held.

From inside, a man, his voice filled with panic, shouted: 'Who is it?'

'Open up!' I shouted. 'Open the door!'

Again, he shouted, 'Who is it!'

'Open the goddamn door!'

'I'm not opening the door till you tell me who it is!'

I reared back, lifted my leg, and hit the door with the heel of my shoe with all I had. The door gave way a couple of inches, only held now by a chain.

In the crack, I could see Ian standing in what appeared to be a small kitchen, dressed only in red boxers, his skin pale and freckly.

He was screaming.

I gave the door another kick and the chain ripped off. I came through the door and shouted at Ian, 'Where is she?'

'Get out of here!' he shouted. 'Get the fuck out of here!'

The kitchen area was part of a larger room that included a couch, a TV and DVD player and game console. It wasn't much of a place, but for a young guy living alone, it was amazingly neat and tidy. No dirty dishes in the sink, no empty beer cans or pizza containers. A small stack of video game magazines were stacked perfectly on the coffee table.

'Where is she?' I asked.

'What?'

'Where is she?' I was shouting at the top of my lungs.

'Get out!' Ian shouted.

There were two doors on the far side of the

room. I shoved Ian out of the way and went to the first one, flung it open, expecting a bedroom or closet or bathroom. But it was an entrance into the back of the florist shop.

I turned to the other door, and as I was putting my hand on the knob Ian pounced on me from behind like a cat. He wrapped his hands around my head, digging his fingers into my eyes and cheeks.

He was slight, which gave him the edge on me when it came to speed and nimbleness. I tried to get my fingers under his and pry him off, but he was hanging on. So I propelled myself backwards and into the wall, crushing the wind out of Ian. He let go and fell to the floor. He was up again in an instant, but this time I was ready for him. I put my fist into his face, catching him below his left eye.

That knocked him back a second time, giving me enough time to throw open the door and enter what turned out to be the bedroom.

It wasn't much larger than a walk-in closet. A small dresser along one wall, a narrow door that must have been a closet, and a second door at the other end that was open and showed a sink and toilet.

There was just enough room for a single bed.

There was a person under the covers, and judging by the shape it definitely looked to be a young woman. Not moving. Drugged, I thought.

Or worse.

The covers were pulled high enough to hide everything but a few locks of blond hair. Despite all the ruckus, she still hadn't moved.

198

Oh dear God . . .

'Syd,' I said. 'Syd?'

I sat on the edge of the bed and was about to pull down the covers when I sensed Ian coming through the door. I turned and pointed and fixed my eyes on him with such fury that he stopped.

'You make one move and I swear I'll fucking kill you,' I said, barely able to get the words out I was panting so hard. Sweat was dripping off my brow, my shirt was plastered to me.

I pulled the covers back down to the girl's shoulders. Something was wrong. Something was very, very wrong. Her skin looked rubbery, had an odd sheen to it.

'What the fuck?'

This girl was not Syd.

This girl was not a girl.

She was a doll.

18

I turned around and looked at Ian, who stood in the doorway staring at me, his face flushed from our grappling and, I suspected, embarrassment.

'Just get out of here,' he said quietly. There was a bruise coming up on his cheek.

'I thought . . . I thought she . . . I thought it was my daughter.'

Ian just stared at me.

'I'm sorry,' I said. 'When I saw you — '

'You were spying on me?'

'I saw you carry something in from your van.'

I put my hand around the doll's arm, raised it up to get a sense of its weight. No wonder it was so easy for Ian to carry it in here. It couldn't have weighed much more than ten or twenty pounds. The inside of the arm felt like pillow stuffing.

I got off the bed and moved past Ian into the main room.

'You bought that next door?' I said.

Ian nodded. His nearly naked body seemed to have caved in on itself. Instead of seeming menacing, he now bordered on pitiful. 'Please don't tell my aunt,' he said.

I lowered my head, shook it regretfully. 'Yeah, sure. I'm sorry.' Then I remembered the command I'd shouted out to Carter as I'd run out of the Just Inn Time. We could probably expect to see the police here any moment.

I said to Ian, 'You keep . . . it . . . here?'

Ian shook his head. 'My aunt's in here all the time, cleaning up, making me things to eat. I got a storage unit in Bridgeport where my family's stuff is. I keep her there and bring her over sometimes, then take her back before my aunt gets here in the morning. Sometimes, we just go for a drive, maybe park down by the harbor for a while and listen to the radio and stuff.'

I didn't want to think about the stuff.

I ran my hand through my hair. Now I understood why Ian had been so odd when I'd spoken to him before. It was because he was, well, odd.

'Listen, Ian,' I said. 'The police are probably going to be here any minute.'

'Oh shit no. That can't happen.'

I felt a bit the same way. Ian, once he recovered from the inevitable mortification, would have every right to charge me with breaking in to his apartment. He could have me charged with assault. I was a regular home invader.

'I don't want the police here,' he said. 'It's not just . . . her.'

'What?'

'I've got weed here, too.'

'OK, look, I'm just going to go,' I said. 'When the cops show up, I'll tell them I thought I saw my daughter hitch-hiking or something.'

Ian, despite all I'd done, managed to mutter, 'Thanks.'

I left without saying anything else. I was expecting to see police cars screaming into the

201

lot out front of the florist shop and XXX Delights, but there was nothing going on. I jogged back to the Just Inn Time, spotting along the way one police car driving up Route 1 at a regular rate of speed. It drove up past the Howard Johnson's and kept on going.

When I walked back into the lobby of my hotel Carter came out from behind the desk and said, 'What's happened, Mr Blake?'

'Did you call the police?'

'Not yet,' he said. 'You ran out of here and didn't say where you were going or what you'd seen. What was I supposed to tell the cops?'

Ordinarily, I'd have been pissed, but not this time. 'No harm done. It was my mistake,' I said and went back up to my room.

★ ★ ★

On my way out in the morning I grabbed a complimentary stale blueberry muffin and coffee from the lobby. There was no sign of Carter, or Veronica, but Cantana, the young Thai-looking woman I'd met here the other morning, was working the breakfast nook. She handed me a takeout coffee cup.

'You can tell just by looking at me that I need coffee,' I said, trying for Mr Amiable. Instead of returning the smile she nodded politely, looked away, and went back to work.

I threw my bag into the back seat of the CR-V, put my coffee in the cup holder and took a bite of muffin, crumbs raining down into my lap. Before turning the ignition I let my head fall back onto the headrest and let out a long sigh. I'd had little sleep since my raid on Ian's apartment. I felt like a damn fool. And worse, I was no closer to finding Syd.

I turned the key and hit the button on Syd's music shuffler. There was an old Spice Girls tune — Syd was too young to have paid much attention to them their first time around, but got interested when they reunited for a tour a year or two ago — and another Beatles tune, 'Why Don't We Do It In The Road', from the *White* album. What father didn't want one of his daughter's favorite songs to be about people having a fuck in the passing lane?

That was followed by — and I was guessing here on some of these — songs by Lily Allen, Metric, Lauryn Hill. Then some familiar chords kicked in and I thought, yes, a band I know and love: Chicago. Too bad the song had to be 'If You Leave Me Now'.

I hadn't cracked the lid on the coffee by the time I'd pulled up to the curb in front of my house a few minutes before eight, but there were muffin crumbs all over my lap and down on the floormats of the CR-V.

There was a police car in the driveway, and parked out front of the house next door, what looked to be Kip Jennings's car. There was no one in the driver's seat, but there looked to be someone sitting on the passenger side.

I took my coffee and as I came up even to the car I saw that there was a young girl sitting there. Twelve, thirteen years old. There was a backpack on the floor by her feet. On her lap was an open textbook. She glanced through the open driver's side window at me.

'Hey,' I said. 'I'm guessing you're Cassie.'

She didn't say anything.

I stood well away from the window. 'Doing some last minute studying?'

'My mom's a cop and she's coming back any minute,' she said.

'I'll leave you be,' I said and turned for my house. Kip Jennings was coming down the driveway.

'Morning,' I said. 'You've trained your daughter well.'

'What?'

'The whole talking to strangers thing. I backed right off.'

'I have to get her to school. I was dropping by here on the way. We're done with your house. You can have it back.'

'Great.'

'It's still a mess.'

'I figured.'

'There are companies you can call to help with the cleanup. I can get you a list.'

'I'll take care of it.'

'You're not going to be charged,' she said. 'The cocaine.'

'Nice to know.'

'And it *was* coke,' she said. 'But cut with so much lactose you'd be one pissed off junkie if you paid very much for it.'

'It wasn't mine.'

She regarded me thoughtfully, then said, 'Doesn't much matter one way or another. The

204

DA would never have gotten a conviction.'

'I think it's important that you know.'

'I'll bet you do,' she said. 'To tell you the truth, I think you're probably telling the truth.'

Probably.

'Because,' she said, 'I believe we were meant to find it.'

'Meant?'

From her car: 'Mom! I'm gonna be late!'

'Hold your horses!' Jennings shouted. 'Yeah. Meant to find it, meant to think it was yours.'

I remembered Edwin Chatsworth advising me not to talk to this woman, but said, 'They tore the place apart like they were looking for something. They knew the moment I came home I'd call the police. Then the police would find the cocaine.'

Detective Jennings nodded back. 'Yeah. And then we put the heat on you.'

I looked at her. 'Why would someone do that?'

'What a coincidence. I was going to ask you that.'

'Mom!'

Jennings sighed. 'She's just like her father.'

'He a police officer too?' I asked.

Something in Jennings's face twitched, even though she tried hard not to show it. 'No,' she said. 'He's an engineer. And he's working somewhere in Alaska, and if we're lucky, he won't ever be coming back.'

I didn't know how to respond to that, so I didn't.

'Divorced, three years,' she said. She puffed herself up a bit. 'And Cassie and I, we're good.'

'She's tough,' I said. 'That comes across pretty quick.'

'Mr Blake,' she said, 'you need to think why someone would go to all the trouble to get you out of town and then see if they could get you framed for drug possession.'

I looked up the street at nothing in particular.

'And you need to keep thinking about the question I asked you before. Just how well did you know what your daughter was up to?'

I said, 'The bloodstains on Syd's car . . . have you found out anything yet?'

'You'll be the second to know,' she said, got into her car and drove her daughter to school.

★ ★ ★

I decided to tackle the cleanup a room at a time.

First, of course, I went upstairs to check for any phone or email messages, even a fax. There was nothing. It occurred to me that with all of today's technologies, there were now more ways than ever to know with absolute certainty that no one wanted to get in touch with me.

Then I went back down to the kitchen. It made sense to put this room in order first. I found some garbage bags under the sink and dumped in food that could not be saved. Items from the refrigerator that had been tossed about and gone bad, spilled cereal that covered the floor.

I'd been going at it for about an hour when I heard someone shouting over the drone of the vacuum cleaner.

'Hello?'

The front door was open. Standing there was a slight man in a suit that had to be five sizes too big for him. You could slip three fingers between his neck and his buttoned shirt collar. His stringy black tie was askew, and it seemed awfully early in the day to look this unkempt. His concave chest made him look as though he was caving in on himself. He was the guy who got sand kicked in his face on the back page of my comic books when I was a kid.

'I rang but you couldn't hear me,' he said.

'Can I help you?' I asked.

'Are you Tim Blake?'

'That's right,' I said.

'Arnold Chilton,' he said. 'I think Bob Janigan mentioned me to you?'

Huh?

Then I remembered. The detective, or security expert, whatever. The one Bob said might be able to help us track down Sydney. I was surprised, knowing how pissed Bob was with me at the moment, that he'd still decided to go ahead with this.

'Bob got in touch with me a few days ago,' he said, 'but I've kind of been swamped getting my mom moved into a nursing home.'

'Oh,' I said. I extended a hand and he took it.

Arnold Chilton whistled as he took in the mess. I hadn't started on the living room yet. 'That must have been some party,' he said.

'It wasn't a party,' I said. 'Someone broke in and tore up the place.'

'Wow,' he said.

'Yeah,' I said.

'You got some time for some questions?' he asked.

'Why don't we go outside?' I suggested. 'There's really nowhere to sit down in here yet.'

'Okey doke,' Chilton said. We walked out onto the front lawn, turned and looked back at the house.

'This is good of Bob to have you look into this,' I said. 'He and I, we don't always see eye to eye on everything.'

'He said something like that.'

'I'll just bet he did,' I said. 'The police are looking into Syd's disappearance, of course, but having someone else on this, that's great. I've been doing everything I can to find her — I even went on a wild goose chase to Seattle this week — but haven't made much headway. You know her car was found?'

'Didn't know that,' Chilton said.

I thought the mention of the Seattle trip and the discovery of Syd's car would have sparked further questions.

'Have you spoken to Detective Jennings?' I asked.

'Who?'

'Kip Jennings,' I said. 'The police detective?'

'I think Bob did mention her, or his wife Susanne did.'

'Susanne is not his wife,' I said. 'We used to be married, but she hasn't married Bob. Yet.'

'*That's* right! I knew that.'

'Did they tell you about Detective Jennings? Did they give you a number for her? Because you're going to want to talk to her.'

'I'm pretty sure they mentioned her. I just don't think I wrote it down.'

'I have her number,' I offered.

'Good,' he nodded agreeably.

'So, are you, what, a friend of Bob's?' I asked. 'Or have you done work for him before?'

'Yeah, I've done some stuff for him in the past,' Chilton said.

I wondered why my ex-wife's boyfriend might have used the services of a private detective. And whatever reason it might have been, did Arnold Chilton actually produce any results? He wasn't inspiring me with confidence.

'So, let's get down to cases,' he said. 'Tell me about the day your daughter disappeared.'

I told the story for the hundredth time. Chilton scribbled into a tattered notebook that had been jammed into a jacket pocket.

'What about friends?' he asked. 'You got some names of her friends?'

'Patty Swain,' I said. 'And there was a guy she used to go out with a few times, Jeff Bluestein. He helped me set up the website.' That reminded me. I had meant to ask him, when he'd popped by the dealership with Patty, to double-check that emails sent to the site were actually getting there. Not fully understanding how all that stuff worked, I was paranoid about things going wrong.

'How do you spell that?' Chilton asked.

I started to spell Bluestein, but he held up his hand. 'The first name,' he said.

I blinked. 'J, e, f, f,' I said.

'OK,' he said, making his notes. 'Sometimes, people spell it with a G, don't they?'

'That's true,' I said.

'But not G, e, f, f. It would be G, e, O, f, f.'

'Yes,' I said. Did I need to tell him it was Syd with a *y* and not an *i*?

'Now,' he said, 'did you notice anything weird with Sydney before she took off?'

'No,' I said. I only hoped he was right, that Sydney 'took off'. Better than her having been taken. 'We had a small argument at breakfast. About some new sunglasses she had.'

'What happened?'

I didn't want to get into it with him. I didn't want to believe it had anything to do with why Syd left, and it wasn't any of Arnold Chilton's business anyway. 'It was no big deal,' I said.

'Was she doing drugs? Like, dealing or something like that?' I thought about the coke found in my room, but said nothing. He continued, 'Hooking, maybe?'

That made me want to punch his lights out. I felt my hands forming into fists. 'Listen, Mr Chilton — '

'Just call me Arnie.' He grinned.

'Arnie,' I said, stretching the word out, 'my daughter was neither a drug dealer nor a prostitute.'

Chilton, clearly a very keen detective, picked up something in my tone. 'OK,' he said, and made a note in his book, muttering under his breath. 'No drugs, no hooking.' He glanced back up. 'And how about yourself? Can you account for your whereabouts?'

'What?'

'At the time your daughter disappeared, where were you?'

I said, 'Arnie, if you don't mind my asking, just what sort of work have you done for Bob? Or anyone else for that matter?'

'Pretty much all my security work has been for Bob,' he said.

'Just what kind of security work was it?' I asked. 'Without,' I added, with mock sincerity, 'violating any sort of confidentiality, of course.'

'No, no problem,' Arnie Chilton said. 'Watching stuff, mainly.'

'Watching stuff,' I repeated. 'What kind of stuff?'

'Cars,' he said.

'So let me get this straight. You were, what, a security guard?'

Arnie nodded. 'The night shifts are the worst. Trying to keep your fucking eyes open, you're almost hoping someone will break into the compound so it'll keep you awake, you know?'

'Sure,' I said. 'Arnie, you mind waiting out here a moment while I make a phone call? I just remembered there's someone I have to get in touch with.'

'That's cool,' Arnie said. 'I'll just review my notes.'

I went back into the kitchen and hit one of the buttons already programmed into the phone's speed dial.

Susanne, clearly looking at the caller ID before picking up, said, 'Anything?'

'No,' I said. 'Is Bob there?'

'Yes,' she said.

'I need to talk to him.'

'I don't think he'll be interested. He's furious with you.' But there was nothing in Susanne's voice to indicate she felt the same.

'Magnum P.I. is here.'

'What?'

'The other day, Bob said he was sending around an investigator to help find Syd. A guy named Chilton.'

'I know. I was spending so much time on this, getting so frustrated with those goddamn crutches and cane, Bob wanted Arnie to do some of the leg work.'

'I need to talk to Bob about him.'

'Hang on.'

She put the phone down. A minute later, Bob picked up the receiver and said, 'What do you want, Tim?' His contempt came through the phone like a virus.

'He's a security guard, Bob.'

'What?'

'He's a fucking night watchman. This Chilton guy you sent over. This so-called security expert you've hired to help find Sydney.'

'You know what your problem is, Tim? You're a snob. You run people down.'

'He's not a licensed private investigator, Bob. He's not some security expert. He's a goddamn security *guard*.'

'Look,' Bob said, lowering his voice so Susanne wouldn't hear, 'he was working for me, and I sold him a Corolla, and he couldn't make all the payments. I thought I'd let him work it off.'

'This guy couldn't find his ass in a snowstorm, Bob.'

'I try to do something to help, and this is the thanks I get,' he said. 'Maybe this is why I'm where I am, and you're where you are. Bad attitude.'

I hung up.

Arnie Chilton was waiting for me in the yard, notepad at the ready.

'Hey,' he said. 'I've thought up some more questions. Good ones.'

'Terrific,' I said. 'But something's come up.'

'What's that?'

'Bob needs you to go to Dunkin's and pick him up a dozen donuts and half a dozen coffees and deliver them to the car lot.'

'Oh, OK.'

'He'll pay you when you get there.'

'Did he say what kind of donuts?' Chilton asked.

I shook my head. 'He said it was up to you.'

Chilton smiled, evidently pleased at being given the responsibility. 'So I can check in with you later, ask you some more questions.'

'Looking forward to it,' I said.

Arnie Chilton walked down to his Corolla, got in behind the wheel. It took several tries before the engine turned over.

As I was walking back into the house, my eye caught something shiny next to the step, down in the garden beds.

I knelt down and brushed away the dirt. It was a cell phone. Black, slender, and off. I opened it, blew away dirt from around the keypad. Who'd lost a cell phone? It could have been any number of people, including all the cops who'd been in and out in the last couple of days. I tucked it into my pocket, figured I could check later.

'Whatcha got there?' said someone from behind me.

It was Kip Jennings.

19

'Excuse me?' I said. Jennings had caught me off guard. I hadn't noticed her drive up the street.

'In your pocket? What was that?'

I pulled out the cell phone. 'I found it in the dirt, by the door there.' I said.

'It's not your phone?'

'No. I just said, I found it on the ground.'

'Can I have a look at that?'

I handed it over to her.

'Looks pretty clean,' she said.

'I just brushed the dirt off,' I told her. She looked up from the phone at me, then back at the phone. She hit a button to power it up and we both waited a few seconds for the little jingle to indicate it was up to speed.

'Maybe it belongs to one of your officers,' I said.

She started playing around with the menu. 'Just checking to see what this cell's number is . . . here we go.' She rhymed off a number with an area code that was, up until recently, unfamiliar to me. 'You know that number?'

'I think so,' I said, and felt something like a chill run up my back.

'Let me check something else here . . . missed calls. Someone made a number of calls to this phone that went unanswered. All from the same number.' And then she rhymed that one off as well. 'That one ring a bell?'

215

'Yes,' I said. 'That's my cell number.'

'This phone,' Jennings said, holding it up as though it were an artifact, 'is the one that belonged to — what was her name?'

'Yolanda Mills,' I said. 'That's the number she gave me to call her.'

'Isn't that something?' Kip Jennings said.

'So it has a Seattle area code and everything?'

'It sure does,' Jennings said.

I was trying to sort this new discovery. 'So there really was someone from Seattle, and whoever it was came back here, broke into my house?'

'I suppose someone could have a phone bought for them out there, then have it FedExed out east,' Jennings speculated. 'For all I know, you can program phones right here in Milford with area codes from anyplace in the country. It'd be something to check out.'

'So, if there was any doubt before, there isn't now,' I said. 'The woman who lured me to Seattle was hooked up with whoever broke into my house.'

Detective Jennings was still looking up different data on the phone's screen. 'It looks like all this phone was ever used for was to call you, and take calls from you.' She dropped the phone into her purse, and then asked, 'Mind if I hang on to this?'

'Of course not,' I said.

'Were you planning to tell me about this phone?' she asked.

'What?'

'Were you going to tell me about it?'

216

'I only just found it. Once I'd figured out what phone it was, yeah, I would have called.'

She nodded slowly. This all had a bad feel to it.

I said, 'Has something happened? You were just here a little while ago. Why are you back?'

'You know someone named Ian Shaw?' she asked.

I swallowed. 'I think so,' I said.

'You think so?'

'He works at Shaw Flowers,' I said. 'For his aunt.'

'So you do know him,' Jennings said.

'Yes,' I said. 'I know who he is.'

'When his aunt came to work this morning . . . by the way, Ian lives in an apartment behind the shop. Did you know that?'

I nodded. 'I get the feeling you already know the answers to these questions.'

The corner of her mouth curled up. 'His aunt called the police today. Ian's got quite the shiner on his cheek. Someone punched him good.'

I said nothing.

'Now, Ian didn't really want to talk about it, but his aunt kind of put the fear of God into him, and he finally coughed up your name. And Mrs Shaw remembered you coming by a couple of times asking about Sydney. And she didn't much like the idea of you beating up on her nephew.'

'There was a misunderstanding,' I said.

Jennings offered up a fake smile. 'Damned if that isn't what Ian said. Just a silly misunderstanding. He says he's not interested in pressing any charges. But his aunt insisted I come by and have a word with you just the same. She told me to tell you to never show your face around there again.'

'No problem,' I said.

'You want to tell me about this misunderstanding?'

'If Ian's not pressing charges, I can't see that there'd be much point,' I said.

Inside the house, the phone rang. 'Excuse me,' I said, ran inside and grabbed the kitchen extension. 'Yeah?'

Susanne said, 'If you thought Bob was pissed before, you should see him now.'

'About what?'

'His detective just showed up with coffee and donuts.'

'Bob should be grateful. Now he knows his guy can actually do something useful.'

'Tim,' she said.

'He's a fucking security guard, Suze,' I said. 'That's how much Bob cares.'

'He does care, Tim. It's just, he doesn't always think things through.'

'If he really cared he'd have a word with Evan. There's something about him, Suze.'

'I don't need this,' Susanne said. 'I don't need all these added complications.'

'I have to go,' I said, seeing Jennings in the doorway.

I hung up and said to the detective. 'Have you ever talked to Evan Janigan about Syd?'

'Yes.'

'Well?'

'He needs a good kick in the ass. But other than that — '

'He's a thief,' I said. 'He's stolen from Susanne.'

'Then she should call the police,' Jennings said. 'Everybody else is.'

★   ★   ★

I was putting back into the cupboard tinned foods and cereal boxes that had survived the invasion when I heard voices by the front door.

'Motherfucker, what happened here?'

It was Patty Swain.

'In the kitchen,' I called out.

I heard a second voice, this one male, say, 'It's like a hurricane or something.' I turned to the door that led into the living room and there stood Patty and Syd's one-time boyfriend, Jeff Bluestein.

'Mr Blake,' he said, nodding, then opening his arms to indicate the mess. 'What happened?'

Patty's eyes were wide as she looked around. 'I can't believe what they did,' she said. 'This is so fucked.'

Jeff said, 'Patty, enough.'

'Someone broke in while I was in Seattle and tore the place apart,' I said.

'Seattle?' Patty said.

'I was out there looking for Sydney.'

Patty, who'd already looked stunned, appeared even more surprised. 'Syd's in Seattle?' she said.

I said, 'I was tricked into thinking she was there, so I'd be out of the house long enough for

219

someone to come in and search it from top to bottom.'

'Oh my God,' Patty said. She wandered into the living room, then up the stairs. All along her route, Jeff and I could hear her saying, 'Oh my God. Oh my God.'

'How you doing, Jeff?' I asked.

Jeff Bluestein was the same age as Syd. He was about my height, just under six feet, but bulkier than I am, with curly black hair and thick black eyebrows. He had a loping quality about him, as though he were dragging somebody else along behind him. He'd always struck me as a nice guy, but Syd had found him moody and unmotivated, and I don't think their three months of going steady, or whatever it was kids called it, was ever very serious. Syd broke it off the end of last summer, but they'd remained friends. Jeff got to know Patty through Syd, and they were friends, too, but nothing more than that.

When Jeff learned Syd was missing, he'd approached me immediately about setting up a website. He was a whiz at that sort of thing. And while that was hardly unique for someone in his age group, I was impressed, and not wanting to have to waste a minute getting the site underway, I turned him loose on it.

I offered to pay him for his time, but he'd refused to take any money. 'I just want Syd to come back,' he'd said. 'That's all the reward I want.'

'I'm OK,' Jeff said in answer to my question about how he was doing. He sounded tired, but

220

Jeff was never what you'd call chipper. He was a bear, just waking up from hibernation, loggy headed, trying to figure out where he was.

'I was going to call you.' I said. 'I wanted to make sure the site's working OK.'

'It's fine,' he said. 'I was checking it this morning. Your mail's working and everything.'

'OK,' I said. 'You want a cold drink or anything? They didn't throw everything out of the fridge.'

'I'll have a look,' he said and opened the appliance door. His body blocked out the interior light. He pulled out a can of Coke and cracked the top. 'I haven't been sleeping so good,' he said.

'Something on your mind?' I asked him.

'Just worried about Syd. I thought she woulda gotten in touch.'

'Yeah,' I said.

From someplace upstairs: 'Oh my God!'

'She's kind of over the top,' Jeff said softly, tipping his head in Patty Swain's direction. I knew he liked hanging around with Patty, but her rough edges made him uncomfortable. I'd never heard Jeff swear, not even a 'damn'.

'She's her own person, that's for sure,' I said.

Jeff stood there looking around the kitchen, not mesmerized by the mess, but off somewhere in his thoughts.

'Why do you think Sydney didn't like me?' he asked. His choice of tense threw me off for a second, but then I realized he was referring specifically to that period when she'd just broken up with him.

'That's not true,' I said. 'I know Syd likes you.'

'But she must have told you something about

221

why she didn't want to go out with me.'

I forced a smile. 'There's clearly a lot Syd hasn't shared with me. Not just about her relationship with you.'

Jeff shrugged. 'I mean, she likes me as a friend, I guess. Lots of girls like me as a friend. Patty likes me as a friend. But that starts to feel a bit pitiful after a while.'

'You're a good guy, Jeff,' I said. 'It can take a long time for the right person to come along.'

He looked at me and I could tell he didn't believe me, but was too polite to argue. 'Sure, I guess.' He guzzled down most of the Coke in one gulp.

'I really hope Sydney comes back soon,' Jeff said, his eyes heavy.

I waited a moment, then said, 'Jeff, all this mess, someone breaking into this house, it all has something to do with Sydney. She's in some kind of trouble.'

'Uh huh.'

'So I'm asking you, I'm asking you as her father, to tell me if there was anything going on that might have made her run off. Maybe something you've thought you should tell me but haven't so far.'

'I just don't know,' he said. 'Like I said, we're just sort of friends now. Maybe, before, she would have told me.'

If she hadn't dumped me, he seemed to be saying, *maybe I'd be able to help you now.*

'If you think of anything . . . ' I said, not bothering to finish.

'I got to take off,' Jeff said. 'I just wanted to

222

come by and see how it was going. Can you tell Patty I had to beat it?'

'Sure,' I said.

About a minute after he left, Patty came back down to the kitchen. 'Where's Jeff?' she asked. 'He go back to the circus?'

'What?'

'You know. The tranquilized bears they train to ride the little bicycles?'

'That's mean, Patty,' I said.

'I say it to his face,' she said. 'He's cool with it. He knows I'm kidding.'

'It's still mean.'

She was all innocent. 'He's a big boy. You should hear the stuff he says about us. About the girls.'

'What sort of stuff?'

'Like we're all a bunch of skanky sluts. But he's just joking around, too. And he's wound up kind of tight, too, you know? Like, you say shit or fuck around him and he gets all weird, like he's a goddamn minister or something.'

'Why would he call Syd a skanky slut?'

'Oh, so, you're not surprised he'd call *me* that.'

I wouldn't be baited. 'Patty, you push the envelope. It's your thing. I'd never call you a skanky slut, but a girl who walks into a house and the first thing out of her mouth is 'motherfucker' shouldn't be shocked by what people might think.'

She tilted her head to one side. 'Go on.'

'But Sydney, so far as I know, didn't do anything to cultivate that kind of an image.'

'Cultivate,' Patty said. 'Yeah.'

'So why would Jeff say that about her?'

Patty actually gave it some thought. 'I think, maybe, because she dumped him, Jeff was thinking, OK, if I run her down, then maybe she was never worthy of me in the first place.'

I nodded. 'That's pretty good.'

Patty noticed some canned goods still on the counter and started putting them away in the cupboard. She followed me around the house for the next couple of hours, helping me tidy, asking me where things went, taking bags of garbage to the side of the house and jamming them into the cans. We worked side by side, and although sometimes we were tripping over each other's feet and bumping shoulders, we got a rhythm going. Patty'd hold a trash bag open, I'd dump stuff into it. I'd get the vacuum out, she'd move a chair out of the way.

She threw herself into it, working up a sweat, a stubborn strand of streaked hair repeatedly falling forward into her eyes. She tried blowing it away, and when that didn't work, tucked it behind her ear until it came free a few seconds later.

We were standing in the kitchen, having a drink of water.

'That thing you said, about DVD players in vans being a sign of the end of civilization?' I said.

'Yeah?'

'You might be on to something.'

She smiled. An honest, genuine smile. It reminded me a little of Sydney's. I fought not to

224

let the thought ruin this moment Patty and I were sharing.

She said, seemingly out of nowhere, but maybe not, 'My dad was a complete asshole.'

I didn't ask.

★　★　★

I called Laura Cantrell and brought her up to date. No Syd, trashed house. Laura said that was too bad. Once she was done with that outpouring of sympathy, she was about to ask when I was coming back to work. I headed her off at the pass and told her I'd be in for the afternoon sales shift, which began at three.

In some ways it made no sense going back to work. The mystery surrounding Syd's disappearance had deepened. I felt I should be out searching for her, but I didn't know where to turn anymore. I felt overwhelmed and powerless.

I couldn't just hang around the house. With Patty's help, I'd made a lot of progress getting the place back in order. I couldn't sit there waiting for the phone to ring or an email to land. People knew how to reach me at the dealership.

I left the house around two-thirty. I plugged Syd's music player into the outlet in the CR-V as I drove along the Post Road to work.

If there was any pleasure in my life these days, it was learning about the music that my daughter enjoyed. Eclectic, to say the least. Punk, jazz, rock, classic pop tunes from the sixties and seventies.

I was haunted by some words sung by Janis

Ian: 'It isn't all it seems, at seventeen.'

And when that song finished, something totally unfamiliar, and less professional, followed. First, some guitar reverberations, like someone was tuning up, getting ready to play. Then a bit of coughing, some giggling, then a young woman's voice taunting, 'Are you going to play it or what?'

Syd.

'OK, OK,' a young man answered. 'Just give me a second. I can lay the voices in right over what's on the computer.'

'Yeah, yeah, it's going,' Sydney said.

'OK, we're good. OK, so, this is a little song I wrote myself that I would like to sing — '

Sydney, adopting a mocking, low voice, interrupted with, 'This is a little song I wrote myself I would like to — '

The boy said, 'Would you knock it off?' Sydney made a snorting noise before the boy continued, 'OK, so, like, this song is called 'Dirty Love' and it is dedicated to Sydney.'

She began to giggle in the background. 'Would you settle the fuck down?' the boy said.

I thumbed up the volume on the steering wheel-mounted control.

The boy belted out no more than a couple of lines. His voice was ragged, a harsh whisper with limited range. He sang, 'She came into my life by chance, with a smile that put me in a trance.'

'OK, stop,' Syd said. 'I'm gonna puke. And I thought you were going to say, 'She came into my life by chance, I can't wait to get into her pants.''

Now they were both laughing.

Sydney and Evan Janigan.

20

I nearly clipped a Ford Windstar when I did a U-turn on Route I and headed flat-out for Bob's Motors.

There wasn't any more to the selection. Once The Sydney and Evan Show finished, the iPod jumped to another song from the *White* album, 'Rocky Raccoon'. I hit the back button to put it on the previous track, then paused it.

The CR-V doesn't exactly handle like a sports car, so when it bumped up over the curb leading into the Bob's Motors lot I nearly lost control. But I gripped the wheel firmly, got the car back on track, and spotted Evan at the far end of a line of cars, a washing wand in his hand. I sped down to where he was, hit the brakes and screeched to a stop.

He held the wand suspended in mid-air, water trickling out the end, and looked over at me through the dark locks that hung across his face.

I killed the ignition and as I got out of the car took the metallic green, match-pack sized music player with me. Without headphones it wasn't as if I could play his song for him, but I thought holding it up for effect would make my point.

It did. The moment Evan saw what was in my hand his mouth hung open.

Even though I was walking, I was coming at him pretty fast. Speaking over the flapping of the multicolored pennant flags strung overhead, I said, 'We need to have a little chat, Evan.'

'What the fuck . . . ' he said.

I closed the distance between us, took the wand from Evan's hand and tossed it to the pavement. 'So you and Sydney weren't that close, huh? All you did was have dinner at the same table.'

'I don't know what your deal is, man, but you're not my fucking father, you know?' he said.

'No, but I'm Sydney's fucking father, and I want to know what was actually going on between you two.' I'd moved even closer, forcing Evan up against a wet, blue Kia sedan.

'I don't know what you're talking about,' he said.

'Tim!' It was Susanne, standing atop the stairs that led up to the office. 'Tim! What's going on?'

I ignored her, and held the music player up to Evan's nose. 'I've been listening to Sydney's tunes the last few days, and guess what just came up? Your little song that you dedicated to her.'

'So?'

'So?' I fired back at him. 'That's all you've got to say?'

'Tim!'

It was Susanne again, moving toward us. She was using her cane and her gait was awkward and unsteady.

'Susanne!' I shouted. 'Just stay there!'

Now Bob was coming out of the office, squinting in the intense sunlight, wondering what all the fuss was about.

'My dad's gonna bust your ass,' Evan said. He was trying to be tough, but his voice squeaked, and his eyes were darting left and right, like he

228

was looking for a way to escape.

Susanne, nearly breathless, had her hand on my upper arm and was trying to pull me away. 'Tim, what the hell are you doing?'

I tried to shake her off gently. 'He's been telling me he hardly ever talked to Sydney. But not according to this.' I held up the iPod.

Evan shot Susanne a look. Susanne looked at him, then back at me. 'What are you talking about?'

'You need to listen to this.'

'It's no big deal!' Evan said.

'What?' Susanne said. 'What is it?'

'He's lied to me about how close he was to Sydney,' I said. 'I wonder what else he's been lying about.'

Bob arrived, slightly winded. Evan said to him, 'Dad, get this asshole away from me.'

Bob grabbed my arm, much harder than Susanne had, and threw me up against the side of a Nissan. It knocked the wind out of me, but that didn't stop me from bouncing back, grabbing Bob around the waist and pounding him into the Kia.

'Stop it!' Susanne shrieked.

'You son of a bitch!' Bob said, trying to find enough room between us to land a punch. 'Didn't you get the message to keep the fuck away from my son?'

He caught me with his right in the side of the head, but there wasn't much power in it. But it made me mad enough to form a fist and drive it into his stomach.

But now Evan was on my back, screaming at

me, locking his arms around my shoulders and pulling me away from his father, who now had a clearer shot at me. As Bob wound up, I shot out with my right leg and caught him right where it counts the most. His punch never connected, and instead he cupped both hands over his crotch and doubled over. 'Oh God!' he said.

'Stop it!' Susanne screamed again. She'd dropped her cane at some point and was using a car to support herself.

I tried to shake off Evan, but he was holding on to me with everything he had, trying to use his weight to drag me down to the asphalt. I managed to get some leverage into an elbow and drove it into his stomach. It made him loosen his grip on me, and I twisted away, stumbled, and fell against the Nissan.

Evan wanted to take another shot at me, but Susanne lurched between us and shouted, 'Enough! Enough!'

The MP3 player had gone flying during the melee and was on the ground near my foot. I reached down, grabbed it and slid it into the front pocket of my slacks.

Everyone took a moment.

Bob, whose face was red and puffy, tried to straighten up, using the Kia's hood for support. But it was still wet, and Bob's hand slipped, throwing him off balance momentarily.

'You OK?' I asked him.

'Fuck off,' he said.

'Are you out of your mind?' Susanne asked me. 'What do you think you're doing?'

'That's what you are,' Evan said, pointing at

me. 'You're out of your mind.'

To Susanne, I said, 'He wrote a song for Sydney.'

'What?'

'They recorded it, she put it on her player. He wrote this song and dedicated it to her.'

Susanne turned on Evan. 'Is that true?'

He shrugged.

'I asked you a question,' she said. 'Is that true?'

'It was just a song,' he said.

Bob slowly stood back up to his full height, but you could see he was still feeling the pain. There's nothing like it. He looked at me. 'I swear to God I'm going to kill you.'

'Shut up, Bob,' Susanne said. That caught both Bob and me off guard.

I said, 'Your boy knew our daughter better than he's been letting on,' I said.

'What are you talking about?' he said.

I took the player back out of my pocket. 'Let's have a listen.' I walked back to my car, turned the key ahead a notch, plugged the player back into the auxiliary jack.

When Syd's voice came on, Susanne's face crumpled like paper. I knew how she felt. I hadn't heard my daughter's voice for weeks, either, until now.

Sydney's and Evan's voices came out of the car speakers, then Evan went into his lyrics. Sydney followed up with the joke about him wanting to get into her pants.

When it got to the end I asked, 'Anyone want to hear it again?'

No one did. But Evan said, 'See? It's not even

a whole song. It's just a couple of lines, that's all. We were just goofing around.'

'Christ almighty,' Bob said to me. 'This is what's got your shorts in a knot?'

But Susanne clearly saw it differently. To Evan, she said, 'Why is Syd making a joke about you wanting to get into her pants?'

Evan's cheeks reddened.

'I'm asking you a question!' Susanne shouted.

'Suze,' Bob said. 'Don't get yourself worked up.'

'Fuck off,' she said to him.

'Susanne, for crying out loud, stop listening to this ex-boob of yours. Don't you see what he's doing? He's using Evan to drive a wedge between us. He wants you back and he figures the best way to do it is to turn you against us.'

'You're an ass,' I said to Bob.

He lunged at me and swung. He caught me in the jaw and I stumbled to the right, tripped over my own feet, and hit the ground.

Susanne screamed at us, 'Stop it!'

She wasn't using a car hood or any of us for support now. She was standing directly before Evan. Her right leg seemed wobbly.

'For the last time,' she said, her voice now not much more than a whisper, 'I want to know what was going on between you and my daughter.'

'We talked some,' he conceded.

'And what else?' Susanne asked. 'What else did you do?'

Evan glanced hopelessly at his father. 'Look, really, nothing happened. We were just getting along OK, all right? We liked to talk. But not

232

when you guys were around. We figured, if our parents knew that we actually liked each other, you'd start freaking out. You'd think it was like incest or something, but it's not.'

I think all the adults exchanged glances at that one. Even Bob and I.

'It was no big deal,' Evan persisted.

'Did you sleep with my daughter?' Susanne asked, point blank.

Ordinarily, that might have been something I'd have wanted to know myself, but I was worried about more than my seventeen-year-old daughter's sex life.

'I don't believe this,' Evan said. 'What a fucking question.'

'How about answering it?' Susanne asked.

'We only . . . we just . . . you know . . . OK, we made out a bit.'

'Great,' Bob said.

'She's not my *sister*,' Evan said. 'Just because you and my dad are getting it on doesn't mean I'm messing around with my sister.'

'You stupid idiot,' Bob said to him. He reached over and grabbed Evan by the scruff of the neck. 'What the hell were you thinking?'

'You moved me into the house with her!' he shouted into his father's face, like it was his fault. On this, we were more or less on the same page. 'What, you think I wasn't going to notice?'

I struggled to my feet and looked at Susanne, but she was avoiding me. Then, to Bob's son, I said, struggling to make my voice as calm as possible, 'Evan, I can't pretend not to care about what you and Syd may have been up to. Any other time, I'd want to kick your ass across this lot.'

Bob, perhaps calmed by the even tone of my voice, if not the words, released his hold on Evan.

I continued, 'But the only thing that interests me right now is finding Sydney. We now know you've been less than honest about how well you two were getting along. OK. Now we want to know if you've been less than honest about where she may be.'

'I swear I — '

'Shut up,' I said. 'If you're not straight with me, right now, right here, I'm calling Detective Jennings and turning it over to her.'

'Honest, I don't — '

'Tell him,' Bob said. 'Tell him what you know.'

All eyes were on Evan. 'She was just, first of all, she didn't like her job.'

'What job?' I asked. 'Where was she working? What was she doing?'

'She told me she was working at the hotel. Same as she told you,' Evan said, looking at me.

'What didn't she like?'

'She said she wanted to quit, see if she could get her job back at the dealership.'

'What else?' I said. 'What else did she say?'

Evan swallowed. 'She was also kind of worried about another thing.'

Again, we waited for Evan to spit it out. Finally, he said, 'She thought she might be late.'

'Late?' I said.

'Oh shit,' said Susanne.

And then she collapsed.

234

21

Bob and I shouted 'Suze!' at the same moment. But even after having been kicked in the nuts, he was down on his knees more quickly than I. He whipped off his sports jacket, folded it over, and slipped it under Susanne's head.

'Are you OK?' he asked urgently. 'Suze?'

It was as though she'd simply crumpled. Her leg or hip or something had momentarily given out and she'd dropped to the pavement like a marionette suddenly without strings. She'd managed to put a hand out to keep her head from striking the ground with any force.

Bob looked at his son and barked, 'Call an ambulance!'

Evan didn't seem to know which way to turn first, whether to grab a cell from one of us or run back to the office. Before he could get his feet to move, Susanne breathed, 'No, no, it's OK.'

'Don't move,' Bob said. He was bent over, cradling her head with his arm. 'What's happened? One of the fractures give way or what?'

'Honestly,' she said. 'It's OK. I just kind of slipped. I don't think I've broken anything again.'

I stood, transfixed, looking not at Susanne, but at Bob. He was focused entirely on my ex-wife. Propping his back against a car, he had lifted Susanne enough to take her entirely into his arms.

'You sure?' he asked, his voice shaking. 'That was a nasty fall.'

'Really,' she whispered.

And then I thought I saw Bob's chin quiver as he struggled to contain his emotions.

'Why don't I get some water?' I said.

'I can do that,' Evan said, and ran.

'I'm just an idiot,' Susanne said. 'I should have been using the cane.'

I found it on the ground, grabbed it, and handed it to Bob.

Bob, still cradling her, said, 'It's OK. There was so much going on.'

'I'm sorry,' I said, not just to Susanne, but to both of them. 'I kind of stirred things up.'

Susanne bristled. 'You did not get me *stirred up*. My leg gave out. Simple as that. Maybe the two of you can stop acting like squabbling children for a minute and help me up.'

We did. We had her on her feet just as Evan returned with a bottled water he'd just cracked the cap on. He handed it to Susanne and she took a sip.

'Thanks,' she said, getting hold of the cane and testing her weight on it. 'I'm OK.'

We all took a moment. Then Susanne said, 'We're not done here.' She had Evan in her sights again. 'Talk to me.'

The implications of Evan's last remark, that Syd was worried about 'being late', had finally sunk in. I wanted to hear what he had to say.

Evan kept his head low, like he was a puppy about to be hit with a rolled-up newspaper. 'It was just the one time,' he said.

'That'll do it,' Bob said.

'But like, a couple of days before she

disappeared, she got one of those get-pregnant-at-home kits,' Evan said.

'Home pregnancy test,' Susanne said, her voice weighed down with dread.

'Yeah,' he said. 'That's it.'

'What did it show?' Susanne asked.

'I think it was positive,' Evan said.

'Oh, God,' Susanne said.

'Or negative,' Evan said. 'Which is the one if you're not pregnant?'

'Negative,' Susanne said.

'Are you sure?' he asked. Susanne glared at him. 'I was thinking, it'd be positive to find out you're *not* pregnant.'

'Was she pregnant or not?' my ex-wife asked.

'I'm not really sure,' he said. 'I wasn't with her when she did the test. You have to go into the bathroom and pee on — '

'I know how it works,' Susanne said.

'So she went and did it and she told me everything was OK, I didn't have to worry about a thing. So I said, so, you're not having a baby? And she said don't worry about it, everything was fine.'

'Did she actually say she wasn't pregnant?' Susanne asked.

Evan's shoulders went up half an inch and dropped. 'I think that's what she meant. I kind of didn't push it, you know? In case she told me something I didn't want to hear.'

Susanne and I exchanged looks. This wasn't the sort of thing you made assumptions about.

'When was this?' I asked.

'Just before she came to stay with you for the

summer,' he said to me.

'*Where* did this happen?' Susanne wanted to know.

Evan kept looking down. 'At Dad's. You guys were both here on the lot that night.'

'You're really something else,' Bob said. 'We welcome Susanne and her daughter into our home and this is what you do?'

'Hold on,' I said. 'Let's not get sidetracked. We can all have a chat later about what Sydney and Evan did, but what matters now is finding Syd. When we get her home, when we know she's safe, there'll be plenty of time for lectures on all this.'

There seemed to be general agreement about that, at least among the adults. I took a couple of deep breaths. 'Let's get back to the job thing,' I said to Evan. 'Why wasn't she happy?'

'Like I said, she didn't really go into it. She just said the job made her sad. She said the people there, lots of them wouldn't talk to her. It's like they were scared all the time. It was creepy.'

'Scared?' said Susanne. 'Creepy?'

Evan shrugged again. 'I don't know. That's what she said. She didn't like to talk about work that much when we were hanging out. It's not like we were hanging out all the time. We've all got lots of stuff to do.'

'What *have* you been doing?' Susanne asked. 'When you're in that room of yours all by yourself?'

Bob said, 'Suze. Come on.'

'I'd like to know,' I said.

'You've already admitted that you've had sex

238

with my daughter,' Susanne said. 'So you might as well tell us about the other stuff.' She paused. 'Why don't we start with the stealing?'

'Susanne, he told you he didn't do that,' Bob said.

But Susanne wasn't looking at him. She still had her eyes fixed on Evan.

'The thing is,' Evan said, now looking at his father, 'I asked you if you could help me out a bit.'

'What are you talking about?'

'I told you I needed some money.'

'I gave you some money. For working around here.'

'I mean, more money.'

'Yeah, I remember,' he said. 'And I said no.'

'Well, I kind of needed some extra cash,' Evan said.

'So you took it from my purse, from the office, and you took my watch,' Susanne said. For someone who'd just collapsed she was on fire.

'But I got it back from the pawn shop,' he said, like he thought he deserved some credit, 'when I had a good stretch.'

'A good stretch?' I said. Evan glanced at me, realizing he'd made a slip. 'A good stretch of what?' I took a shot. 'Luck?'

'I guess.'

'What?' Susanne said to me, sensing I had figured something out.

'Gambling,' I guessed. 'Online gambling.'

'It's just once in a while,' Evan said. 'Just for fun.'

'So you're stealing money to pay off your

credit card bills,' I said.

Evan didn't respond. His father jumped in. 'I gave you a card for emergencies, not for playing poker on the Internet.'

'How much do you owe?'

'Just, like, a thousand or so.'

'Or so?' Bob said.

'About four thousand,' Evan muttered.

'Christ on a cracker,' Bob said.

'Evan,' I said, 'did you ever steal any money out of my house?'

He shook his head violently. 'Never, swear to God, I never took anything from your place.' He paused. 'But . . . I've borrowed some from friends.'

'In addition to the four grand on your Visa?' Bob asked.

Evan nodded sheepishly. 'Like, about six hundred.'

All of us, except Evan, were doing a variation of the same thing. Looking down, shaking our heads, thinking, is there no end to the kind of shit that kids can get into?

Susanne turned to me and said, 'Can I talk to you for a minute?'

We took a few steps back in the direction of the office. I let her put some weight on my arm.

'This thing, the gambling debts?' she said. 'That's Bob's problem.'

I wasn't sure. I wondered whether Evan's debt problems could have drawn Sydney in somehow. But I let Susanne continue.

'Maybe the reason she's gone, is she's pregnant. She's too afraid to tell us and she's run off to have the baby.'

I wasn't buying it, although, in some ways, it would be a relief to learn this was the reason for Sydney's disappearing act. At least it would mean she was OK. That she was alive. I could welcome home a pregnant daughter if there was a pregnant daughter to welcome home.

And yet.

'Why run off now?' I said. 'If she is pregnant, it's just at the beginning. Is she going to be gone for eight months? If she were going to run off to have a baby, wouldn't she have waited a little longer?'

Susanne nodded. 'I know, I know. Maybe she ran off to have it dealt with. To get an abortion.'

'She's been gone for weeks, Suze. How long would she need to do that? And don't you think, even if she was scared, and embarrassed, that eventually she'd screw up her courage and come to us for help? Something like this, wouldn't she have come to you, if not me?'

Susanne was starting to tear up. 'Maybe not if she blamed me. Because I'd moved us in with Bob and Evan. Because she'd think it was my fault.'

I thought there was something to that, but kept it to myself.

'It doesn't explain other things,' I said. 'What about that van you said has been watching your house? Syd's abandoned car? Or me being tricked into flying to Seattle? My house getting torn apart?'

Susanne shook her head in frustration. 'The van, that's probably just my imagination. I'm so tense, I'm seeing things that aren't there. You know?'

241

'Maybe,' I said.

'And it could have been kids who broke into your house. Just stupid vandalism.'

I didn't bother to tell her about the phone I'd found, how that discovery tightened the knot that brought all these things together.

'And maybe the Seattle thing,' Susanne continued, 'was just some prankster. You know there are some pretty sick people out there. It could have been someone who saw the website, just wanted to mess with you.'

How comforting it would be to believe what Susanne wanted to believe, that our daughter was out there, pregnant but safe, just waiting for the right time to come back home.

'Suppose I talk to Detective Jennings,' I said, 'and tell her they should check with Planned Parenthood offices, abortion clinics, that kind of thing. See if anyone there has seen Sydney.'

Susanne sniffed and nodded. 'OK.'

'It's worth a shot,' I said.

'OK,' she said again.

'Excuse me.' It was Bob, with a contrite Evan standing at his side. Susanne and I looked at the two of them without saying anything. 'Evan has something he'd like to say to the both of you.'

Susanne and I waited. Evan cleared his throat twice and said, 'I'm sorry.'

Bob offered up several small nods, smiled. Susanne and I looked at each other, then back at Evan.

'Well,' I said. 'Everything's just peachy now, isn't it?'

22

I left a message for Kip Jennings on my way to Riverside Honda. I pulled into the dealership a little after three, settled in behind my desk and fired up the computer. Following my routine of the last few weeks, I checked the website for any tips about Sydney, and, finding none, checked my work voicemail. There were three calls from people wondering how much they could get for their used cars. I made a note of their numbers so that I could call them back.

The hell of it was, I still had to make a living. I had bills to pay, not the least of which was a round trip to Seattle.

Andy Hertz had his head down at his desk, writing down some numbers on a yellow pad. 'Hey,' I said to him. It wasn't like him to be antisocial.

'Hey,' he said, glancing up. 'Welcome back.'

'Anything going on?' I asked.

'Not much.'

'Sell any cars?'

'It's been kind of slow,' Andy said. 'This idea of yours, to call up people selling their used cars, that hasn't worked worth a shit.' Then, remembering, 'You find Sydney?'

'No,' I said.

I got back behind my desk, unable to think about anything but my daughter. But I'd been able to go through the motions before when she was the only thing on my mind, so I got to it. I dug out my book of recent leads — people who'd taken test drives, asked for brochures, made low offers and walked away. I took a breath, and started dialing numbers.

I didn't leave messages when no one picked up. The chances that anyone would return a car salesman's call were about the same as a Prius winning the Indy 500. You had to talk to people directly.

A rich stockbroker from Stamford told me he was still mulling over whether to get the Honda S2000 he'd been salivating over a few weeks ago. I put him in the 'call back' list. An elderly couple from Derby had changed their mind about getting a car now that the husband had been diagnosed with cataracts.

And then I'd come to Lorna and Dell. The couple who'd looked at just about every car on the market and couldn't reach a decision. They'd come close to driving me mad with their indecision, but some sales you just had to work harder for than others.

I glanced at the clock, saw that it was after four, and took a chance Lorna might be home from her teaching job.

She picked up. 'Hello?'

'Hello, Lorna,' slipping into my car salesman voice, which is not far off from my regular voice, except that it sounds as though I've just had some cough syrup. 'Tim Blake from Riverside Honda.'

'Oh, how are you today?'

'I'm just great, how about yourself?'

'We're terrific. We're loving the car.'

I almost asked her to repeat herself, but calm prevailed. 'That's just great,' I said. 'I've been off a few days, you know. Just what did you end up getting?'

'We bought a Pilot. We spent all this time looking at sedans, and then we thought, maybe we could use a little more room. Are you feeling better?'

Evidently I had been ill. 'Yes, much better,' I said. 'I trust you were well looked after in my absence.'

'Oh yes. We came in looking for you, and that nice boy Andy helped us out.'

'That's great,' I said. 'Be sure to drop by and say hello when you're in for service.'

I hung up.

How it's supposed to work is this: if a customer you've been working with for some time finally decides to buy, and he shows up on your day off to make the deal, the salesperson who helps him splits the commission with you. That is, if he's not a scumbucket.

I poked my head around the divider and said to Andy, 'Hey, you want to go grab a coffee and get some air?'

Andy looked up nervously. 'Now?'

'Sure,' I said. 'I could use a coffee before I start making any more calls.'

We walked over to the communal coffee pot, poured ourselves each a cup, then walked around to the back of the dealership where there was shade from some tall oaks on a neighboring property.

'Nice day,' Andy said.

'Oh yeah,' I said, taking a sip of the hot coffee.

'Laura's sure been on the warpath,' he said. 'Leaning on everyone to get their numbers up. But sometimes, you know, things are just slow. What are you gonna do, right?'

'Sure,' I said. 'It happens.'

'Yeah,' he said, like we were two buddies, just shootin' the shit.

'So, you gonna tell me?' I asked.

'Hmm?' said Andy.

'You going to tell me about the Pilot you sold to Lorna and Dell?'

Andy coughed up a nervous laugh. 'Oh yeah, I was going to.'

'Were you?' I said. 'You seemed to have forgotten about it when I asked you how things had gone the last few days.'

'It just kind of slipped my mind, that's all. Don't worry, I'll split that commission down the middle with you.'

'Let me tell you something, Andy,' I said. 'You're still relatively new, so I'll cut you some slack today, but you ever pull a stunt like that again I'll slam a hood down on your fucking hand.'

'Sure, you bet,' Andy said. 'Won't ever happen again. You gonna tell Laura on me?'

I shook my head. 'Laura's sales manager. She doesn't give a shit who gets the commissions as long as the cars get sold. She'll just let us sort it out, and that's what I'm doing now. Understand?'

'You bet.'

246

I tossed my full coffee into an old oil drum and went back inside. There was a guy hanging around my desk. The girl at reception caught my eye as I walked into the showroom and said, 'That gentleman asked for you.'

He was sandy-haired, trim, mid-thirties, smart clothes. I put out my hand as I approached. 'Tim Blake,' I said. 'You were looking for me?'

He nodded and returned the handshake. 'Eric Downes,' he said. 'I got your name from a guy I work with who bought a car from you a few years ago.'

'Who was that?' I asked.

'Dan?' he said. 'I don't even know his last name.' He laughed self-consciously. 'You'd think I'd know a co-worker's last name.'

'No problem,' I said. I could recall two or three Dans off the top of my head, but it didn't really matter which one. 'What can I help you with?' I asked.

'I've been seriously thinking about a Civic coupe,' Eric Downes said.

'The regular coupe, or the Si?'

'Oh, the Si,' he said.

'Nice vehicle,' I said. 'Six-speed, alloys, 197 horsepower. It really goes, and at the same time, you're going to get respectable gas mileage with it.'

'Everyone's thinking about that these days,' Eric said. 'I've been reading up on them online, I've looked at other people's, but this is the first time I've been into a showroom to look at one. Thing is, I've also been looking at a Mini, and a GTI. The Volkswagen. But I wanted to check the

Si first. You have any in stock?'

'I don't have one on the floor here,' I said, 'but I have one in the lot, a demo.'

'What I'd really like to do,' he said, 'is take one for a test drive, but like, do I have to put down a deposit first to do something like that?'

'No, of course not,' I said. 'I can arrange for you to take one out if you'd like. I just need a copy of your driver's license, and it'd be my pleasure to ride along with you to show you the car's features.'

Not that Eric would be able to pick up a load of manure with an Si, but I wasn't going to make that mistake again.

Eric glanced at his watch like he had some place to get to, then shrugged and said, 'What the hell, let's do it.'

While I was arranging to have one of the summer hires bring the red demo we had up to the door, I watched Andy skulk in and slink into his chair. He didn't look over at me, or my customer. He was an OK kid. He just still had a lot to learn. Unless, of course, his ambition was to be a slimy car salesman. If that was the case, he was ahead of the game.

Shannon, at reception, made a copy of Eric Downes's license, gave the original back to me and I handed it over to him while he inspected other new cars on the lot. A couple of minutes later, the red Civic Si rolled up.

'What are you driving now?' I asked Eric.

'I've got a Mazda,' he said. 'I've had good luck with it, but I feel like a change.'

'You'd be looking to trade it in?' I asked.

'I'm actually at the end of a lease,' he said.

'They call this Rallye Red,' I said, pointing out some of the Honda's exterior features for Eric. The rear spoiler, the Si badging. I opened the door for him to get behind the wheel, then joined him on the other side.

'Nice,' he said, running his hands over the leather-wrapped steering wheel. I directed his attention to the navigation and audio systems, the side bolsters on the racing-style bucket seats.

'Start 'er up,' I said.

Eric turned the engine over, gave the accelerator a couple of light taps to hear the revs, pushed in the clutch and worked the gearshift around, getting an idea where all the gears were.

'Can I smoke in here?' Eric asked, about to reach into his jacket.

'Once you own it,' I smiled. 'But for now, no, if you don't mind.'

'No problem,' he said.

'Let's go out that way,' I said, pointing right. 'Then we'll head up to the turnpike, get an idea how it performs on the highway.' I got the navigation screen set up so we could keep track of our movements. 'You ever had a car with one of these built in to the dash?' I asked.

'Yup,' said Eric. He didn't seem particularly impressed.

While Eric waited for a break in traffic, I happened to look across the street at the vacant lot there. There's usually nothing there, which probably explains why the dark blue Chrysler van with tinted windows sitting there caught my eye. I didn't give it another thought after that.

There are only a few thousand of those on the road in Milford alone.

Eric put the Civic into first, eased up on the clutch, and took us out onto Route 1. But instead of turning right, as I had suggested, he went left, front tires squealing. This is one of the first things you learn in the car selling business: test drive routes have as few left turns as possible. You don't want someone unfamiliar with the car making turns in front of traffic. That goes double when the car has a stick instead of an automatic.

I said, 'No, I thought we'd head — '

'I want to go this way,' he said.

Eric tromped on the gas, pushing the car up through the gears until we were cruising in sixth, weaving from lane to lane, zooming past motorists with more conventional driving habits. I glanced over at the digital readout on the dash, saw that the car was topping out at more than sixty.

'Eric, I know the car goes like stink and it doesn't feel like you're going as fast as you are, but I think you might want to let up a bit on the pedal there before we get a ticket or something worse.'

Eric glanced over and flashed me a grin, but there was nothing friendly about it.

'Why don't you just sit back and enjoy the ride,' he said, 'and tell me where the fuck your daughter is.'

23

When I didn't immediately say something — I was too stunned to respond for several seconds — Eric said, 'It's got good handling, I'll grant you that. You don't really think of that with a Civic, at least I never have. I like the road feel. Comes right through the steering wheel. Some cars, they're all mushy, you know? I like a car where you feel connected, you get what I'm saying?'

He glanced over. 'Huh?' he prodded. 'You know what I mean?'

'Who are you?' I finally managed to say, my hand gripped tightly around the brushed aluminum passenger door handle. My heart, which had already started pounding when Eric Downes hit the gas, was going like a trip hammer now.

He flashed that grin again. 'I'm Eric.'

'What's happened to Sydney?'

'Hello? Timmy, my man, did you hear what I asked you a second ago? I asked *you* to tell *me* where your daughter is.'

'I don't know where she is.'

'You know what? I tend to believe that. We've seen your website, we know you've been looking for her. We've been watching you, watching your wife's place, haven't seen your daughter. Not one titty tit tit. But I figured, hey, I had to ask, you know? Give you a chance to tell us where she was before we consider other courses of action.'

'Who's we?' I asked.

Eric downshifted, turned hard left at a yellow light that was in the process of turning red, and gunned it up a residential side street. We were still doing sixty, but now we were doing it in a thirty. 'You know what kind of suspension this baby's got?' he asked.

'What kind of trouble is Sydney in?' I asked.

'She's in a whole *fuck* of a lot of trouble,' Eric said. 'She's got her tit one hundred per cent caught in the wringer, you know what I'm saying?'

'Tell me what it is,' I said. 'Tell me what the problem is. If I can solve it, make you happy, then my daughter will come home and we can forget all about this. If it's about money, just tell me how much and I'll make it right.'

'You want to make me one satisfied customer, is that the idea? I tell you what your daughter's done, and you'll throw in free rustproofing?'

Eric chuckled, swerved sharply to avoid a parked car. I tightened my grip on the door handle and pressed my right foot reflexively to the firewall, as though I had a brake pedal of my own. Glancing over, I caught a glimpse of a gun butt in his inside left jacket pocket.

'Do you know if Sydney's OK?' I asked. 'Has she been in touch with you?'

Eric came to another side street, hit the brakes, turned right, let the front-wheel drive pull the car so the back end hardly fishtailed. Every few seconds he'd glance over at me, but most of the time he had his eyes on the road.

'I still don't think you're getting it,' he said. 'We haven't heard from her. If we had, maybe we could have worked something out with her, come to some kind of an arrangement, you know? And if you're not able to tell me where she is, it's going to make that very difficult. Because we'd have liked nothing better than to put all this business behind us.'

'What business?'

Eric sighed. 'You know what I think? I think you never tried hard enough. If she was my daughter, I'd have been out there looking for her twenty-four-seven, not sitting around being Mr Car Salesman, slicking back my hair, wearing my plaid jacket, adjusting my white belt, trying to sell Jap cars.' What was with the past tense? Why was he talking like I was done searching? 'What the hell kind of father you been, anyway?'

'You lousy son of a bitch,' I said. Even with the A/C blasting in my face, I felt hot with anger. If this guy hadn't been sitting behind the wheel, I'd have tried to grab hold of him around the neck.

Eric shot me another glance, then looked forward. Without taking his eyes off the road, he launched his shifting hand blindingly fast, backhanding me on the nose.

The pain was instantaneous, and tremendous. Most people go their whole lives without getting punched in the nose, and up to that moment, I'd been one of them. I shouted out in pain, cupped my hands over my face. Blood trickled into my palms.

'Try not to get anything onto the upholstery,' Eric said. 'I'm not going to buy this car if it's got

253

blood all over the seats.'

'Jesus!' I said. 'You son of a bitch!' If this had been my own car, I might have been able to find a box of tissues in the glove box, but there'd be nothing in there but a crisp, new, unopened driver's manual. Blood dripped onto my pants as I reached into my pocket for something to blot my nose.

'Don't be rude, Timmy, or I just might not buy this car. Can I ask you something? Does it come with a decent warranty, or do you have to buy those extended things, because, personally, I think those things are a huge fucking ripoff.'

I closed my eyes a moment, winced, opened them. Through tears, I surveyed the navigational screen. We were heading north through Stratford on Huntington, almost to the Merritt Parkway. Eric slipped a cigarette from a pack in his pocket, put it between his lips and lit it with a silver lighter.

'I know what you're thinking,' Eric said, breathing out smoke. 'Maybe you want to grab the wheel or something, show you're a tough guy, be a big hero, that kind of thing. Well, I'm better at this sort of shit than you are. You sit in your little showroom day after day, handing out brochures, filling out forms, trying to talk people into buying options they don't really need, you probably don't run into somebody like me every day. Somebody who can mess you up really, really bad. And the thing is, there's not just one of me. There's a whole fucking bunch of us, OK? So don't go doing something stupid. You do something stupid, you're not just putting yourself in jeopardy, but your daughter, too, got it?'

I dabbed some tissue under my nose. 'Yeah,' I said.

'The fact is,' Eric continued, 'it's time for a change of approach. More direct, more up front.' He smiled. 'The Seattle thing, that was OK at the time, but things have escalated, you catch my drift?'

I glanced over.

'Can I ask you a question?' he said. 'Seriously? Did the cops even *find* that coke?'

'Yes,' I said slowly.

He slapped his thigh. 'I win the bet,' he said. 'The others said, no, it was too well hidden, and I said, fuck, if it's sitting right in the open, who's going to believe that it wasn't found when the place was torn apart? You get what I'm saying?'

'Yes.'

'But my other question is, what the fuck are you doing, walking around? Why didn't the cops arrest you?'

'They didn't buy it,' I said.

He banged the steering wheel with his fist. 'Shit.'

'Why'd you do that? Plant cocaine in my house?'

He shook his head angrily for a moment, then became almost philosophical. 'Honestly? The coke thing was kind of an afterthought. Mainly, we just wanted you out of town for a while, get you out of the way. Buy us some time, maybe your kid would show up while you were gone. Be a lot easier to deal with her with no daddy to run home to.'

He smiled to himself. 'But once you were gone, I had what you might call an inspiration. Figured, tear your house apart, plant some coke. I thought, hey, once you came back, you'd have a whole 'nother shitload of problems to deal with, including having to explain to the cops why there was coke in your house.'

The anger returned. 'Fucking stupid cops! Laid it all out for them! House torn apart like somebody was looking for something, the cops find the coke, they start leaning on you. It's simple. I can't believe they're so fucking stupid!'

'If they'd bought it, wouldn't that have made them stupid?' I asked.

'That just really pisses me off. I was in a good mood up to now.'

'Why'd you want me out of the way, for the police to arrest me? What have I done to you?'

Another glance. 'You just won't quit. Going here and there, bugging the shit out of everybody, looking for your kid. You're a fucking problem waiting to happen. A goddamn liability.' He banged the steering wheel again. Then, 'Did you happen to find a phone, by the way? It might have slipped out of somebody's pocket.'

'Yeah,' I said.

Eric chortled. 'Well, no biggie. We got no fucking use for it any more.'

Eric guided the Civic onto the ramp for the eastbound Merritt Parkway. 'Let's see what this baby'll do,' he said, downshifting, hitting the gas, and merging into traffic. 'How much one of these run?'

I was still blotting my nose, thinking.

Eric glanced over. 'You know what? I bet I know what's on your mind.'

I just looked at him.

'Why hasn't your daughter gotten in touch with you? Or even the cops? Am I right?'

After a moment, I said, 'Maybe.'

'Fact is, I don't think your daughter's got much to gain by talking to the cops.'

'What do you mean?'

'You ask me, smartest thing she could do is pretend none of this ever happened.'

'I don't understand.'

'I'm sure you don't.'

'What do you want with my daughter? What's she done?'

'She's not the little angel you think she is, that's for fucking sure.'

I wasn't sure I wanted to know. But I had to.

'What's she done?' I asked. 'She stolen something from you?'

'Oh, Timmy, if only it was that,' Eric said. 'Don't you think, if all she'd done was take something from us, she might have gotten in touch with you?'

I didn't say anything.

'I mean, she's got to be scared shitless and all. That's part of it. But my theory is, she's just ashamed.'

I blotted up some more blood. Neither of us said anything for about a mile.

It was Eric who broke the silence. 'I think we'll take the next exit, find us a nice place in the woods to continue our discussion. Fact is, I had another one of those inspirational moments

257

when I was on my way to see you today, about what to do if you didn't know where your girl was, which clearly you do not. I thought to myself, what if we had some sort of an event that would make her want to come home. Then we don't even have to look for her. We just wait for her to show up. You get what I'm saying?'

'No,' I said.

'You ever read that book?' he asked. 'The one where they talk about trusting your gut instinct? How going with the idea that just comes to you is usually a better plan than the one you think over for months and months? You ever read that book?'

'Yeah,' I said. 'I read that book.'

'Well, that was what I had before we left. One of those '*Ah ha!*' moments. Sometimes, you know, the simplest ideas are the best ones.'

'I still don't know what you're talking about,' I said.

Eric grinned and tossed his cigarette out the window. 'Well, if you were a little girl on the run, wouldn't you come home for your daddy's funeral?'

The next exit would take me to my execution. Eric Downes was going to take that gun out of his jacket and kill me in the woods.

I didn't, at that moment, see a lot of options, save one.

I yanked up on the emergency brake.

'*Shiiitttt!*' Eric screamed as the car suddenly decelerated and lurched toward the shoulder. He threw both hands back onto the wheel as a car coming up from behind laid on the horn and swerved past, narrowly missing the back end of the Civic.

As Eric's hands went to the wheel I unbuckled my seat belt with one hand, threw open the passenger door with the other, and catapulted myself out of the car.

We probably weren't going much more than five or ten miles per hour at that point, but jumping out of a car at any speed is an insane thing to try. Except, perhaps, when the guy behind the wheel is getting ready to shoot you.

I tried to maintain my balance as I hit the gravel, but I lost my footing on the loose stones and did a simultaneous tumble and spin, something that might have earned me a 7.2 in Olympic skating, right into the tall grasses beyond the shoulder. I rolled twice, then raised myself on my knees, gave my head a quick shake in a bid to get my bearings, and saw that the Civic had come to a stop on the shoulder about thirty yards up the highway.

Horns blared from several other cars speeding past. One driver stuck his middle finger out through the sunroof.

The driver's door flew open and Eric jumped out of the Civic, gun in hand. He ran to the back of the car, scanning the side of the road, but I'd thrown myself onto the ground, flattened myself out. I could just make out Eric between the blades, but felt relatively sure he could not see me.

Now Eric was glancing at the traffic, and you could see the wheels turning. Motorists see a guy at the side of the road waving a gun, someone's going to pick up their cell and make a call.

He knew he had to get out of there. There wasn't time to hunt me down.

He ran around to the other side of the car, slammed the passenger door shut, then got in the driver's seat. The car took off, kicking up gravel as it swerved onto the pavement.

I stood up and brushed myself off. Maybe, because my nose still hurt so much, I didn't notice all the other aches and pains that come from jumping out of a moving automobile.

I got out my cell phone and called the dealership. 'Andy in sales,' I said when someone picked up.

A moment later, 'Andy Hertz.'

'It's Tim,' I said.

'Oh, hi,' he said.

'I need a lift.'

24

I could have asked Andy Hertz, who was still feeling guilty about the stolen commission, for a lung right about then, but a ride was all I needed. I gave him directions and about twenty minutes later he found me alongside the Merritt Parkway.

'What the hell happened to you?' he asked as I got into the air conditioned Accord.

I turned the mirror around to get a look at myself. My nose and left cheek were swollen and decorated with small red shreds of tissue. And my clothes were dusted and grass-stained.

'What are you doing out here in the middle of nowhere?' he asked.

'Take me back,' I said.

'What happened to the Si you went out in? Did the car get stolen?'

'Just drive, Andy.'

'Do you need me to take you to a hospital or something?'

I turned in my seat and said patiently, 'No more questions, Andy. Just get me back.'

He did as he was asked, but that didn't stop him from looking over every few seconds. While I'd been waiting for him to show up I'd put in a call to Kip Jennings, and still had the phone in my hand, hoping she'd call back any second.

As we approached the dealership, I glanced over at the 7-Eleven parking lot, where I'd noticed the Chrysler van when Eric — or whoever he really was — and I left for our test drive.

The van was gone. But sitting right next to where it had been parked was the red Civic.

'Pull in here,' I instructed Andy.

He wheeled the Accord into the vacant lot and I got out. The Civic was unlocked, the keys in the ignition. I went around to the passenger side, opened the door, saw dark splotches of blood on the dark gray fabric seats. I reached in, took the key, waited for a break in the traffic, and ran across the street to the dealership, leaving Andy to get back across with the car by himself.

As I entered the showroom my cell rang. I flipped it open, put it to my ear, and said, 'Yeah.'

'Jennings.'

Once I started talking I couldn't keep my voice from shaking. 'Some guy just tried to kill me.'

'Are you hurt?'

'He acted like he wanted to buy a car, we got out on the highway, he wanted to know where Syd was and then he was going for a gun — '

'Where are you?'

'The dealership.'

'Are you OK?'

'Yes. Well, no, but mostly yes.'

'How long ago?'

I had no idea. I glanced at my watch. 'It all started more than an hour ago. He dumped me on the Merritt Parkway about three quarters of an hour ago.'

'Five minutes,' she said and hung up.

I heard sirens in three.

262

Jennings was looking at the photocopy we'd taken of Eric Downes's driver's license prior to the test drive.

'It's a fake,' she told me.

'How do you know?'

'Trust me,' she said.

'Let me see,' I said. I studied the photo on the license. It was a man with roughly the same facial shape and hair color as the one who'd tried to kill me, but it wasn't him. The more I looked, the more I realized it wasn't even close.

'That's not the guy,' I said. 'He handed over his license to me, I didn't even look at it before I gave it to Shannon to copy. He could have handed me my mother's ID and it would have worked.'

Jennings didn't bother to lecture me on the obvious holes in our system.

'He said they were looking for Syd,' I said.

'Who's they?' Jennings asked.

'I don't know,' I said. While I was telling her my story, a team of cops descended on the red Civic across the street.

'You have surveillance cameras here?' she asked, looking about the showroom. 'We might be able to get a look at him.'

'We only turn them on when we're closed,' I said.

'Super,' Jennings said. She leaned in and got a closer look at my nose. 'You should see a doctor.'

'I don't think it's broken,' I said. I had been, for as long as I could stand it, holding an ice pack on it. Laura Cantrell had found one in the lunchroom fridge.

Jennings asked countless questions. Not just about the man's appearance, but his voice, his clothes, mannerisms, patterns of speech.

'He knew all about the Seattle thing,' he said. 'He admitted he was in my house. They planted the coke, thinking you'd arrest me, that'd be one more headache for me to deal with.'

'Why would they want to do that?'

I paused. 'He said I was a problem waiting to happen. Because I won't stop looking for Syd.'

'A problem for who?' she asked. 'Aside from that guy from the flower shop?'

'Just about everyone else who runs a business near the hotel,' I said.

Jennings eyes were piercing. 'Have there been others?'

'Other what?'

'Other misunderstandings? Like the one you had with Ian Shaw?'

'No,' I said.

Jennings didn't look convinced. She was about to ask me something else when her cell rang. She dug her phone from her purse, looked at who was calling, and said, 'I have to take this.' She turned and stepped away.

I took the opportunity to go into Laura Cantrell's office with my warm, damp, ice pack.

'Thanks,' I said.

She took it from me gingerly, looking for a place to put it down where it wouldn't leave a wet spot, and finally set it atop a crinkled copy of *Motor Trend*.

'I'm taking a leave,' I said.

'Tim,' she said.

'I'm going to look for Sydney and I'm not coming back until I've found her. If I have to I'll put my house up for sale to keep myself afloat.'

'I guess you do what you have to do,' she said. 'But you know, at the end of the day, I can't hold on to your job for ever.'

'I'd expect nothing more.'

'Jesus, Tim, I know you're going through a lot but you don't have to be an asshole.'

'I'll turn my contacts over to Andy. He can have my customers. He's already got a head start.'

'I was going to tell you about that,' she said.

'I don't care, Laura,' I said.

I was about to turn and leave when Laura said, 'This is kind of difficult, Tim, but . . . '

'What?' I asked.

'You *are* driving a company car.'

I wanted to see whether she could look me in the eye and ask for my keys, and damned if she didn't. 'I can help you out as best I can, but I can't justify giving a car to someone on a leave,' she said.

Riverside Honda had plenty of used cars to choose from, but suddenly I didn't want to give my own employer the business. 'Give me a day or two?'

'Of course,' Laura said.

'I'll give Bob a call,' I said, half grinning to myself. 'I'll bet he can put me into something.'

Detective Jennings was waiting by my desk. Her cell phone was tucked away.

'Tell me again why you think this guy was going to kill you,' she said.

'To get Syd to come back. I guess he figured she'd hear, somehow, if I was dead, and she'd feel she had to come back to the funeral.'

Jennings didn't say anything for a moment.

'What?' I asked.

'That tends to support the idea that Syd *is* alive.'

I blinked. 'You got some reason to believe that she isn't?'

'That was the lab calling,' she said. 'We got the DNA results, on the blood from your daughter's car.'

I was feeling faint.

'We got two hits. One was your daughter.'

★ ★ ★

I was already feeling woozy. Jennings put me in my own desk chair, then sat down across from me.

'Some of the blood on the steering wheel and door handle of Sydney's car turned out to be hers,' Jennings said.

'That doesn't mean she's dead,' I said. 'It just means that she lost a bit of blood. She could have had a cut finger or something.'

'That's true,' Jennings said.

I was trying hard to focus, and thought back a couple of sentences. 'Some?' I said.

'Some what?'

'You said some of the blood on the steering wheel was Syd's.'

266

'We've acquired quite a database over the last few years of suspects and convicted criminals.' She paused. 'And from the deceased. When we get a DNA sample we run it against what we already have, see if we get lucky.'

Lucky.

She nodded. 'The other blood belonged to Randall Tripe.'

I looked at her oddly. 'Should I know that name?'

'I mentioned him the other day, remember? He'd been involved in everything from identity theft to human trafficking. He was found dead in a dumpster in Bridgeport a day after you reported Sydney missing. Shot in the chest.'

'That doesn't make any sense,' I said. 'Sydney's car was found up in Derby. That's quite a hike from Bridgeport.'

'Whoever dumped his body in that dumpster might have taken him from the car in Derby,' Jennings said. 'But the way I see it, there's two ways to explain two different kinds of blood on the car. One, an injured Mr Tripe had your daughter's blood on his hands and took off with her car, or two, an injured Sydney Blake had Mr Tripe's blood on her hands and took off in her own car.'

'But we know Tripe is dead,' I said.

'Bingo. That's why I tend to go with number two.'

'But if Syd had Tripe's blood on her hands . . .'

'Yeah,' Jennings said. 'That's something to think about, isn't it?'

I thought about what 'Eric' had said. That Sydney hadn't gotten in touch because she was ashamed of something she'd done.

★ ★ ★

It was dark by the time I got home.

After the kind of day I'd had, I was on high alert, like a mouse slipping through the forest at night wondering how many owls are overhead. I kept checking my rearview mirror, looking for vans, scanning the faces of pedestrians I passed on the street, hunting for people in the bushes, looking for lights that were on that should be off, lights that were off that should be on.

I'd asked Jennings whether I was entitled to some sort of police protection, and she'd said she'd put a call into the Secret Service. I took her sarcasm to mean the Milford police did not have a lot of extra officers to go around. So I was my own bodyguard, and I didn't exactly feel up to the job.

As I pulled into the driveway, the house appeared in order.

I unlocked the door, went inside, flipped on the front hall light switch. The house looked almost as it had before I'd gone to Seattle. Things back in place, carpets vacuumed, floors swept. I double locked the door behind me.

My nose was throbbing, my head pounding. I went looking for Tylenol in its usual place in the kitchen cupboard, but after the cleanup many things were not where I expected to find them. I hunted around, finally found the bottle, and washed down a couple of pills with some cold water from the tap.

I stood there, leaning up against the counter, pondering what I would do next. I'd made a decision to devote every waking hour to finding Syd. Now all I had to do was figure out how to use them productively.

I wondered how Arnie Chilton's parallel investigation was coming along. Perhaps, by this time, he'd tracked down a Boston cream donut.

It wasn't until I was standing there, alone in my kitchen, that I realized how weary I was. I felt as though I had nothing left to give, at least right now.

I decided the smartest thing to do, for myself and for Syd, was to head straight to bed, get a good night's rest, start fresh on this in the morning.

I finished drinking the water, set the glass in the sink. And then, perhaps not sure whether I really should go to bed, I sat down at the kitchen table.

Put my head down for a moment onto my folded arms. Turned it to one side so my injured nose wouldn't rub up against my arm.

Maybe I didn't need to go to bed yet. Maybe, if I just rested for a few moments, it would be enough to recharge my batteries. Then I could spend the rest of the evening coming up with a plan to find Syd. Even though this Eric character didn't know where she was, maybe if I knew more about him, that would tell me more about what Syd had been into, and then . . .

I'm not sure how many times the phone rang

before I heard it. I jerked awake, looked up at the clock. It was after midnight. I'd been asleep at the kitchen table for nearly three hours. I pushed the chair back, stumbled over to the phone and snatched up the receiver.

I put it to my ear and said, groggily, 'Hello?'

There was some background noise. Music, people shouting. And then a voice.

A girl's voice.

She said, 'Help me.'

25

'Syd?' I said. 'Syd, is that you?'

At the other end of the line, crying. 'I need you to come and get me.' Her words were slightly slurred. The background music made it difficult to hear her clearly.

'Syd, where are you? Tell me where you are!' I was feeling over-whelmed, as though my entire body wanted to cry. 'I'll come and get you. Just tell me where you are.'

'It's not *Syd*.'

'What?' I said.

'It's me. It's Patty.' She sniffed. 'Can you come and get me? Please?'

'Patty?'

'Can you get me?'

'What's happened, Patty? Are you OK?'

'I hurt myself.' Her words continued to slur.

'What happened?'

'I fell down.'

'Are you drunk, Patty?'

'I might have had, maybe a few, I don't know. I'm pretty good.'

'Patty, you should phone your mom. She'll come get you. If you want, I'll call her for you.'

'Mr B, like, this time of night, she'll be more shitfaced than I am.'

'Have you got money for a cab?' I asked. 'Tell me where you are and I'll send one to take you home. Or I'll pay him before he heads off.'

'Please just come get me,' she said.

I heard a boy talking to her. 'Shit, whaddya do to your leg? Why don't you stop bleeding all over the place and come with us.'

'Fuck off,' Patty told him.

'And why don't you suck this,' the boy said. That was followed by raucous male laughter.

'Patty,' I said. She wasn't going to have to ask me again. I didn't like the sounds of things. I'd go get her.

'Huh?'

'Tell me where you are. Right now. Where are you?'

'I'm on, like . . . Hey!' She was shouting at someone. 'Where the fuck is this?'

Someone yelled something back that sounded like 'America!'

'Very funny, asshole!' Patty shouted. Then she called out to someone else, and then said into the phone. 'OK, you know that road that goes along the beach? Broadway? East Broadway?'

'Sure.' It was five minutes away, tops. 'Where are you along there?'

'There's like, a bunch of houses.'

It was all houses along there. 'Do you see a street sign, Patty?'

'No, wait, yeah, Gardner?'

I knew where she was. 'I'll be right there,' I told her. 'Don't move.' I hung up the phone, grabbed my keys, locked the house on the way out, and got into the CR-V.

It had turned into a muggy night, but instead of flipping the air on I put down the windows. Fresh air blowing through the car would help wake me up. The drive down to East Broadway only took a few minutes. I trolled slowly down the street. Quite a few young people were walking along the sidewalk, a few wandering down the center of the street, a few holding bottles in their hands. Clearly, a big party had taken place somewhere, no doubt in one of the beach houses where the parents were away.

I drove slowly, not just because I was trying to spot Patty. I didn't want to run anyone over.

I slowed to a crawl as I reached Gardner, then came to a full stop. There were twenty kids or more milling about behind one of the houses on the south side of the street that was right on the beach. All the lights were on and loud music blared from inside. Up at the far end of the street, a police car was making its way.

I spotted Patty standing on the curb, a tall boy towering over her, bending down, talking into her ear. She had her head turned, like she didn't want anything to do with him. I wondered why she didn't just walk away, then noticed the boy had a grip on her arm.

'Patty!' I called.

She didn't hear me. The boy was yelling at her.

I had the door open and one foot down on the pavement. 'Hey!' I shouted. 'Let go of her!'

The boy glanced over, still holding on to Patty. His head wavered a bit and he struggled to focus on me.

'Patty!' I shouted.

She ripped her arm away from the boy and started off in my direction. The boy stumbled after her, saying, loud enough for me to hear,

'Come on, come with me.'

She turned back to him, made a jerking gesture with her fist, said, 'Do it yourself.'

'Fuck you,' he said.

Her hair was scraggly and as she approached my car I could see she was walking with a decided limp. She was wearing black shorts that fit her like a second skin, her legs brilliant white in contrast, except for the area around her right knee, which was dark and slightly shiny.

'Hey, Mr B,' she said, approaching my window. 'Whoa, nice nose job.'

'Get in,' I said. The boy stood in the street, watching us through clouded eyes. 'Get lost,' I said to him and got back into the car.

Patty loped around the front of the car, fumbled with the door handle on the passenger side, and got into the car. She smelled of alcohol.

'Home, James,' she said.

I pulled a U-turn in the street and started heading back toward the center of Milford. Even though I didn't know where Patty lived I wanted to get away from all these kids hanging around.

'Where do you live, Patty?'

That seemed to sober her up almost immediately. 'Shit, no, we can't go to my house. Take me to your place.'

'Patty, I have to take you home.'

'If I go home like this my mom will kill me.'

'I thought you said your mother'd probably already be passed out.'

'If I'm lucky. But if she's awake she's going to have six shit fits seeing me like this.'

She reached down and tentatively touched her

274

knee. 'God does that hurt. I bet it hurts almost as much as your face.'

I flicked on the interior light and glanced over as I drove. Her knee was a mess. 'Who did that to you?'

'OK, so this asshole Ryan or whatever his name was, he drops his beer on the sidewalk just as I'm walking by, right, and there's glass all over the place? And I'm trying to walk around it, and there's this bunch of girls who aren't even from around here, they're like these skanks from Bridgeport or something, and they start saying something about my hair, and I turned to give them the finger and tripped, right? I hit the sidewalk and there's this little bit of glass right under my knee but I think I picked it out but what a bunch of assholes, right, they — '

'You might need stitches,' I said. The Milford Hospital was only a minute away. 'I can take you to the ER, let them have a look at it.'

'Oh man, no, you can't do that to me. Then there's going to be this whole sideshow, right? They might even call the cops because I'm not old enough to drink. There'll be some big lecture or they might even fucking charge me.'

'You need a big lecture,' I said.

Patty shot me a look. 'You think I'm a loser, don't you?'

'No,' I said. 'But you make a lot of bad choices.'

'That's supposed to make me feel better, right? That *I'm not* stupid, I make stupid *choices*. Well, if you make stupid choices all the time, doesn't that make you stupid?'

'Who was that guy grabbing your arm?'

She shrugged. 'I don't know. Just some guy wanted me to blow him.'

When I reached Bridgeport Avenue I turned in the direction of the hospital.

'I know where you're going,' she said. 'I won't go in. And if you drive me home, I'll just take off. Let me crash at your place tonight.'

It wasn't a good idea. At the same time, I wasn't about to let a teenage girl who'd had too much to drink wander off on her own. So I didn't continue on to the hospital, and I didn't ask Patty for directions to her mother's house. Instead, I took her back to my place.

I parked and came around to Patty's side. She had the door open and was getting out, but between the drinking and the banged up knee, she was unsteady on her feet. She slipped an arm up over my shoulder and I led her across the drive and up the path to the front door.

I heard a car coming down the street. It slowed as it approached my house, as though the driver was intending to turn into my drive. It was a silver Ford Focus, and I was guessing that Kate Wood was behind the wheel.

She slowed long enough to get a good look at me half-carrying a young girl into my house. Then she hit the gas and kept going on up the street.

'Oh, Christ,' I said.

'What?' asked Patty.

'Never mind. I'll deal with it later.'

I took her upstairs to the bathroom Syd used and instructed her to kick off her shoes and sit on the edge of the tub with her feet inside. 'Can you sit there without falling over?' I asked.

'I'm fine,' she said tiredly. 'I can really hold my liquor.' There was a hint of pride there.

'I'll get the first-aid kit.'

She was still perched on the edge of the tub when I came back, but she looked even younger than her seventeen years. In her bare feet, head hanging low, streaky, multicolored hair dangling in her eyes, with her knee scraped and bloodied, she looked like a little girl who'd fallen off her bike in the rain.

She looked up at me, her eyes moist.

'You OK?' I asked.

'I think about Sydney all the time,' she said.

'Me too.'

'All the time,' she said. Then, 'What happened to your face?'

'I had a bad test drive with somebody,' I said.

'Wow. The car hit a tree or something?'

'Not exactly. Let's worry right now about getting you patched up.'

Running some lukewarm water from the tap, I got down on my knees and managed to get Patty's knee cleaned. Using some fresh white towels from under the counter, I gently blotted the wound. The towels quickly became stained with blood.

Next I applied some disinfectant, then some bandages.

'You're good at this,' Patty said, leaning into me just slightly.

'I haven't done a skinned knee in a long time,' I said. 'The last time was when Syd was little, and she had rollerblades.'

Patty was quiet for a moment, sitting there, feet in the tub. I felt the weight of her body leaning into mine. When I was done with her wound, I lacked the energy to get up so I sat on the floor, my body held up by the vanity.

'You've always been really decent to me,' Patty said.

'Why wouldn't I be?' I said.

'Because I'm not like Sydney,' she said. 'I'm not a good girl.'

'Patty . . .'

'I'm a bad girl. I do all the bad things.'

'Yeah,' I said. 'You do bad things. But it doesn't make you a bad kid.'

'We're back to the bad choices thing,' she said, mockingly.

'If you're trying to convince me not to like you, it's not going to work,' I said. 'I think you're a special person, Patty. You're an original. But you haven't got a lot longer to get your act together. You keep getting into shit like whatever that was tonight, and you're going to run yourself off the rails permanently.'

She thought about that. 'I know you look down on me.' I started to say something but she held up a wobbly hand. 'But you don't do it in a way that makes me feel like I'm worthless.'

'You're not worthless, Patty.'

'I feel that way sometimes.' Without looking at me, she said, 'What if Sydney doesn't come back?'

'I can't let myself think about that, Patty,' I said. 'Starting tomorrow, I'm going to spend all my time trying to find her.'

'What about your job?' she asked.

'I can always sell cars. I don't know how much time I have to find Syd.'

Patty reached down to the floor for one of the damp, bloody towels, and used it to dry her feet before she swung them out of the tub.

'You need to call your mom and let her know where you are, that you're OK.' I said.

A small smile crossed Patty's face. 'You think everybody's family is like yours.'

'What do you mean?'

'You think all families care.'

I didn't have anything to say to that.

'I know what it's like for Sydney,' Patty said. 'She acts like it's a big pain in the ass, you guys calling her when she's late, her checking in to let you know where she is, you looking out for her and all that shit. Sometimes, mostly when she's with me, she acts like that stuff embarrasses her, but I think she just acts that way because she doesn't want me to feel bad because nobody's waiting up for me, wondering where I am, dragging me out of dumbass parties like that one I went to tonight, because no one gives a shit, you know?'

'I'm sorry.'

'My dad, one time — this was before I was six and he took off? He almost killed me.'

Maybe, when you're already carrying a heavy burden, there's always room for a little more. 'What did he do?' I asked.

'It wasn't usually his thing to take me to daycare, right? But this one day, my mom, she had this really early morning meeting to go to, so my dad had to drop me off, only he forgot, you know? I guess I was three, and I'm in the back, and I guess I fell asleep, and instead of going to the daycare to drop me off he just kept driving to work, and it was really hot out.'

'Oh, no,' I said.

'So he went into work and it was like eighty degrees out but like a fucking million degrees in the car, and I guess when I woke up I was all dehydrated and shit, and my super-terrific dad didn't remember I was out there until about two hours later. So he runs out and gets me out and runs me into the building and I'm totally like almost passed out and he gets me some water and makes me drink it and this is the thing, right, the first thing he says to me, and I can still remember this, even though I was three years old, he says to me, 'Let's not tell your mother about this.''

I was slowly shaking my head.

'But she found out anyway, because just before my dad runs out, some lady saw me in the car and she wasn't strong enough to smash in the window so she'd called the fire department. So everybody found out, my mom too, and that was the beginning of the end of their so-called marriage.'

'That's an awful story,' I said.

'You know why I think he did it?' she asked.

I sighed. 'It happens,' I said. 'You just get into this kind of trance, you do the things you always do in the morning, and dropping you off was something different. He was on auto-pilot. I'm sure he never meant to do it.'

'OK, maybe he didn't mean to do it,' Patty said. 'I mean, it wasn't like he got up that morning and decided, hey, I think I'll kill my little girl today. I know he didn't actually do *that*. It was more like a subconscious thing. At this really dark level in his brain, he didn't care what happened to me, because the son of a bitch isn't even my real father.'

I didn't have it in me to take this child's pain away. Even if I'd had the energy to want to deal with it, she'd never be able to unload all of it. Right now, I didn't want to know about her mother's extramarital affairs, or whether she was adopted, or any of that stuff. The simple truth was, if I let my head touch the bathmat, I'd fall asleep right here on the bathroom floor.

'Did you ever cheat on Mrs B?' she asked.

'That's kind of personal,' I said.

Her face cracked. 'So you *did*. I thought you were different. I thought you were like, all upstanding and shit like that.'

'The answer is no,' I said. 'I was always faithful to Mrs B — Susanne — while we were together.'

'You're shittin' me.'

'No,' I said. 'I am not *shittin'* you.'

I struggled to get up off the floor. 'Patty,' I said, 'I have to get some sleep. And you need to get to bed. Take Syd's room. In the morning I still want you to call your mother.'

'You hear my cell phone ringing?' she asked. 'You hear anybody wondering where I am?'

'No,' I said.

As I moved to leave the bathroom, Patty said

281

to me, 'I have this really great idea.'

I stopped. For a second, I wondered whether she'd suddenly had an insight into where I might find Syd.

'What's that?'

'Why don't I just live here? While you're out during the day finding Sydney, I can watch the place, make sure nobody breaks in again and fucks around with things, take phone calls, keep an eye on the website, have something ready for you to eat when you get home.'

Her eyes had brightened. She had a hopeful smile on her face.

'I can't do that, Patty,' I said. 'It's a kind offer, but I have to say no. It wouldn't be right.'

'What's the big deal? You afraid people'll think if I'm living here you're doing me?'

As much as I liked Patty, she was wearing me out. I'd done all I could for her tonight.

'I've already got one daughter to worry about,' I said. 'I don't need two.'

She held my gaze for several seconds. The words seemed to have opened a new wound in her, bigger than the one in her knee.

'OK, then,' she said frostily. She grabbed her shoes and brushed past me on her way to Sydney's bedroom. 'I didn't mean like it had to be for ever.'

'Patty,' I said to her, firmly but not unkindly, 'in the morning, I'm happy to give you a lift wherever you need it, but you have to leave.'

And she did. Before I got up.

26

I slept till half past seven. Before heading into the ensuite off my bedroom, I went down the hall and looked in Sydney's bedroom. The door was wide open. The bed was empty, and made. I wasn't even sure Patty had slept there.

After telling her she'd have to leave in the morning, I'd gone into my own bedroom and closed the door. I'd fallen asleep almost instantly. It was possible, I now realized, that she had left then.

I went down to the kitchen to look for any signs of her, but there was none. The only glass in the sink was the one I had used to take some Tylenols the night before.

'OK then,' I said quietly to myself. I went to the front door, found it unlocked. Patty would have had to unlock it to leave, and without a key, had no way to send the bolt home when she stepped outside.

Before hitting the shower I checked the computer to see whether anyone had tried to get in touch with me about Syd. And of course, every time I sat down to the computer what I was most hoping to find was a note from Syd herself.

This morning, as was most often the case, there was nothing.

But the phone did ring just before eight.

'Hey,' Susanne said. 'I was just sitting here, wishing the phone would ring with good news.'

'I wish I had some,' I said. I filled her in on a couple of things. That I'd quit my job until I'd found Syd. That the blood on Syd's car belonged to Syd and some hood who had been found dead in Bridgeport. That someone who'd been involved in the break-in at my house had come by the dealership looking for Syd, and had tried to kill me.

'What?' Susanne said. 'And I'm hearing about all this *now*?'

I thought I had plenty of excuses. Exhausted. Traumatized. Overwhelmed. But I didn't think any of them would fly.

I said, 'I'm sorry. If I'd had good news, I'd have called.'

'This man who tried to kill you, who was looking for Syd,' Susanne said. 'Who was he? Are the police looking for him? If they question him won't they know why Syd's missing?'

'They're working on it,' I said. 'They have to find him first. He used a fake license when he took the car for a test drive.'

'Oh,' she said, the air coming out of her balloon.

'Any news on your front?' I asked.

Susanne seemed to be pulling herself together on the other end of the line. All my news, particularly the attempt on my life, had left her shell-shocked. Finally, 'Bob's going all Spanish Inquisition on Evan.'

'Good,' I said.

'He owes more money than he's saying. He managed to get a fake credit card from one of his friends, he won't say who, to play some of his gambling on the computer.'

'A fake card?'

'It's the data from someone else's card, but on a new card? He used it for a couple of days, until the person whose card it was found out about some fishy charges and cancelled it. Then Evan went back to using his. He even snuck Bob's card out of his wallet a couple of times and used that.'

'Maybe Bob will find out something that links Evan's problems to Sydney. Maybe he owes someone money and they told him they'd hurt her if he didn't pay up. I'm just grasping at straws here, Suze.'

'I know,' she said.

'About Bob,' I said.

'Yes?'

'Look,' I said, finding it difficult to come up with the words, 'tell him . . . tell him I'm sorry about how I handled things with Evan.'

'OK.'

'He has to know we've all been going through a lot.'

'Sure,' Susanne said.

'And I think . . . I think maybe he's good for you.'

'Pardon?'

'When you fell . . . there was something . . . I think he really loves you, Suze.'

Susanne didn't say anything. I had a feeling she was finding it hard to say anything for a moment.

'And another thing,' I said. 'I need to talk to Bob about a car.'

'What car?'

'Laura's taking mine. I need wheels.'

'You need a car, from Bob?' Susanne said. 'He's going to just love this.'

* * *

I replaced the receiver and was about to turn away from the phone when something from the night before came back to me. I dialed Kate Wood. I tried her cell, figuring she might already be on her way to work.

'Hello,' she said. It sounded as though she was driving. A radio broadcasting traffic reports in the background got turned down.

'Hey,' I said. 'It's Tim.'

'I know,' she said.

'You drove by last night.'

'Maybe.'

'I need to explain what you saw,' I said.

'I didn't see anything,' she said.

'That was Syd's friend Patty,' I said.

'I see,' Kate said. 'So you've decided you like them a lot younger.'

'She was hurt,' I said, recalling that Patty, limping because of her injured knee, had her arm around me for support as I took her into the house. 'She hurt herself at some party down on the beach that got a bit out of hand, called me and asked her to pick her up.'

'Of course she did,' Kate said.

'Anyway, I got her knee bandaged, and offered to let her stay in Syd's room, but I think she must have taken off right after I went to bed.'

286

'Kind of funny, don't you think?' Kate said.

'What? What's funny?'

'That you'd actually go to the trouble to call, after you told me it was over, and tell me this. You don't call me any other time, but this, this you want to phone me about.'

'Kate, I just thought you should know.'

'I'll just bet you do. You know, things are really starting to come together where you're concerned, Tim.'

'I don't know what you're talking about, Kate.'

'I'm not stupid, Tim. I can figure things out.'

'OK, Kate, whatever you say. I thought an explanation was in order, but clearly you've got some other scenario going on in your head and I don't imagine there's much I can do to change it, so you have a great day.'

I hung up.

I put on a pot of coffee and made myself a fried egg sandwich, leaving the yolk runny. I was scanning the headlines of the *New Haven Register* that had been tossed onto the front step that morning when the doorbell rang. I set down the paper and went to the front door, still in my bare feet, and opened it cautiously.

It was Arnie Chilton. When he saw my nose he did a double-take.

'What happened to you?'

'And good morning to you, too,' I said.

'Seriously, what happened? Did Bob do that? I know he thinks you're a dick.'

'No,' I said. 'I had a run-in with someone else.'

'Oh,' he said, then, as if remembering why he'd come knocking in the first place, said,

'Bob's right, you know. You really are a dick.'

'And here I thought you weren't good at finding things out,' I said.

'That was a shitty thing to do, making me do a coffee and donut run,' he said. He didn't look angry so much as hurt. I actually felt a twinge of guilt.

'Sorry,' I said. 'I think I was trying to stick it to Bob more than you.'

'You used me as an instrument of ridicule,' he said.

I stared at him with some wonder. 'Yeah, I guess that's what I did,' I said. I opened the door a bit wider. 'You want some coffee?'

'OK,' he said, and followed me into the kitchen.

Arnie took it black. I poured him a cup and set it on the kitchen table. I sat back down and took another bite of my sandwich.

'You eaten?' I asked.

'Yeah,' he said, blowing on the coffee. 'You think that just because I was a security guard, I'm an idiot.'

'No,' I said. 'Just underqualified.' He looked up from his coffee. 'No offense.'

Arnie looked like he wanted to say something, but wasn't sure what, so he went back to his coffee.

'You just come by to tell me I'm a dick?' I asked.

'That was just the first item on the list,' he said. 'But I also want to ask you some questions.'

'So you're actually still on this,' I said.

'I'm going to stay on this until I work off what

I owe Bob,' he said.

'He hasn't called you off?' I'd wondered if Bob might have fired Arnie as a way of sticking it to me. But, assuming Arnie had even a remote chance of finding anything out about Syd, that would be punishing Susanne, too. And I didn't think, anymore, that Bob had that in him.

'No,' he said, surprised. 'I'm an honorable person, you know. Someone asks me to do something, I do it.'

I popped the last of the egg sandwich into my mouth. 'OK.'

'So you know Sydney had this boyfriend? This kid named Jeff Bluestein?'

'I know. He dropped by yesterday.'

'What do you know about him?'

'About Jeff?'

'Yeah.'

I shrugged. 'Not that much. Knows computers, helped me set up the website. Kind of quiet. Has a bit of a confidence problem.'

'You know he got in some shit, right?'

Suddenly, he had my attention. 'What sort of shit?'

Arnie Chilton looked pleased with himself. 'Jeff had this part-time job over in Bridgeport waiting tables at Dalrymple's.' It was a moderately priced family restaurant, like an Applebee's. 'So they caught him doing this thing with customer credit cards. They'd give him their card, and before he swiped it through the restaurant's cash register, he ran it through this thing called a wedge.'

'A wedge?' I said.

'Small thing, not much bigger than a pack of smokes. You swipe a card through it and it stores all the data.'

'OK,' I said.

'Later, you download all the data out of the wedge and transfer it to the magnetic strips of new, fake cards.'

'Son of a bitch,' I said, thinking back to a conversation I'd had only moments earlier.

'So, anyway, this Jeff character, he was doing this, the manager spotted him, fired him on the spot.'

'When was this?'

'Shit, months ago,' Arnie said. 'Might have been last summer.'

'And he wasn't charged?'

'The manager was going to charge him, but first he thought, he didn't need the bad publicity, right? People find out your place has been ripping off customers' credit card data, they stay away. Plus, Jeff, he was just a kid, right, and then his dad — who works at one of the radio stations Dalrymple's buys time on — he came to see the manager and said his son was never going to do anything like this again, that he was going to scare the living shit out of him, and that if the restaurant pressed charges it could ruin the kid for life, that whole song and dance thing, you know? Plus, he'd see that the restaurant got a whole bunch of free spots during the drive-home show.'

'Arnie,' I said, 'how did you track this down?'

He looked a bit sheepish. 'The manager at the Dalrymple's is my brother.'

'You're kidding me.' I had to laugh.

'I'm kind of in debt to him, too. I'm over there a lot, doing cleanup. He used to have lots of other people working there for next to nothing, but not any more. I do it in between my private eye jobs.' He grinned.

'Of which this is your first,' I said.

He nodded. 'The thing is, I was over there talking to him, telling him about Bob asking me to try to find your daughter, and I happened to mention she'd had a boyfriend named Jeff, and he goes, we used to have a Jeff kid working here, what was his name, and I tell him, and he goes, no shit?'

'Small world,' I said.

'Pretty sure it was the same guy.'

'You mentioned this to Bob and Susanne yet?' I asked.

'Uh-uh. I was going to report back to them later today or tomorrow. Thing is, I'm going to go home and get some sleep. I was up late last night, having drinks with my brother.'

'You talked to Jeff about this?'

He shook his head. 'Not yet.'

'You mind if I do that?' I asked.

'Sounds good to me. Thing is, that's kind of why I thought I'd mention it to you. These young kids, they kind of scare me. Some of them can really get in your face, and I'm not really good at dealing with that.'

Jeff, while a big boy, didn't strike me as much of a potential threat, even to Arnie. 'I get what you're saying,' I said.

'You think this might have anything to do with

291

what happened to your daughter?' Arnie asked.

'I don't know,' I said.

'My brother, he's had to deal with a lot of crap in the restaurant business, let me tell ya. After he told me about this Jeff kid, he started getting into all the problems he has getting help. You know all the talk, these last few years, about immigration and all these illegals working in the country?'

'I watch Lou Dobbs occasionally,' I said.

'OK, so some people, they've been saying, what they should have is a law that if you hire someone you know is an illegal, then they can charge you, or shut your business down, you've heard about this?'

'Sure.' I thought of something Kip Jennings had said about Randall Tripe. That he'd been involved in, among other things, trafficking in illegals. 'You ever hear of a guy named Tripe? Randall Tripe?'

'Huh?'

'Never mind, go on with your story.'

'So my brother figures, he doesn't need that kind of shit, right? He wants to run a place on the up and up. But there was a time he'd hire people like that, no papers, no background check. To wash dishes, clear tables, that kind of thing. I tell ya, I wouldn't want to work in the restaurant business for anything.'

Arnie seemed to have wound down.

'I'm sorry about the thing with the donuts,' I said. Arnie shrugged, like it was nothing. 'Can I ask you one last thing?'

'I guess,' he said.

'If Bob's the one who hired you, why you

coming to me with this?'

Arnie shrugged. 'The thing about Bob is, he thinks owning a bunch of used car lots is on the same level as being the Pope or something. As big an asshole as you are, sometimes I think Bob's an even bigger one.'

★ ★ ★

Sydney, sixteen. Only a few months ago.

She's passed all her driving tests and now wants to take out the car solo. She has more opportunities at her mother's house than at mine. Susanne works conventional hours compared to me, so there's a car available more often for Syd to practice with in the evenings. When Syd's staying with me, and there actually happens to be an evening when I'm home and the car's in the driveway, I'm more hesitant about letting her take it out. I attribute this to the fact that I haven't had as much chance to get comfortable with the idea of her being out there on the road, alone.

This is before she gets her summer job at the dealership, where she shows herself to be quite adept at getting into a strange car and whipping it around the lot, driving it into the service bay, lining it up over the hoist.

I'm driving a Civic this particular week. Sydney says she wants to drive it to her mother's house to pick up some homework she's left there, and drive back. On her own.

'Come on,' she says.

I give in.

About an hour later, there's a knock at the door. I find Patty standing there, smiling nervously. She and Syd have been friends a couple of months now.

I open the door.

'Can I come in?' she asks.

'Syd's not home,' I tell her. 'She drove over to her mom's to pick something up.'

'Can I still come in?'

I let her in.

'OK, the first thing you have to know,' Patty says, holding her hands in front of her as though she were patting down a cloud, 'is that Sydney's OK.'

I feel the trap door opening beneath me. 'Go on.'

'She's fine. But this thing happened, and you need to know that it wasn't her fault at all.'

'What's happened, Patty?'

'On the way back from her mom's, Sydney picked me up and we decided to go to Carvel for some ice cream?' It's just down the hill from us. Patty must have walked up here from there. 'So, she's parked, and she's not even in the car, and this guy, this total asshole, he's driving some beatup old shitbox, and he's backing up, and he goes right into the car door.'

'You weren't in the car? You and Syd?'

'Like I said, we saw the whole thing happen while we were getting our ice cream. And then the guy, he just takes off before we can get down a license plate or anything. But it was totally not Sydney's fault.'

I started going for my coat.

'You're not going to be mad at her, are you?' Patty asked.

'I just want to be sure she's OK.'

'She's cool. Mostly, she's worried about you. That you're going to freak out.'

Later, I say to Syd, 'Is that what you thought I was going to do? Freak out?'

'I don't know,' she says.

'Why'd you send Patty?'

'Well, she offered, first of all. And I kind of thought, OK, because, ever since you and Mom got divorced, well, even before you got divorced, every time there's anything about money, it's like, watch out, it's freak-out time.'

'Syd — '

'And a dented door, that's going to be a fortune, right? And you're not going to want to put it through insurance because they'll put your rates up, and like I'd pay for it but I don't have any money anyway, and you'll ask Mom for half but she'll say it's your car, you let me drive it, you should pay for it all, and you'll get all pissed, and it'll be like it was when you had the dealership and everything was going wrong and every night you and Mom were fighting and she said this was all supposed to give me a better life and it was like if it wasn't for me you wouldn't be fighting all the time and — '

The next day I ask Susanne to meet me for lunch.

'Truce,' I say.

'OK,' she says. And, it turns out, she means it.

295

27

After Arnie left, I called the cell number I had for Patty. First, I wanted to be sure she was OK, that she'd safely gotten home — or someplace — after she'd left my place. She wasn't answering. Probably saw my number and figured, drop dead, dickwad. I knew I'd been firm with her the night before, but there were probably others who'd accuse me of not being firm enough. Drinking underage, staying up late, not phoning home, there was plenty of material there for a lecture.

I didn't feel that was my role. I'd felt an obligation to make sure Patty was OK, but it wasn't up to me, certainly not at the moment, to turn her life around.

I had two numbers for Jeff. Home and cell. I called his home.

A woman answered. 'Hello?'

'Mrs Bluestein?' I asked.

'Yes?'

'Tim Blake here.'

'Oh my, hello.'

I'd found that people who might normally ask how you were didn't where I was concerned. I asked, 'Is Jeff there?'

'Not at the moment. Is this about the website?'

'I had a couple of questions for him, technical stuff I really don't understand.'

'Oh, I don't get any of it, either. He's always doing something on the computers and I haven't the foggiest notion what it is.'

'I've got his cell number. I'll try that.' I hung up, dialed again.

'Yeah?'

'Jeff, it's Mr Blake.'

'Yeah?'

'We need to talk.'

'Yeah? I mean, yeah, sure, I guess. What's up? Has the site gone down or something?'

'Nothing like that. I just wanted to talk to you about a couple of other things.'

'Sure.'

'What are you doing?'

'Huh?'

'Right now. What are you doing?'

'I'm on the train. Some friends and I decided to go into the city for the day.' By city, I guessed he meant Manhattan.

'You're going into New York?'

'Yeah. Just something to do.'

'When are you coming back?'

'Tonight, I guess,' he said. 'We're going down to SoHo to the Kid Robot store.' I had no idea what that was.

What I wanted to talk to him about I didn't want to do over the phone. I didn't know that his Dalrymple's misadventure had anything to do with Syd, but I wanted to talk to him face to face when we went over this. Whatever intimidation skills I possessed might not work that well over the phone.

'OK, we'll talk tomorrow,' I said. 'For sure.'

'For sure,' Jeff said, but he didn't sound at all excited.

* * *

'*You* want to buy a car from *me*,' Bob Janigan said that afternoon.

'Consider it my way of making amends,' I said.

The two of us were standing on the lot, pennants flapping overhead.

'It's not true, by the way,' I said.

'What? You don't want to buy a car?'

'I'm not trying to drive a wedge between you and Susanne,' I said. 'I still care about her. I still love her, but not . . . the same way. But it's not my intention to come between the two of you.'

'I'll think you're full of shit,' Bob said.

I nodded, gave that a moment, then said, 'So what do you have?'

He pointed to a faded blue Volkswagen New Beetle, about ten years old, one of the first of the retro-designed models off the line. 'What about that?'

'You're joking,' I said.

'No, I'm not joking. It's got relatively low miles, it's priced fairly, and it's pretty good on gas.'

'It's a birthday car, isn't it?' I asked.

Bob pretended not to know what I meant by that. It was what people in the business called a car that had been sitting on the lot so long it had been through an entire calendar year. 'A birthday car?' he said.

'Come on, Bob,' I said. 'I've noticed this car

sitting here for months. You can't unload it. There's a puddle of oil under it, and the two front tires are bald.'

'It's got tinted windows,' he said. 'And there's a six-pack CD player in the trunk.' He handed me a thick remote key. 'Go ahead, start it up.'

I got in, turned the ignition, flipped the lights on, then left the car running while I walked around it.

'Headlight's out,' I said. 'And you hear that knocking sound?'

'It just has to warm up.'

'And you're expecting to get forty-five hundred for it?' I asked.

'It's a good deal,' he insisted. 'Best deal on the lot.' He added, 'Your price range.'

'I'll give you thirty-eight, you put some decent tires on the front, replace the headlight, find what's leaking underneath, we got a deal.'

Bob let out a long breath of exasperation. 'Bite me, Tim.'

'You should say that on your commercials,' I suggested.

I went back, killed the engine, then pulled up the lever that released the seatback to allow access to the minuscule rear seat. It snapped off in my hand. I held it up for Bob.

'Thirty-nine hundred,' he said.

'You replace the headlight, the bald tires,' I said, tossing the lever onto the floor of the back seat.

'Deal,' he said. 'Anything to get this thing off the lot.'

I went into the office, where Susanne was

engaged in paperwork. She looked up, couldn't take her eyes off my nose.

'Bob thinks he sold you the Beetle?' she asked.

'Yeah. I had to bargain hard to make him think I wasn't getting the car for free.'

'I'll just hold onto the check,' she said. 'He won't notice for weeks that it hasn't been deposited. And by then, maybe you won't need it, you'll be back at the dealership, and you can return it.'

'I'll pay you for the tires and the new headlight,' I said. 'I don't want you out of pocket.'

'I'll let you know how much,' she said.

'You're OK, Suze,' I said.

'Go find our girl,' she said.

★ ★ ★

When I stepped out of the office I spotted a dark blue sedan pulling in off the street. There was one man behind the wheel, another riding shotgun. The car lurched to a stop and the two doors opened simultaneously. As they got out, the passenger pointed toward the far end of the lot, where Evan was once again washing cars.

The men who got out of the car were young, a year or two older than Evan. They began walking in Evan's direction.

As soon he spotted them, he put down the wand he'd been using, and stood there, frozen. I could tell he was wondering whether to run, calculating the odds that he could get away from these two.

I poked my head back into the office and said to Susanne, 'Find Bob.'

I went down the steps and started walking after the two men. They weren't running, but their walk was purposeful and full of menace. Evan seemed to grow smaller the closer they got.

They penned him in between a Land Rover and a Chrysler 300 that were backed up to a chain-link fence. 'Hey Evan,' said the one in the lead.

'Hey,' he said. 'I tried to give you guys a call.'

'No shit? I didn't get a call.' He turned to the second guy. 'Did you get a call?'

'Nope,' said the other one.

'It beats the shit out of me that anyone still uses that excuse,' the first guy said. 'My phone here, it lets you leave messages? You heard of that? And it even tells me who's called. And guess what, fucknuts? You didn't call me.'

'I was going to,' Evan said.

'Maybe we should just take your phone and shove it up your ass.'

'What's going on here?' I said, coming up behind the two men.

They both turned.

'The fuck are you?' the second one said.

'Is there some kind of problem?'

'Just a private business matter,' said the lead guy. He and his friend both crossed their arms menacingly.

'Evan?' I said.

For maybe the first time, he seemed pleased to see me. 'Hey, Mr Blake,' he said.

'What's going on?' I asked him.

'It's no big deal,' he said.

To the lead guy, I said, 'How much does he owe you?'

He cocked his head to one side, seemingly impressed that I had caught the essence of the situation.

'Five hundred,' he said.

I got out my wallet. 'I've got a hundred and sixty dollars I can give you right now. You come here tomorrow at the same time he'll have the rest.' I looked past them to Evan. 'Right?'

'That's right,' he nodded.

I fished out the bills and the young man snatched them from me. 'He better fucking have the rest tomorrow.'

He and his buddy brushed past me and went back to their car as Bob ran up, breathless.

I said to Evan, 'Gambling?'

Sheepishly, he shook his head. 'I've owed them for some weed for about three weeks now.'

Bob said, 'What? Who were those guys?'

I said to him, 'Let me know when the Beetle's ready.'

★ ★ ★

I spun my wheels, literally and figuratively, for the rest of the afternoon.

I drove around Milford. I drove around Bridgeport. I drove up to Derby. I went into youth shelters, fast food joints, corner stores, showing Syd's picture to anyone who'd look at it.

Struck out everywhere.

Heading home, I popped into a ShopRite for an already roasted chicken and a small tub of potato salad and took it home. I stood at the kitchen counter, broke off parts of the chicken with my hand and put them into my mouth, ate the potato salad right out of the container. At least, for that, I used a fork. It occurred to me, once I'd nearly finished off the entire chicken, that my caveman-like behavior was related to skipping lunch.

There'd been no calls waiting for me when I got home, and there were no emails of note coming in from Syd's website.

I went to the phone and dialed Patty's cell. I hadn't spoken to her since rescuing her from that street party and bringing her back here to bandage her knee.

Was that only last night?

Patty's cell rang until it went to message. I was about to leave one, then decided against it.

After cleaning up the kitchen, I dropped onto the couch and turned on the news. I didn't even last until the weather teaser. I passed out.

It was dark when I woke. I turned off the TV and went up the stairs to my bedroom. My bag, the one that had been to Seattle and the Just Inn Time and finally back home again, was resting on a chair. I'd never completely unpacked it.

Something twigged, and I looked into the bag.

'Where the . . .'

I dumped everything left in the bag — a couple of pairs of socks, some underwear, a pullover shirt — onto the bed.

'Son of a bitch,' I said.

303

I left my room and went into Syd's, thinking maybe I'd already found what I was now looking for, had put it back in its place, but forgotten.

I gave Syd's room a quick look, came up empty.

'Where the hell are you, Milt?' I said aloud.

I grabbed my keys, went outside and unlocked my car. I looked in the trunk, the back seat, under the seats, but Sydney's favorite stuffed moose was nowhere to be found.

'The hotel,' I said to myself.

I had placed it on the bed when I'd spent my night at the Just Inn Time. Then, when I'd grabbed a pillow to rest my head on the window, Milt had taken a tumble.

I didn't have the energy to go over there now, but made a mental note to pop in the next time I was driving by.

I went back inside, and up to my room. It made sense to go to bed, but I felt so overwhelmingly frustrated. Sure it was late, but I should be doing something. Making calls, going to more shelters, driving to —

A noise.

I heard something outside. A thump, a bump, something.

Maybe it was just a car door opening and closing.

But if I could hear it, it probably wasn't one of the neighbors. It had to be someone in my driveway, or out front of my house.

I went down the stairs, trying not to make any sounds of my own, and was getting read to peek out the front window when the doorbell rang.

My heart jumped.

I went to the door, peered through the window at the side. A man was standing there, holding something boxy — about the size of a car battery — in his right hand. I threw the deadbolt, opened the door.

'Mr Blake,' the man said.

'Mr Fletcher,' I said.

'You remembered,' he said.

'I never forget someone who uses a test drive to deliver manure.'

'Yeah,' Richard Fletcher said, and extended the arm that was holding the package. I could see now that it was a six-pack of Coors, in cans.

I accepted the package. The cans were warm to the touch, and he said, 'First time I came by, I'd just come from the store, and they were cold. But they've warmed up since then.'

'You've been by before?' I said.

'A couple of times, earlier in the day,' he said. 'I figured out your address from the card you gave me. Matched the home number to an address in the phone book.'

'You might as well come in,' I said, and opened the door wider.

I led him into the kitchen, motioned for him to take a seat, and took out two cans. I tossed him one, cracked the tab on mine and sat down opposite him.

We both took a sip of beer.

'It would have been better cold,' he said.

'Yeah, well,' I said.

He nodded. Finally, he said, 'I'm not really in the market for a new truck.'

'I figured.'

'I promised a guy I'd deliver him some manure, but then my truck wouldn't work. He was promising me forty dollars.'

'Sure,' I said, taking another sip of the Coors.

'I didn't have money to rent a truck,' Fletcher said. 'And there wasn't anybody I could borrow one off of.'

'Sure,' I said.

'So,' Fletcher said, 'that's why I did it.'

I nodded.

'Next time,' he said, 'I could try the Toyota dealer.'

I smiled. 'I'd be grateful.'

He returned the smile. 'So, that's what I came by to say.' He struggled a moment. 'Sorry,' he said. 'I never meant any harm.'

I took another sip of the warm beer. 'What's your daughter's name?' I asked.

'Sofia,' he said.

'That's a pretty name,' I said.

We each took another sip of our beers.

'I should be going,' he said. He looked down at the can. 'I don't think I can finish this. I used to be able to sit down and drink half a dozen of these, but now it's all I can do to finish one.'

I got up and walked with him to the door, followed him outside to the driveway. We stopped briefly behind the CR-V. I stuck out my hand, and he took it. We shook.

'When I win the lottery I'll buy a car off ya,' he said.

'Sounds fair,' I said.

As I turned to go back into the house, there

was a distant squeal of tires, the gunning of a car engine.

The sound got louder. Someone was coming up the street very, very fast.

Just as I turned to look, there was a popping noise. Before Fletcher came at me, I caught a glimpse of a van barreling up the street.

As Fletcher took hold of me around the waist and pulled me down onto the cool grass, I heard more pops, then glass shattering.

'Head down!' Fletcher barked into my ear.

I managed to turn my head toward the street, caught another glimpse of the van as it sped off.

Once the van was gone, Fletcher got off me. I stood up, saw that the back window of my car had been shot out.

'I'd been thinking maybe the beer wasn't enough,' he said, 'but now I definitely think we're even.'

28

I ran into the house to call the police. When I came back out, Richard Fletcher was down at the bottom of the driveway, only a few feet away from his yellow Pinto. I had to run to catch up to him before he turned the key.

'Where are you going?' I asked as he rolled down the window.

'Home,' he said.

'The police are on their way,' I said. 'They'll want to talk to you. You're a witness.'

'I didn't see nothin',' he said. 'I've got enough problems getting by and raising my girl without getting dragged into whatever mess you're in. If you tell the police I was here I'll deny it.'

He turned the key. The engine wheezed three times before it turned over. He gave me a final nod, and drove off down Hill Street, the Pinto sputtering and gasping.

★   ★   ★

It wasn't long before the street looked like a cop convention. At least a dozen cars out front of the house, rotating roof lights casting a strobing red glow on the houses and trees. Further up the street, a news crew van. Neighbors were milling about, talking in hushed tones to one another, trying to figure out what had happened while the police strung yellow tape around the scene.

They were roaming all over the inside of the house, too. They should know their way by now.

Standing out front of the house with me, Kip Jennings said, 'So you're standing out here talking to who again?'

'Richard Fletcher,' I said. 'He lives on Coulter.'

'And where's he?'

'He went home.'

'This guy saves you from someone doing a drive-by, and then he just goes home.'

'Yeah,' I said.

'What was he doing here in the first place?'

'He dropped by with a peace offering,' I said. 'He took a pickup out on a test drive, used it to deliver manure. I called him on it, and he came by tonight with a six-pack of Coors. The drive-by happened as he was leaving.'

'He set you up?' she asked.

I shook my head. 'I don't think so. He saved me. If he hadn't tackled me I'd be dead now.' I paused. 'He said if you go see him he's going to deny being here. He doesn't need the hassle.'

'Really,' she said. She decided to tack in a different direction. 'You said you saw the car?'

'Speeding off, yeah. A van. I just caught a glimpse of it. It might have been the same van that was parked across from the dealership, the one that belonged to the guy who wanted to kill me.'

'Maybe he's going to keep doing this until he gets it right,' Jennings said.

A uniformed cop came out of the house and said to Jennings, 'There's something upstairs you should see.'

Jennings looked at me, like I should know what the officer was talking about. I shrugged. I followed her, and the uniform, into the house and up the stairs. The cop stopped outside the bathroom door in the upstairs hallway and pointed inside.

'We found those,' he said.

He was pointing to some bloodied towels, wadded up and tossed onto the floor beyond the toilet.

Jennings looked at me. 'That your blood?'

'No,' I said. 'But — '

'We're going to have to get that bagged,' Jennings said to the cop. 'Forensics here yet?'

'Just arriving,' the cop said.

Jennings said to me, 'I thought you said no one got hit.'

'I can explain those,' I said. 'You don't have to do anything. I mean, forensics-wise.'

'Come with me,' Jennings said, heading back downstairs and into the kitchen, where there was less traffic. 'Explain.'

'You know Sydney's friend, Patty Swain?'

Jennings, who had what I would call a poker face most of the time, did something with her eyes. They seemed to pop for a hundredth of a second.

'Yes,' she said.

'She called me late last night. She was at a party down on the beach strip. She'd had a lot to drink and she'd hurt herself.'

'Go on.'

'She asked me to come and get her. When the phone rang, and I picked up, I thought it was

310

Syd calling for a second. They almost sound the same on the phone.'

'And why did she call you?'

'I guess she felt she didn't have anyone else.'

'Why's that?'

'Her father left years ago, and she says her mother's a bit of a — this isn't me saying this, this is Patty, and Syd's made comments in the past — she says her mother's a bit of a drunk. Said even if she called home, her mother wouldn't have been able to come and get her.'

'So you went,' Jennings said.

I sighed. 'Yeah. I was pretty exhausted, but it's not like she was calling from far away. So I drove down, found her, and brought her back here. It was pretty ugly down there, guys getting a bit aggressive, you know? I offered to drive her back to her own place, but there was no way she'd let me take her there. Her knee was cut up pretty bad.'

'What happened?'

'She fell on some broken glass.'

'And you patched her up?'

'I brought her into the house, got her cleaned up in the bathroom up there. I blotted up some of the blood with the towels, tossed them in the corner, forgot all about them when I headed out this morning.'

Jennings was wearing a very serious expression.

'What?' I asked. 'It's not a big deal. I mean, set your forensics people loose on the towels if you want, but that's all it was.'

'What happened after you took care of her knee?'

311

'OK, well, I bandaged it up, and then I offered again to take her home, but she didn't want to leave, so I said she could sleep in Sydney's room for the night.'

'Really,' Jennings said.

'Maybe that was stupid,' I said. 'But she said that if I drove her home, she'd just run off someplace, and the idea of a teenage girl, who'd been drinking, wandering around town on her own in the middle of the night, that didn't seem like a good idea to me.'

'Of course not.'

'The fact is, I don't know whether she stayed here for the night or not,' I said. 'I went straight to bed and when I got up in the morning she was already gone and the bed didn't even look as though it had been slept in. She'd let herself out, the front door was unlocked.'

'What time did you get up?'

'About seven-thirty,' I said.

'Did she talk to you about anything?'

'What do you mean?'

'Just, anything.'

I shrugged. 'A bit about her father. She doesn't much care for him, but it sounds like she hasn't seen much of him for years. Her mother, the drinking. She offered to stay here, look after the house, until Syd comes back.'

'Did that seem odd to you?' Jennings said.

'I don't know. Maybe. It's like she wants to live here instead of her own house. She's spent a lot of time here since she and Sydney became friends. I told Patty that wouldn't work. And I told her she had to be gone first thing in the

312

morning, so maybe I pissed her off and she left right after I went to bed.'

'Is there anyone who can back this story up for you?' Detective Jennings asked.

'Why's that necessary?'

'I'm just asking.'

Kate Wood. She could back up the first part of my story. She saw me going into the house with Patty. But was Kate someone I wanted to put the police onto? Would talking to her make things any better?

'Look, there is someone,' I said hesitantly. 'But I have to tell you, she's a bit, you know, she's a bit of a flake.'

'Is that so?' Jennings said.

'A woman I used to see, her name's Kate Wood. She drove by here when I was bringing Patty into the house. And I talked to her later, explained what was going on.'

'Why did you feel the need to do that?' Jennings asked.

Because it looked bad.

'Just, I don't know, I thought she might have gotten the wrong idea,' I said. 'Kate probably wanted to drop by, have a talk — '

'Why would she do that? Didn't you say you used to be seeing her?'

'Yes,' I said. 'That's true. But I guess, I don't know, I guess she thought there were still issues to resolve.'

Jennings said, 'Is there anything else you want to tell me? Anything you want to get off your chest?'

'What? No. I mean, yes, there are things I

313

want to talk about. I want to know what you're doing to find Sydney. You're always asking me questions, but you never have any news for me.' Other than Sydney's blood being on the car, of course. 'I've been driving all over the place today, showing Syd's picture to hundreds of people. How many people have you shown her picture to today?'

Jennings held my gaze momentarily, then said, 'We'll talk more in a minute.'

She was taking out her cell phone as she left the kitchen. By the time she was talking to whoever she wanted to talk to, she was outside, where I couldn't hear her.

I leaned up against the fridge, tried to get my head around what had happened here in the last hour.

Sydney was still out there.

People who wanted to know where she was were trying to kill me.

Just call me, Syd. Tell me where you are. Tell me what's going on.

Jennings returned a moment later, pocketing her phone. 'I'd like to go over this again. When you picked Patty up, when you brought her home.'

'Why's this a big deal?'

'She's missing,' Kip Jennings said.

29

This much Kip Jennings told me:

Patty had a part-time job in that accessories store in the Connecticut Post Mall, two or three shifts a week. She was due in at ten that morning, and no one thought much about it when she hadn't shown up by ten-thirty. Patty had a somewhat cavalier attitude about things like punching in on time.

But when it got to be eleven, they started to wonder whether she didn't realize she was scheduled to work, so they tried her cell. When they didn't get any answer there, they tried her home. No luck there, either.

One of the staff knew where Patty's mother, Carol Swain, worked, so a call was put in to her at a glass and mirror sales office on Bridgeport Avenue. She hadn't seen her daughter since the afternoon of the day before, and while it was not unusual for Patty to get home late, her mother was surprised not to find her home in the morning. And then for her not to show up for work — while she was often late, she'd eventually show up — that was definitely out of the ordinary.

When Carol Swain got home, and Patty was not there, she tried her daughter's cell herself. When that failed to raise her, she considered calling friends of her daughter's, then had to admit she didn't know very much about Patty's friends. Patty didn't tell her a damn thing about the kids she hung out with. Carol was telling all this to one of her friends, a woman she sometimes went drinking with after work, and the friend said, 'Carol? Has it occurred to you your daughter might actually be in some trouble?'

So around six o'clock, Patty's mother called the police. Almost apologetic about it. Probably nothing, she said. You know what girls are like today. But had there been, you know, any teenage girls who looked like her daughter run down at an intersection or anything?

The police said no. They asked Carol Swain if she wanted to file a missing person's report on her daughter.

She thought about that a moment, and said, 'Hell, I don't want to make a federal case out of this or anything.'

The police said, 'We can't do anything to help you find her if you're not going to report her missing.'

So Carol Swain said, 'Oh, why the hell not?'

Jennings told me all this, finishing up with, 'I just made a couple of calls in the last few minutes, and she hasn't turned up.'

'I tried to call her a couple of times today,' I said. 'She never answered.'

'At the moment,' Jennings said, 'it seems that you're the last person who's seen her.'

That seemed to be more than just an observation. 'What are you saying?'

'Mr Blake, you seem like a decent enough guy, so I'm just trying to be straight with you. We've

316

found bloody towels in your house that you say were used to help a girl who hasn't been seen in nearly twenty-four hours.'

'I've been totally straight with you,' I said.

'I hope so,' she said. 'Now we've got two missing girl cases, and you're at the center of both of them.'

★ ★ ★

In the morning, I phoned Susanne at work.

'Has Bob got that Beetle ready?' I asked.

'Yeah,' she said. 'New tires, new headlight.'

'Oil leak?'

'I'm not a miracle worker, Tim.'

'I need a lift.'

'You had to give the car back already?' she asked.

'It's gone,' I said. But it was the police who had it, not Laura Cantrell.

'I'm on it,' Susanne said.

I hoped she would come pick me up herself. I thought it was unlikely she'd send Bob.

I was surprised to see Evan drive down my street in the Beetle. There was an ominous rattling sound coming from under the hood. The short wheelbase allowed him to do a tight U-turn in the street, bringing the passenger door right to me.

I got in and he said, 'What's with the police tape around your house?'

I said, 'Are you going to be able to pay those guys when they come back for the rest of their money?'

317

'Yeah,' he said, glancing back at my house as we pulled away.

'From your dad?'

'Yeah.' He cleared his throat. 'Thanks for that yesterday.'

'I considered letting them have a go at you,' I said.

'Why?'

'Maybe you need to have the shit beat out of you. It might smarten you up.'

He kept his eyes on the road ahead. 'Maybe,' he said.

'You do drugs, you steal, you're addicted to online gambling,' I said. 'And you slept with my daughter.'

He shot me a look. 'Maybe she saw something in me that you don't.'

'She must have,' I said. I didn't know whether Evan was trying to be on his best behavior because he had me in the car, but he signaled all his turns, kept to the speed limit, and made no improper lane changes.

I said, 'Have you seen Syd's friend Patty in the last couple of days?'

'Huh?' he said. 'No. Why?'

I shook my head, not interested in answering his questions since I had more of my own. 'You used a fake credit card,' I said. 'To pay for some of your gambling.'

'Yeah.'

'How does that work? If you win, doesn't the money go back to the account of the guy whose card number you've ripped off?'

'I hadn't really thought it through. It's the

318

actual playing that matters, not whether there's money coming in.'

Once you put yourself in the head of a gambler, that actually made some sense. 'Where'd you get the card?'

'I don't want to get anyone in trouble,' he said.

'It was Jeff Bluestein, wasn't it?' I said.

Evan glanced over. 'How did you — ' And then he cut himself off.

'I didn't,' I said. 'Not until now.' I leaned back into my seat. 'He's my first visit today.'

Evan seemed to break out almost instantly into a sweat. 'Don't tell him I said anything.'

I said nothing for a moment. I was listening. Finally, I said, 'Does the engine sound funny to you?'

* * *

I slipped in behind the wheel of the Beetle after we pulled into Bob's Motors. Susanne, still on the cane, came out of the office as Evan slunk away.

'What'd you say to him?' she asked.

'Nothing,' I said. I told her, as I always did, that if I found out anything I'd be in touch. Even though, sometimes, there were things I chose not to tell her. Like what had happened last night at my home.

'What can I do?' she asked.

'Be here,' I said.

'What are you going to do?'

'Poke around,' I said.

As I'd told Evan moments earlier, I planned to

319

start with Jeff Bluestein. I knew where he lived. I'd dropped Sydney off there the odd time before either of them had drivers' licenses.

I parked the Beetle out front, strode up to the front door and leaned on the bell. Jeff's mother appeared at the door and smiled.

'Good morning,' she said. Her smile seemed forced, like she really didn't want to see me. I don't think she'd liked it, from the very beginning, that her son had been helping me. I was a man with problems, and nothing good could come from letting your son associate with a man like that.

'Hi,' I said.

'Jeff's still sleeping.'

'Wake him up, if you don't mind. He knows I wanted to see him this morning.'

Still standing in the doorway, Mrs Bluestein said, 'If this is just some technical questions about the website, can't it wait until later?'

'I'm afraid not,' I said.

'Just a moment,' she said, letting the storm door close. It was a one-storey house, and I watched her cross the living room, go down a hall, and tentatively enter a door on the right side. She was in there about half a minute, then came back.

'Just another half hour? He's very sleepy.'

I moved past her and went down the hall, Mrs Bluestein trailing after me, saying, 'Excuse me! Excuse me!'

I pushed open the boy's door, saw Jeff huddled under his covers, and said, making no effort to keep my voice down, 'Jeff.'

320

'Hmm?'

'Let's talk.'

He blinked his eyes several times, getting me in focus. 'It's really early,' he said, hunkering down.

'Throw some clothes on. We'll go get some breakfast.'

'Mr Blake!' his mother shouted. 'He was out late with his friends.'

I leaned in close to Jeff, putting my mouth to his ear, enduring his early morning breath. 'You get your ass out of bed and come talk to me or I'm going to ask you all about Dalrymple's in front of your mother.'

I didn't actually know whether she knew about what had happened with Jeff's restaurant job, but judging by how that made him jump under the covers, I was betting not.

'Mr Blake,' his mother persisted, 'please leave right now.'

I backed away from her son. He was already throwing off his covers. He said, 'It's OK, Mom. I just kind of forgot when we were supposed to meet.'

I flashed his mother a smile. 'See?' To Jeff I said, 'I'll be out front. Five minutes.'

'Yeah,' Jeff said.

Mrs Bluestein attempted to ask me if this was about something other than the website, but I deflected all her questions. I went out to the car, got in behind the wheel, and would have passed the time listening to the radio if the knob hadn't broken off in my hand.

Jeff came out in four minutes, walked across

the lawn, and got in next to me.

'What do you want?' I asked him.

'Huh?'

'For breakfast.'

'I'm not really hungry,' he said.

'McDonald's it is, then,' I said, and cranked the engine.

I drove us to the closest one, led the way inside, and ordered an Egg McMuffin with coffee and a hash brown. As we slipped into a booth sitting across from each other, I noticed Jeff eyeing my hash brown.

'You want that?' I asked.

'I don't know,' he said.

'Take it,' I told him, and he did.

'How did you hear about Dalrymple's?' he asked.

'That's not important right now,' I said. 'But I want you to tell me all about it.'

'Why?'

'Because I do,' I said.

'What's it to you?'

'I won't know that until you tell me,' I said. 'Maybe nothing, but maybe something.'

He took a bite of hash brown. 'It's got nothing to do with Sydney. I mean, that's why you're asking, right?'

'What did you do?' I asked.

'It was no big deal. Nobody really got ripped off. The credit card companies don't make people pay for stuff they don't buy.'

I wasn't up for giving a lecture in how theft drives up the price of everything, so I let it go.

'You'd been doing it for a while before the

322

manager caught you, is that right?'

'Not that long, but yeah, it was for a while.'

'If it had been somebody else who caught you, it'd be a different story now, wouldn't it? We might be holding phones and looking at each other through a pane of glass.'

Jeff looked mournful. 'I know it was a stupid thing to do. I did it to make some extra money.'

'Tell me what you did, exactly,' I said.

Jeff hung his head down, ashamed, but not so ashamed that he couldn't finish the last bite of my hash brown. I took a sip of coffee.

'I had this little thing, you could swipe Visa and Master Card and American Express cards through it, and it kept all the data, you know, like the numbers and all that stuff. It could hold the information from lots and lots of cards.'

'Who gave it to you? Who wanted you to do it?'

'I don't know.'

I put down my sandwich and leaned across the table, so close our heads were nearly touching. 'Jeff, I'm not fucking around here. I want answers.'

'You've never liked me, have you? Like, when Sydney and I were going out, you didn't like that.'

'Don't try that with me, Jeff. Maybe you know how to pull your mother's heart strings, make her feel guilty, but I don't care. Does she even know about any of this? Did your dad tell her?'

'How do you know my dad knows?'

'I'm guessing that means no. You want me to go back and tell her what you did?'

'No,' he whispered.

'The thing is, you're not the only one in trouble any more. Evan, for example?'

'What's going on with Evan?'

'His little online gambling problem? That's out in the open now. He's been stealing money to pay off his debts. And he used at least one fake credit card that he got from you.'

'Oh, man,' Jeff said. 'He wasn't supposed to tell anybody about that.'

'Did you give him money, too?'

'I loaned him some, the odd time. He's never paid me back.'

'There's a surprise.' I shook my head tiredly. 'Look, I'm not interested in getting you in any more trouble than you're already in.'

'You don't understand,' he said. 'I could get in a whole lot more trouble.'

'What do you mean?'

'The guy, the one who was paying me to rip off the credit cards in the first place, he was kind of creepy. Like, smarmy?'

'What was his name?'

'I don't remember,' Jeff said.

'How'd you get in touch with him?'

'He gave me a cell phone number.'

'What do you mean, the guy was smarmy?'

'Like, I just got this vibe off him, like if you crossed him you'd really pay for it.'

'He must have been pissed when you got caught.'

'I only heard from him once after that. He was pissed, but when he found out I wasn't being charged, and that my dad got the manager at

Dalrymple's to forget about it, I guess he thought it was better not to stir things up.'

'What about your dad? Didn't he want to find out who the guy was?'

'He was so mad, right? But he didn't want my mom to know, because she'd have totally freaked out about it, so he decided it was better to let it go.'

'So this guy,' I said. 'What'd he look like?'

Jeff shrugged. 'Just a guy, you know?'

It was like pulling teeth. 'Was he tall, thin, fat, black guy, white guy?'

'A white guy,' Jeff said, nodding, like that should do it.

'Fat?'

'No, he was in pretty good shape. And he had kind of light-colored hair, I guess. And he had pretty decent clothes. He smoked.'

'How old was he?'

'He was pretty old,' Jeff said.

'Like what, sixties, seventies?'

Jeff concentrated. 'No, I think thirties.'

'How much was he paying you?'

'Well, he gave me the thing, you know, the wedge he called it, and he said he'd give me fifty bucks for every card I swiped through it. But mostly he wanted them to be high-end cards, like gold cards and stuff like that. So in a single shift, I could make a thousand bucks. Dalrymple's, they were paying, like, just minimum wage, plus tips, but some nights they were good and some nights they weren't, although I always told my mom they were big so she wouldn't wonder why I had so much money.' He paused. 'While it lasted.'

It wasn't hard to understand the appeal for a young kid looking for some fast cash.

'But that last night, when Roy — '

'Roy?'

'Roy Chilton, the manager? When he saw me swiping the card an extra time through the wedge, he knew right away what it was and went all ballistic on me.'

'Why'd you do it, Jeff?' I asked. 'You're a good kid.'

He shrugged again. 'I wanted to get a laptop.'

I stared out the window for a moment, watched the traffic go past. I asked, 'Did Sydney know about this?'

'No way,' he said. 'I never told her anything about it. I kind of didn't want anyone to know. I told Sydney I got the job at Dalrymple's, but when I got fired right away I told her I dropped a family's entire order all over the floor and that was why they got rid of me. And I made Evan swear not to tell Sydney anything about the card I gave him.'

I could recall Syd mentioning something about Jeff losing his job, but never the reason why.

'You're not saying anything,' Jeff said. 'You pissed at me?'

I laid my hands flat on the tabletop and closed my eyes for a moment. When I opened them, Jeff was looking at me warily, wondering, I think, whether there was something wrong with me.

'You probably weren't the only kid this guy had doing this,' I said. 'That's a lot of fake cards, a lot of identities getting ripped off for a lot of money.'

'One time,' Jeff said, 'he made some mention, it was to get some people started, people who'd just come to the country, so they could get things and stuff.'

I thought about that a moment.

'You still have that cell number for this guy?'

Jeff shook his head.

'You sure you don't remember his name?'

Jeff struggled for a moment. 'Thing is, he told me his name once, but then when he answered his phone, he said, like, 'Gary here'.'

'But Gary wasn't the name he gave you before?'

'No, it was something else.' Jeff wrinkled his nose, like the answer was out there and all he had to do was sniff it out. 'It mighta been Eric.'

'Eric,' I repeated.

'I think that was it.'

'How'd you hook up with him the first time?'

'Someone told me that if I was looking for a way to make some extra money to give this guy a call. I thought, maybe I could do something different than the Dalrymple's thing, or work this other job on the side. Turned out the two of them went together.'

'Who?' I asked. 'Who told you this?'

'Please, Mr Blake, I don't want to get anyone else in trouble.'

Maybe, if he hadn't mentioned the name Eric, I'd still think it was possible Jeff's problems were in no way connected to Sydney. Now, I had the feeling there was a very strong link.

'Spill it, Jeff,' I said. 'Who tipped you to this guy?'

Jeff ran his index finger sideways under his nose, then said, 'You know him. He sells cars where you work? Andy?'

I blinked. 'Andy Hertz?'

'Yeah, that's him. But don't ever tell him I told you.'

I sat there, trying to put it together. Jeff looked at me and said, 'Hey Mr Blake, you seen Patty around lately?'

30

Driving Jeff back to his home in my Beetle, I said, 'How do you know Andy Hertz?'

'Last year, when Sydney was working at the dealership, she got to be friends with everybody,' Jeff said. 'Sometimes, when Syd and I and Patty and some of our other friends got together, Andy would hang out with us. He was older than everybody else, but he was kind of cool, and plus he could buy beer for us.'

'Isn't that great,' I said.

'Yeah,' Jeff said. 'He's a pretty good guy.'

'So, Andy just told all of you how to make a little extra money?'

'No,' Jeff said. 'Just me. I mean, the only one I know that he told was me. I got talking to him alone once about trying to find a job, and he said he had a number for a guy he'd run into a couple of times, that he could fix me up with something.'

'Really,' I said.

'Yeah.'

'Did you tell Andy what happened?'

'Like I said, I didn't want anybody to know, so no, I didn't tell him. My dad said I couldn't ever tell anybody. I never even told Andy I got in touch with the guy in the first place.'

I did my best to concentrate on the traffic ahead of me. I could feel the blood pulsing in my temples. I very much wanted to have a chat with Andy Hertz.

'You OK, Mr Blake?' Jeff asked.

'I'm fine,' I said.

'You're not going to mention to Andy that I told you this, are you?' he asked worriedly.

I glanced over and said nothing.

Despite his size, he seemed to sink in his chair. In the fishbowl-like interior of the Beetle, he still had plenty of headroom. Jeff was quiet for another moment, then said, 'I wonder if I did something to piss Patty off. She usually calls me back.'

★ ★ ★

I dropped Jeff off — his mother was standing at the door and had been there the whole time for all we knew — and as I was backing out of the driveway, intending to head straight over to Riverside Honda and have a few words with Andy Hertz, my cell went off.

'Hello?'

'Mr Blake? Detective Jennings. Where are you?'

'Driving to work.'

'I need you to come in to police headquarters.'

'Can it wait? I need to go to the dealership and talk to — '

'You need to come in now.'

Panic washed over me. 'What's happened? Is it Sydney? Have you found Sydney?'

'I'd just like you to come in,' she said.

I wanted to tell her I might have a lead on finding Eric, whose real name might be Gary, but decided to wait until I got to the station.

'I'll be there in a few minutes,' I said.

She met me at the door of the police building. 'I appreciate you coming right away,' she said.

'What's happened?' I asked. 'Have you found Syd?'

'Come with me,' Jennings said, and I followed her down a tiled hallway, around a corner, and into a simple, unadorned room with a table and chairs. 'Have a seat,' she directed me.

I took a seat.

She left the door open, and a couple of seconds later we were joined by a barrel-chested man in his fifties with a military-style brush cut.

'This is Detective Adam Marjorie,' Jennings said. He didn't look like the kind of guy who took much ribbing about his last name. 'He's . . . now involved in the investigation.' Her tone suggested he was higher up the departmental food chain, and was stepping in to show how things were done.

'What's this about?' I asked.

'Detective Marjorie and I would like to review the incidents of a couple nights ago,' she said.

Not last night, when someone took a shot at me?

'What do you want to know?' I asked.

'We want to ask you about Patty Swain,' Marjorie said. His voice was low and gravelly.

I was starting to get an inkling of what was going on here. I was in an interrogation room. This was going to be an interrogation. And this Marjorie character, he was going to be the bad cop.

'I told Detective Jennings everything I could,' I

said. Looking at her, I pleaded, 'Didn't I?'

If Marjorie was going to be the bad cop, surely it only followed what Jennings's role was supposed to be?

'Tell us again about the phone call you got from her,' she said.

I told my story again. Patty calling for a ride, how she'd hurt her knee falling on some cut glass. I also gave them some details about the boy who was bothering her, holding onto her arm. Jennings made a couple of notes about that, but Marjorie didn't appear to care.

'What sort of shape would you say she was in when you got her to your house?' he asked, moving around the side of the table, only a couple of feet from me.

'What do you mean?'

'Was she aware of what was going on? Was she lucid? Was she conscious?'

'Yes. Yes to all those things.'

'Are you sure?' he asked.

'Of course I'm sure. What the hell?' I looked back and forth between the two of them.

Jennings sat down across from me. 'Didn't you have to practically carry her into your house?' she asked.

'She was limping,' I said. 'Because of her knee.'

'So you were in physical contact with her,' she said.

'Huh? Yes, I had to be, to help her into the house, so she wouldn't fall over. She'd also been drinking.'

'Where'd she get the booze?' Detective Marjorie asked. 'You give it to her?'

332

'That's right,' I said. 'It's so hard for teenagers to get booze, they need me to buy it for them.'

'Don't get smart, asshole,' Detective Marjorie said.

I looked at Jennings, stupefied. 'Who is this guy?'

Marjorie didn't like that. He leaned in close enough that I could feel his hot breath on my face. 'I'm the guy who thinks it's odd that a man as old as you takes a young, drunk girl into his house late at night supposedly to help her out. What did you do with her when you got her inside?'

'I don't believe this,' I said. I turned again to Jennings, thinking naively that maybe I'd find an ally in her, but there was nothing in her expression to suggest she was on my side.

'I think you should answer the question,' Jennings said.

'She hardly needed me to get her booze,' I said. 'She'd been at a party down on the beach strip. She could have gotten it from anyone. In fact, by the time I got Patty to my place, she was sobering up. Still a bit drunk, but relatively coherent.'

'There was a fair bit of blood on those towels,' Marjorie said.

'Her knee was bleeding,' I said. 'Most of the cuts were fairly superficial, but one or two of them were deeper and they bled quite a bit. Come on, what are you suggesting? That I did something to Patty, and then left bloody towels on the bathroom floor where you could just walk in and find them?'

333

Jennings leaned back in her chair and folded her arms. 'We spoke to Ms Wood.'

'OK,' I said.

'She said you called her the next morning about what she saw.'

'She drove past the house when Patty and I were going inside. I think she might have been intending to stop, but when she saw I wasn't alone, she drove on. So the next day, I gave her a call.'

'Why?' Jennings asked. 'You're not still seeing Ms Wood, are you?'

'No, I'm not.'

'So why would you owe her some explanation?'

'I was worried she might have the wrong impression.'

'So you were worried. About what she might have thought was going on? Carrying a girl into your house? You felt that needed to be explained. That she might naturally get the wrong idea about that.'

'I wasn't *carrying* her,' I insisted. 'I told you, I was helping her.'

'Ms Wood saw it differently,' Marjorie said.

I shook my head and rolled my eyes. 'She was driving past, at a good clip, at night. She didn't see things the way they happened.'

'OK,' Jennings said, her voice trailing off for a second, like she was collecting her thoughts. Then, 'Tell us again about when you first heard from this Yolanda Mills person in Seattle. The one who said she'd seen your daughter out there.'

334

What did Yolanda Mills have to do with Patty?

'It was an email,' I said. 'She'd seen the website I'd had set up. That was what she claimed. But the whole thing was a setup. We've talked about this.' I said this looking right at Jennings. 'You already know it was a trick to get me out of town.'

'And then you emailed her back?' Like she hadn't heard a word I'd just said.

'That's right. I wanted to know where I could get in touch with her, and then whoever it was emailed back with a phone number, and I called her.'

'And spoke to someone,' she said.

I nodded. 'I don't know who it was. And of course there was no such person when I went out there.'

'Yes, I know,' Jennings said. She seemed to be working up to something. 'Kate Wood, she was at your home when you received the first email correspondence from the Mills woman, is that right?'

I said yes.

'And then she was on your computer when the second email came in from her, is that right?'

I said yes again.

'Where were you at that moment?'

'What do you mean?' I said. 'I was right there.'

'In the same room with Ms Wood?'

I thought back to that night. 'I was downstairs, in the kitchen.'

'And what were you doing?' Marjorie asked.

'I was phoning shelters, drop-in places for runaways in Seattle,' I said. 'I was using my cell while Kate was making calls upstairs.'

'And where were you getting the phone numbers from?' Jennings asked.

'I'd grabbed Syd's laptop and taken it downstairs. The house is set up for wireless, so you can use the laptop anywhere.'

The two detectives glanced at one another, then looked back at me.

'So it was while you were downstairs on the laptop that Ms Wood shouted down to you that you'd received another email from Yolanda Mills.'

'Yes,' I said. Where the hell were they going with this?

'And then what happened?' Jennings asked.

'I ran back upstairs, read the email, and there was a phone number, so I called it and talked to that woman.'

Jennings nodded. 'Was Ms Wood in the room at the time?'

'Yes.'

'And did she listen in to the phone call at all? Was she on an extension?'

'No. She wasn't.'

'Would you say she was able to listen to both sides of the conversation?'

'I don't understand the point of these questions,' I said.

'Could you just please answer them?' Jennings said.

'Should I have a lawyer? You said the other night I might want to give my lawyer a call.'

Marjorie cut in. 'You think you need a lawyer?'

'I don't know.'

'Why would a guy with nothing to hide need a lawyer? I mean, if you've got something to hide, we can shut this down right now and you can get your lawyer in here if that's the way you want it.'

'I don't have anything to hide,' I said, knowing as the words came out of my mouth that I was a moron if I let this go on much longer.

'You want to answer that last question?' he asked.

'I'm afraid I don't — what was it?'

'Could Ms Wood hear both sides of the conversation you claimed to be having on the phone with Yolanda Mills?'

Claimed?

'Um, I don't know. Probably not.'

Now it was Jennings's turn. 'Tell me about the phone,' she said.

'What phone?'

'The phone you had in your pocket when I dropped by your house the other morning.'

'That's the phone that was used to call me from Seattle. Or at least, it had a Seattle number.'

'That's right,' Jennings said.

'If you know this why are you asking me?'

'How long had you had that phone?'

'I hadn't had it any time at all. I found it just before you showed up. I found it in the dirt. That man who was going to kill me, he even mentioned it, said they forgot it there.'

'I'll just bet,' Detective Marjorie said.

'Look, if you'd given me a second, I'd have handed it over to you,' I said.

'We weren't able to find any fingerprints on it,

other than yours,' Jennings said casually.

Marjorie had moved away from me and was slowly pacing the room, which suddenly seemed very small, as though the walls were closing in.

He asked, 'Did Ms Wood just drop by, or were you expecting her?'

We were back to her now?

'When are we talking about now?' I asked.

'Same as a minute ago,' he said, shaking his head, like I was an idiot who couldn't follow a simple conversation. 'The night you were getting all this news from Seattle.'

'We'd talked on the phone earlier,' I said. 'She was going to bring Chinese food.'

'Did you tell her to come right away?' Jennings asked.

Again, I tried to think back. 'I asked her to give me an hour.' I let out a long sigh. 'I went out for a drive. I do that a lot, looking for Sydney.' I remembered what I had done on that drive. 'I stopped by Richard Fletcher's house.'

'Who's that?' he asked.

I glanced at Jennings, who already knew this story. 'He took a truck for a test drive, but he really just wanted it to deliver a load of manure.'

'You sure he wasn't delivering this story of yours?' Marjorie asked. 'Because it amounts to the same thing.'

'We spoke to him,' Jennings said. 'About the shooting at your house.'

'Yes?' I said hopefully.

'It was just like you said,' Jennings said. 'He denies dropping by. Says he doesn't know anything about it. He says he was home all evening with his daughter, and she says the same thing.'

'She's a kid,' I said. 'Of course she's going to say what her father wants her to say.'

'All we have at the moment is your word against his,' Jennings said.

I was about to say something in protest, but Marjorie cut me off. 'You own a gun, Mr Blake?'

'A gun? No. I don't own a gun.'

'I'm not talking about a licensed gun. Any gun.'

'I don't own a gun,' I said. 'I never have.'

'Never even went hunting with your dad as a kid?'

'No.'

Marjorie looked unconvinced.

'I'd really appreciate it if you'd tell me what this is all about,' I said. 'I don't understand the point of all this.'

'There never really was a Yolanda Mills, was there?' Marjorie said.

'No,' I said. 'I thought we'd pretty much established that. She's an invention. She was made up by these people, the ones working with that guy who wanted to kill me, who probably shot up my car. They wanted me out of town so they could plant that cocaine in my house. They tore the place apart so it would look like someone had been searching the place for it, but missed it. Their whole plan was for the cops to find it, and arrest me. Then I'd be out of the way.'

'And just who is it who wants you out of the way?' he asked.

'I don't know,' I said.

Detective Marjorie grinned and shook his head.

'My daughter's missing and you think the whole thing is a fucking joke,' I said.

'Do I?' Marjorie said. 'I think it's a joke? You give me a story that's straight out of *The Twilight Zone* and I'm the one making a joke? OK, let me ask you something very serious then, Mr Blake. Did you make up Yolanda Mills?'

It was like getting hit in the side of the head with a two-by-four.

'I'm sorry?' I said.

'You heard me.'

I looked at Detective Jennings. 'Is he fucking kidding?'

Jennings held my gaze. 'Answer his question, Mr Blake.'

I said to her, leaning closer to her, 'From him, I can accept this kind of horseshit. But you? From the beginning, I've always thought you were in my corner.'

'This will all go a lot better, and be over a lot quicker, if you just answer the questions,' she said.

'No,' I said, sitting upright. 'I did not make up Yolanda Mills.'

Marjorie said, 'You sure? You sure you didn't make her up, and use Kate Wood to back up your story? Use her as a witness?'

'What the hell did she tell you?' I asked.

'There's something you need to know about Kate Wood. No, two things. First, she's got it in for me because I didn't want to see her any

340

more. And second, she's a nutcase.'

'Isn't it possible,' Marjorie said, 'that you waited until she came over to discover that first email, then later when you took the laptop downstairs, you sent yourself an email from a bogus Hotmail account in Yolanda Mills's name, which Ms Wood discovered upstairs? And then you placed your call to her, but you didn't really place a call to anyone? That you faked it, all for Ms Wood's benefit?'

Now it was my turn to smile. Not with amusement, but astonishment. I said to him, 'And you thought my story was inventive. You're out of your fucking mind.'

Jennings remained stone faced, but Marjorie's cheeks flushed red with anger.

'That's not exactly answering the question, Mr Blake,' Jennings said.

'You have to understand something about Kate Wood. She sees conspiracies all over the place. She thinks everyone's got it in for her, like everyone gets up in the morning and has a meeting to figure out how they're going to stick it to Kate Wood today. That's why I felt I had to call her. Because I know how her mind works.'

'So that's your defense,' Detective Marjorie said. 'She's a nut.'

'I'm just saying you need to know how she sees the world. Is this really what she believes, or did you lead her this way? Because I know it wouldn't take much. Does she honestly think I was manipulating her? That I set this whole thing up so she'd corroborate some crazy story?' I looked directly at Jennings. 'You saw my house

341

when I got back from Seattle. You saw what they did to it.'

She nodded thoughtfully. 'It is possible, in theory,' she said slowly, 'that you could have done that before you left for Seattle.'

'Is that what you believe?' I asked her point blank.

'You have to admit it's possible,' she said.

'That's not exactly answering the question, either,' I said. 'Is that what you believe?'

She grimaced, as though she didn't want to have to answer. Was that because she didn't want Marjorie to know she thought I was innocent, or because she didn't want me to know she'd given up on me?

'Why would I do something like that? Set up a call from someone who didn't exist? Tear up my house and make it look like someone else did it? Plant cocaine so you could find it? Where would I get cocaine? And if I could get my hands on some, why would I do that? What possible reason could I have for doing something like that?'

Neither of them said anything. I guess they wanted me to figure it out on my own.

'Mr Blake,' Jennings said, 'what started out as an investigation into your daughter's disappearance has fanned out in a number of directions. For example, there's this man named Eric who supposedly was trying to kill — '

'Supposedly?' I said, pointing to my nose. 'Does that look like a *supposedly* busted nose?'

Jennings continued, 'And now a second missing girl. Who's a very close friend of your daughter's. You know what the common thread

342

in all these incidents is?'

'Yes,' I said. 'Sydney.'

'That's one way of looking at it,' Detective Marjorie said. 'The way I see it, what's most common is you. You know what I think?'

I waited.

'I think you're a pretty smart guy, but not smart enough. I think it's even possible there are some people hunting for you. Maybe you've jerked some people around and they're looking for payback. That part I haven't worked out yet. But I do think it's possible you've staged some of these things to make it look like your daughter was mixed up in something. Divert the attention away from yourself.'

'Why the hell would I want to do that?'

'You're at the center of everything,' Marjorie said. 'You're the last one to see your daughter. The last one to see Patty Swain. We're not stupid, Mr Blake.'

'No,' I said. 'You are.' I shook my head. 'Whatever you're getting at, this is crazy.'

'Is that why you had to get rid of Patty?' Detective Marjorie asked. 'Because she figured out you killed your own daughter?'

I didn't even think about what I did next. Even if I had, I can't say that I would have behaved any differently.

I do know it was something instinctual. Someone suggests you killed your own daughter, that you took the life of the person more dear to you than anyone else in the world, what else are you going to do but try to get your hands around his neck and choke the life out of him?

343

I came out of the chair like it was an ejector seat and went straight for Marjorie, my hands outstretched. I wanted to kill him. And not just for what he was suggesting about me. I was doing it for Syd. Here these people were supposed to be helping find her, but weren't getting anywhere because they — maybe not Jennings, but I was no longer sure about her — were wasting their time trying to find a way to put the blame on me.

'You son of a bitch,' I said, reaching for his throat.

But I couldn't get my hands around it. You weren't a cop for as many years as I guessed Detective Marjorie had been without learning a thing or two about how to defend yourself. He took hold of one of my arms and used my own force and momentum against me and threw me into the wall behind him.

Then he turned, grabbed hold of my hair with his meaty fingers and shoved my face up against the wall. My neck felt like it was going to snap.

'Adam!' Jennings shouted at him.

'You motherfucker,' he breathed into my ear.

'Adam,' Jennings said again. 'Let him go.'

'You just assaulted a police officer,' he whispered. 'Nice going, dickhead.'

'I didn't kill my daughter!' I shouted, my lips moving on the pale green surface.

'Adam,' Jennings said. 'Let's talk.'

He held me another second for effect, then let me go. Then he and Jennings left the room. I heard the door lock.

I leaned up against the wall, panting, trying to

regain my composure. I stood there a good five minutes before the door opened and Detective Jennings came in alone.

'You're free to go,' she said, holding the door open.

'What, that's it?'

'You're free to go.'

'I don't believe you people.'

'Mr Blake — '

'Let me guess. Your friend wants to hold me, to charge me, but there's no evidence against me. Just his whacko theories.'

'Really, Mr Blake, you should just go.'

'He'd like to charge me with assault, but he's thinking if you let me go, maybe I'll make some sort of mistake, something that'll stick.'

Jennings didn't speak.

'I'll tell you the mistake I made. The mistake I made was trusting you. I mean, I know parents are usually primary suspects when something happens to their kids, but I never got the idea I was one in your eyes, not until now. But now, if you're thinking the way he's thinking, then I guess I can't count on you for help any more. I guess I'm on my own to find my daughter.'

She was still holding the door open. I went through it.

'Thanks,' I said.

31

I was in a sweat as I walked out into the police station parking lot. It wasn't just from anger. It was hot. I turned on the A/C when I got into the car and powered up the windows. I adjusted the vents so they'd be blowing on me, but even after a couple of minutes, all that was coming out of them was hot air. I tried adjusting the settings on the A/C controls, but things didn't get any better.

'Goddamn it, Bob,' I said under my breath.

I drove into the Riverside Honda lot, circled around until I saw a demo — a blue Civic hybrid — I was pretty sure Andy Hertz was using these days, and parked next to it. I walked into the showroom, heading straight for Andy's desk, but when I passed Laura Cantrell's office she called out: 'Tim!'

I whirled around.

'Bringing back the CR-V?' she asked.

'Try the cops,' I told her.

Andy was leaned over his desk, on the phone. I reached over his shoulder, tapped the receiver base and disconnected him.

He saw my arm and followed it until he realized who'd cut him off. 'What the fuck, Tim? What are you doing?'

'We're going to have a chat,' I said.

'I had a solid lead there,' he said. 'Guy wants to get his wife a Pilot for her birthday and — '

I grabbed him under the arm and yanked him out of his chair. 'Let's go,' I said.

'Where? Where we going?'

'Tim! What are you doing?' It was Laura, hands on hips, trying to look like she was running the place.

I ignored her and steered Andy toward the door. I took him outside and walked him around the back of the dealership, where I'd chewed him out for stealing a commission from under me.

'What's with you?' he asked. 'I didn't swipe any more of your customers. Besides, you're not even working here now so if someone did come in and dealt with you before, what the fuck am I supposed to do about it?'

'Think back,' I said, putting my face into his. 'A year ago. You put Jeff Bluestein in touch with someone for a job.'

'Huh?'

'Jeff. You remember. He and Sydney were going out for a while.'

'Yeah, I know who he is,' he said defensively.

'I'm guessing you know Syd and all her friends. Jeff tells me you used to hang out with them.'

He protested that. 'Aw, come on, a few drinks was all.'

'That was the other thing he mentioned. That you used to buy booze for them since they're underage.'

'Jeez, Tim. Shit, you were their age once, weren't you? Didn't you have someone buy beer for you when you were sixteen?'

'Any other day, Andy, I'd carve you out a new

347

one for getting booze for my daughter, but I'm worried about bigger things right now. I want to know about this guy you put Jeff onto.'

'It was just some guy,' he said.

I pushed him up against the side of a minivan. 'I want a name.'

'I only knew his first name,' Andy said. 'It was Gary. Just Gary. That's all I knew.'

'Where'd you know him from?'

'I used to see him at this bar I go to, kept seeing him there, then one day, I'm walking into the Dairy Queen, and he's sitting there having a milkshake with Patty.'

'What?'

'Yeah. They were just kind of hanging out and talking. Patty waved and I went over and said hi, told Gary I recognized him from that place, and that was about it.'

'Patty?' I said. 'Patty Swain?'

'Yeah.'

'Did you ever ask Patty about him?'

Andy shook his head. 'Not really. I just figured they knew each other. Anyway, not long after that, I ran into the guy at a bar, I go, 'Hey, I know you.' It's like we already know each other, and we got talking.'

'What'd this guy do?'

'He was like, a businessman, you know? He was into a lot of things. Asked me if I wanted to make some extra money, but that was around the time I started here and things were going pretty good, you know? But I said if I knew anybody who was looking for some work I'd send them his way.'

'So the guy gave you a number?'

'He gave me a card, but it wasn't his own business card. It was another card he happened to have on him, so he wrote his number on the back.'

'You still have that card?'

'Yeah, probably, at home. I've got a jar I toss business cards into.'

'You remember whose card it was?'

'I don't know. Like I said, it wasn't his own card. It could have been for a body shop or a hotel or something, maybe a lawyer's. I just don't remember. It was a whole fucking year ago!' I still had his head pressed up against the minivan, his neck arched at an awkward angle. I moved back half a step so he wouldn't have to contort himself.

'OK, tell me about Gary.'

'He said he remembered Patty saying I worked with cars. He wondered what, exactly, that entailed. Like, did I service them? Run a Mobil station, what? And I told him I sold cars, and he said I wasn't the kind of guy he was looking for. He wanted people in the restaurant business, gas stations, convenience stores, that kind of thing, a place where there are lots of transactions.'

'You didn't wonder what that was about?'

'Not really,' Andy said. 'He wasn't interested in me, so I wasn't interested in what he was looking for.'

'Go on.'

'So, you know, one night I'm hanging out after work with Sydney, and Jeff, and Patty, and Jeff is going on about how he wants to get some really cool laptop, one of the new Macs that are really thin or something, and I said hey, you work in a restaurant, right? And Jeff said yeah, so I gave him the number of this guy — I guess I still had his card at that time — and said he might have something for him. And that was it.'

'Did you ever give that number to anyone else?' I asked him.

'What do you mean?'

I moved in closer again. 'I mean, did you ever give that number to anyone else?'

'I don't know, maybe. Like who?'

'Did you ever give that number to Sydney?'

Andy licked his lips, like his mouth was dry. 'Look, Tim, like, I give a lot of numbers out to a lot of people. How do you expect me to remember something like that?'

'I swear to God, Andy, I'm — '

'OK, OK, uh, let me think. Honestly, I don't think I ever did. But one time, Patty said she was thinking of switching to some other job, and I remembered I still had that guy's number, and I went to offer it to her, but when she looked at it she goes, oh that guy, I already have his number. So I guess, if she knew it, she could have given it to Sydney.'

That was certainly possible.

'What's the big deal about this anyway?' Andy asked. 'So I gave Jeff the guy's number, and I offered it to Patty, and maybe she gave it to Sydney? If they got some work out of it, why are you all over my ass about it?'

'Do you know what this guy wanted Jeff to do?' I asked.

350

Andy shook his head. 'I don't know. I never heard any more about it. Didn't it work out?'

'He wanted Jeff to rip off credit card numbers.'

'Well shit, that's not legal,' Andy said.

Maybe, another time, I might have laughed. Instead, I asked Andy, 'Did you see that guy I went for a test drive with two days ago? He said his name was Eric, but it was a fake name. Could that have been Gary?'

Andy shook his head. 'I didn't see the guy.'

'Do you have any idea whether Sydney might ever have gotten in touch with him?'

He gave half a nod. 'A few weeks ago, before summer started, she dropped by to see you, stopped by my desk, and I asked whether she was going to be working at Riverside Honda again for the summer. She said no, she needed a bit of distance from her dad, that Patty had put her on to something else, maybe she got that number from her, and the bonus was you got paid in cash so you avoided all kinds of tax and shit.'

'And it never occurred to you to mention this to me? To the police?'

'I didn't know it meant anything,' he said. 'Swear to God.'

I backed away from him, exhausted. 'Have you seen Patty around lately?'

His face seemed to flush. 'No,' he said.

'When was the last time?'

'I don't know. Probably that day she dropped by to see you.'

'Probably?' I asked. Andy seemed to be hedging.

'No, really. I'd see her the odd time, but I

351

haven't seen her in a while. Why?'

'No one's seen her for a couple of days,' I said.

Andy's face flashed with worry. 'Shit. She's gone, too?'

'Yeah,' I said. 'How well do you know her?'

'Not . . . really well,' he said.

'What are you not telling me?' I asked.

He shrugged uncomfortably. 'We hooked up a couple of times,' he said. 'It was nothing.'

'Hooked up? You slept with her?'

'Listen, it's not like she's Mother Teresa, you know? I mean, she's been with more guys than I've been with girls, and she's like five years younger — '

He stopped himself.

'Yeah,' I said. 'She is like five years younger than you are. What's the problem, Andy? Can't get dates your own age?'

'I do OK,' he said.

I didn't want to ask, but felt I had to. 'What about you and Sydney?'

He shook his head adamantly. 'No way, man. I never touched her. I mean, with your desk next to mine? I didn't want to hook up with her in case you found out and, you know, wanted to pound the shit out of me or something.'

He was dumb enough to steal my customers, but not that dumb.

'You're going to do something for me,' I said.

'OK,' he said.

'You're going to find this Gary for me.'

'How'm I supposed to do that?'

'What's this bar where you'd see him all the time?'

'JD's,' he said. I'd seen it out on Naugatuck Avenue, although I'd never been inside. It had been a long time since I'd hung out in bars. 'I could go after work, see if he's there, ask around for him.'

'Good idea,' I said. 'If you see him, or get a lead on him, you're going to call me right away. Understand?'

'Sure. Then what? You going to call the cops?'

'We'll see. We're not exactly on speaking terms at the moment.'

32

Andy still had to finish out his shift, which went to six. He said he'd head over to JD's after that, but wasn't hopeful that Gary, if he showed up at all, would make an appearance before eight. But if he saw any other patrons that he could remember being in Gary's company in the past, he'd ask where he might be able to find him.

In the meantime, there were others I wanted to talk to. Patty Swain's mother, for one. A visit to see her seemed long overdue.

I went back into the dealership, wound my way through the showroom of gleaming, tightly packed cars, and dropped into the chair behind my desk. Laura didn't appear to have found anyone to use it temporarily, so I made myself at home long enough to look up some phone numbers.

I found a Milford address for a Swain. In all the time Syd and Patty had been friends, I'd never actually driven to Patty's house, never had to drop Sydney off or pick her up there. I made a note of the address and wrote it down.

I was getting up from my chair when I found Laura Cantrell standing in my path.

'A moment?' she asked. I followed her into her office and she asked me to close the door. 'What's going on with you and Andy?'

'That's between us,' I said.

'Where's my car?'

By that, she had to mean the one I'd not returned. 'The police have it,' I said. 'The back end got shot up.'

'Shot up? What do you mean? With *bullets*?'

'Yeah.'

'Tim,' she said slowly, 'I've been patient with your situation, I really have. And I get why you want to take a leave. But if that's what you're going to do, take it. But now I find you're getting company cars damaged, and you keep popping in here to deal with your shit, and it's getting disruptive.'

'My shit,' I said.

'I've got cars to move. I can't do it if you keep dropping by to harass my salespeople. Promise me you're not going to bring your troubles around here any more.'

'Thanks, Laura,' I said. 'At the end of the day, you've always been there for me.'

★ ★ ★

I was heading down Route I, about to turn into the Just Inn Time to see if anyone had found Milt in the room I'd rented a few nights earlier, when my cell went off.

'What are you doing right now?' It was Arnie Chilton.

'Why?'

'There's some stuff you should hear.'

'What?'

'Look, I'm at my brother Roy's restaurant. You know, Dalrymple's?'

'Yeah.'

'You know where it is?'

'Yeah.'

'Where are you now?' Chilton asked.

'Can you tell me what it's about, Arnie? Because I've kind of got a lot on my plate at the moment.'

'I think Roy's got something you might find interesting.'

I turned off before I got to the hotel and headed for Dalrymple's.

★ ★ ★

My phone hadn't been back in my jacket three minutes when it rang again. Thinking it was Arnie calling back, I didn't look at the call display.

'Yeah,' I said.

'Hey.'

Kate Wood.

'Hello, Kate,' I said evenly.

'Look,' she said, 'I think I might have done something I shouldn't have.'

'What might that be, Kate?'

'OK, you're going to get mad, but I think I need to give you a heads up about something.'

'Really?'

'The thing is, I was talking to the police, and now I'm starting to think I may have given them the wrong idea.'

'About what, Kate?'

'You know how, sometimes, I kind of overreact a bit to things? How, once in a while, I get carried away a little?'

I paused. 'I think I know what you're talking about.'

'Well, when I was talking to the police, they might have gotten the idea that maybe there really was no call from Seattle. That maybe you were making the whole thing up.'

'Whoa,' I said.

'I think, OK, what I think is, I think maybe when I saw you helping that girl into your house the other night, that made me kinda mad, and got me thinking all sorts of crazy things. So I'm calling to tell you, you might be hearing from the police about this, and I'm really sorry if it causes you any problems.'

I didn't say anything.

'So I was thinking,' she said, 'that maybe there's some way I could make it up to you? To prove to you I'm sorry? I know the other night, when I brought over Chinese, things kind of went to shit and all, but I was thinking we could try that again, I could bring over — '

I flipped the phone shut and returned it to my jacket.

⋆　⋆　⋆

Dalrymple's was a roadhouse with weathered beams and fishermen's nets out front. Inside, the walls were adorned with paintings of ships sailing the high seas, lifesavers, and other bits and bobs of nautical gear. The place was hopping, most of the tables filled, wait staff busily crisscrossing the floor.

Arnie must have been watching for me,

357

because he appeared out of nowhere, all smiles.

'Hey, great, thanks for coming,' he said, shaking my hand. 'Roy's in his office.'

He led me down a hallway, past the two restroom doors, then opened a third door marked 'Office'.

Seated behind a desk was a large bull of a man, hairless except for a thick moustache.

'This is the guy,' Arnie said.

'Close the door,' Roy said. Arnie did so, and the restaurant din faded away immediately. 'You're Tim Blake?'

'Yes.'

The restaurant décor was carried through to the office. More nautical art, and several scale models of sailing ships dressed the shelves. One particularly spectacular one, with magnificent tall sails, sat on Roy Chilton's desk. He noticed me looking at it.

'The *Bluenose*,' he said, coming around the desk and shaking my hand. 'A schooner from Nova Scotia. A fishing vessel that was also a racing ship.'

Roy Chilton moved his tongue around the inside of his cheek. 'So, my brother tells me your daughter's missing.'

'Yeah. She's in a lot of trouble, and I need to find her right away.'

'Arnie here thinks I might have something important to tell you, but I don't know that it's got anything to do with your daughter.'

'Just tell it,' Arnie said.

'Arnie says he already told you about that Bluestein, what I caught him doing here.'

358

'Yes.'

'I'd appreciate you not spreading that around. I kind of made a deal with the little shit's dad to keep the lid on it.'

'Sure,' I said.

'Kid caused me a lot of grief. I've still got the credit card companies nosing around. They've red-flagged us.'

'Is this about Jeff?' I asked.

Roy shook his head. 'Not really.' He cleared his throat. 'You get a lot of turnover in this business. People come and go. Worst is when a chef quits on you. Those you can usually hang on to for a while, maybe years, if you're lucky. But wait staff, dishwashers, cleaning staff, they come and go. And you gotta be careful who you hire. Illegals, that kind of thing. Some managers, they don't give a rat's ass. So what if someone doesn't have papers or a Social Security Number. You pay them dirt cheap under the table, who cares. Truth is, I used to operate that way, but not any more.'

'Problems?'

'I've seen things,' he said.

'What sort of things?'

'For a while there, I was getting workers through a guy. He came by, made a pitch, said he could get me help for less than I was normally paying people, and I thought, great. So he brings in these people, I don't know where the fuck they were from. One from India, I think, a couple from Thailand or China. Let me tell you something. These people, they worked their fucking asses off. Did any job you told them. But

359

you think they'd talk to you? Have any kind of conversation? I mean, OK, English was not exactly their first fucking language, but they wouldn't even look you in the eye. They couldn't wait tables. Didn't speak English good enough. Had them in the kitchen, and cleaning up. You know what the thing was about them?'

'No. What?'

'They were always scared.'

'Because they were here illegally,' I said.

'Yeah, but it was more than that.' He went back behind his desk, but stood. 'This guy supplying them, he'd drop them off at the beginning of their shift and pick them up at the end. I drew up a schedule, so they'd know what days they had off, and the guy says oh, fuck that. You can work 'em seven days a week if you want. And he says, don't worry about long shifts. You want to work 'em twelve, fifteen hours, that's OK, too. I tell him, listen, that's against the law, and he says, you don't have to worry about that. He says his workers aren't covered by those laws.'

'Who'd you pay? Him, or the workers?'

Roy Chilton cast his eyes down, as though ashamed. He looked back up. 'Him. Because it was his agency. So I'd pay him — cash — and then I assumed he'd pay the workers.'

'You think they got the money?'

He shrugged. 'So, he'd bring them over at the beginning of shift, and he'd be here to get them at the end. All these people saw was the inside of that van and the inside of my restaurant. You'd look in their eyes, and I swear to God, they all looked dead. Their eyes were fucking dead. Like they'd all given up. Like they'd lost hope.'

He swallowed, looked down again, took a breath. Like he was gathering strength. 'One time, there was a girl working here, Chinese I think she was. Really pretty, or at least she would have been, if she ever smiled. She worked in the kitchen, and I sent somebody to get her, bring her in here. Someone else had booked off sick, and this girl, she worked her ass off all day, you know, and I just wanted to tell her, if she could even fucking understand me, that she did a hell of a job and I really appreciated it. So she comes in, and she closes the door, and I start to tell her she's done good, right? And I can tell she doesn't get what I'm saying. But she comes around the table here, she gets down on her knees, like she's getting ready to, you know . . .'

'I get it.'

'And I tell her, no, get up, I don't want that. But she just assumed this was part of the job.'

I said nothing.

'One night, he's picking up one of the girls from the kitchen, it's like two in the morning, and she was so wrung out, totally fucking exhausted. And she heads out, and I see she's forgot her jacket. So I run out to the van, and that guy's holding her head down in his lap, you know?' He sighed. 'She had to do anything he asked. She had to put up with that shit. And you know why?'

'Why?'

'Because he *owned* her,' Roy Chilton said. 'He owned all these people. They were goddamn slaves to him. He was just renting them out like they were fishing boats.'

'Human trafficking,' I said, thinking out loud.

'Huh?'

'Human trafficking. You lure people to this country, get them to pay thousands of dollars up front with the promise of living the American dream, and once you get them here, you own them. You control them.'

'I didn't want any part of it,' Roy said. 'Told that guy the next day, no thanks. I'd find people elsewhere.'

'He'd just take them to another restaurant,' I said. 'Or turn them into full-time sex trade workers.' I paused. 'But why are you telling me all this?' I looked at Arnie. 'Why'd you want me to hear all this?'

'You mentioned a name when I was at your place,' Arnie said. 'A weird name, that's why I remember.'

It wasn't immediately coming back to me.

'Tripe,' he said. 'Randall Tripe. But you never said another thing about him.'

I looked at Roy. He was smiling and nodding. 'That's the guy. I'd been telling Arnie all about this, happened to mention the name — '

'And I go, hey, where'd I hear that before?' Arnie said.

'I'd heard about him since then,' Roy said. 'Read about him in the paper couple of weeks ago. Somebody shot him, left him in a dumpster. You put a guy like that in the garbage, it makes the other trash look good.'

33

Driving away from Dalrymple's, I felt like I was nibbling around the edges. I knew Randall Tripe was involved in this somehow. His blood was on my daughter's car. That was *definitely* a connection.

Had Syd somehow gotten mixed up in his little slave labor business? Had she found out about his involvement in human trafficking? And if so, how? In what circles had Syd been moving to find out about a scumbag like Tripe?

Was it possible he'd tried to make Sydney one of his workers? I could recall a TV documentary on human trafficking, how its victims weren't just illegal immigrants, that criminals who made their living this way often preyed on people — particularly young ones — who were born right here in the United States. As long as they could find a way to control you, they didn't care where you'd come from.

I wasn't quite sure what to do with the information Roy Chilton had given me. I wanted to pass it along to Kip Jennings, but I felt so betrayed by her I wasn't confident she could help me any more.

Driving back into Milford, I decided to continue on with what I'd been about to do when Arnie Chilton phoned. I drove to the Just Inn Time, parked close to the front doors, and went into the lobby.

Today, Veronica Harp was on the front desk with Owen. She smiled warily as I came in. Our last encounter, when she'd offered to make me forget my troubles — at least temporarily — by slipping between the sheets with her, made this meeting feel slightly awkward.

'Mr Blake,' she said professionally, what with Owen only a couple of feet away fiddling with a fax machine, 'how can I help you today?'

I explained that when I'd rented my room, I'd had Syd's stuffed moose Milt in my bag, and now I couldn't put my hands on it.

'When she comes home, I want it to be there for her,' I said.

Veronica nodded, understanding. 'Let me just check our lost and found,' she said, and disappeared into an adjacent office.

I paced the lobby, five steps this way, five steps back. I did that three or four times before Veronica came back, empty-handed.

'Nothing's been turned in,' she said.

'Is the room in use? Could I go up and have a look?'

Veronica consulted the computer. 'Let's have a look-see . . . The room's empty at the moment, but our damn system for making new keys is down for a minute. I'll come up with you and let you in with my pass key.'

'Sure,' I said. 'Thanks.'

She came around the counter. She had her cell phone in one hand, like she was expecting a call, the key card in the other.

We went to the elevator together. 'It's possible, if one of the maids found it,' she said, 'they might not have turned it in.' She gave me a sad smile. 'It happens.'

'Sure,' I said again.

'You think it's possible you might have lost it someplace else?' she asked.

'Maybe,' I said. 'But I think it was here.'

The elevator doors parted. As we started down the hall, Veronica's phone went off. She glanced at the ID, hit the button, put the phone to her ear. 'Hang on a second,' she said. She extended the pass to me and said, 'You mind? I really have to take this.'

I nodded and took the key as Veronica Harp hit the elevator button to go back down, phone stuck to her ear.

I reached my former room, inserted the key, waited for the little light to turn green, and went inside.

The room was all made up, waiting for the next guest. Stepping into the center of the room, I didn't see Milt anywhere. It was possible, of course, that one of the housekeeping staff found Milt and, rather than turn him in to the office, decided to keep him. Milt was pretty threadbare from years of hugging, but then again, the staff here probably didn't make a fortune, and coming home with any stuffed toy for your daughter, even one whose antlers were nearly falling off, was better than coming home without one at all.

I walked around the room, glanced under chairs, opened the drawers of the dresser — all empty.

Then I got down on my hands and knees and

peered under the bed. Clearly, vacuuming under here was not something hotel management insisted be done on a daily basis. There were dust balls the size of, well, golf balls.

I found a skin magazine, a package of cigarette papers, a paperback novel by John Grisham. Where the bed met the wall there was a dark blob. I reached my arm under, grabbed hold of it tentatively.

It was furry.

I pulled it out. It was Milt. I picked the larger bits of dust off him and tried to blow off the rest.

'Got ya,' I said, holding Milt, looking into his goofy face, touching the right antler that was hanging by a thread. 'I thought I'd lost you.'

And then, suddenly, sitting there on the hotel bedroom floor with Milt in my hands, I felt overwhelmed.

Cried like a baby.

I allowed myself three minutes to feel bad, then got to my feet, went into the bathroom to splash some water on my face, dried off with a fresh towel, and left the room.

★　★　★

I was heading back to the elevator, Milt in hand, when I heard muffled screaming coming from a room at the end of the hall.

A woman's screams. Short ones. Every few seconds.

Not frightened screams. Not screams of terror. They were cries of pain.

I started heading to the end of the hall,

pausing at the doors, trying to figure out which room the cries were coming from.

'*Aww!*' a woman shouted. Nothing for a few seconds. Then, '*Aww!*'

That meant waiting a moment at each door, listening for the next cry to determine whether *this* was the room.

I was hearing another voice now, another woman. She was shouting. 'You don't go home! You here to work! You try to run away again, they make me do this even harder!'

I had the right door.

Then a noise that sounded like *thwack*.

And then the woman screamed, '*Aww!*'

Something horrible was happening in that room.

I reached into my pocket, felt the key card. Veronica had called it a pass key. I took that to mean that it would let me into any room, not just the one where I'd stayed.

I like to think I would have gone through that door to help any woman who was in trouble, but at that moment, I was going through that door because I thought it might be Syd.

I put the card into the slot, waited, hoped, for the light to turn green.

It did. I withdrew the card, turned the handle, and burst into the room.

'What's going on in — '

And I stopped, tried to take in what I was looking at.

Standing in front of me was the woman I'd run into in the hotel breakfast nook. Cantana. She was in her hotel uniform. She was holding in

367

her right hand a thin, chrome wand, or stick. I looked a little closer and realized it was an old car antenna.

The other woman in the room was kneeling at the foot of the bed, bent at the waist so that her upper body and arms were splayed out on the bedspread. She was dressed similarly to Cantana, but the big difference was, there was blood seeping through her uniform on her buttocks. She turned her head toward me, and there were tears on her cheeks. She was Asian, mid-twenties.

'What you want?' Cantana asked me. 'How you get in here? What you doing with that?'

She was pointing at Milt.

I was speechless. I started backing out of the room, Cantana still yammering at me. 'What you doing in here? Can't you see we having a meeting?'

Once I was all the way into the hall, Cantana slammed the door in my face. I stood there, dumbstruck, then turned around slowly.

What the hell was that?

That was when I found myself staring directly at the fire extinguisher station recessed into the opposite wall. The extinguisher sat behind a labeled glass door.

The letter 'I' in the word 'FIRE' was nearly worn away.

34

The picture.

The picture that was emailed to me, to make me think that Syd had been spotted in Seattle.

It had shown Sydney, in her coral scarf, walking past a fire extinguisher station. And the 'I' in 'FIRE' had been worn away, just like this one was.

I didn't have that picture in front of me right now, but I was certain this was the spot. This was where Syd's picture had been snapped.

She'd been in this hotel.

She'd worked *here*.

She'd been working here all along. She hadn't been lying.

It was everyone else who had been lying. Everybody here had been primed to tell the same story. To say they didn't know Syd, they'd never seen her.

Everybody here was covering their collective ass.

But if that was the case, then I wasn't safe here. Not if I gave any indication that I'd figured out the truth. Especially after walking in on Cantana disciplining that other hotel employee. Whatever had been going on in there, it wasn't some kinky sex scene. The woman bent over that bed was in genuine distress. Her screams had been real. She'd broken the rules and was paying the price for it.

I had to get out of here. Once I was out of here, then I could call —

'Mr Blake?'

I hadn't even heard the elevator open. I looked down the hall and saw Veronica Harp stepping off.

'Have you gotten yourself lost?' she asked. 'The room you were in was at the other end of the hall. But — oh! — I see you found it!'

She was pointing to Milt.

'Yes, yes, I did,' I said, walking towards her.

'What were you doing down here?' she asked.

'I was just . . . a little distracted. I had Milt in my hands here and walked right past the elevator without noticing.'

'Do you have my key?' she asked.

I reached into my pocket and handed it to her. 'Thanks,' I said.

'Don't want this falling into the wrong hands!' she joked, putting it into her own pocket. I hit the elevator button. The doors, which had just closed, popped open again. Veronica boarded the elevator with me.

'Are you OK?' she asked. 'You look a little . . . rattled.'

'I'm fine,' I said. 'I mean, you know, as fine as I can be, considering.'

'Sure, sure,' she said. 'I understand. Listen, about the other evening, I want to apologize.'

'No, don't worry about it.'

'No, I think I came on a bit strong.'

'It's OK, really.'

We reached the first floor and the doors parted.

'Take care,' I said to Veronica, rudely getting off ahead of her and hot-footing it to the lobby doors.

'Well, so long to you, too,' she said.

★ ★ ★

I got in the Beetle, putting Milt in the passenger seat, and drove out of the Just Inn Time lot as quickly as I could. I had to put some distance between myself and this hotel. I had to think about what this all meant.

If I'd felt I was nibbling around the edges before, now I felt as though I was taking huge bites.

Close to finding answers, close to finding Syd, or both?

Of that, I was less sure.

Something was going on at the hotel, and now I was guessing that Syd had stumbled on to it. And given that Eric — or Gary, or whatever his name was — was looking for her, I felt the odds were she was still out there, somewhere.

Syd, for crying out loud, just call home.

I needed help with this. I couldn't do it all alone.

I was going to have to call Kip Jennings.

Detective Marjorie had it in for me. But maybe, just maybe, there was a part of Kip Jennings that still believed in me, that still believed my daughter was still alive, and genuinely in danger.

I had to put some trust in her now. I had to tell her what I'd found out.

371

I pulled the car off Route I into a plaza parking lot. I felt too on edge to attempt driving and talking on the cell at the same time. I got out the phone and keyed in the number I'd used to get in touch with Jennings before.

I got her voicemail.

'Listen, Detective Jennings, this is Tim Blake. Something's happened, and I think I know what's going on. I need to talk to *you*. Not that asshole Marjorie. I don't honestly think you believe I've done what he thinks I've done. It's *you* I want to talk to, because I think you'll believe me and I think you'll do something about it. I'm this close to finding Syd. I really think I am. You have to call me when you get this message. Please.'

I flipped my phone shut, gripped the top of the steering wheel and rested my head on my hands.

I still wanted to talk to Carol Swain about Patty. It was easy to forget, with all that was happening, that Patty was missing, too. I couldn't help but feel that Patty's disappearance was linked to Sydney's, and hoped that talking to Patty's mother might offer up some new clue about what might have happened to both of them.

But first, I was going to go home, find that picture in my emails of Sydney walking past that fire extinguisher. I'd print it out, show it to Jennings, take her to the hotel, show her the worn 'I' on the glass door. She'd come around.

'Oh no,' I said as I turned onto Hill Street.

Up ahead, out front of my house parked next

to the curb, was Kate Wood's silver Focus.

'Perfect,' I said under my breath.

As I pulled into the drive I noticed that Kate's car was empty. She wasn't sitting in it waiting for me. I'd never given her a key to the house. Maybe she was sitting around back in one of the lawn chairs, waiting for me to come home and let her in.

I turned off the Beetle. Instead of walking in through the front door, I walked down the side of the house to the backyard.

I spotted the brown bag of Chinese food first. It lay on the grass, on its side, the top ripped open. It looked as though someone had reached in and helped themselves to a couple of things and left the rest.

The sliding glass door that leads from the living room to the backyard patio had been broken. There was glass on the carpet inside the house. Someone had smashed the glass so they could reach in and unlock the door.

I slid the door open and stepped in.

I called out, 'Kate?'

There was no reply.

Broken glass crunched under my shoes. I moved through the living room and into the kitchen.

She was on the floor, on her back, her arms stretched out above her head, her legs twisted awkwardly. Blood was pooled around her.

I was guessing it must have come from the hole in the middle of her forehead.

35

Suddenly overwhelmed, I bolted from the house through the open back door. I put a hand up against the siding to support myself and threw up. Seeing Kate, that way, had done more than fuck with my head. My stomach was doing somersaults. When I was sure I was done, I stepped away from the house. But wooziness swept in, and I had to put my hands on my knees and hold my head down for the better part of half a minute.

This was not happening.

Except, of course, it was. There was a dead woman in my kitchen. A woman I had, at least at one point, cared about, been intimate with, shared some small part of life with.

And now she'd been shot through the head.

I was stunned, horrified. I felt strangely cold, almost shivery, and noticed a tremor in my hands. I was so shaken, it took a few moments before I was able to focus enough to figure out what had happened. Not that it took a rocket scientist to put it together. They — or, more likely, the man known as Eric or Gary — had been here, waiting for me, but Kate had showed up instead.

Maybe the noise of the shot made him panic, think the police might turn up, so he took off, decided he could always try again later.

I stood outside, not knowing what to do. I

couldn't go back in there. I was — and there's no sense soft pedaling this — too goddamn scared to enter my home. I couldn't look at Kate Wood again, see her that way.

When my cell went off, it might as well have been wired directly to my heart, it gave me such a start.

I fished the phone out of my pocket, but my hand was shaking so badly it landed on the grass. I retrieved it, flipped it open, and put it to my ear without looking to see who it was.

'Yeah,' I said, my voice so quiet I could barely hear it myself.

'Mr Blake?'

Kip Jennings.

'Yeah,' I said.

'I'm returning your call,' she said. 'You have some new information for me or something?'

'Yeah,' I said.

'So, what is it?'

I'd been in shock only seconds before, but now my mind was suddenly focused. *Think this through very carefully*.

There had been several developments in the past few hours:

Syd had been at the hotel, and it now seemed likely everyone who worked there had been lying to me. The police, too. Veronica Harp and everyone else had been covering up from the beginning.

Randall Tripe was involved in some kind of human trafficking scheme, and the fact that his blood — and Syd's — were on her car connected them.

Andy Hertz was beating the bushes trying to get a lead on this Gary character, who'd not only tried to kill me, but might be the one who'd given Syd the lead on the hotel job.

I'd felt, up until the moment I'd discovered Kate, I was getting close, that I was getting somewhere. It was why I felt it so urgent to finally talk, face to face, with Patty's mother, Carol Swain. Maybe she'd know some small detail about her daughter, or mine, that could end up tipping things in my favor.

What I couldn't afford was losing time answering questions from the police about how Kate Wood ended up dead in my kitchen.

'Mr Blake?' Jennings said. 'Are you there?'

I had a pretty good idea how Jennings and Marjorie would put this together.

Kate Wood is found dead in *my* house a very short time after I learn she's tipped police to what she thinks is suspicious behavior on my part. I've told the police she's a nut. I'm angry, can't believe she'd point the police in my direction. Kate drops by my house, wanting to patch things up. I'm not interested in an apology. I flip out. After all, look how I reacted when Detective Marjorie suggested I'd killed my own daughter.

They wouldn't be bringing me in for questioning. They'd be arresting me.

And no one would be looking for Syd. They'd be more than happy to find a way to conclude I'd killed her.

'Mr Blake?' Jennings said again.

'I'll have to get back to you,' I said, and flipped the phone shut.

When the phone rang again a few minutes later, I checked the ID before answering.

'Yeah,' I said, starting up the Beetle and driving away from my house as quickly as that shitbox would take me.

'Hey, Tim. It's Andy.'

'Yeah, Andy.'

'You OK? You sound weird.'

'What's going on?'

'OK, so, I'm at that place? And I don't see Gary around. I asked a couple of people who might know him, but they haven't seen him lately.'

'They know how to find him?' I hung a right, then a left, putting my neighborhood behind me.

'No. But what I thought I'd do is, I'll hang in long enough to have a couple beers and eat some wings. What I was wondering is, would you pay me back for that?'

Paying Andy's bill was the least of my concerns. 'Sure, whatever.'

'OK. Thanks. I'll check in with you later.'

I flipped the phone shut. And then I lost it.

★ ★ ★

My eyes started brimming over with tears to the point that I couldn't see where I was driving. I managed to veer the Beetle over to the shoulder, put it in neutral and yanked up on the emergency brake. Then I put both hands back on the steering wheel, squeezed as hard as I could and made my arms go rigid, as though I could channel all

377

the tension from my body into the car. My breathing, fast and shallow, seemed to be accelerating, like it was trying to keep pace with my heart.

'Oh God,' I was saying under my breath. 'Oh God, oh God, oh God.' It was turning into a mantra.

Was this what a heart attack felt like? Or was that what this actually was?

All the pressure of the last few weeks had come to a boil. A missing daughter, attempts on my life, and now, a woman murdered in my own home. There was only so much one person could endure.

I was a goddamn car salesman, for fuck's sake. Nothing in my life had even remotely prepared me for dealing with the things that were going on around me now.

Pull it together.

I pried my fingers from the steering wheel, wiped the tears out of my eyes. The trouble was, the tears were still coming. If I wasn't careful, I was going to go into convulsions right here at the side of the road.

It's about Syd. You have to get it together for Syd. Have your little meltdown, then suck it up and move on. Because if you're not out there trying to find her, who the hell else do you think's going to do it?

I wiped my eyes some more, dried my hands on my shirt. My breathing was still rapid, so I concentrated on slowing it down. I took deeper breaths, tried to hold them a second, let them out slowly.

'You can do this,' I said under my breath. 'You can do this.'

Gradually, my breathing started to return to, if not normal, something approaching that. The pounding in my chest eased off.

'Syd,' I said. 'Syd.'

I put the car in gear, took my foot off the brake, and got back on the road.

★   ★   ★

Minutes later, I pulled into the driveway of what I believed to be Patty Swain's mother's house. It was in one of Milford's older neighborhoods, west and inland from the harbor, where the homes have a beach house feel about them even if they aren't right on the sound.

There was no car in the driveway, so I wasn't surprised when no one answered my knock. I thought about leaving a note inside the screen door, with my name and number, but just as I was slipping one of my business cards out of my wallet, a rusted mid-nineties Ford Taurus pulled in next to my Beetle.

I stood on the doorstep and watched a fortyish woman get out. She grabbed a couple of bags of groceries and a purse from the passenger seat, dragging everything with one hand, her keys in the other, teetering on high-heeled sandals. 'Can I help you?' she called out. She had on oversized sunglasses and pulled them off as she approached.

'Are you Patty's mom?' I asked.

'Yes, why — ' She stopped in mid-sentence when it seemed that she had a good look at me. I'd never met this woman before, but she seemed to recognize me. Or maybe she was looking at my bandaged nose and bruised cheek.

'I'm Tim Blake,' I said.

'I'll bet that hurts,' she said.

'You should see the other guy,' I said. 'Actually, he looks fine.'

I came off the step and offered to take her bags. She let me. She was probably a knockout, once. She still had an impressive figure, but her legs, exposed in her white shorts, were bony, the skin weathered from too much time in the sun. Her cheeks were pale, her blond hair dry and stringy. I could see Patty in her face, the strong cheekbones, the dark eyes.

I could hear bottles jangling against each other in one of the bags I'd taken from her.

She still hadn't said anything, so I continued. 'Patty's good friends with my daughter Sydney. You probably know all about her being missing. And now, I understand Patty hasn't been seen in a couple of days.' I sensed that my voice was shaking slightly, maybe not enough for this woman to notice, but it was there. 'I'm sorry, I don't recall your name, but — '

'It's Carol,' she said. 'Um, I thought, at first, maybe you were from the police, until I got a good look at you.'

I took that to mean that, even in plainclothes, I didn't look like a cop, but asked, 'We've never met, have we?'

'No, we haven't,' she said. 'Listen, why don't you come in.'

She got her key into the door and scurried ahead of me into the house, picking up several empty bottles in the front room and taking her bags into the kitchen. 'I haven't had a chance to clean up in the last couple of days,' she said. It looked more like the last couple of years. 'What with all that's been going on.'

'Have you heard from Patty?' I asked. 'Has there been any sign of her?'

'Huh?' she said from the kitchen, where I could hear bottles being tossed into a recycling container. 'No.' She came back into the living room. 'I guess you've heard all about that?'

'Patty and Syd being friends, yeah, the police have talked to me about it,' I said.

'I didn't even know, until Patty didn't come home and the police told me they were friends, that they even knew each other,' Carol Swain said.

'You're kidding,' I said. 'They've been friends for a while now. Patty didn't talk about her?'

'Patty doesn't talk to me about what she does or who she sees, and I'm pretty sure she doesn't talk to any of her friends about me,' Carol said. 'At least if she does, she doesn't have anything good to say.'

'You and Patty aren't close,' I said.

'Not exactly the Gilmore Girls, I'll tell you that,' she said, and laughed. 'Can I get you a beer or anything?'

'No, thanks,' I said. I almost reconsidered. Maybe a drink was what I needed. My nerves could use some calming. But I also wanted a clear head. 'Patty didn't tell you one of her friends was missing?'

'She said something about it, yeah,' Carol said. 'But I don't remember her saying her name, exactly. I hope you won't think me a terrible host if I pour myself something?'

'Go ahead,' I said. I had a feeling that anything Patty might have told her mother would not necessarily have registered.

Carol Swain went back into the kitchen, opened and closed the fridge, and returned with a Sam Adams in her hand. It didn't take long for beads of sweat to form on the bottle.

'So Patty's been hanging around with your daughter for how long?' she asked.

I had to focus. 'Over a year,' I said after thinking a second or two.

She was shaking her head puzzledly over this. 'Son of a bitch.'

'Why should that be a surprise?' I asked.

'Hmm? No reason. That girl of mine . . . She's a pistol, isn't she?'

'Yes,' I said. 'She is. A pistol. Pretty independent minded.'

'Gets that from her father,' Carol said. 'The fucker.'

'I take it he's not in the picture,' I said.

'He pops in now and then, but not long enough to make an impression, thank Christ. Not since Patty was a little one. It's kind of amazing, her hooking up with your kid. A year, you say?'

'Yeah.' The word came out short and clipped.

'You OK?' she asked.

'It's been a . . . yeah, I'm OK.'

She looked at me skeptically, then put our conversation back on track. Her eyes rolled up slightly into her head, like she was counting off months, circling dates on a calendar mentally. 'So how exactly did they meet?'

'In summer school,' I said. 'A math class.'

'Summer school?' Carol said, shaking her head. 'Math?'

I nodded.

'Patty's always been pretty good at math,' she said.

'Syd's not bad at math, either, but if they don't do the homework, they don't get the marks,' I said.

'Ain't that the truth. So you're telling me they hit it off?'

'Yes,' I said.

She nodded, thinking about it. 'I guess that does kinda make sense,' she said. I had no idea what she meant by that. 'That girl, I swear.'

'I like Patty,' I said. 'She's a good kid.'

'Clearly you need more than a year to get to know her,' Carol Swain said. 'The time and energy I've put into that child, and what does she do? Cause me nothing but grief, that's what.' She sighed. 'The cops came to see me today. Jennings? She said she'd been talking to you. She told me you were the last one to see Patty.'

'It seems that way,' I admitted.

'She tell you where she was running off to?' she asked, taking a pull on the beer.

'No. If I knew that, I'd have told the police. I'd tell you.'

'It's not like she hasn't run off before. A day here, maybe two. But when she didn't show for work, that seemed strange. She doesn't give a flying fuck about a lot of things, but she always

383

turned up for work, even if she didn't manage to get there on time, even if she'd gotten hammered the night before. Where I work, if you're late, they dock you. Even if you've got a good excuse. Like if you're sick, or hung over, or something.'

'Patty hasn't called you.'

'Nope.'

'Are you worried?'

'Aren't you? About your daughter?'

'Yes. Very.'

'There you go. You and I don't look like we'd have much in common, but there's something right there.' She took another drink. 'Maybe we have more in common than you think.'

'Maybe,' I said, not really thinking about it. 'I wanted to talk to you because, I thought if you had some idea what might have happened to Patty, it might be the same thing that's happened to Sydney.'

'I can tell you this much,' she said, flopping down onto the couch. 'I'll bet it's something bad.'

I set aside some discarded newspapers and took a chair opposite her. 'What do you mean?'

'My girl, sometimes she doesn't always do the smartest things.'

'What do you mean?' I asked again.

'Anything the other kids are into, Patty's into it a year sooner. All I ever wanted was the best for her. I wanted her so badly to begin with. She was my little gift from God, you know? I didn't think I'd ever even have a baby, and then when my prayers were finally answered, I went and screwed it all up.'

'Screwed it up how?' I said.

'Maybe, if Ronald had hung in — '

'Ronald?'

'My husband,' she said. 'If he'd hung in to be a father to her, maybe that would have made some difference. You know how hard it is to raise a child alone?'

Susanne and I had been working independently the last five years, but we were still able to count on each other where Syd was concerned.

'It's hard enough for two,' I said. 'It's a heavy load for one.'

'And trying to make a living, and run a house.' She made a grand gesture with her arms, as though keeping this place running efficiently were on a par with maintaining a Hilton. Then she set her beer down on the coffee table, but it caught the edge, and hit the floor. Carol was like lightning, righting the bottle before she'd lost much of it.

'Shit,' she said.

I sat and looked at her.

She leaned back against the couch, caught me staring, and mis-interpreted. 'I'm not much now,' she said. 'But I had my day.'

'I'm sorry,' I said. 'I was just thinking how much you look like Patty.'

'Yeah,' she said. 'Although I have to say, she seems to favor her father some, too.'

'Do you have *any* idea where the girls might be?' I asked.

Carol shook her head. 'I told the police everything I could think of. I wish the hell I knew. I'm hoping, maybe she just met some guy, she's run off with him for a week or something, and she'll come on back. Knocked up, probably, but at least she'll be back.'

'Is that what you think's happened?'

She put the beer down and studied me. 'I don't know.' She kept looking at me, examining my features.

'What is it?' I asked.

'You're a good looking man,' she said. 'Even with your nose all broke.'

I couldn't think of any way to respond to that. So I said nothing.

'What, you can't say thanks?' she said.

'It just seems an odd thing to say,' I said, honestly.

'You probably think I'm coming on to you or something,' she said.

'I don't know what to think,' I said. I felt numb.

She snorted. 'That's rich. Believe me, I'm not. I was just noticing, that's all. It's the first time I've really gotten a good look at you.'

'Excuse me?'

'I came into where you worked once to see you. This would be a good ten years ago.' I was selling cars at a Toyota dealership back then. 'You were one of the top salesmen, right?'

I had no idea where this was going. 'So we *have* met? You said a moment ago that we hadn't, but — did I sell you a car? I'm usually pretty good with faces, I'm sorry, but I don't remember you.'

'No, no, you didn't sell me a car. I came into the showroom, saw you at your desk, and once I had a look at you, I decided to get out before I changed my mind and went over and talked to you. I guess I lost my nerve.'

'Mrs Swain, I'm afraid I don't understand.'

'No, I don't expect you would,' she said. 'I didn't want to make any trouble for you at the time. But boy, you know, I really just wanted to say hello, that's all. I just wanted to thank you.'

'Thank me for what?'

'For being Patty's father,' she said.

36

Sydney, age four:

I am tucking her into bed. She usually asks for a story, but for some reason, not tonight. I've put in a long day, and think maybe I've caught a break here, because one story is not usually enough to satisfy Syd. If you pick one too short, she'll demand a second. If you pick one too long, there's not a chance she's going to nod off before you're done. The trick was to find one that was just right. A book that Goldilocks would like.

But I haven't caught a break after all. Sydney has something on her mind.

'Why is there just me?' she asks as I pull the covers up to her neck.

'What do you mean, why is there just you?' I say. 'You don't see me here? Your mother's coming up in a minute. There's your friends, and — '

'I mean in our family. Why is there just me? Why isn't there anybody else?'

'You mean, like brothers and sisters?'

She nods.

'I don't know,' I say. 'Maybe some day you will have a brother or a sister.' But I'm not really so sure about that. Susanne and I, things just aren't clicking between us the way they once did. Lots of talk about money, about the future, about whether I'm going to reach for the next rung of the ladder or just stay where I am now.

'All my friends have brothers and sisters,' Syd says.

'Do they like having brothers and sisters?'

She thinks about that. 'Anita hates her brother. He's older and he snuck up behind her and put dirt in her pants.'

'That's not very nice.'

'And Trisha says her little sister gets all the attention since she got born and she hopes she moves out.'

'I think that's kind of unlikely.'

I hand Syd her stuffed moose. Milt. She wraps her arm around him and draws him close.

'If I had a sister, I wouldn't hate her,' she says.

'Of course you wouldn't,' I say.

'But I don't think I want one,' she says, quickly reconsidering.

'Why's that?'

'Because you and Mommy would run out of love,' she says. 'There wouldn't be enough.'

I lean in and kiss her on the forehead. 'That wouldn't be a problem. We'd just make up some more.'

She nods. I think she's picturing the kitchen, that love is like brownies. You make up a batch whenever you feel like it.

'OK then,' she says. That's good enough for her.

★   ★   ★

I sat, breathless for a moment, sitting there in Carol Swain's house, before I said, 'I'm sorry, what?'

'You're Patty's father,' Carol Swain repeated. She grinned. 'You should see your face right now.' She added, 'The part that's not *already* red.'

'Mrs Swain, we've never even met,' I said.

'Well, you had to know from the outset that that wasn't exactly necessary, right?' she said, smirking.

I shook my head and got to my feet. The wooziness I'd felt after finding Kate was returning. I wavered slightly, put my hand on the wall to steady myself.

'Whoa,' said Carol. 'Steady on there, pardner.'

'I think I should go,' I said, pushing myself off the wall, willing the room to stop spinning. 'We're not making any sense here.'

'You pretend you don't know what I'm talking about, but I know you do.'

'No,' I said, feeling my pulse quicken again. 'It's not possible.'

Really? Is that what you honestly believe?

'What's not possible? That you could be my daughter's father, or that I could have found out it was you?'

I wanted to leave but felt rooted to the floor.

'You put all that information on the form,' she said. 'Not your name, of course. But everything short of that. What would you like me to tell you about yourself?'

'You don't have to — '

'Your father died at the age of sixty-seven — you were just nineteen at the time, that must have been rough — of lung cancer, but that was attributed to him being a heavy smoker, so it's

390

not like you necessarily had a genetic disposition, you know? Your mother at that time was sixty-four, reasonably healthy for that age, and no signs of heart disease even though there was some history of it in her family. How am I doing so far?'

'Pretty good,' I said.

'You were in good shape yourself, although how much of a history does someone have at twenty? That's how old you were, right?'

'Yes,' I said.

'You'd had chicken pox and measles and all those other childhood diseases, and your tonsils removed when you were six. They don't do that very much any more, do they? I can't remember the last time a kid had his tonsils out.'

I didn't bother nodding, but she was right on all points.

'You were going to Bridgeport Business College, although that wasn't actually on the forms. It was easy to figure out, since it was the closest school to the clinic. Just down the street. That was where a lot of their donors came from. Sometimes you wonder if they do that deliberately, set up close to a college where they know the boys are desperate for money. So, anyway, we started the search there, and it paid off.'

I breathed in and out, slowly, half a dozen times before sitting back down. Carol waited until she was sure I wasn't going to keel over or anything.

'This is all very exciting,' she said, but then her smile turned downward. 'At least it would be, under different circumstances.' She leaned forward on the couch. 'I bet you could use that drink now.'

'No, it's OK,' I said. 'It was all supposed to be confidential.'

'And it was,' she said. 'No one at the clinic ever told me you were the sperm donor. But when I was making a choice as to whose sperm I would pick, they provided all these forms that you had to fill out when you, you know, made a deposit. There was all that family history, ages, educational profile, race. You wrote down that you'd excelled in math in high school and college, which was another reason why we zeroed in on the business college.'

'We?'

'Me, and the detective I hired.'

'Let me guess,' I said. 'This would be about ten, twelve years ago?'

'That's right,' Carol Swain said. 'How did you know that?'

'I got hints that someone had been asking around about me. I wondered if it was some kind of credit history check. But then it stopped, and I didn't think about it again. Until the last few weeks, when my ex-wife reminded me about it. But even then, I kind of let it go. It didn't seem to have any bearing on what's going on now.'

'It doesn't really,' she said.

'Why did you hire a detective?'

'I wanted to know who Patty's real father was. A few years after we got married, Ronald and I decided to have a child. Turns out his little swimmers weren't up to the job. At first we thought it must be me.' She laughed. 'Ronald always felt anything that didn't go right around here was my fault, and not being able to get pregnant was just added to the list. So I went to the doctor and turned out that everything was just fine, so then Ronald finally agreed to go, and then we found out just whose fault it was.'

'Go on.'

'So finally I ended up going to the Mansfield Clinic. They said I could be artificially inseminated, and I thought, hey, that could work, but it took Ronald a long time to come around to the idea, no pun intended.'

'Not being the real father, that didn't sit well.'

Carol thought about that. 'He just wasn't sure he could come to love a child that wasn't really his. Even if it was half mine. But we talked about it, and he finally said he was OK with it, that even if he wasn't, technically speaking, the father, he'd be a father to our child. So I had it done, chose you from the samples they had in the freezer, and then guess what happened?'

'He never really felt she was his daughter.'

'Yeah. We had this beautiful baby girl named Patricia, and he tried, but he just didn't have it in him. You know he nearly killed her?'

'Left her in a locked car in the heat,' I said.

'Patty told you that story?'

'Yes.'

'Well, it's true. Stupid bastard. Claimed he just forgot, and I have to give him the benefit of the doubt, I suppose, but honestly, you had to wonder. The marriage was already on the skids by that point, but that was it for me. I wanted him gone, and he was happy to oblige.'

'I'm sorry,' I said.

'Don't be,' she said and waved her hand. 'I was better off without him. We were both making pretty good money in those days. He was at Sikorsky, I was assistant manager of a company that made plastic molds. Even after we split, I managed to look after me and Patty, and Ronald sent along the odd check, but his heart wasn't in it, supporting a kid he had no real connection to. I kept wishing I had a decent man in my life, someone who could be a real father to Patty, because I believe from the bottom of my heart that it takes a mother and a father to raise a child, but it also has to be a mother and a father who give a shit, you know what I'm saying?'

'I know what you're saying,' I said.

'So I started wondering, who *is* Patty's real father? What kind of man is he? Is he a good man? Would he make a good father to Patty? Wouldn't he want to see his daughter, and once he did, wouldn't he fall in love with her and want to look after her?' She reached across the coffee table and touched my hand. 'Didn't you ever wonder? Didn't you ever stop and think, is there a kid out there who's mine and I don't even know what he or she looks like? Didn't you ever wonder, when you went to the supermarket and there was some kid stocking shelves, could that be my son? Could that kid taking my order at Burger King be carrying my DNA? Didn't you?'

I took a moment to find my voice. 'Yes,' I said. 'Occasionally.'

'Didn't you want to know?'

'Sometimes,' I said. 'But learning something like that . . . I don't know how to put it . . . would come with some obligations. I mean, once you knew, you'd feel you should reach out, something.'

'Yeah,' Carol nodded, taking her hand away.

'And it was so long ago,' I said. 'I never thought about it all that much, not back then. At the time, it seemed meaningless. A way to make a few extra bucks.' I sighed. 'Beer money for the weekend. It's only later in life that you start thinking about the implications of things.'

'Did you ever tell your wife? That there might be other kids out there who are yours?'

'No,' I said. 'I never have.'

'So,' she said, picking up her story, 'there was no father on the scene, and I couldn't stop thinking about finding out who Patty's real father was. I had this fantasy that if I could find you, you'd fall in love with us. That you'd fall for me and Patty and come into our lives and everything would end up just like in the movies. A friend of mine knew someone who was a private detective, a man named Denton Abagnall, and it took me a couple of months to work up the nerve to call him. I asked him if it was even possible to find out, that the clinic was very strict about confidentiality, but when I showed him the form you'd filled out with the background information, he said he might be able to figure out who you were through a process of elimination. He started with the college, got the names of all the male students over a three-year period, checked all their names against death records, looking for any of them who were nineteen when they lost a father at the age of sixty-seven, and he started putting it all together. Once Mr Abagnall was sure he had the right student, he had to move ahead six years or so, and he tracked someone down with your name working at a Toyota dealership. He went in, got one of your business cards with your picture on it, and the minute I saw your face, I knew.'

It had never occurred to me that Patty and I looked anything alike. But I was pretty sure there had been times when it had occurred to me — almost subconsciously — that she and Sydney shared certain characteristics. The way they arched their eyebrows, twitched their noses.

'Mr Abagnall wrote up an entire report for me, and that's when I found out that you were married, that you had a daughter of your own. That's when the fantasy died for me. I knew I couldn't turn your life upside down. I didn't want to take away another little girl's father to give my daughter one.'

'But still you came into the dealership.'

'I just had to see you. In person. Just once. Then I put it behind me. I moved on.'

I sat back in my chair, trying to take it all in.

And then it hit me. I didn't have one daughter missing, and in danger.

I had two.

37

'So you must have told Patty all of this,' I said.

'No, never,' Carol Swain said. 'I didn't want her to know.'

'But she must have found out,' I said. 'How else could she have connected with Sydney?'

'I've been thinking about that from the moment you turned up in my driveway. You know how once in a while, you read some story in the paper, about a couple who meet and fall in love and then find out that they're brother and sister? You think, what are the odds, but it happens. At least in this case, it wasn't a brother-sister thing, thank God.'

'I don't know,' I said. I wasn't a big believer in coincidences, although I knew they could happen. 'When the detective reported everything back to you, he must have included the names of my wife and daughter.'

'He did.'

'So when Patty said she had a friend named Sydney, didn't that set off any bells?'

'In the report I got, your daughter's name was down as Francine,' Carol Swain said.

Francine was Sydney's first name, the name that showed up on her birth certificate. But when she was just a toddler, her second name, Sydney — and ultimately, Syd — just seemed to suit her better, and we stopped calling her Francine altogether.

I explained this to Patty's mother. 'So there was never a time that I suspected,' she said. 'Maybe, if Patty had ever brought your daughter around, I'd have noticed some similarities.'

'This report you got from the detective,' I asked. 'Do you still have it?' She nodded. 'Is it here, in the house?' She nodded again. 'So then maybe Patty found it.'

'I don't think so,' she said. 'It's hidden.'

'Hidden where?'

She set down her beer and went upstairs. I heard her moving around up there, then she came back downstairs clutching a thick manila business envelope with her name printed on the front. She tossed it onto the coffee table. 'There it is. Everything anybody ever wanted to know about Timothy Justin Blake. It was in this secret-like zippered compartment in a travel bag I keep under the bed.'

I slid the envelope's contents out onto the table as Carol sat back down and resumed her relationship with the beer.

There were quite a few pages. Photocopies of birth certificates, my father's death certificate, a photo of me from a Bridgeport Business School graduation ceremony, a picture of the house I grew up in and the house I had been living in at the time. All that, and a copy of the bill for services rendered from Denton Abagnall.

'Have you spoken to Mr Abagnall lately?' I asked.

She shook her head. 'He got killed a couple of years ago. It was in all the papers. He'd been hired by that woman whose family disappeared when she was a kid.'

I remembered reading something about that at the time. 'So you never showed this to your daughter?'

'I'm telling you, no,' she said.

'Who else might have known?' I asked. 'That you'd hired someone to find out I was Patty's biological father?'

Carol Swain shook her head. 'No one,' she said. 'Unless Abagnall told someone. And I don't think he would have done that. He seemed like a real professional, you know?'

'What about your husband, Ronald?' I asked.

'I don't see how . . . ' she said, but then her voice drifted off. 'No, I don't think so.'

'Do you and he still keep in touch?' I asked.

'Yes,' she said. 'Off and on.' There was something in the way she said it. Her eyes did some kind of twinkle.

'What do you mean?' I asked. 'Off and on?'

She looked away, drank some beer. 'It's just . . . He's a total asshole, OK? I know that. It's just that, sometimes, we hook up. You know? No strings, just get together for old time's sake.' She rolled her eyes. 'It's not like I'm going to get pregnant or anything with the guy shooting blanks.'

'How often do you see him?'

She shrugged. 'Every few months. Maybe, if it's been a long time for either one of us, someone gets an itch that needs scratching, we kind of send out a little email, you know, like, what's doing?'

'When was the last time?'

'Maybe eight, ten months ago. It's been a while. And the last time before that was, way more than a year ago, for a few days.'

'He came here?' I asked.

'His wife wouldn't exactly be crazy about it if I went and stayed with him at their place.'

'Ronald stayed here for a while? More than a year ago?'

'He had a blowout with his own missus, needed a place to camp out. So I shipped Patty off to stay with my sister in Hartford for a bit so I could have some peace and quiet. Seemed like a good time for a bit of a reunion with Ronald.'

'He slept in your room?'

She looked at me and said, 'Duh.'

'I'm just asking because he'd have been in the same room with this file.'

She shook her head. 'You're wrong.'

'I'm not accusing him of anything,' I said. 'I'm just saying it's possible. He might have gone looking through your things, looking for something else — '

'What, a pair of my panties to try on?'

'I was thinking more like money. And instead, he came across that envelope. Maybe he'd have thought there was money in it, looked inside, found something else.'

'Anyway,' she said dismissively, 'it's not like it would be a huge shocker, even if he had looked inside. He already knew he wasn't Patty's father.'

'But he'd never known the actual identity of Patty's biological father. And that I had a daughter of my own, about Patty's age.' My mind was racing, trying to see whether any of these pieces fit together. 'If he did see the file, do you think he would have told Patty?'

This time she was more definite. 'No way,' she said. 'Even though he was a piss poor father to her, he still felt he was more her father than anyone else was. He wouldn't have wanted to admit you existed.'

That made sense to me. 'But if he read the file, is there any way he might act on the information?'

'Like what?'

'I don't know,' I said. 'I'm just thinking out loud here. Do you think he might have engineered a way for the girls to meet each other?'

'Why?'

'I'm telling you I don't know. I mean, would he do it out of mischief? Because he liked the idea that he knew they were half-sisters, even if they didn't know?'

And did it have anything to do with the fact that they were both, now, missing? I didn't pose the question out loud. I felt I was already too far down a strange road without a map.

'That sounds crazy to me,' Carol said.

'Have you been in contact with Ronald since Patty went missing?'

'Yeah, the first day, before I called the cops,' she said. 'I felt like an idiot doing it, because I knew what the chances were. So I call him at work and say, you know, has Patty been by your place or anything, and he says, you're kidding, that'd be a first.'

'She doesn't keep in touch with him,' I said.

'No. And he couldn't be happier. He's not bad in the sack, but as a dad he's a complete and total washout.'

I tossed the various pages of the report onto the envelope and stood up, paced back and forth a few steps. 'We need to talk to him,' I said.

'Huh?'

'We need to go talk to Ronald.'

'What's the point of that?'

'I want you to introduce me. Just tell him the truth. That I'm Tim Blake, my daughter Sydney is a friend of Patty's, the two of them are missing. I want to see his face when you tell him who I am.'

'You think that'll prove something,' she said.

'It might,' I said. 'He still work for Sikorsky?'

'In his dreams. He works at a liquor store.' Right, I thought. I did know that. 'He's probably still on. I'd shop there, but the son of a bitch doesn't give me a discount. So I take my business elsewhere.'

My cell phone rang.

'Hello?'

'You said you were going to get back to me.' It was Detective Jennings.

Hearing her voice made me feel as though a trap door had opened under me. 'I've kind of had a lot on my plate,' I said. 'When I get a minute I'll call you.'

'Where are you, Mr Blake?' she asked.

'Out and about,' I said. Carol Swain looked at me curiously.

'I want to talk to you right now,' Jennings said. 'In person.'

'Why's that so important?'

'I dropped by your house,' she said.

I swallowed. 'Oh,' I said. 'Like I said, I've been out, looking for Syd.'

'I'm not asking you to come in,' Jennings said firmly. 'I'm telling you. You're coming in right now, or we're going to find you and bring you in.'

I decided to take a shot at playing dumb. 'I don't understand the urgency.'

'Mr Blake, one of your neighbors saw you come home less than an hour ago and leave again in a hurry. I know you were here.'

'I really have to go.'

'Mr Blake, let me lay it out for you. Kate Wood is dead. Are you hearing me?'

'I hear you.'

'Unless you can tell me something to persuade me otherwise, you're the lead suspect in a homicide.'

'I didn't do it,' I said. Carol was still looking at me.

'That's not what I'd call persuasive,' Jennings said. 'Call your lawyer, Edwin Chatsworth. He can arrange a surrender so no one has to get — '

I closed the phone and said to Carol Swain, 'Let's go see your ex.'

★ ★ ★

I put Milt in the back seat so Carol wouldn't crush him when she got into the Beetle. She gave me directions to a store in Devon, not far from the dealership, that was sandwiched between a

403

courier franchise and a distributor of appliance parts.

At a four-way stop, we waited for a police car to go through ahead of us. I gripped the wheel a little tighter and held my breath, trying to will myself into a state of invisibility as the patrol car went past.

Carol picked up on my anxiety. 'Somebody looking for you?' she asked.

'I'm fine,' I said. I figured it would take a few more minutes for Jennings to put the word out to every cop in Milford to be on the lookout for me. It wouldn't take her long — a call to Susanne or Bob would do it — to find out what I was driving now that the CR-V had been hauled in for a forensics examination.

It was getting to be dusk as I pulled into a spot out front of the liquor store. Carol Swain was out of the car before I'd turned the ignition off. She was making a beeline for the door and I told her to wait up.

An elderly, unshaven man clutching a brown-bagged bottle shuffled out the door as we went in. The old guy had evidently been the sole customer. The only one left in the store was the man behind the counter.

The guy who scratched Patty's mother's itch every eight to ten months might have been a good-looking man, once. About five-ten, strong jaw, blue eyes. But he was thin to the point of emaciated, his hair was thinning, and he'd gone a day or two without shaving. He peered at me though a pair of cheap reading glasses.

'Hey,' he said. He noticed his ex first, me

second, and my nose third. He didn't look puzzled, surprised, annoyed, intimidated, you name it. There was nothing there.

'Hey, Ron,' she said.

'Hey,' he said.

I thought he might ask Carol if she'd heard from Patty, but he didn't.

'Ron, this here's Tim Blake.' He just looked at me. 'He's been trying to find his daughter, Francine?'

That had been my idea, to refer to Sydney by her first name, the one that the detective had used in his report.

Ronald's expression stayed blank.

'She was a friend of Patty's,' Carol Swain continued. 'Now the two of them are missing.'

'Kids,' he said dismissively, shaking his head. He asked me, 'Did they run off together?' It seemed a genuine question.

'We don't know,' I said. 'I came by to talk to Carol, see whether she had any idea about where either one of them might be.'

'I don't know what your daughter's like,' he said, 'but Patty's the kind of girl, she's probably just blowing off some steam, getting a little wild for a couple of days. I'm sure she'll turn up. And if your Francine is with her, they'll probably come back together.' He looked at his ex-wife and said, 'Joyce is going to give me a lift home when I lock up so, you know, you might not want to be hanging around when . . .'

'It's OK,' Carol Swain said. 'We just wanted to pop in, in case you'd heard from Patty, you know?'

'Yeah, well, no,' he said, looking back and forth between us.

I said, 'Mr Swain, do you know who I am?'

'What do you mean?'

'Do you recognize my name?'

He looked at me a moment and finally said, 'Yup.'

'Where from?'

He glanced at Carol, then back at me. 'You're the one supplied the juice to make Patty.'

From Carol Swain, a sharp intake of breath.

'How would you know that?' I asked.

Ronald Swain offered up half a shrug. 'It was all in the report. The one the detective did. It was hidden in a suitcase under Carol's bed.'

'You son of a bitch,' Carol said. If Ronald was hurt by the name-calling, he didn't show it.

'When did you see that report?' I asked.

Another shrug. 'A year ago? Something like that.'

I tried to probe a bit. 'What did you think when you read it? Were you angry?'

'Not really. I mean, I knew I wasn't Patty's father. Somebody had to be.'

'You were never curious?'

He shook his head. 'I mean, when I found the report, I was interested enough to read it. But that was about it.'

'What about my daughter? Were you curious about her? Were you interested in Patty's half-sister? Did you think about trying to get the two of them together?'

There was almost nothing in his dull eyes. 'Why would I want to do that?'

'Did you ever show that report to Patty?' Carol asked. 'Did you ever tell her about it?'

Ronald Swain sighed tiredly. 'Both of you have evidently mistaken me for someone who gives a damn. Why would I tell Patty? The only thing I might have done, if this had been ten years ago, is go knocking on your door — ' he looked at me ' — with Patty in tow and seen if you wanted to take her off our hands. Might have kept the two of us together. But now, with her grown up and all, what would be the point of that?'

Carol Swain looked from Ronald to me and offered up half a shrug, as if to say, 'There you go.'

Ronald, looking at Carol, said, 'You should give me a call. But here, not at home.'

'When this whole thing with Patty blows over,' she said, giving him a wink as she turned away.

It didn't feel as though we'd been in the store all that long, but it was noticeably darker out when we got back into the car.

'Well fuck me,' she said.

'Excuse me?'

'He read the file.' She shook her head. 'He's never been much of a reader.'

38

There was a police car sitting in Carol Swain's driveway when we turned the corner. I hit the Beetle's brakes.

'Whaddya suppose they're doing there?' she said. 'Maybe they brought home Patty.'

She had her hand on the door handle, getting ready to bolt. I reached for her arm and held her.

'They're probably looking for me,' I said. 'Checking all the possible places I might turn up.'

Carol settled back into the car. 'What do they want with you?'

'It's a long story,' I said.

'I can hoof it from here if you want,' she said.

'I'd appreciate that,' I said. 'And if they ask if you've seen me — '

'Seen who?' she said, and smiled. 'I couldn't turn in my daughter's real life father. What kind of mother would I be if I did that?'

'If the police find me right now,' I said, 'they're going to slow me down trying to find Syd.' I paused. 'And Patty.'

'You think Patty's mixed up with what happened to your girl?'

'I don't know. I hope not.' I didn't want to tell Carol I had a bad feeling about Patty. 'Thanks for your help,' I said.

'No problem,' she said. She had her hand on the door again but didn't push it open. 'It was good to finally meet you. I mean, I know the circumstances are kind of shitty and all, but I'm glad to be able to talk to you, to tell you what you did for me, after all this time.'

I smiled awkwardly.

'I don't blame you for not saying anything,' she said. 'I wouldn't know what to say either.'

'I had to know I might be the biological father of some child out there somewhere,' I said. 'So that part's not a surprise. I guess I never expected to actually know the identity of one of them.'

She smiled ruefully. 'There might be more. Maybe there's hundreds of them running around out there. Little Tims and Timettes all over southern Connecticut.'

'I doubt that,' I said. 'I think they limit just how much of the stuff they spread around.' I winced. 'That didn't sound right.'

Carol smiled. 'That's OK. But I can't help wondering, if you'd been her father in every way, not just the biological, if she'd have turned out different. Whether she would have been such a screwup. So ungrateful, always getting into trouble.'

I felt maybe I was being blamed here. I wanted to ask whether Patty might have turned out differently if Carol's husband had hung in, if Carol hadn't turned into an alcoholic over the years.

That was what I wanted to say to her. But I didn't because I did feel the blame.

I felt responsible.

Patty existed because of me. But I'd done

nothing to help her since she came into the world.

I rested my hands on the steering wheel, looked at the Swain house shrouded in darkness, the cop car out front. 'You make decisions years ago, not thinking they mean a great deal, and then years later . . . '

'It's a bitch, isn't it?' she said. Then, impulsively, she leaned over and kissed me on the cheek. Tentatively, so as not to put any pressure on my injury. 'If you find my girl, tell her to get in touch with her goddamn mother, would you do that for me?'

'Sure,' I said, my cheek cool where her lips had been.

As she slipped out of the car, my cell phone went off again. This time, I looked at the ID. I didn't want to talk to Jennings again.

'Hello?' I said.

'Tim?'

'Yeah.'

'It's Andy.'

'Yeah, Andy.'

I'd almost forgotten Andy was out there trying to find this elusive Gary. There'd been a lot of events in the last couple of hours that seemed to have overtaken his errand.

'OK, so, I ended up leaving that other bar. Some guy said Gary didn't hang out there any more, he mostly goes to Nasty's? You know the place?'

'I know of it.'

'So then I went there, and hung around a bit, and had a couple more beers, asked if anyone

410

had seen him there and I got a lead on where I can find him.'

'What'd you find out?'

'OK, um, it's kind of complicated, but I'm going back to the dealership to check something out.'

'The dealership?'

'OK, so, I'm thinking, actually, that this guy might have gone for a test drive last summer with Alan?' One of the other salesmen. 'And Gary's card, with a work address and number, might be in Alan's Rolodex on his desk.'

I wasn't sure I wanted to turn up at the dealership. The police might be looking for me there.

'What's his last name, Andy? What did you find out about him?'

'OK, I didn't get a lot, and I can't really talk right now. But can you meet me at the showroom? By the time you get there I might have the info.'

'The showroom's going to be all locked up.'

'I've got a key,' he said. 'Give a loud rap on the service door and I'll let you in.'

I wasn't crazy about the idea. For a second, I wondered whether Andy could be setting me up. Maybe Jennings was behind this call. But I was so desperate for leads I decided to take the chance. 'OK,' I said. 'Twenty minutes?'

'See you then.' Andy ended the call.

I started up the Beetle, listened to the engine rattle, then backed up to the corner so I wouldn't have to drive past Carol's house, where the police car still sat in the driveway.

411

Any info Andy had learned about Gary — a full name and maybe an address — might tip things in my favor. Even if it wasn't something that led me directly to Syd, maybe it would be something that would give me leverage. Regardless, I had to avoid the police. They were more interested in finding me than Syd. I believed the only one who had a hope of finding her was me.

I drove past the dealership once, looking for cop cars, marked or unmarked. The used cars in the west end of the lot sparkled as brightly as the new models under the lights. Never buy a used car at night, my father used to say. All cars look good at night under streetlamps. While the lights in the lot were turned up, the lights inside the building were turned down. The showroom lighting was dimmed at night to save on the electric bill, but not to the point that you couldn't see the cars or people moving around in there. I could just make out Andy sitting at his desk up near the glass.

I went down the road a block, turned around and came back. The glare from the Beetle's headlights caught Andy's attention. I parked around back, and before I even had a chance to bang on the service door, Andy was pushing it open from the inside.

'Hey,' he said. 'Right on time. Where you been?'

'Around,' I said as I slipped inside and made sure the door was locked behind us. As we were walking past the service counter in the direction of the showroom, I said, 'So did you find this card in Alan's Rolodex?'

412

'Yeah,' Andy said, staying ahead of me. 'I got it.'

'That's great.'

Maybe I should have felt excited, but Kate Wood's death and constantly looking over my shoulder for the police had ratcheted up my anxiety level.

We were in the dimly lit showroom now. Andy headed over to his desk. He seemed distracted. Every time I asked him a question, he answered while keeping his back to me.

'So what's his last name?' I asked, standing just behind him and to one side as he looked through some papers on his desk.

'The card must be here someplace,' he said. 'I just found it.'

I jumped when I heard the familiar sound of car doors opening. Not outside, in the lot, but right here in the showroom. You didn't expect to hear that when there were no customers or other salespeople in the building.

The drivers' doors of an Odyssey van, a Pilot, and an Accord all opened at once. A man got out of each vehicle. Two of them were holding guns. One of them was Carter, from the front desk of the Just Inn Time. The second was Owen, the young man with the acne-scarred face who'd been on the desk with Carter that first night I'd come looking for Syd. And the third was the man who'd taken me for the test drive in the Civic.

'You're looking for me,' he said, standing behind the open door of the Accord.

'So, you're Gary,' I said. I looked from him to Carter, standing by the van. 'Hey,' I said. Carter

413

had nothing to say. Nor did Owen, getting out of the Pilot.

I looked at Andy, who'd finally turned around, but couldn't look me in the eye. So he had set me up, but not with the cops. That, I thought in retrospect, might not have been so bad.

'Sorry, man,' he said.

39

'What happened, Andy?' I asked. 'They promise to buy a car if you set me up?'

He looked hurt. 'They were going to mess me up, big time,' he said. 'I asked a couple of people at the second bar about Gary, and someone made a call, and then he showed up with these other guys.' He sniffed. 'Look, they just want to talk to you.' To the others, he said, 'Isn't that right?'

Gary, a lit cigarette dangling from between his lips, stepped forward, keeping the gun trained on me. He looked at the nose he'd damaged and grinned. 'Can I ask you something?' he said.

'Sure.'

'Where's your girlfriend get her Chinese food from? They got awesome egg rolls.'

'Did she find you or did you find her?' I asked.

'I was waiting for you, and then she came by with the food. She got a bit hysterical when she found me in the house.'

'You didn't have to kill her,' I said.

'Figured the neighbors might have heard the shot, decided I'd have to get you later.'

'Hey, hold on,' Andy said. 'We had a deal. You said you just wanted to talk to him.'

'Shut up, Andy,' Gary said, turning the weapon on him briefly. Andy shut up.

I happened to glance up at one of the closed circuit TV cameras. Gary saw where I was looking and said, 'Your friend here disabled that for us. He's been super helpful.'

'What do you want?' I asked him.

'I want you to stop nosing around the hotel,' he said. 'For ever. We don't need someone like you drawing attention to what we're doing there, messing things up for us with the cops or the INS or anybody else.'

'I've never seen you there,' I said to him. I nodded toward Carter and Owen. 'You two, yeah.'

'I work off site,' Gary said. 'I'm what you call hotel support.'

'Support for what?'

He shrugged. 'Hotel brings in the workers — '

'Illegals,' I said.

'And before we find them work, we need to get them clothes and food and shit, and I help with the financing of that.'

'By getting kids to rip off people's credit cards.'

With his free hand, he took the cigarette from his mouth and blew smoke toward my face.

'My daughter did work at the hotel,' I said. 'And everyone there covered it up.'

'The fact is,' Gary said, 'your daughter should be grateful we covered up the truth.'

I waited.

'I mean, if you killed somebody, would you want the cops to know?'

Slowly, it started to make some sense. 'Randall Tripe,' I said.

Gary nodded.

'Whatever my daughter did,' I said, 'she must

416

have had a very good reason.'

'I'll tell you what she did. She shot the fucker. Her aim was off some. A little closer to the heart and he could have gone out quicker.'

'What was he doing?' I asked. 'Why did she have to shoot him? You think I'm going to believe she just shot him for no good reason?'

Gary mulled that over some. 'OK, maybe. But dead's dead. If she'd just minded her own business and done her job, none of this would have happened.'

'What was her job?'

'Front desk, like these two clowns,' Gary said. That's what Syd had always said. 'The hotel's lousy with Chinks and slopes and Pakis doing the grunt work and getting rented out to other places, but you need people up front who can speak English. So when Sydney was recommended to us, she seemed just fine. She shouldn't have interfered in other parts of our business.'

'What happened with Tripe?'

Gary grimaced, like he didn't want to get into it. 'Look, sometimes Randy got a bit, well, randy. But the guy had a point. He figured, hey, we're giving these people the American dream, and they should be grateful. Randy had a way that he liked them — the ladies in particular — to show their gratitude. Your little girl got in the way of that.'

'What are you saying? Sydney shot this guy while he was raping someone?'

Gary didn't want to talk about this any more. He waved his gun at Andy, but asked me.

'How'd you know to send this dipstick to look for me? How'd you make that connection?'

I said nothing.

'Let me guess. You were talking to that kid. The one who fucked things up for me at Dalrymple's. That how you did it?'

I didn't want to get Jeff in any more trouble than he was already. Gary took my silence as admission.

'That stupid fucker,' he said. 'I was thinking we wouldn't have to worry about him.'

'What about Patty?' I asked.

'Hmm?'

'Patty Swain. What's happened to her? Where is she?'

He smiled. 'You don't have to worry about her any more.'

Part of me died at that moment.

'And as far as your daughter's concerned,' Gary added, 'it's just a matter of time now before we solve that problem.' He glanced at his watch. 'They might even be there already.'

'You know where she is? You know where Syd is?'

Gary snapped his fingers at Owen. He approached, and I saw that he held in his hand a roll of duct tape.

'Stick out your hands,' Owen said. With Gary pointing the gun at me, I didn't have much choice but to comply. He wrapped the tape around my wrists half a dozen times.

Andy said, 'Listen, guys, come on, what are you doing here?'

'Shut up,' Gary said to him again.

'Jesus Christ, you're not going to kill him, are you? That's insane! You can't just kill the guy!'

'No?' said Gary, who then raised his weapon to Andy's forehead and pulled the trigger.

The bullet didn't even knock him back all that much. His head snapped back, but the bullet went through him so quickly the rest of his body barely had a chance to react. His face had no time to register surprise. He dropped to the floor, his head landing on the tile, dark blood starting to pool almost instantly.

Gary took the cigarette from his mouth, blew out more smoke. 'Fuck. There I go making an even bigger mess for myself. That is *so* me.'

Some droplets of blood, warm and wet, had splattered back onto my cheek.

I wasn't the only one startled. Carter and Owen had jumped back when Gary pulled the trigger.

Carter said, 'Jesus.' Owen was staring wide-eyed. The shot was still ringing in my ears, and must have been for them, too.

'So,' Carter said, 'what now?'

'What do you mean, what now?' Gary snapped.

'Tell me we don't have to drag him down to a dumpster in Bridgeport, too. If we get pulled over along the way, we're fucked.'

Gary was agitated. He'd been fairly composed up to now, but having lost his cool with Andy seemed to have thrown him off his game.

'Let me think, let me think,' he said.

'I won't say a word,' I said to him. 'Just leave Sydney alone. Let her come home alive. She'll never tell anyone what you've been doing at the hotel. It's like you said. She's killed someone. She's not going to want to talk to the police.'

'Oh please,' he said. He pointed his gun down at Andy's body and said to me, 'You know, that's *your* fucking fault. If you hadn't sent him looking for me he wouldn't have ended up like that.'

There was some truth in that.

'Put this asshole somewhere while I think!' he shouted to Owen, who shoved me through the front door of the minivan and slammed the door so hard I got my foot out of the way just in time.

Carter said, 'If that's really what you want to do, we can take both of them, dump them in the garbage. We just drive slow so nobody pulls us over.'

Ashes dropped from Gary's cigarette as he shook his head. 'No, no, wait a second. We just fuckin' leave both of them here. We don't have to dump them anywhere. Let the cops come here and think what they want. The TV cameras are off. No one has to know we was even here.'

I'd been tossed so hard into the van I was hanging over the open area between the driver and passenger seat. Slowly, and awkwardly, with my wrists tied together, I tried to right myself behind the steering wheel. Once in a sitting position, I looked through the windshield. The van was surrounded by other vehicles; a Pilot directly ahead, a Civic to the rear, an Accord off to the right, a boxy Element to the left. Gary and Carter and Owen were in front of the van, off the right fender, debating how to handle this new predicament.

Andy's body lay just ahead of the Element.

He was just a boy.

Duct tape had been wound around the outside of my wrists, but not looped around the insides. Below the steering wheel, I started twisting my arms back and forth, trying to create some play in the tape. I'd have had a go at the edge of it with my teeth, but one of the three might notice.

I wasn't quite sure what I hoped to accomplish even if I got my hands free. There were three of them, two with guns. I could try to make a run for it, but I didn't like my chances. The showroom doors that led outside couldn't be opened without a key. I'd have to stay ahead of them all the way through the service department to get to a door I could push open.

'I think we just need to get out of here,' Carter said. 'Kill Blake and we go.'

'Yeah,' said Owen. 'I don't want to hang around here.'

Gray was nodding. 'OK, OK.'

I kept twisting at the tape. Even with my wrists bound, maybe, when one of the three approached the door, I could kick it open, knock one of them back, jump out, run like hell.

I wouldn't stand a chance.

I could lean on the horn. But how much attention was that likely to attract, really? And how long did I think I'd be able to lean on it before they dealt with me? A quick bullet through the windshield would put an end to it.

Horn aside, how long did I have, anyway?

I looked down, checked what progress I was making with the tape. Another minute and I thought I'd have it. The tape pulled at the hairs on my arm, but the pain didn't mean much in the overall scheme of things.

Something about the center console caught my eye.

It was open just a crack. Just wide enough to see something shiny inside.

I felt my heart start to pound. I swung my two hands over to the right and tipped the compartment door back another inch.

A set of keys.

I leaned over slightly, caught the keys between the thumb and index finger of my right hand, and carefully removed them from the compartment without jiggling them. Awkwardly, I maneuvered my wrists so that I could slide the proper key into the ignition.

I was going to need my hands separated to pull this off. Because the moment I turned the ignition with one hand, I was going to have to lock the doors and power up the windows with the other.

I hoped, first of all, that I'd be around so Laura Cantrell could give me shit for what I was about to try, and second, that there was some gas in this goddamn van.

40

I'd loosened the tape enough that I was able to slide my right hand through the loop. I took my left hand, tape hanging loose about the wrist, and positioned it over the controls on the driver's door. I could have hit the power lock button now — the key didn't have to be turned to make it work — but Gary and Carter and Owen would have heard the thunk of all the locks engaging and wondered what I was up to. That would give them a one-second head start, maybe enough to get to one of the two open windows and make a grab for me through them. A lot of vans on the market didn't have power rear windows. This one did, but I'd caught a break there. They were already in the up position.

Of course, bulletproof glass was not currently an option. Even with the windows up, I was hardly going to be immune.

I got my other hand on the key.

The three of them were milling around the front of the van, looking down at Andy's body, then at me. Carter and Owen were looking at Gary. He gave them a subtle nod.

They turned and glared at me behind the windshield.

I twisted the key forward.

The engine turning over would have sounded loud anyway, inside the showroom, where

423

sounds bounce off the glass and the other cars. But under these circumstances, it was like a bomb going off.

The three men jumped as the engine roared only three feet away from them. It took them a good half-second to realize what I'd actually done.

By that time, I had the two windows halfway up.

Carter moved first. He ran for my door, reached for the handle with his left hand, couldn't open it, tried to hit me with his right, which was still holding the gun. He slipped his hand through as the window was about three-quarters of the way up.

The window kept moving.

Owen had run after Carter, but there was nothing for him to do but watch what was happening. He slapped both hands on the front fender, as though he had superhuman strength and could hold the van there should it start to move.

Carter fired.

The gun went off about six inches from my left ear and sounded like a cannon blast, but with the way the window was traveling and forcing Carter's hand higher and higher, his shot went north and into the ceiling of the van.

Gary, still standing near the front of the van, screamed, 'What the fuck!'

The driver's window went as high as it could, trapping Carter at the narrowest part of his wrist. He screamed.

I grabbed the shift lever mounted on the

center on the dash, put the van into reverse, and floored it. I might normally have been inclined to watch where I was driving, but as the van began to move backwards, I kept staring straight ahead at Gary, who had tossed his lit cigarette and was raising his gun, getting ready to fire.

The van took off with a squeal, the front tires spinning on the tile floor. To my left, Carter's face slammed against the window as he was dragged along. Owen leapt backwards.

It was a short trip.

Ten feet into the journey the van smashed broadside into the Civic. The crash momentarily drowned out Carter's screams. My head slammed back into the headrest.

Carter squeezed off another shot. I wasn't sure where it went, exactly, but I didn't feel a bullet tear through my brain, so I grabbed the shifter again and threw the automatic transmission down into first.

I tromped onto the accelerator, interrupting Carter as he banged on the driver's door window with his free hand, trying to shatter it so he could free himself. Maybe, if he'd been hitting it with something harder than his own fist, he could have broken it. Owen, unarmed, was shunting back and forth, like the target in a game of dodge ball, clueless about what to do.

I realized we now had a soundtrack. There was a cacophony of car alarms going off.

As the car jumped toward Gary, he got off a shot just before diving off to my left. The windshield instantly spider-webbed, the bullet hitting in the windshield's upper right corner.

Gary's foot slipped in the blood leaking from Andy Hertz's brain. He went sprawling onto the floor, just beyond the van's path.

Still dragging a screaming Carter, I slammed broadside into the Pilot. I must have knocked the back end of it a good two feet across the floor. I knew the air bag in the steering wheel in front of me was bound to deploy at this point, but it was like when you know the flash is going to go off when your picture is being taken. You think you can keep from blinking, but you can't.

So it was still a shock when the white pillow exploded in front of me, a cloud moving at jet speed. It enveloped my face. Unable to see for the few seconds it took the bag to deflate, I blindly put the car into reverse, turned the wheel a bit to the right, and floored it again.

My head slammed into the headrest a second time. I'd hit the Civic once again, this time more to the front. The gun Carter had been holding slipped from his grasp, bumped my shoulder, and dropped down between the door and the seat.

I didn't really have a moment to look for it.

I patted down the airbag so I could see what was happening. Carter I didn't have to worry about, especially since he'd lost his gun. He was just coming along for the ride, wherever I decided to go, at least until his hand came off.

Owen had run to the far corner of the showroom, on the other side of the Pilot, just beyond my desk. Gary, still down on the floor next to Andy's body, his shirt and pants smeared with blood, took another shot. He didn't have time to aim and it went wild. A bullet *pinged* someplace into the sheetmetal.

I heard a kind of primal screaming, almost animalistic. It took a moment to realize it was coming from me.

Gary was slipping as he struggled to his feet, preparing to get off another shot. I threw the car back into drive, pulled the wheel, hit the gas, and went straight for him.

He fired and this time his aim was better, hitting the windshield midway, about a foot left of center. The glass shattered into a million tiny pieces but at least I could see clearly now. Gary dived to my right, in the direction of a bank of offices, including Laura's, and the van plowed into the back end of the Element, to the left of the Pilot I'd already pretty much destroyed. Glass shattered, the hood of the van buckled upwards to the point where it was starting to obstruct my view.

Carter's wrist was starting to bleed. He was still banging on the glass, screaming at the top of his lungs.

I needed to get out of there.

I hit the brakes, put the van in reverse, took a millisecond to plot a way out. I needed to find a wide expanse of glass, an area without any partitions, if I wanted to drive out of here. I was thinking it would be almost better to smash my way out in reverse; otherwise the shards of glass coming through the space where the windshield had been could end up beheading me.

With enough speed, I might be able to blast a hole between the Civic and a metallic blue

Accord that had, so far, escaped any damage.

'Please!' Carter screamed. 'Put the window down!'

I glanced at him long enough to say, 'Fuck you.'

I shoved my foot down on the accelerator. Carter, anticipating the move, tried running alongside, but I'd altered my course a little, heading for the back end of the Accord, squeezing in past the end of the Civic.

The front end of the Civic knocked Carter's legs out from under him. As I sped past the front of the car, Carter continued to be dragged over it by his wrist.

The Accord moved a few feet, but not enough to clear me a path.

Somewhere, I thought I smelled gasoline.

I looked ahead, and Gary was on the move, closing in at two o'clock. I moved the shift lever back into drive, steered right and went for him. He dove further right but I kept on going, smashing through the door and frosted window glass of Laura's office. Shards flew across the crumpled hood and slid over the dashboard.

Carter, no longer screaming, was hanging off my door like a rag doll.

The rear window on the passenger side suddenly exploded. It had been shot out. I didn't have time to see where Gary was. I backed out of Laura's office at high speed, went barreling halfway across the showroom, and smashed into the other end of the Element, threw the van back in drive and hurtled forward, this time taking out the office next to Laura's. The leasing manager's.

He would not be pleased.

More shots rang out. Gary was running around to the far perimeter of the showroom, using the smashed cars as cover. I was leaning over as far as I could while driving, using the van's doors and the dashboard for my own cover.

Car alarms continued to whoop.

Again, I put the van into reverse and my foot to the floor. The only thing I didn't want to hit was Andy's body, and I was worried the van was heading in that direction, so I pulled left on the wheel, glanced back, broadsided the Element again, and before I'd even turned to look forward I'd put the car in drive and given it gas.

I swung my head around, looked ahead, and there was Gary.

He was between the van and the Accord. He was holding the gun in both hands, arms outstretched, taking a bead on me.

He shifted slightly to the left. I turned left and kept on going.

The gun fired, but it went off just as the van connected with Gary, so the bullet angled up toward the ceiling. There was, maybe, a hundredth of a second when all Gary was feeling was the front of the van barreling into him. By the time that hundredth of a second had passed, he was feeling the Accord at his back.

If he made a sound when the life was crushed out of him, it couldn't be heard for the tearing and wrenching of sheetmetal. At the moment of impact, the gun flew out of his hand and sailed over the van, landing somewhere on the showroom floor behind me.

Gary's mouth was frozen into a grotesque grin, his face smeared with blood.

I sat there a moment, letting the engine idle. I looked out my window. Carter appeared to be as dead as Gary. It must have been when his lower body hit the Civic and was dragged across it. Maybe the impact severed his spine. I powered the window down an inch, freeing Carter's wrist and allowing him to slide to the floor.

The engine was still running, the alarms were still blaring, but a moment of calm washed over me.

'Don't move, motherfucker!'

I glanced up in my rearview mirror. It was Owen, holding the gun that had flown out of Gary's hands.

I don't know quite how to explain this. I'd been terrified through everything that had happened so far, but now . . . now I was just annoyed.

I put the car into reverse and gave it everything I had.

The tires squealed again and the van powered its way past the Pilot, kept on going, took out my desk, and then there was a huge crash as the tail end went through the massive plate glass window.

The ass end of the van dropped two feet to the ground, the front end went skyward. The front wheels, suspended in mid-air, spun at high speed.

I looked down between the seat and the door, knowing Carter's gun was there someplace.

Now there was a new noise added to the mix.

Going through the showroom glass had activated the building's security alarm.

The van was so out of kilter I couldn't get a look at the showroom, didn't know where Owen was. I twisted in my seat, shoved my right arm down in the narrow space between the door and the seat.

I found the gun. I slipped my fingers around something cold and slender, what had to be the barrel. I fished it up between the seat, thought I had it, but as I tried to clear the gun butt past the seatback adjustment lever, it slipped from my hand and dropped back down, further out of reach than it had been before.

Beneath the sirens, I thought I could hear someone walking across broken glass. Owen was working his way around the van.

'You're not going anyplace now!' he shouted.

Through the open windshield, there was the flickering of light. It took a second for me to realize it was from flames.

I jammed my hand down into the space again, hunted around for the gun. It was caught under the edge of a floor mat. I got my fingers around the barrel again, pulled the gun back up, turned it around so that I had my hand wrapped around the butt, the finger around the trigger.

Suddenly, my door was yanked open. The crash must have somehow unlocked it.

Owen said, 'Hey, asshole, I'm going to — '

I shot him.

'Fuck!' he screamed, toppling backwards onto the asphalt just outside the showroom window. Gravity swung the door closed, but I kicked it

431

open with my foot and scrambled down to the ground, the van's engine still running.

Fire was spreading through the showroom.

Owen was splayed on his back. I could see red blossoming on his left shoulder. So I hadn't fired a fatal shot. His right hand still held the gun, but before he could train it on me I stood over him and pointed Carter's gun directly at his head.

'Throw away the gun,' I said.

'What?' he said. There were so many alarms blaring he couldn't hear me.

'Throw it!' I said.

He tossed it a few feet away.

'Where's my daughter?' I shouted at him. 'Gary said he knew where she was!'

'I don't know!' he said.

I fired the gun into the ground between his legs.

'Jesus Christ!' he said.

'Gary said they were on the way to get her. Where is she?'

'I can't tell you,' he said. 'I can't.'

'I'm going to shoot you in the knee if you don't tell me,' I said.

'Listen, if I tell you they'll — '

I held the gun over his knee and pulled the trigger. The resulting scream, momentarily, drowned out the various alarms.

'The next one goes in your other knee,' I said. 'Where is she?'

'Oh God!' he screamed, writhing on the ground.

'Where is my daughter?' I asked.

'Vermont!' he wept.

'Where in Vermont?'

'Stowe!' he said. 'Somewhere in Stowe!'

'Where in Stowe?'

'They don't know! Just somewhere!'

'Who's going for her?'

Before he could answer, he passed out. Or died.

I walked over and picked Gary's gun up off the ground. I might need two. As I was heading back to the Beetle, the entire showroom erupted into flames behind me. A car's gas tank exploded. A fireball blew out one of the other plate glass windows.

I got into the car and took out my cell, punched in a familiar number. In the distance, I could hear sirens.

Susanne answered. 'Hello?'

'Hi Susanne,' I said. 'Could you put Bob on?'

'Oh my God, Tim, the police have been here and — '

'Just put Bob on for a second.'

Ten seconds later, Bob, sounding annoyed, said, 'Jesus, Tim, you've got the entire police force looking for you. What the hell have you — '

'What are you doing right now?' I asked. 'I need a different car. One I can count on, and it needs to be fast.'

41

I was driving the Beetle along Route I when I noticed, in my rearview mirror, a patrol car that had been heading in the other direction put its brake lights on. I kept glancing at the mirror.

'Don't turn around, don't turn around,' I said under my breath.

The cop car turned around.

It was still quite a ways back, so I eased down on the accelerator, trying to increase the distance between us without appearing to take off at high speed. Not that the Beetle was exactly up to that.

The cop car straightened out, and the flashing lights went on.

I hung a hard right down a residential street, then killed my lights so there weren't two bright red orbs glowing from the back of the car. The streetlights were bright enough that I could see where I was going. I looked in the mirror, saw the police car take the right as well.

I took a random route. A right, another right, a left. I kept looking up at the mirror, looking not just for the car, but the pulsing glow of its rooftop lights.

The driver of that car was probably on the radio now, asking for other cars to close in on the area.

I wasn't safe in this car. The odds are I wouldn't make it to Bob's house without getting spotted.

I made another left, another right, and found myself down near the harbor, not far from Carol Swain's house. I couldn't go back there.

I was coming up on a cross-street, and a police car zoomed past, siren off but lights flashing. If I'd had my headlights on, I'd have had a perfect look at the driver's profile.

I wasn't even going to get out of this neighborhood, let alone to Bob's house. I wheeled the Beetle into a stranger's driveway, pulling it up as far as it would go next to the house, killed the engine, grabbed the two guns I'd acquired, plus Milt from the back seat, and got out of the car.

Would it be safe to call Bob and ask him to come pick me up here? And would he even do it? Clearly, the police — maybe Jennings herself — had been to see them. Even if Susanne and Bob didn't know why, exactly, the police were hunting for me, they had to know it was serious.

I started running in the direction of the harbor. Bob's house wasn't far from the sound. Maybe I could steal a small boat, head up to the Stratford shore near where Bob lived, beach the boat, then hoof it the rest of the way to his place. Then, with any luck, I could talk him into giving me another car so I could start driving up to Stowe.

I got to the harbor. It was a warm evening, and many people were sitting on their boats, having a drink, chatting with friends, their voices coming through the night like soft background noise. Stealing a boat might not be all that simple.

I was skulking around a parking lot that edged up to some tree cover. I was tiptoeing across gravel to the most remote end of the lot, wondering if there was any chance someone might have left their keys in a car — did anyone do that any more? — when something about a van I was walking past caught my eye.

Stenciled on the rear windows were the words 'Shaw Flowers'.

As I came up around the driver's side of the vehicle, I could see what appeared to be two people up front, leaning into one another over the console.

I tapped the driver's window with the barrel of one of my acquired weapons. He jumped, and as he turned to see who it was, his blond-haired companion slumped forward lifelessly onto the dashboard.

'Hey, Ian,' I said through the glass.

He powered the window down. 'Oh my God, it's you,' he said.

'It's OK,' I said. 'I can see that's not my daughter with you.'

'My aunt made me tell,' he said quickly, defensively. 'She made me tell who hit me. But I told the police it was all a mixup.'

'I know,' I said. 'I appreciate that. And I never told anyone about your friend.'

'Thanks,' he said quietly. 'What do you want? What are you doing here?'

'Unlock the back door,' I said. 'I need you and Mildred there to make a delivery.'

I got into the back. I set the guns on the floor, and put Milt on the seat. Surprisingly, it was the stuffed moose that caught Ian's attention.

'And you think I'm strange,' he said.

★ ★ ★

We spotted three cruisers wandering the neighborhood before we got back up to Route 1.

'They all looking for you?' Ian asked while I looked around in the back of the van, trying to stay below the window line.

'The less you know, the better,' I said. 'You've got a wrapped-up bouquet sitting back here.'

'Yeah,' Ian said. 'Been trying two days to deliver it. The people are away.'

I gave him directions to Bob's house. 'Drive down the street once, see if the place is being watched. Cop cars, or what look like unmarked cop cars. We do that a couple of times, and if it looks clear, pull into the driveway.'

'OK.' He paused. 'You know, I don't normally deliver flowers this late. Won't that look weird?'

'Let's hope not,' I said.

It didn't take long to get to Bob's neighborhood. 'Houses are really nice around here,' Ian said. 'I've delivered up around here before.' He paused. 'I don't see anything that looks funny.'

'Let's do it,' I said. 'I want you and Mildred to hang in for a minute.'

'Her name's Juanita,' Ian said.

He pulled into Bob's very wide driveway, right next to the Hummer. I grabbed the wrapped bouquet, slipped out the side of the van, walked up to the front door.

Susanne looked shocked when she opened it. At first, I thought it was the late-night floral delivery, then realized she was looking at me.

'My God, what happened to you?' she asked,

437

Bob standing in the hall a few feet behind her. She took the flowers from me and set them on a nearby table.

At first I was thinking, she'd already seen my nose. It hadn't occurred to me that I'd sustained more injuries. I glanced in the front hall mirror. My cheeks had several small cuts in them. My forehead was bruised. Shards of broken window glass and hitting your head on the steering wheel will do that to you.

And there was still duct tape hanging off one of my wrists.

'I don't have time to explain,' I said. To Bob, I said, 'What have you got for me?'

'Where's the Beetle?' he asked, peering out into the drive and seeing only the van.

To Susanne, I said, in a rapid-fire delivery, 'I know where Syd is. She's in Vermont. In Stowe. There are people already on their way to get her. They might already be there. I need to get there fast.'

I thought she'd pepper me with questions, but she instantly grasped that my taking time to answer them would not be in Syd's best interest. She said, 'Just take Bob's car. Go. Now.'

She was referring to the Hummer, Bob's massive SUV. I didn't like the idea of heading up to Stowe in that beast. It stuck out like a sore thumb, was lumbering and slow to respond, I'd lose too much time stopping every hundred miles to fill it up with gas, and before long the police might be looking for it.

'Something else, Suze,' I said.

She nodded, instantly understanding. 'On the

438

lot, we just took in a Mustang. Has a V8 under the hood.'

'Come on,' Bob protested, 'you can't be serious.' He looked at me. 'You know the police have been by here twice tonight looking for you? What the hell's going on, Tim?'

'A lot,' I said. 'But at this point, all that matters is that I get on the road to Stowe.'

Susanne put her hand on the doorknob for support. 'The Mustang's in good mechanical shape,' she said to me. 'Good tires.'

'And it's fast?' I said.

She nodded. 'In a straight line. Not so hot cornering, but it's interstate all the way to Vermont.'

'Let's get it.'

'I don't like this,' Bob said. 'If the police are looking for him, this is tantamount to helping a fugitive.'

Susanne looked long and hard into Bob's face. 'I can do this alone, or you can help me.'

Evan came down the stairs. 'What's going on?'

'We'll be back in a bit,' Bob said grudgingly. 'If the phone rings, answer it.'

'No, don't,' said Susanne. 'And if the police come to the door, you haven't seen Tim, and you have no idea where we are.'

'So you want me to lie to the cops,' Evan said, half to himself. 'Cool.'

As the three of us went out of the house toward the Hummer, Bob said, 'Honestly, Tim, I think you owe us an explanation here of just what the hell's going on. You call late at night, demand a car, have some story about Sydney being up in Vermont, you can't — '

'Hang on,' I said, changing direction and heading over to the van. 'I have to get my guns.'

That shut Bob up, at least for a while.

* * *

I thanked Ian and told him to take off. In addition to the guns, I grabbed Milt, whom I gave to Susanne for safekeeping. On the way to Bob's Motors, I laid it out for Susanne in point form. Bob, behind the wheel of his Hummer, listened, then made some noises about how what made the most sense was to call the police, here and in Vermont. I argued that the police were so focused on me right now we'd waste valuable time persuading them to move on Stowe.

Susanne said to Bob, 'I'll put my money on Tim, for now, if you don't mind.' Then, to me, 'That man you shot in the knee. Is he dead?'

'Owen?' I said from the back seat. 'I don't think so. If an ambulance got to him in time, he'll live. But the two with him? Gary and Carter? They're goners.'

'And Andy,' Susanne said from the passenger seat.

'Yeah,' I said. 'And it gets even worse.'

'What?'

'Patty,' I said. 'I don't know how she was involved in any of this, but something happened to her in the last forty-eight hours. No one's seen her. And one of those three who tried to kill me, he said I didn't have to worry about her anymore.'

'Oh my God,' Susanne said. 'Oh my God.'

'Yeah,' I said, feeling the pain of what had happened to Patty in a way I could not bring myself to tell my ex-wife. At least not now.

'I can't believe this,' Susanne said. 'It can't be happening . . . '

We went the next few blocks in silence. Then Susanne said, 'So someone really was watching the house.'

'Yeah,' I said. Behind the wheel, Bob looked chagrined. 'They thought if Syd tried to come home, to your place, they'd get her then.'

'Why hasn't she just called us?' Susanne asked. 'Found a way to get in touch?'

'One reason,' I said slowly, knowing there was no real way to prepare Susanne for this, 'is that she may have killed someone.'

Susanne started to form some words to respond, but nothing came out.

'I think it may have been self-defense, or she was trying to help someone else who was being attacked.'

'But . . . ' Susanne struggled. 'Even if, even if that's true, I can't believe she wouldn't call. For help.'

'I don't know,' I said. 'I don't know.'

I wondered whether we were thinking the same thing, that something had happened to Sydney, something even the bad guys didn't know about, that had kept her from letting her parents know where she was.

'Maybe because, on top of everything else, she's pregnant,' Susanne said.

Bob tightened his grip on the Hummer steering wheel.

'I don't think so. I mean, yeah, maybe, but I don't think that has anything to do with why she hasn't called.'

Bob's used car dealership was just up ahead. He pulled into the lot and parked just beyond a dark blue Mustang, late nineties vintage I thought. 'I'll get the key,' Susanne said, getting out and heading for the office.

'You never even paid for the Beetle, did you?' Bob asked.

'Is that your biggest concern at the moment, Bob?' I asked.

I was resting my head against the seatback. I was suddenly very exhausted. Stowe had to be a good four-hour drive. I needed some sleep, but I didn't have time for it.

I also didn't know where to begin looking for Syd once I got to Stowe.

'Look,' Bob said, 'do what you have to do. But it's not fair to drag Susanne into this. Not if you're wanted by the police. You're really a piece of work, you know?'

'Did the cops tell you what they want me for?'

'All they said was more questioning. It was Detective Jennings, and this other cop, big guy with a girl's name. What do they think you've done?'

'There's a list,' I said. 'But the man who tried to kill me tonight killed a woman named Kate Wood earlier today. The police like me for it, at the moment.'

'Jesus Christ.'

I closed my eyes and rested my head. I opened them when I heard rapping at my window.

Susanne was dangling a set of car keys.

I climbed down from the Hummer and took the keys for the Mustang. 'Any gas in it?' I asked.

'I doubt it,' she said. 'It's not exactly Bob's policy to include a tankful with every purchase.'

I hit the remote button and unlocked the doors of the Mustang. I got inside, left the driver's door yawning open, and turned the engine over. It roared. I glanced at the gas gauge and saw that there was a little under half a tank.

'Gas up now and you should be able to make it the whole way there without stopping if you get lucky,' Bob said.

'You mind grabbing the guns?' I said to Bob.

He went back to the Hummer. She said to me, 'I'm going with you.'

'That's not a good idea,' I said. 'You're not up to this.'

'Don't tell me that.'

'Susanne,' I said, lowering my voice so she'd lean in close to me. 'I'm going to get Syd out of this thing. But if something happens to me in the meantime, I want her to have you to come home to.'

'Tim, don't say — '

'No, listen to me. I mean it. You have to stay here, be here for Sydney when she comes back, if she ends up coming back alone. And I may need to get in touch, need you to find out things for me. Right off the bat, when you get home, I need you to look up some directions for me for getting to Stowe. I'm going to hit 95, then 91 north, but I could use some pointers along the way.'

Susanne's eyes were glistening. 'I love you, you

know. I always will.' She sniffed. 'What should I do about the police?'

'Don't tell them a damn thing. But if it's Jennings . . . you can tell her what went down at the dealership. Just not where I've gone. They'll try to stop me. Jennings'll be waking up every Connecticut state police officer trying to find me. I don't know how much time I have to find Syd, but I don't need Jennings holding me up.'

Susanne understood.

'If that guy I shot wakes up, she may find out soon enough that I'm on the way to Stowe,' I said. 'If she pressures you, tell her I'm still in the Beetle. At least then they won't be looking for this car.'

Susanne nodded. She said, 'I can't let you go alone.'

'Suze, you can't come.'

'Then you have to take Bob.'

Bob had just shown up with the two guns. He was holding them like they were made of plutonium. 'What?' he said.

'You're going with Tim.'

'Oh no, no, no, I don't think that's a good idea.'

'Just this once, I gotta agree with Bob,' I said.

'If you don't go,' she told him, balancing on her cane, 'I will.'

He stood there a moment saying nothing. Then, guns still in hand, he gave Susanne an awkward hug and walked around to the passenger door of the Mustang, opened it and got in.

'Let's go,' he said, gently putting the guns on the floor mat in front of him.

42

By the time we'd gassed up and got onto I-95, it was around ten-thirty p.m. Once I'd merged the Mustang onto the highway, I put my foot down. The needle on the speedometer climbed until I had the Ford up to ninety. I could feel the car floating a bit, but I was confident it was a speed I could maintain, and decided to hold it there for the time being.

'We don't even know where we're going,' Bob said. 'I mean, once we actually get to Stowe. I was there once, years ago, with my first wife, Evan's mother, and the place is lousy with resorts and all these places tucked up into the mountains.'

'I doubt Sydney's staying at a resort,' I said.

'Maybe she got a job at one,' Bob said. 'A lot of those places, they'd pay a kid like Sydney cash under the table. She wouldn't have to give her real name or anything, which, considering she's a kid on the run, would kind of be appealing to her.'

What he said made some sense.

He continued, 'I think one of Evan's friends had a summer job up there once. Stowe does a pretty big winter business, the skiing and all, but it's pretty nice in the summer, too.'

While I was thinking about what Bob had to say, I was also trying to concentrate on the road. When you're doing ninety — and nudging up above that — you need to pay attention to what you're doing. Especially at night.

As if reading my mind, Bob said, 'You know, if a deer or something runs out in front of us at this speed, we're fucked.'

'I'd rather take my chances in this than that Beetle,' I said.

'Still, we hit a deer, the goddamn thing'll come right through the windshield.'

I glanced over. 'If you want, Bob, I can drop you off at the next service center.'

'I'm just saying, you're not going to be much help to Sydney if you've got an antler through your brain.'

He leaned forward in the dark and picked up one of the two guns I'd brought along for the ride.

'Be careful with those, Bob,' I cautioned.

'Don't worry,' he said. 'I'm not an idiot.' He was peering closely at the gun in the darkness. What light there was came from the glow of the instrumentation. 'Can I turn on the light for a second?' he asked.

'No,' I said. I didn't want an interior light interfering with my night vision, such as it was.

'You know what I think this is? This and the other one? I think these are Rugers.'

'I don't know anything about guns,' I said.

'Well, I know a little. These are impressive pistols. I think they hold a ten-round magazine.'

'Huh?' I said.

'Ten bullets,' he said. 'The clip holds ten bullets. The gun can hold eleven if there's already one in the pipe. Semi-automatic,

.22-caliber. These guys who were gunning for you had nice taste in weapons.'

'Yeah,' I said.

'You know whether these are fully loaded?'

'Considering that they were shooting at me with them, I'd have to say no,' I said. 'The one guy, Gary, I think he fired the most shots, so the gun that he was using, there might not be any rounds left in it at all. The other one, that was the one Carter was using. He got off a couple of shots into the ceiling of the van, but I think that was about it. Then I fired . . . ' I had to think back. 'I think I fired three shots with it.'

'So these guns might be empty,' Bob said.

'Yes, Bob, those guns might be empty.'

He powered down his window, suddenly putting us in the eye of a mini-hurricane. Gripping one of the guns, he rested his arm on the door and fired off into the night.

'What the fuck!' I shouted. 'Don't do that!'

He brought his arm in and powered the window back up. 'That one still has some ammo in it,' he said.

'It did!' I shouted. 'What if that was the last bullet?'

'Well, if it was,' he said, 'you really couldn't have hoped to accomplish much anyway with just one bullet.'

I was ready to get out my phone and tell Susanne to come pick up her boyfriend along the side of I-91 about twenty miles north of New Haven, but restrained myself.

'I think I can figure out how to remove the magazine to check,' Bob said.

'Jesus Christ, Bob,' I said. 'Please don't end up killing us here in the car.'

I had my eyes on the road but was pretty sure he gave me a look. 'I know what I'm doing,' he said. 'You just press this little button here and the clip falls out. There, see?'

He displayed the candy-bar-shaped magazine for me. 'It's got like a little slit in the side here so you can see how many bullets you have left. You gotta turn on the light for just a second, OK?'

Reluctantly, I reached up and flicked on the interior light. If Bob was going to inspect the guns, I supposed it made sense that he be able to see what he was doing, for both our sakes.

'OK, hang on,' he said, pulling the magazine out of one gun and examining it. 'There's one bullet left in this one. And let's have a look at this other one here. Hang on, OK, there's three in this one. So we've got four bullets between us.'

'Great,' I said.

'How many bad guys you figure we're going to be running into?' he asked.

'I don't know,' I said.

'Well, if there's more than four, we'll ask them to stand in front of each other.'

That nearly made me smile. 'How come you're so laid back about this?' I asked.

He shrugged. 'Come on,' he said. 'What are the odds that we're really going to run into a bunch of badass gunslingers?'

Maybe, if Bob had had the kind of evening I'd had, he wouldn't have asked a question like that.

★ ★ ★

My cell rang.

I held onto the wheel with one hand, fumbled the phone to my ear with the other.

'It's me,' Susanne said. 'Thought I'd check in.'

'Bob's shooting at trees, but other than that, we're fine.'

'I went online. Getting to Stowe's pretty simple. You just stay on 91 for a dog's age. Then, when you're well into Vermont, when you get to 89, you take that northwest, follow signs to Montpelier. You go past Montpelier a few miles, look for the Waterbury exit, go north, Stowe's just up there. Do you need me to go over that again?'

'No,' I said. 'Thanks.'

'The computer say it's more than four hours to drive there.'

'I think we can cut an hour off that,' I said. 'So long as we don't get stopped by the cops.'

'Speaking of which,' Susanne said, 'Detective Jennings called again.'

'Oh yeah.'

'She sounds pissed.'

'There's a shocker.'

'She's tearing apart Milford trying to find you. I think she'll be calling your cell next.'

'What did you tell her?'

'I told her what went down at the dealership. But not where you're going.'

'She didn't like that.'

'No. Like Bob predicted, she accused me of aiding a fugitive.'

'Did she say whether the guy I shot was dead?'

'She didn't get into it with me,' Susanne said.

'But she did say someone was taken to Milford Hospital.'

If the guy was able to talk, he might tell Jennings Sydney was in Stowe. Then she'd send out the troops to intercept me.

'How do you think they know Syd is up there?' Susanne asked.

'I don't know.' Bob was making motions to hand the phone to him. 'Hang on, Bob wants to talk to you.' I gave him the cell.

'Hey,' he said. 'You remember one of Evan's friends had a summer job up in Stowe? Ask him about that. Ask him who it was, where the place was.' He said to me, 'If Sydney heard about it, maybe she might have gone there to hide out for a while.'

Then he got very quiet. He said, 'It's OK . . . I do . . . You know I do . . . OK.' He stayed on the phone a moment more, then handed the phone to me.

'Hey,' I said.

'If I hear anything more, I'll call,' she said.

'OK,' I said, and flipped the phone shut. Tentatively, I asked Bob, 'Everything OK?'

Bob said nothing for a moment, then, 'She just . . . she was just thanking me for going with you.' Long pause. He glanced over at me, the gauges casting soft light across his face. 'She thinks she made a mistake, leaving you.'

'I doubt that,' I said.

'It's true,' he said. 'And now, with all this shit with Evan, I wouldn't blame her if she moved out and tried to patch things up with you.'

I watched as the dotted lines came zooming

450

toward the Mustang and then slipped away. 'I know you love her,' I said. 'I saw it when she collapsed that day.'

We went another mile or so before Bob said, 'I know you think that I think I'm better than you. But I have to compete with your ghost every day.'

My cell rang. I flipped it open.

'Yeah,' I said.

'Mr Blake.'

'Detective Jennings,' I said.

'Do you know where I am right now?'

'I'm guessing the hospital, or the dealership.'

'The dealership,' she said. 'At least what's left of it. The whole place is ablaze. Your wife tells me that once this fire is out, we're going to find three dead people inside. We've got a man in hospital in serious condition. Shot in the shoulder and the knee. But I gather I'm not telling you anything you don't already know.'

'I know Susanne's told you that two of the men in the building tried to kill me. So did the one you found outside, the one you took to hospital. A man named Gary executed Andy Hertz. Shot him point blank in the head. Same way he shot Kate Wood.'

'We need to talk about that.'

'Soon,' I said.

'How did the other two men in that building die, Mr Blake? Did you kill them?'

'You're kind of fading in and out,' I lied.

'Wherever you are, turn around and come in right now.'

'I can't do that. Maybe, if I had any faith that you and Detective Marjorie weren't trying to pin

451

everything on me, I'd feel differently. The fact is, there's been a goddamn human trafficking operation going on at that hotel right under your noses. Why don't you work on that till I get back?'

'Human trafficking? Is that what your daughter's gotten mixed up in?'

'She was working there all the time,' I said. 'Everybody there was told to lie. And they did a pretty convincing job of it.'

'Mr Blake, *please*, come in. We'll take over looking for Syd and — '

'You need to go through that hotel,' I pressed. 'Room by room.' I felt a lump in my throat. 'You need to see if there's any sign of Patty.'

'You think she's hiding there?'

'I think . . . I think she's dead.'

Jennings waited.

'Gary said she was dead,' I said.

Jennings didn't say anything.

'Detective?'

'I'm here,' she said.

'You got anything to say?'

Another pause, then, 'We obtained Patty's cell phone records.'

'I've been calling her cell,' I said. 'She's not answering.'

'There had been several calls, over the last few weeks, to her phone from a number in Vermont. From Stowe, specifically.'

I tried to keep my voice even. 'Whose phone?'

'Pay phones. A couple of different numbers, actually. Someone made the calls using prepaid phone cards.'

'What about the other way?' I asked. 'Were

452

there any calls from Patty's phone to Stowe?'

'No,' Jennings said.

'Well, I suppose it could have been anyone,' I said. 'A boyfriend, a relative.'

'Mr Blake, is that where you're headed? To Stowe?'

'No,' I said. 'I have to go, detective.' And I flipped the phone shut. Seconds later, it started to ring. Jennings calling back.

'You're not going to answer that?' Bob asked.

I shook my head. 'No.'

★ ★ ★

A few miles later, Bob shouted: 'Tim!'

'Huh?' I said.

The Mustang had rolled onto the shoulder. I jerked hard on the wheel, bringing the car back onto the road.

'Jesus Christ!' Bob shouted. 'You fell asleep!'

I blinked furiously, shook my head. 'I'm OK, I'm OK,' I said.

'Let me drive for a while,' he said.

I was going to argue, but realized it was the smartest thing to do. I pulled the car over to the side, left it running as I got out and stretched in the cool, night air. Bob came around, got behind the wheel. I slipped into the passenger seat and was doing up the seatbelt as Bob pulled back onto the road.

'You know the way?' I said.

Bob looked at me. 'I know you think I'm a fucking moron, but I know how to drive.'

'The thing is, now I'm awake,' I said.

Thirty seconds later, I was out cold.

453

43

Somewhere around Brattleboro Bob decided we needed to start looking for a gas station. It was the middle of the night and it was clear we weren't going to make it all the way to Stowe without refilling. Holding the car at ninety was sucking up the fuel pretty quickly.

We found an all-night station, a rundown place that was light on the amenities, including a working rest room. Bob ran off into the bushes to take a whiz while I filled the tank at the self-serve. When he came back I ran off into those same bushes.

Bob, pretty tired himself now, tossed me the keys. When I got into the car he handed me a Mars bar and held up a coffee, which he then fit into the cup holder. 'This, along with your nap, should keep you going.'

'You know how I take it?' I asked.

'Black, I know. Half the time Susanne makes me coffee, she serves it to me that way, leaves out the cream, thinks she's still married to you.'

I tore off the end of the candy bar wrapper as I barreled up the ramp and back onto the highway. I took a huge bite and chewed contentedly while Bob sipped his own coffee. I could not remember when I'd last eaten. I set the bar down on my lap and carefully brought the coffee up to my lips. Bob had already pried back the plastic lid so I could get at it.

I took a sip.

'Wow,' I said. 'That has to be the worst coffee I've ever had in my entire life.' I had to suppress a gag reflex as it went down my throat.

'Yeah,' said Bob, nodding. 'If that won't keep you awake, nothing will.'

I took my eyes off the road for a second, still holding the cup close to my mouth. 'Thanks,' I said.

Another mile on, I said, 'I know I've sometimes been, you know, where you're concerned, a bit — '

'Of an asshole?' Bob said.

'I was going to say, a bit reluctant to show you much respect.'

'Sort of the same thing,' he said, leaning back in his seat, glancing into the passenger door mirror.

'Well, I don't really think that's going to change any,' I said. Bob found himself unable to stifle a laugh. 'But I want to thank you for taking such good care of Susanne.'

'Shit,' he said.

'No, really,' I said. 'I mean it.'

'And I mean shit, you've got a cop on your ass.'

I glanced into the rearview mirror. Flashing lights. Way back there, maybe as far as a mile, but unmistakably cruiser lights. I felt my heart hammer in my chest. After all I'd been through today and I was worried now about a speeding ticket?

Unless it was worse than that. Maybe Jennings had figured out where we were going, and what kind of car we were in, and put the word out.

'Shit,' I concurred. The thing was, we were lucky to have gotten this far along without getting pulled over.

There was nowhere to go, out here on the interstate, and no upcoming exits that might allow me to lose the police. I eased my foot off the gas, allowing the car to coast back down to something close to the legal speed limit, hoping that by the time the cop caught up with us, he'd think he'd made a mistake about how fast we were going.

And if he did pull us over for something as simple as speeding — and wasn't after me for the mayhem I'd left behind — I'd take the damn ticket.

'What are you doing?' Bob asked as the car slowed. First to eighty, then seventy-five.

'I'm dropping down to the speed limit,' I said.

'No, no, you've got to lose him,' Bob said.

'How am I supposed to lose him? Which side street would you like me to turn down?'

'OK, here's the thing,' he said, measuring his words. 'I'm not sure, technically speaking, whether the registration for this car will hold up.'

'What are you talking about?'

'I'm just saying it would be better, all around, if we weren't pulled over.'

'Bob, is this car stolen?'

'I'm not saying *that*,' he said. 'I'm just saying the registration might not hold up to close scrutiny.'

I was still letting the car slow down. The flashing light behind me was getting closer.

'Honest to God, Bob, you told me your days of Katrina cars were over. That you were on the up and up. I swear — '

'Calm down,' he said. 'It might be OK, I don't know.'

'This is a stolen car,' I said.

'I do not have personal knowledge that this car is stolen,' he said.

'Those are fucking weasel words if ever I heard them,' I said.

I felt sweat breaking out on my forehead. I didn't see as we had any choice but to pull over and see how this played out.

We could hear the siren now.

'I'm just saying, while this is a legitimate car, its history is a bit clouded,' Bob continued.

'How many cars on your lot are like this?' I asked. 'Have you got them grouped? These cars over here, these were in a flood, these ones over here were stolen, these ones over here come with a free fire extinguisher because they're likely to burst into flames?'

'This is what I mean about you being an asshole,' Bob said.

The cruiser was nearly on top of us now, lights flashing, siren wailing.

'You know,' Bob said, 'there's also the matter of these two guns we've got.'

'Oh, God,' I said. 'Speeding, a car with a murky registration, and weapons we don't have licenses for that can be traced back to actual murders.'

'Nice going,' Bob said.

And then a miracle happened. The cop car

457

moved out into the passing lane and blasted past us.

'What the hell?' said Bob.

About another mile on, we came upon a pickup truck that had rolled over into the median. The cruiser was pulled over onto the left shoulder, the officer helping a couple of people standing about, apparently not seriously injured.

'You see?' Bob said. 'Everything's OK.'

The rest of the way, I held the Mustang to just a few miles per hour over the limit. It seemed safer that way.

★　★　★

There was a long stretch after that where neither of us said much of anything. I finished my Mars bar, even drank the bad — now cold — coffee Bob had bought. When there was nothing to do but stare at the road up ahead and fall into a trance watching the dotted lines zip past, I had time to think.

About Syd's disappearance. Gary and Carter and Owen. Andy Hertz.

And while Syd was always there right in front, I also couldn't stop thinking about Patty. The girl I now knew to be my biological daughter. And within minutes of learning the truth about my connection to her, came the news that I had lost her.

It was a lot to take in.

Bob would never have been my first choice of someone to open up to. But at that moment, he happened to be the only one available.

I said, 'What would you do if you found out there was a child out there who was yours, a grown-up kid, and you'd never known about this person before?'

Bob glanced over nervously. 'What have you heard?'

'I'm not talking about you,' I said. 'I'm just saying. How would you handle that? Finding out there was this person and you were the father?'

'I don't know. I guess that would kind of blow my mind,' he said.

'And then,' I said, slowly, 'what if, right after you learned this, you found out that something had happened to this kid. And any kind of connection you might have wanted to make, you'd never be able to do that?'

'What happened?' Bob said. 'To this supposed, imaginary kid?'

'She died,' I said.

I could feel Bob looking at me. 'What are we talking about here, Tim? You're not talking about Evan and Sydney, and anything that might or might not have happened there, are you?'

'No,' I said.

'So what, then?'

I shook my head. I had to blink a few times to keep the road in focus. 'Nothing,' I said. 'Forget I said anything about it.'

★ ★ ★

We headed north at the Waterbury exit, past the Ben and Jerry's ice cream factory on the left. There were hardly any cars on the road. It was, after all, coming up on three in the morning.

The road wound leisurely up and over graceful hills, through wooded areas and clearings. A couple of times, the headlamps caught the eyes of night creatures — raccoons, most likely — at the edge of the road, starry pinpoints of light.

About fifteen minutes after getting off the interstate the road curved down and to the right, taking us into the center of Stowe. Colonial-looking homes and businesses crowded up to the sides of the road. We came to a stop, a T intersection. There was an inn on the right, a church and what appeared to be a government building just up ahead and to the left. Turning left would take us over a short bridge, with a pedestrian walkway on the right side modeled after a covered bridge.

'Where the hell do we start?' Bob asked.

A cell phone went off. I grabbed mine out of my jacket, but it wasn't the one ringing.

'Oh,' said Bob, and fished out his own phone. 'Yeah? We just got here, just pulled into town a few minutes ago. Yeah, we're OK, although we nearly got pulled over, Jesus. Uh huh. OK. OK. Did Evan know any more than that? OK, OK, great. OK, yeah, of course we'll be careful. OK. Bye.'

'What?' I asked as he put the phone away. I noticed, at the gas station on the corner, a pay phone. I wondered whether any of the calls made to Patty's cell had come from it.

'Susanne talked to Evan, and then he tried to find this kid he knew, name of Stewart. He just found him, woke him up in the middle of the

460

night. Stewart said yeah, he used to work up here at a motel or inn or something.'

'What was the name of it?' I asked.

'The Mountain Shade,' Bob said. 'Stewart said it was a good job, because they paid in cash.'

This underground economy was everywhere.

'Did Stewart know Sydney?' I asked. 'Did he ever tell her about the place?'

'Evan says yeah. A few months ago, they ran into each other at a Starbucks or something, and Sydney was asking about it. I guess this was before she found something else to do for the summer.'

I thought about that. If Syd was on the run and knew she'd have to support herself while things got themselves sorted out, it would be the perfect job for her. A place where she could make some money and stay below the radar.

'So where the hell is this place?' I asked.

There weren't exactly a lot of tourist information places open this time of night. The gas station was closed as well. I went straight ahead, but in less than a mile we were driving out of Stowe, so I turned around and came back to the T intersection, turning right onto Mountain Road and across the bridge with the covered walkway.

This route was filled with places to stay. I scanned to the left as Bob read off the names of places on the right.

'Partridge Inn . . . Town and Country . . . Stoweflake . . . '

'Up there,' I said. 'You see the sign, just past the pizza place?'

'Mountain Shade,' Bob said. 'Son of a bitch.'

I pulled into the lot, the tires crunching on the gravel. As I reached for the handle to open the door, Bob said, 'Hey, you want this?'

He had a Ruger in each hand and held one out to me. 'Which one is this?' I asked. 'The one with one bullet, or three?'

He glanced down at one, then the other. 'Fuck.'

I took the gun from him. Once we were out of the car, we tried to figure out what to do with them.

'It won't fit in my jacket pocket,' I said.

'Try this,' Bob said, turning to the side and demonstrating how he could tuck the barrel of the gun into the waistband of his pants at the back.

'You'll shoot your ass off,' I said.

'That's how it's done,' he said. 'Then you hang your jacket over it, no one knows it's there. It's better than tucking it in the front of your pants. If it shoots off by mistake there, you got a lot more to lose.'

So, nervously, I tucked the gun into the back of my pants. It felt, to say the least, intrusive.

The night air was so still that when we closed the doors the sound echoed. There was a light over the office door, but no light on inside.

'What are we going to do?' Bob asked.

'We're going to have to wake some people up,' I said.

I banged on the office door. I was hoping that whoever ran the joint had quarters adjoining the office and would hear the ruckus. You ran a place

462

like this, you had to be prepared for the unexpected. A burst pipe. A guest with a heart attack.

I waited a few seconds after the first round of knocking, then started up again. Somewhere down a hallway a light came on.

'Here we go,' I said. 'Someone's coming.'

A shadowy figure started trudging down the hall, flipped the office light on, and came to the door. It was a man in his sixties, gray hair tousled, still drawing together the sash on his striped bathrobe.

'We're closed!' he shouted through the glass.

I banged again.

'Goddamn it,' he said, unlocked the office door, swung it open a foot and said, 'Do you know what time it is?'

'We're really sorry,' I said.

'Yeah,' said Bob.

'I'm Tim Blake, this is Bob Janigan, and we're trying to find my daughter.'

'What?' said the manager.

'My daughter,' I said. 'We think it's possible she might be working here and it's very important we find her.'

'Family emergency,' Bob chimed in.

The manager shook his head. The gesture seemed designed to wake himself up as much as to display annoyance. 'What the hell's her name?'

'Sydney Blake,' I said.

'Never heard of her,' he said and began to close the door.

I got my foot in. 'Please, just a minute. It's

possible you might know her by another name.'

'What?' he said. 'What other name?'

'I don't know,' I said. I was reaching into my jacket for one of the photos of Syd I carried around with me everywhere I went. I reached through the door and handed it to him.

Reluctantly, he took it between his fingers and squinted at it. 'Hang on,' he said and went around to the office desk, where a pair of reading glasses lay. That allowed us to open the door wider and take a step inside.

He peered through the glasses at the photo.

'Hang on,' he said again, and I felt my pulse quicken. 'I've seen this girl.'

'Where?' I asked. 'When?'

'She came in here, I don't know, two weeks or more ago. Looking for some part-time work. I didn't have anything.'

'Did she tell you her name?'

He shrugged. 'Maybe, but I don't remember it. I told her to try another place, one of their summer staff quit all of a sudden, they were looking for help.'

'What place?' I asked.

'Uh, hang on. Touch the Cloud.'

'What?' Bob asked.

'The inn. That's the name of it, the Touch the Cloud Inn. It's further up the road, on the way to Smugglers' Notch, where the road starts climbing.'

'Do you know if she got a job there?'

'Beats me,' he said. 'Now you can go wake them up.' He ushered us out of the office and killed the light.

Back in the car, the guns removed from the backs of our pants, we carried on up Mountain Road, driving slowly so as not to miss any of the signs.

'Whoa, go back!' Bob shouted. 'I think it's in there.'

I backed up the Mustang about thirty yards. Even at night, it was clear to see that the Touch the Cloud Inn had seen better days. The towering rustic sign out front needed paint, a mock split rail fence around the garden below it appeared to have been used for bumper impact tests, and one of the bulbs over the office door was burned out.

We parked again, tucked the guns into our waistbands, and did the whole routine all over again.

A second after the first knock, a small dog started yapping. I heard nails skittering across the floor, saw the shadow of something small scurrying across it. *Yap yap! Yap yap yap!*

Even before the lights came on inside, a woman was shouting: 'Mitzi! Mitzi! Stop it! Be quiet!'

She was in her forties, streaky blond hair, good-looking — not easy to pull off this time of night in a frayed housecoat and no makeup. She was also very wary. She looked at us through the glass of the still-locked storm door and asked, 'Who are you?' We introduced ourselves. 'What do you want?' she shouted over Mitzi's yapping.

I said, loud enough to be heard through glass and over Mitzi, 'We're trying to find my daughter. It's an emergency.' I said I thought she might be working there, and gave her Sydney's name.

'Sorry,' she said. 'I've got no one here by that name. Mitzi, Jesus, shut up!'

The dog shut up.

I pressed Syd's picture up against the glass. The woman leaned in, studied it, and said, 'That's Kerry.'

'Kerry?' I said.

'Kerry Morton.'

'She works here?' I asked.

The woman nodded. 'Who'd you say you were again?'

'Tim Blake. I'm her father.'

'If you're her father, how come her last name's not the same as yours?'

'It's a long story. Listen, it's very important that I find her. Do you know where she's staying?'

The woman kept studying me. Maybe she was looking for some sort of family resemblance. 'Let me see some ID. Him, too.'

I dug out my wallet, pulled out my driver's license and put it up against the glass. Bob did the same.

The woman was debating what to do. 'Hang on,' she said. She left the office and could be heard in a nearby room saying, 'Wake up, wake up, pull some pants on.' Some male grumbling. 'There's a couple chuckleheads here want me to walk off into the night with them and there's no way I'm going out there alone.'

A moment later she reappeared with a young, shirtless and barefooted man who looked like

466

he'd just walked out of an Abercrombie and Fitch ad. Washboard stomach, rippling arms, hair as black as the woods. The faded jeans he'd just pulled on were zipped but unbuttoned. Bob and I traded glances. A boy toy. But a boy toy who didn't look like he should be messed with.

'This is Wyatt,' she said. He blinked sleepily at us. 'He's joining us.'

'Great,' I said.

'We got several out-of-town kids working here,' she said. 'Wyatt's one. We got a few mini-cabins out back for them.' Evidently Wyatt was favored with better accommodation, at least tonight. 'Kerry's staying in one of those.'

'Where?' I asked. 'Do they have numbers? Can you tell me where — '

'Hold your horses,' she said and, along with Wyatt, led us down a sidewalk, around the side of the building to a row of cabins dimly lit by some lamps attached to wooden poles. They all backed on to a wooded area. I hoped Wyatt was groggy enough not to notice the bulges under the backs of our jackets. It was dark out, so I figured we were OK.

'It's this one over here,' she said. 'This better be a real emergency because she's going to be pissed, getting woke up in the middle of the night. I know I am.'

I didn't have anything to say. I was so excited about finally finding Sydney that my body was shaking.

The woman reached the door and rapped on it lightly with her knuckle. 'Hey Kerry, it's Madeline. Kerry?'

The windows stayed dark. I didn't hear any stirring inside. I came up to the door and called out, 'Sydney! It's Dad! Open the door! It's OK!'

Still nothing. 'Open the door,' I said to the woman I now knew to be Madeline.

'I'll have to go back and get the — '

Bob had come around behind her and kicked the door in. 'Hey!' she said.

'Whoa!' said Wyatt. It was the first word we'd heard from him. He grabbed hold of Bob's arm, but Bob shook him off and reached around inside the door, found a light switch and flicked it on.

It was, at best, six by nine feet. A cot, two wooden chairs, an antique washstand. No running water, no bathroom. A quaint prison cell, in many ways. There were a few toiletry items on the washstand, a hair brush, a set of keys, a pair of sunglasses. The cot didn't look slept in.

'Where the hell is she?' Madeline asked. 'She needs to be stripping beds first thing in the morning.'

I stepped over to the washstand, picked up the keys. There were three house keys — that made sense; my house, Susanne's, and now Bob's — plus a remote and a car key, both stamped with the Honda emblem. I touched the hair brush, then picked up the sunglasses.

They had 'Versace' written on the arms.

'This is Sydney's stuff,' I said to Bob, trying to keep my voice from breaking.

I began looking about the cabin for any other clues, anything that might give me a hint as to where she was now.

'When did you last see her?' I asked Madeline,

who was huddling up close to Wyatt.

'Sometime today,' she said vaguely. 'I don't really keep track. Kerry usually works an early shift, finishes up mid-afternoon. After that she can do what she wants.'

'So she did work today?' I asked. 'You actually saw her.'

'Yeah, I saw her.'

'What was she like? How was she?'

'You mean today, or since she got here?'

'Both, everything.'

'She's just about the unhappiest girl I ever did see. Mopey and down, skittish, always looking over her shoulder, you come up behind her and say something and she jumps out of her skin. Cries all the time. Something's wrong with that girl, you don't mind my saying.'

I'd felt so hopeful moments earlier, now very uneasy. We'd come so close to finding her. Where would she have gone in the middle of the night?

What if someone else had already found her?

I looked in the corners of the cabin, in the washstand, under the cot. I found some shorts, underwear, a couple of tops. What few items there were looked brand new. Syd had left Milford without packing, after all. There were a couple of prepaid phone cards she must have used to make long-distance calls, and some sheets of paper with material that had been printed off the Internet. Some of it was from the website I'd set up to find her. There was an online version of a *New Haven Register* story on her disappearance.

'You have a computer here people can use?' I asked.

'There's one in the office I let the kids working for me borrow. Send emails home, that kind of thing.'

'Has Sydney — Kerry — used it?'

'Yeah, she sneaks some time on it every day. And yeah,' she said, nodding at the papers in my hand, 'she's printed some stuff off it, but I don't know what it's about. She was always clearing the history every time she was done.'

I asked, 'Did you hear anything unusual tonight, see any people around you didn't recognize?'

'I run a tourist business,' Madeline said. 'I see different people around here every day.'

'How about you?' I asked Wyatt.

The boy shrugged. 'I never talked to her,' he said.

I turned to Bob. 'I don't know what to do,' I said.

He stood there in the dim light of the cabin, shaking his head. He didn't seem to have any ideas either.

'Maybe it's time to let Detective Jennings in on things,' he said. 'Tell her where we are, see if she can get the locals involved.'

'Locals?' Madeline said.

'How about some of the other people you have working here?' I asked. 'You have other kids working for you for the summer? Kids Sydney might have talked to?'

Madeline said, 'Two cabins down, there's a girl here for the summer from Buffalo. I've seen the two of them talking a few times.'

'We need to talk to her right now,' I said.

Madeline looked as though she was preparing to argue, then said, 'What the hell.' With her housecoat flapping in the light breeze, she led us to the door of the other cabin and knocked on the door.

'Alicia? Alicia, it's Madeline!'

A light flicked on inside, and a few seconds later a sleepy-eyed girl, black, nineteen or twenty years old, opened the door. She was in a T-shirt and panties. When she saw that it wasn't just Madeline at the door, but three men, she narrowed the opening to about six inches, showing nothing but her face.

'What's wrong? What's going on?' Her eyes shifted from Madeline and Wyatt to Bob and me and back again.

'These men need to talk to you about Kerry,' Madeline said.

'Why?'

'I'm her father,' I said. 'We need to find her. It's very important.'

'She's in the cabin two doors down,' Alicia said, like we were all idiots.

'No,' Madeline said. 'She's not. She's gone.'

Then Alicia began to nod slowly, like maybe that made sense to her. 'OK,' she said, drawing the word out.

'What?' I asked.

'Well, OK, Kerry's already pretty jumpy, right?' She looked at Madeline for confirmation, who nodded. 'But today, she was totally freaked out. I was just sitting out front, reading Stephen King, and Kerry comes running up from the main building, she looks like she's seen a ghost, you know? She was totally freaked out about something. She goes into her cabin and I went in to see her and she was putting on her backpack and I asked her what's going on and she wouldn't say anything. She just said she had stuff to do and she had to go right away.'

'She didn't say why?' I asked. 'She didn't say what had freaked her out?'

'No, but it was something, that's for sure.'

'When was this?' I asked.

'Like, late this afternoon?'

'Where did she go?'

'I don't know. She started walking one way, then she looked over toward the parking lot, stopped all of a sudden, turned around and started going the other way. And she was walking along the trees there, you know? Instead of going down the pathway. Like she didn't want people to see her.' She looked directly at Madeline. 'Is she gone? Am I going to have to do all her chores in the morning?'

'We'll talk about that later,' Madeline said.

I asked, 'Did you talk to Syd? I mean, Kerry? Before this thing today? Did you talk to her much?'

'Some. A bit. I guess.'

'What did she tell you about herself? Did she tell you why she was here? Did she talk about anything? Why she was on edge?'

'Not really. But she's majorly screwed up, honestly. She doesn't want to do any jobs where she has to go into the dining room or work the front desk. She only wants to do stuff where she won't run into people. I don't think she really likes people. I mean, she's the first person I ever met didn't have a cell phone. She said she didn't use them any more, that they weren't safe. I know they say if you talk on them too much they make your brains get cancer or something, but I think they're safe.'

To Madeline, I said, 'You have a pay phone here?'

'No. There are a few around town, but we don't have one.'

'If you wanted to use a pay phone, where would you go? I saw one at the main intersection downtown.'

'You wouldn't have to go that far. Just down the road, where the pizza place is, they've got one there.'

I looked at the sliver of Alicia in the open doorway. 'Thank you for your help. I'm sorry we troubled you.'

She said, 'Did you say Syd? A second ago?'

'Yes,' I said. 'That's my daughter's name. Not Kerry, Sydney.'

She vanished for a moment, then, when her face reappeared, she extended her hand out. There was a piece of folded paper in it.

'This got slipped under my door earlier,' she said. 'Someone got the wrong cabin, but I didn't know anyone named Sydney so I didn't know who to give it to.'

I took the paper and unfolded it. It read:

Syd: I'm here to bring you home! Meet me by that little covered bridge in the center of town! Love, Patty.

44

'What?' Bob said. 'What does it say?'

I handed the note to him. It had filled me with a mixed sense of hope and puzzlement. He read it a couple of times and said, 'Didn't you say Patty was dead?'

'Yeah,' I said. 'But maybe I was wrong. I hope I'm wrong. But this note could be some kind of trick. It might be from someone else, meant to lure Sydney out into the open.'

I asked Alicia, 'You didn't see who left this? You haven't seen anyone around? A girl with streaks in her hair?'

Alicia shook her head.

So I thanked her again, and walked back to the office with Madeline and Wyatt. I had her take down my cell number in case Syd reappeared, or anything else happened. Then Bob and I returned to the Mustang, fishing the guns out of the back of our britches before we settled into the seats. I wanted to study the note, so I gave him the keys.

'We'll check out the covered bridge,' I said, once we were in the car.

'Yeah,' said Bob.

The note was handwritten. I was trying to recall whether I'd ever seen a sample of Patty's handwriting. If I had, I couldn't remember. It was hard to tell from the note whether it bore any of the trademarks of a teenage girl's style. It appeared to have been hurriedly written, and on a rough surface, as if the paper had been held against the side of the cabin when the pen was applied.

'If it isn't Patty who wrote this,' I said, 'whoever did write it will be looking for Sydney, not us. And if it is Patty, she'll certainly know us when she sees us.'

And, I was thinking, if it really was Patty, what the hell was she doing? How did she know Sydney might be up here, and why was she trying to mount a solo rescue?

'The thing is, Sydney may not be around any more,' Bob said, interrupting my thoughts. 'Something spooked her, made her run.'

'Maybe,' I said. 'And if she's worried about being seen, she may not want to be standing at the edge of the highway with her thumb out.'

'You think she has a car?' Bob asked.

It was possible. I was guessing she ditched the Civic because she was afraid the bad guys would be looking for it. Did she grab another car? Did she hitchhike to Stowe?

'I don't know,' I said. 'Let's assume she's still around, otherwise there's no point in our being here. And if she's going to call anyone, maybe she'll use that pay phone by the pizza place.'

'That's an idea.'

We turned the car around, powered down both of the windows, and pulled onto Mountain Road, heading in the direction of the town's center. Bob was taking it slow, scanning the sides of the road, attempting to peer onto porches, down side streets, occasionally glancing into the

475

rearview mirror in case a car started bearing down on us in a hurry.

We were looking for not one girl now, but two.

'Sydney might have gotten a room somewhere else,' I said.

'Maybe,' Bob said, watching out his side.

I continued my scan. Bob said, 'Take a look behind us. Is that a car back there, with no lights on?'

I twisted around in my seat, looked out the back window. 'Hang on, I'm just waiting for it to go under a streetlight . . . Yeah. You're right. Looks like one of those new Chargers. That, or a Magnum. It's got that big grill, you know?'

'Yeah,' Bob said, his palms sweaty on the steering wheel. 'I think it might have picked us up just after we got back onto the main road.'

'It's definitely holding way back.'

'Covered bridge, dead ahead,' Bob said.

I turned to the front. It was odd, as covered bridges went. Only the pedestrian walkway, on the left side, was protected with a roof. The roadway itself was uncovered. In darkness, it was impossible to tell whether anyone was hiding under the covered part.

'You want me to pull over?' Bob asked.

'No,' I said. 'Not if that other car's following us. Try to get past it, turn a corner or something, I'll jump out and run back to the bridge.'

'OK,' he said. 'Do you know my cell number so you can call me back?'

I took out a pen and wrote it on the back of the note that had been left for Sydney, wrote my own number on a corner of the page, tore it off and handed it to Bob.

The Mustang rolled over the bridge. The other car, a dark, menacing shadow, was about twenty car lengths back.

'OK,' Bob said, 'get ready.'

He made a stop at the sign, turned left and floored it. Then he hit the brakes, and I prepared to jump out and run down between two buildings.

'Gun!' Bob whispered.

I nearly fell over reaching back into the car as Bob handed me one of the Rugers. Whether it was the one with one bullet, or the one with three, I had no idea. I tucked it into the back of my pants.

I scurried off into the shadows as the Mustang pulled away.

The car with its headlights out slowed at the intersection without signaling or stopping and continued on after Bob. It was a Charger, with tinted windows. I couldn't tell who was behind the wheel, or whether the driver had company.

Once that car was a safe distance up the street, I ran across the road and down the other street in the direction of the bridge. All there was to hear was the sound of my shoes hitting the pavement, and my hurried breathing.

I got to the end of the bridge, entered the covered portion, and waited a moment for my eyes to adjust.

'Patty?' I called. Not too loud, but loud enough.

I waited two seconds for anyone to respond.

'Patty?' I called again.

'Mr B?'

I could detect movement on the bridge, at the midpoint. I started walking, quickly. 'Patty!' I said.

I thought she might run toward me, but as I approached I could see that she looked frightened, as though she doubted it was really me. But when I got to her, and threw my arms around her, held her next to me, she said, 'The fuck are you doing here?'

'You're OK,' I said, holding on to her, not wanting to let go. 'You're OK.'

'Yeah, I'm OK,' she said, and now she was hugging me, too. Her hands touched the gun in the small of my back and pulled away suddenly. 'Why wouldn't I be OK?'

I let go of her enough to look her into her eyes. 'I thought you were dead.'

'Fuck, no, here I am,' she said.

I gave this girl — this girl I now knew to be my daughter — another hug.

'What's the deal, Mr B?' she said. 'You're crying.'

'I'm sorry,' I said. 'I'm just glad to find out you're OK.' I tried to focus. 'Everyone's been worried sick about you. We were thinking the worst.' I thought about Carol Swain, whose level of concern wasn't exactly off the scale, but she needed to know that her daughter was all right. 'You have to call your mother,' I said. 'You have to let her know you're safe.'

'Yeah, sure,' Patty said, rolling her eyes.

'You do. But Patty, have you seen Syd?'

Patty shook her head. 'What are you even

478

doing here?' she asked me. 'How did you . . . '

'What about you?' I asked. I needed to get past my emotional response, and ask some questions. 'What are *you* doing here?'

Patty seemed to be struggling for an answer. 'I'm here looking for Sydney.'

'I figured that,' I said. 'But how did you know?'

'She called me,' Patty said quickly. 'She called and told me she was here.'

'When?'

'Just, like, yesterday?' Patty said.

'How is she? Is she OK?'

'Yeah, yeah, she's cool, she's good.'

I felt relief starting to wash over me, but I still had many questions. 'How did you get up here?'

'I, you know, I hitched. Took a while.'

'Patty, why didn't you just tell me? If Syd told you where she was, why didn't you let me know? I could have brought you up here.'

Her mouth twitched. 'I . . . I was pissed at you. About the other night. I wanted to make you proud of me. I wanted to bring Syd back myself.'

'Oh, Patty,' I said. 'Is that why you weren't answering my calls?'

She nodded. 'I wanted to do it myself. Syd got a job up here, and I went there to find her, but she was gone. I turned my cell off for a day or so. I didn't feel like talking to anybody.'

'You left Syd a note,' I said.

'Yeah, but I guess she didn't get it.'

'You left it at the wrong cabin.'

'Shit.'

479

'How long have you been on this bridge?'

'Off and on, for hours,' she said.

'Sydney got scared off,' I told her. 'She ran away from the inn. I think she saw one of them, looking for her.'

Patty looked scared.

I took hold of her by the shoulders. 'This is something you can't do alone, Patty. These people, the ones who've been looking for Syd, they're very dangerous. They're killers, Patty. And I think they're up here right now. There's been a car following us around.'

'Us?'

'I'm here with Bob. We started driving up when we learned Sydney was here in Stowe.'

'How did you know that?'

'I found out from one of them. Patty, I shot a man tonight. I shot him to find out what he knew. And he told me Sydney was up here.'

Something Jennings had told me shortly after Bob and I started heading up from Milford came into my head.

'Patty,' I said. 'This call you got from Sydney. Telling you she was up here. You got that when?'

'Yesterday,' she said.

'Was that the first call?'

'Huh?'

'Was that the first time she called you? Yesterday?'

'Yeah, of course,' she said.

'Because the police, they've been looking for you for the last couple of days, and they were checking your cell records.'

'Yeah . . . '

'And they said there were other calls from Stowe. Much earlier ones.'

'That's crazy,' she said. 'They must have that wrong.'

'No, I don't think so.'

'It doesn't make any sense,' she insisted.

'Did Sydney call you before? Has she been keeping in touch with you? You haven't known all along where she's been, have you?'

She opened her mouth, but nothing came out. Not for a second, anyway. 'What?' she said. 'Are you crazy?'

'I'm just trying to figure it all out,' I said. 'And I can't figure out why Sydney would call you to come and get her. Why wouldn't she have called me, or her mother?'

'I don't know!' she shouted. 'I don't know! Shit!'

'Patty, what's going on? I need you to be honest with me. I need you to tell me what's going on.'

'Honest?' she said. 'You want honest? I'll give you honest. My whole life has been one long fucking joke. It's been shit, that's what it's been.'

'Patty.'

'And you know why? You know whose fault it is?'

'Patty, this isn't the time. We have to find out where — '

'It's my fucking parents' fault, for sure, but you know who else? Huh? You know who else? *You.* That's who. That's who's fucked up my entire life. You.'

'Patty,' I said again.

481

'Because you're the reason I'm here,' she said. 'You're the reason I *exist*.'

I let that one hang out there a minute before I said, 'I know.'

'What?'

'I know. I saw your mother. I know about the file. You found the file, didn't you? The detective's report.'

She stared at me, stone-faced. 'Yeah. I saw it.'

'You're my daughter,' I said.

'Yeah,' she repeated. 'Big whoop.'

'You should have told me. When you met Sydney, when you came to our house, you must have figured it out.'

'I knew before,' she whispered. 'That's why I got to know her, kind of snuck into that math class. Because I wanted to get to know *you*. I wanted to know who my real father was. And now I know. I found out the other night. I saw the real you. When you told me you had one daughter and that was enough.'

'Patty, I didn't know. If I'd known — '

'If you'd known, what? What would you have done? You'd have freaked out, that's what you would have done. And listen, don't even worry yourself about it. Because I really don't have any father, OK? All you are is just some guy who had it off with a cup.'

'I'm sorry,' I said. 'You make decisions when you're young, you never think about the ramifications of — '

'Oh fuck off,' she said. But while she sounded angry, I could see, in the limited light, that she was crying.

482

'Patty,' I said, 'when did Sydney first call you?'
She wouldn't look at me.

'How long have you known she was up here?
What did you tell her? Why have you been
keeping — '

My cell phone rang.

'Yeah?'

'Tim? It's Bob. I've got her. I've got Syd.'

45

I heard the phone being rustled. 'Daddy?' Sydney said. 'Daddy?'

'Syd!' I said while Patty watched me. 'Oh my God, Syd, I can't believe it's you! Are you OK?'

'Yeah, yeah, I'm OK!'

'How did Bob find you?'

'I found *him*!'

'What?'

'I've been hiding out all over town for hours after I got spotted at the inn. So I saw this car drive by, and the window was down, and I was sure it was Bob, so I phoned him!'

'That's great, honey! That's fantastic!' I brought my voice down a touch. 'They're still around. There's some car prowling around with its headlights off.'

'I know, I know,' she said. 'Did you find Patty? Bob said Patty left me a note?'

'I'm with her right now.'

'Oh thank God,' Sydney said. 'Is she OK?'

I smiled at Patty, who seemed to be studying my facial reactions. 'She's good. She's OK.'

'Patty's been so great,' Sydney said. 'Right from the beginning. I mean, it's been awful, hiding out like this, but at least you knew I was OK.'

I looked at Patty. I wasn't sure whether she could hear Sydney's voice coming out of the cell. I turned slightly away. 'What's that, hon?'

484

'Whenever I called Patty she kept me posted on everything. How the people from the hotel were watching you and Mom, about the fake website you got Jeff to set up to make them think you really didn't know where I was. How the hotel people had our phones all tapped and were listening in on everything. Patty said as soon as it was safe to call you, and come back, she'd let me know. I can't believe it's finally over.'

'Yeah,' I said. 'I can't believe it, either.' Patty tried to inch closer to me, wanting to hear what Sydney was saying. I said, 'You've been up here the whole time?'

'Pretty much,' she said. She was trying to hold off crying, but she was unable to stop her voice from shaking. 'The first day, after it happened . . . Oh God, Dad, I swear I didn't mean to shoot that man. I was walking down the hall and this girl was screaming, and when I used the pass key to go into the room, this man, he was doing these awful things to one of the Chinese women who worked there, he had her tied down and — '

'It's OK, honey.'

'And I started to scream, and then this guy got off the bed and started coming after me. That's when I saw the gun sitting on the dresser, so I grabbed it, and — '

'It's OK. You can tell me all this later.'

Full out crying now. 'I shot him. I couldn't believe I'd done it. Then Carter and some of the others came in, and I was freaking out, you know?'

'I know, I know.'

'I told them we had to call the police. I knew I

485

had to call them. But then, they all started freaking out, too. Said we couldn't call the police. Said they couldn't find out what was happening.'

'OK,' I said. 'And then what?'

'So they took my cell, and they left me in the room with the dead man and Owen was standing outside the door so I couldn't get away, and they ripped out the wall phone so I couldn't call anybody. I was so scared, and I couldn't think what to do, and I knew Patty was coming over, because we were going to hit the mall real quick when I finished work. So I thought, maybe that dead man had a phone on him, and I reached into his jacket, and oh Daddy I got his blood all over my hands — '

'It's OK,' I said softly.

'And I called Patty with his phone and told her I was in trouble.'

I looked at Patty. She wasn't making eye contact.

'So Patty, she had this idea. She snuck into the hotel, pulled the fire alarm, snuck back out, and then I guess everybody was running around, and then she ran around to the window of the room I was in — it was on the first floor. I slid it open, it only went about ten inches, and there was a screen, and Patty kicked out the screen, but I couldn't squeeze through, so Patty grabbed my arm and pulled and pulled and it just about killed me but she got me out.' Syd took a moment to catch her breath. 'But she told you all this, right?'

'Sure,' I said.

'And Patty, she could see everything so clearly, she was so cool. She told me to just go, and keep going. Because, I'd shot a guy, right? She said the police would never understand, that they never believed teenagers, and those bad people at the hotel would be after me, too. Patty told me not to think about anything but getting away, and she'd explain to you and the police what happened before everybody, you know, started flying off the handle. So I got in the car and just started driving away like crazy.'

Another breath, then, 'So I ditched the car, because I figured everyone'd be looking for it, and hitched my way up to Stowe. I remembered this friend of Evan's talking about living up here, getting a job, so I figured it'd be as good a place as any to hide until you told Patty to tell me it was safe to come home.'

'Syd,' I said, 'tell Bob I'm on the bridge with Patty. He can scoop us all up, we can get the hell out of here, sort it all out on the way back.'

Patty had her back to me. She had her cell out and was punching in a number.

'Hang on,' I said to Sydney. To Patty, I said, 'Who you calling?'

'Like you said,' she snapped. 'I'm calling my mom.'

I almost reached out and took the phone from her, but instead said to Syd, 'Hon, put Bob on for a second.'

'Hang on.'

Then: 'Yeah?'

'What about that car that was following us?' I asked him.

487

'I did a couple of quick turns, think I lost it. I'm parked with the lights off in some driveway by a hotel.'

'OK. When you think it's safe, whip down to the bridge and we'll all get the hell out of here.'

'Sounds like a plan,' Bob said. 'Hey, I know there's a lot of bad shit coming down, but there's some good news.'

'What?'

'I asked Sydney here if Evan had knocked her up, if she was pregnant. But she's not.'

'Bob!' Sydney shouted, and grabbed the phone back from him. 'What's wrong with him?'

'Don't worry about it,' I said. 'The only thing that matters is that you're OK.'

Patty, talking into her own phone, was saying, 'Yeah, I'm here with Mr Blake, on the bridge, and Bob and Sydney are going to be here in just a second, and then we're all supposed to head back.'

Now Bob was back on the phone. 'Hey, Tim,' he said, 'doesn't some of what Sydney just told you sound kind of goofy?' To Syd, he said, 'No offense.'

'Yeah,' I said, looking at Patty. 'It does.'

Patty said, 'OK, see you soon.' And she put her phone away.

I said to Bob, 'Get here quick.'

'Give us a minute to make sure the coast is clear,' he said.

I put my phone away. Patty eyed me nervously. 'So that's great,' she said, trying to smile. 'We're all going back.'

'What's this game you've been playing?' I

asked her, keeping my voice level. 'Telling Sydney to stay up here until it was safe? What was going on in your head?'

'Don't yell at me,' she said.

I took hold of her by the shoulders. 'You think this is yelling? Patty, why did you do this?'

She tried to wriggle away but I held on to her. 'I hate you,' she said. 'I thought I could love you, but I hate you.'

I wasn't letting go. 'Why did you do it?'

She stopped fighting me, but wouldn't look at me. 'At first, I thought if she came back, I'd be in deep shit.'

'You? Why would you be in trouble?'

'Because . . . I gave her the tip to work for the hotel. I put her in touch with somebody.'

I thought about what Andy had told me, about finding Gary and Patty meeting over a milkshake.

'You knew Gary,' I said. 'Andy saw you together.'

Now she looked at me. She was puzzled. 'Knew?'

'Gary's dead,' I said.

'Dead?' Patty said.

'How did you know Gary?'

'I did some work for him. Couple of places I worked.'

'Stealing data off credit cards?'

'It was no big thing.' She looked away. 'But I knew if Sydney came back, and told everybody everything, it'd come back on me. How Syd got the job, that I knew Gary, that I used to rip off numbers for him. I'd be in deep shit.'

'Patty, Patty, Patty,' I said softly, thinking of all the anguish she'd put me, and so many others, through the last few weeks. 'Didn't Gary, and the others at the hotel, didn't they think you'd know where Sydney was? Because you were friends?'

'They didn't know we were that close. I mean, they came to see me, right? I wasn't going to tell them where Sydney was, but I had to give them something, so I told them they should watch your house and Sydney's mom's place, but so what? I knew Sydney wasn't going to show up, because she was listening to me. She'd call me every few days and I'd tell her to keep laying low, right? And come on, let's face it, she's been safe all this time, right?'

I heard a car pull up, a door open and close.

'But you still could have told me,' I said. 'It didn't make any sense to trick Sydney into staying away.'

'The thing is . . . '

'What?'

She bit her lower lip. Then, 'I liked it that she was gone.'

I felt a chill that had nothing to do with the night air. I thought of all the times Patty, since Syd's disappearance, had dropped by to see me. Showed up with dinner. Popped into the dealership.

Patty wanted to take Sydney's place. She could be my daughter if Sydney didn't come back.

Then why had Patty finally decided, in the end, to come to Stowe to bring Sydney back?

Unless that hadn't been the plan at all.

490

That's when I realized that someone was standing on the covered walkway only a few steps away. I'd been so focused on Patty, trying to figure out what she'd done, that I'd failed to notice we were no longer alone.

I whirled around. There was a woman standing there. She was holding a gun, and it was pointed at me.

It was Veronica Harp.

46

'You little bitch,' Veronica said to Patty. 'You mean you knew where she was all along? You waited until *yesterday* to tell us? You couldn't have mentioned this a couple of weeks ago?'

So, there it was.

Patty had led Veronica here. To get Sydney. I could guess when she decided to make her betrayal of Sydney complete. After I'd told her I had one daughter, and didn't need another.

'He has a gun,' Patty told Veronica.

Great.

Veronica, keeping her weapon trained on me, said, 'Take it out slowly and toss it over the railing.'

I reached behind me, pulled the Ruger from behind my belt, and did as I was told. A second later we heard it splash into the creek.

'Do your Yolanda Mills voice for me,' I said to Veronica. She held back a smile. 'Emailing me that picture was what really clinched it.'

'That was a bit of luck,' Veronica said. 'I really was trying to figure out how to take pictures with my phone. I'm not very technical, you know, but I want to be able to take lots of shots of my grandson, and I don't want to have to carry a camera around if the phone will do the trick. So I was fiddling with it up in the hall when Sydney walked by. Who knew it would come in handy later.' To Patty she said, 'You told me you hardly

492

knew this Sydney kid. You're friends?'

More than that, I thought.

'I didn't want something to happen to her,' Patty said. 'Then.'

Veronica sighed. 'Working with children, I swear.'

I said, 'I don't get it.'

'You don't get what?'

'How does someone like you, a goddamn grandmother, sleep at night doing what you do? Bringing people into the country, farming them out as slave labor. Taking all their rights away. Turning them into prostitutes and God knows what else.'

Veronica became indignant. 'They get lots of good jobs. Nannies, hotel work, restaurants, construction. Let me tell you something. They've got it a lot better here than they did back in the countries they came from. You see any of them trying to go home?'

'Would you let them? What do they pay you to come here? What kind of horseshit stories do you tell them to convince them they're going to have a better life when they get here?'

Veronica had nothing more to say. When it was clear she wasn't interested in debating with me any longer, I said to Patty, 'You know she's going to have to kill Sydney. And me. And Bob.'

Patty said nothing.

'And probably you, too,' I said.

'Don't listen to him, Patty,' said Veronica. 'You fucked this up, but you've been a lot of help to us. You made the right decision, telling me how to find your friend.' She was agitated. 'Where are the rest of them?'

'They should be here any second,' Patty said. 'If they see your car — '

'It's across the street, behind a gift shop. Go out onto the road, flag them down, tell them to come onto the bridge, that Mr Blake has turned his ankle, something. You're good at lying.' She smiled. 'Aren't you, sweetheart?'

Patty took a couple of hesitant steps.

'Go!' Veronica hissed.

Patty ran.

'The shit's hit the fan back in Milford,' I said. 'Have you heard?'

She looked at me.

'Gary's dead. Carter is dead. Owen's in hospital.'

I could tell that she didn't know about this. She was trying to hide her surprise.

'The whole thing's unraveling, Veronica. You'd be smarter to forget about us and just get in your car and drive as far away as you can.'

'Shut up,' she said.

'You can't go back. I'll bet the hotel is swarming with police right now. When Owen's able to, he'll probably tell them everything if it means he can cut some kind of a deal. I'll bet he gives you up first.'

'I have friends,' Veronica said, but her voice lacked confidence.

'Out in Seattle, maybe? Did one of them send you that cell phone in the mail?'

'Just shut up.'

'I don't care how many friends you have. I don't like your odds now. I think, basically, you're fucked, Veronica.'

Her eyes dazzled angrily as she held the gun on me. 'I don't think so.'

We could both hear a car approaching. Then, in the distance, Patty yelling, 'Over here! Over here!'

My gun was down in the creek, but Bob would still have his. The problem was, he had no idea he was going to need it. If I didn't think I could get the drop on Veronica — she was careful to stand several feet away from me — I would have to wait until I was sure Bob and Sydney were out of the car before I started shouting.

I heard the echo of a car door closing, then some girlish squealing. Patty and Sydney embracing. Sydney genuinely excited, Patty giving an Oscar-worthy performance.

They needed to quiet down, just for a second.

I could hear them approaching the end of the covered walkway.

'Run!' I shouted as loud as I could.

'Fuck!' Veronica said, and fired.

I was already moving, but not quite fast enough. My left ear suddenly felt very hot and my hand went up to it instinctively. I could feel blood trickling out between my fingers. The bullet had nicked the top of my ear. The shock of it bounced me off the walkway wall and down to the floor.

Instead of scaring everyone away, the shot brought people running.

Bob was in the lead, reaching around to his back, which suggested to me that he had the Ruger with him. He could see me down on the bridge, and Veronica, gun still in hand.

He brought out the weapon, fired one shot wild, using all the skill he'd employed when he'd taken a shot out the window of the Mustang.

Veronica threw herself up against the wall and fired back, even though Sydney and Patty were already on the bridge behind Bob, and at risk of getting hit.

Bob, as it turned out, was an effective cover for both of them. 'Oh shit!' he shouted. The gun fell out of his right hand. He grabbed his upper right arm with his left hand and tripped over his own feet. 'Jesus!' he said. 'I'm fucking shot!'

Sydney screamed.

Now Veronica was running down the bridge, away from me. Sydney turned to run, but Patty blocked her way long enough for Veronica to grab her. She took hold of her by the arm and started dragging her back to where I was leaning up against the walkway wall.

Veronica said to Patty, 'Get that gun!' Meaning Bob's, which had slid away from him. He was in too much pain to try to reach it.

Patty did as she was told, held the weapon down at her side in her right hand.

Veronica turned on Sydney and said, 'Get over there.' She kept pushing Sydney along the bridge, then shoved her down when they reached me.

Syd threw her arms around me and immediately felt blood on her fingers.

'Dad, are you OK? Are you shot?'

'It's OK,' I said. 'I'm OK.'

'Why is Patty helping her?' she asked. 'What's going on?'

I put an arm around Sydney, pulled her into

me. I wanted a chance to hold her before Veronica ended up killing all of us.

'It doesn't matter any more,' I said. 'We're together. I love you. I love you so much.'

Veronica looked down at Sydney. 'God, what a pain in the ass little bitch you turned out to be. All we wanted was a nice, English-speaking face on the front desk, and look at the trouble you got us into.'

'He was a bad man,' Sydney said through her tears. 'Mr Tripe was a very bad man.'

'You think I've been hunting you down to get even for that?' Veronica asked. 'I just want to shut you up, once and for all. As long as there was a chance you might come back, tell the police about the hotel . . . ' Veronica shook her head, called over to Patty, 'Bring me that other gun, would you, love?'

Patty approached.

The gun hung from her right arm. I wondered if Bob had ended up with the Ruger with only one bullet left in it. If so, it was empty now. That would mean at least Patty was not a threat.

But how many bullets did Veronica still have in her weapon?

Patty stopped a few feet away, gun still in her hand.

'You know how this is going to go,' I said to Patty. 'If you ever thought there was going to be a chance for us to connect, to have anything, it's not going to happen. She's going to kill me. And your sister.'

Sydney said, 'What?'

'Just shut up,' Patty said.

'She's your sister,' I told Sydney.

'Shut up! Shut up!' Patty shouted.

I was still looking at Sydney. 'Patty is . . . Patty's my daughter.'

Sydney couldn't find any words.

In the distance, a siren. People, no doubt, had heard the shots.

'Shit,' said Veronica. 'We have to get out of here.'

It sounded as though more than one siren was approaching. A cop car, probably an ambulance, too.

'I'm sorry,' Patty whispered. She looked at Syd and me. 'I'm sorry. I really really fucked this up. This isn't how I wanted it to go.'

A solitary tear ran down her left cheek.

Veronica pointed her gun at my head. 'We have to run,' she said. 'Bye bye.'

I got ready. I tried to pull myself over Sydney, to somehow protect her.

And then the shot came. Loud.

But it didn't come from Veronica's gun.

Then there was another shot.

Bob, evidently, had taken the gun with three bullets.

Veronica's body was thrown up against the railing. Feebly, she raised her weapon and fired it once at Patty before she slid down to the planks of the covered walkway.

The one shot Veronica managed to get off had caught Patty in the chest. The gun fell from Patty's hand as she collapsed against the wooden beams, then slumped down into an awkward sitting position.

I lunged for Veronica, grabbed her wrist and

slammed it against the railing. But there was no fight in her. The gun went over the side and down into the creek. Veronica didn't move.

Syd was screaming.

I got my arms around her. 'It's OK, it's OK, it's OK,' I said. I kept telling her it was OK, that it was over, that we were going home, that she was going to see her mother, that everything was going to be OK, that the nightmare had come to an end.

Even thought the sirens were closing in, suddenly it seemed very quiet.

I kept holding Syd. I wanted to hold her forever, never let her out of my arms again, but we weren't totally out of the woods yet. People were hurt. Patty. And Bob. Even though I'd only been nicked in the ear, I was feeling very faint.

No doubt a large part of that was emotional. This rollercoaster ride we'd been on for weeks was coming to an end. I felt like I was shutting down.

'Sydney,' I said softly, trying to calm her. 'It's over. You're coming home. You know that, right?'

I felt her head go up and down.

'We're going home. We're going home now.'

'I know,' she whispered. 'I know.'

'The police, the ambulance, they're coming,' I said. 'They might see Bob, but they won't know anyone's in here.'

Another nod, a sense that she was pulling herself together, at least slightly. 'I'll tell them,' Syd said.

'I'll stay here with Patty,' I said. 'She's shot pretty bad.'

'You, too,' Syd said, looking at the blood running down from my ear.

'It's not that bad. But . . . I'm feeling a bit weird.'

Then we both looked at Patty. There was a huge black spot rapidly spreading across her chest.

'Daddy,' Syd said, not able to take her eyes off the blood, her voice shaky. 'You said she was my — '

'Hon,' I said. 'Go. Now.'

She looked at both of us a moment longer, sniffed, nodded, then started running down to the end of the bridge.

I slid over, put my arm around Patty, pulled her into me, felt the warmth of the blood that was soaking her clothes.

If only I'd known. If only I'd known.

'They're coming,' I said to her. 'Just hold on.'

'I'm sorry,' she said.

I barely made out the words. They came out raspy, bubbly.

'Don't talk,' I said, trying to comfort her, putting my face up against her cheek, tears coming together. 'Don't talk.'

'I just wanted you to love me,' Patty whispered.

'I love you,' I said. 'I do.'

I stayed and held Patty as she drew her last breaths while my other daughter flagged down the ambulance and the police.

We do hope that you have enjoyed reading
this large print book.

Did you know that all of our titles
are available for purchase?

We publish a wide range of high quality
large print books including:
**Romances, Mysteries, Classics
General Fiction
Non Fiction and Westerns**

Special interest titles available in
large print are:
**The Little Oxford Dictionary
Music Book
Song Book
Hymn Book
Service Book**

Also available from us courtesy of
Oxford University Press:
**Young Readers' Dictionary
(large print edition)
Young Readers' Thesaurus
(large print edition)**

For further information or a free
brochure, please contact us at:
**Ulverscroft Large Print Books Ltd.,
The Green, Bradgate Road, Anstey,
Leicester, LE7 7FU, England.
Tel:** (00 44) 0116 236 4325
Fax: (00 44) 0116 234 0205

Other titles published by
The House of Ulverscroft:

TOO CLOSE TO HOME

Linwood Barclay

When the Cutter family's next-door-neighbours, the Langleys, are gunned down in their house one hot August night, the Cutters' world is turned upside down. That such brutal violence could be visited on an ordinary suburban family is as shocking as it is inexplicable — but at least the Cutters can comfort themselves with the thought that lightning is unlikely to strike twice in the same place. Unless, of course, the killers went to the wrong house . . .